I0780226

The Gloaming

ISBN: 978-1-961615-10-6
Imprint: Thornewood Studios

The Gloaming

By S.L. Thorne

Book 2 of
The Gryphon's Rest

TABLE OF CONTENTS

DEDICATION

For those who have supported my continuing efforts to tell this immense tale. For those who have helped me with characters and timelines. For all those who bore with me from the last book and have come back for more. For all those who let me read to them, and those who begged me to. For all of my editors who forgot that they were supposed to be making corrections and got swept up in the story instead:

Thank you.

And mostly, for my husband, who put up with my working on this and completely forgetting other things (like feeding him and laundry).

1

Jonny Sorrow stood alone on the stage. His long white hair flowed over his shoulders as he made the polished fiddle in his hands weep. The stage was dark save for the single, pale blue light; before him, the audience: silent, en-rapt. In the middle of the dance floor a single woman danced. Her red skirt was slung low on her hips, beaded fringe flying as she undulated. Her black hair flew unbound about her like a raven cloud, her sorrow and pain written in her movements for the world to see. She was breathtaking.

In the shadow of the stairwell, on the last step, An stood listening to the music. The pits of fog that served her for eyes watching only the dancer. She could just see Solitaire through a gap in the mortals crowding the edge of the floor. Her heart was filled by the music, knowing whose hands wrung that soulful sound from simple strings. She could not bring herself to look at the musician.

Roulet came down behind her, set a hand on her shoulder as much a warning of her presence as comfort. She wrapped her arms around An from behind and watched her twin dance away her pain. An settled back into the embrace, knowing Roulet needed comforting too. It had been several months since Henry's death and the fight in the woods, and Solitaire was still torn deeply, still had to be watched carefully.

"She'll be all right, eventually," An said softly, the lilt of her accent as light as her voice.

"I know," Roulet breathed. "It just hurts to know she's hurting. It was so damned senseless."

"Why *did* Henry go harin' off after that boggart? I never found out," An asked.

Roulet let go, turned and sat on the stairs. An sank to join her, resting the tip of Cipín, her shillelagh, on the step below her and the rest against her shoulder. "The damned thing brought him a Christmas present. It knew what it had. Skye saw the thing backing up after Henry took the package, trying to be all subtle about it. Inside was a short lanyard woven from wolf fur, Raigne's we've discovered. On it was the key to Henry's house and an earring Solitaire lost there one night."

An's hand covered her mouth, fully understanding the implications. Aislynn came downstairs in the form of a small monkey and curled up in her lap.

"Yeah," Roulet said, leaning back against the wall. "That particular threat to Solitaire was what set Henry off. He knew who'd sent it. Raigne had been chasing him for over a year and never liked it much that he was dallying with my sister. Granted, Henry chased nearly anything in a skirt, but he really cared for Solitaire.

"Did you know that in his will he called her his 'unwedded wife'? Said he should have just married her. That, I think, is part of her problem right now, why she's taking it so hard."

"He gave her th' house though," An said, remembering. "Has she even been in it? Since?"

Roulet shook her head. "Too scared. We don't know if Raigne was the only one who had a key. That and memories. He gave her Reign of Depravity, too."

An frowned. "What's that?"

"A strip club," Roulet laughed. "We used to work there, when we first escaped." She shrugged, "It was what we knew. I danced there off and on for special promotions after Liberty and I opened this place, but Solitaire was there more often. Mikey's helping her run it now. Ian asked him to step in for security reasons. So many ways for the Bratva to start poking holes in it. Already had Cass and Dukes in three times in the last two months. Thankfully they never find anything to the complaints. We're careful."

"The Chief told me th' Russians are bad news."

Roulet nodded. "They want something, they won't hesitate to take it by whatever means necessary. Nothing is sacred."

She looked out over the club, from the audience now clapping in a frenzy for her sister and Jonny to the bar where two individuals were headed. She groaned, pulled herself to her feet.

"What is it?" An asked.

"Speaking of the devils."

Aislynn climbed up to her shoulder as An followed Roulet to the bar.

"Evening, Cass, Dukes," Roulet said cheerfully. "This an official visit or are you off duty?"

Dukes, the shorter of the two men snorted and gave her a grudging 'evenin'. Cass smiled, apologized for his partner. "Actually we're looking for a spot of dinner. We're tired of the fast food garbage we've been eating and I remembered you have a full service kitchen and fast service. And excellent coffee."

"We were in the neighbourhood," Dukes growled, ordering a coffee and the night's special from Tori.

An looked long and hard at the two men, frowning. They were... perfectly normal as far as she could tell, but she could see them. They were like Tori... sort of, ghostly, but in a different way. The two men were just a little more than human.

As Tori set a cup of steaming black coffee in front of Dukes, he looked over at An, frowned at what sat on her shoulder. He narrowed his eyes, trying to understand what he was seeing. "That's got to be some kind of health violation."

Tori responded before Roulet could, glancing up at who he was referring to. "Service animals are allowed everywhere by law," she replied.

"That's not a service animal," he growled, moving closer. "That's a... what is that?"

Cass stopped him before he got too close. "Stop being an ass, Paul."

Paul really saw An for the first time. "Shit, you're one of *them*," he snarled and went back to the bar to drink his coffee.

Cass hung his head a moment. "Um... I'm sorry about him. He's... a little bitter."

An gave him a soft smile and a nod. "'Tis all right."

Roulet just raised her eyebrows in Paul's direction. "Won't your eating here kinda compromise you two?" she asked.

Cass chuckled, "What better way to keep an eye on the place? Besides, you're an official eatery and open late."

Roulet smiled, "And we provide discounts to all active service personnel. That includes military, police and fire. ...And we are open for lunch, so let the department know. The more this place is known for a cop hangout, the less trouble I'm going to have from the Russian mob trying to muscle in."

An excused herself politely, went to her table where Jonny now sat. There was a cluster of young women and at least one young man fawning over him, but she approached anyway. They were dismissive of her at first, seeing her as just another rival for his attentions, but when he rose and pulled out a seat for her, taking her hand and guiding her around the obstacles, most of them drifted away. As for the few who remained... well, it was lucky An could not see the looks they were giving her. A waitress brought out a tea tray with two cups, a full pot and a third, miniature teacup for the 'monkey', along with a plate of confections, and the last of them finally got the picture and wandered away.

Once she could tell they were alone, An spoke softly to Jonny as she poured the tea. "The two policemen at the bar," she began. "I can see them, but ...they look mundane and it's confusing."

Jonny glanced in that direction, smirked as a blonde woman in a camouflage tank top and low slung jeans came up to flirt with the taller of the two detectives. "I wouldna ken. Not my area of expertise, such sights. Could be they're just special somehow, like Tori. Th' world holds many flavours of 'extra-ordinary'. Ours is but one."

An tipped her head in acknowledgement as she added a spoonful of honey to her tea and slowly stirred. Setting the spoon down, her attention was caught by a young woman on the stage singing a fair rendition of "Right Kind of Wrong" and she smiled. She sipped her tea in silence with a look of amusement.

Jonny brushed back the fall of her honey-brown hair so he could see her fair Irish face and the fog-filled hollows that served her for eyes. "And what is it that has ye in so fair a mood, Ceobhránach?"

"Nothin', really. I'm still worried about Solitaire, but ...I was listenin' to th' words," she nodded in the singer's direction. He looked up at the stage and the woman upon it. "I think they fair say my piece."

He gave her his sad smile, toyed with the lock of hair still entwined in his fingers, "Aye. Ye may come to regret it."

She turned to gaze at him, taking in everything from his tanned skin and high cheekbones to the earth-brown eyes that seemed to see right through her. His snow white hair fell like a cloud around him. "Never. Oh, I may hurt, aye. But love... 'Tis nothing to regret. If at the end of my life I can say I was loved for even an hour... then I have lived a worthwhile life."

She watched the petty drake selecting a decorated cookie from the plate with extreme care. An couldn't bring herself to look at Jonny when he watched her like that. She blushed enough as it was.

His voice was snow on silk soft when he spoke, his eyes still on her face, the sorrow in them deep. "I can't promise ye that."

She tilted her face to regard him. His finger stroked her cheek. The coldness of his skin felt good against the flush of her face.

They were interrupted by a new artist on stage as the usual in-between singer playback screeched to a halt. He was a large, rough-looking black man dressed up like the stereotypical gang-banger. His voice was gruff and gravelly and sent a shiver up An's spine as he all but barked out his rap.

"I'm the Dark Man's Hound
I'll take your ass to the pound
Unless I want 'em to, my paws don't make a sound
But when I howl, bitch, you can feel it in the ground
You can feel my breath and I can smell your fear, BOO!
Just keep on screaming 'cause no one can hear you!"

Done, the man howled. It was piercing, carried a primordial threat eliciting a primordial terror in those who heard and had the means to understand. For the mortals, it was just a cheap thrill and some folk howled with him, laughing off their fear.

At the bar, An noted the two detectives watching the man with narrowed eyes, one of them with his hand at his hip, wanting to reach for his weapon. Even the young woman hitting on the taller one shivered. As the singer bulled past their table, An could smell asphalt and smoke and sulphur and tar and all the worst smells of a hot city swelter. She looked to Jonny, saw his tightened lips and the faint pallor beneath his tanned skin. She touched his hand, her question unasked.

"That does not bode well," he said low.

"Who was that?" she whispered, stroking Aislynn's scales as she finally peeked up over the table from where she had taken refuge in An's lap.

"Hellhound. One o' th'... Dark Man's minions. What he's doing on this side...." He shook his head, refusing to finish the sentence.

"Sendin' a warnin', sounded like. He huntin', ye think?"

Jonny twisted his hand in that gesture that was the closest to a shrug as he got.

An turned back to observing the foggy darkness that surrounded her, found her teacup by its heat and sipped. Occasionally she could see something or someone flit across her vision and she would know whatever it was to be touched by magic of some sort. It was a gift from the fey children she had once served as governess, in compensation for losing her own eyes saving their lives. There were other gifts, less often used but equally useful.

Conversation occurred all around them, as Courtz was always busy on Friday nights. Karaoke was popular. An could not hear most of the discussions, and truthfully, would not have listened if she could, but from the tiny twinges and occasional skipped heartbeats she knew lies were being told all around her. All the more reason to tune them out.

Instead, she sat with Jonny, enjoying his company in silence. They drank the tea, ate what they wanted from the plate, and Jonny drank his pint. It was Guinness tonight, not his usual Nut Brown. It was comfortable as they listened to the various singers. Most were fair, expressive if not technically pleasing, and the genres encompassed all kinds. An made note of songs to learn for herself later.

It was after midnight when a tattooed man with a coarse, wiry beard got up on the stage and began to scream out something by a black metal band. An winced and Aislynn buried herself in An's vest, trying to block out the noise. An leaned over to Jonny, was bolstered a little by the look of pain on his face. She had to raise her voice more than she liked just to be heard. "Will ye walk me t' ma door? I can't... I can't take this," she said with a gesture towards the singer she could hear but not see.

He nodded and stood. Leaving a few bills on the table, he took her hand and helped her through the crowd, at the edge of what had become a mosh pit. He started to lead her to the stairs, but she turned him right, towards the front door. He obliged, and both of them took a breath of relief as they stepped to the pavement and the door closed behind them, shutting off the sound. The street was far from quiet, but even that noise was a welcome change.

"I don't mind a bit o' th' metal if 'tis melodic or lyrical. "Nothing Else Matters" for instance. But screamers with no melody just fer th' point o' screamin' offend me," he said softly.

An chuckled as Aislynn crawled out of her vest and up to her shoulder, enjoying the light breeze of early Spring on her face. "Drawbacks of bein' a Bard, I'll assume."

"Perhaps. ...Didn't ye come from upstairs?" he asked as they reached the corner.

"Aye," she replied, feeling shy of a sudden. "I... wanted a walk, if ye don't mind. 'Tis hard t' talk in there sometimes and 'tis a nice night."

"That it be," he agreed, and led her across the street into the neighbourhood beyond. "So what is it my lady wishes to talk about?"

She blushed now, though she smiled at his astuteness. "Not sure it's all that... specific. I've... been noticing things lately, and it calls to mind... questions. And before ye ask, they're not the kind I can just blurt out."

He smiled at that, but let her be. "And what is it ye've observed?"

She took a moment to think about it, how to put it. "Spring bein' in th' air for one. Everyone is pairing up it seems. Even Foxfire with that raccoon girl we found in the woods. Raven's been cozyin' up to that new gentleman, the patchwork?"

"Patches?" he supplied.

"That what he's chosen?" she asked, unimpressed. "They say he's one of the contenders for th' Holly King. Along with... Mikey, Fox (though I think that be a mistake), Barry..."

"Barry *would* be a mistake. He's worn that crown afore and it wasn't pretty. He's... gotten bitter since his lover died."

An did not press for details, merely nodded. "Even Liberty and Skye are gettin' a mite cozy," she smiled. "And, well, ...ye said sommat before Hellhound interrupted, and it made me think."

He waited a moment before asking, "An' yer question would be?" If she hadn't been so close or paying attention, she would never have heard the words.

"Us. What... what is it ye want of... us? How ye feel? Ye said ye 'can't promise me that'. What did ye mean?"

He took in and let out a deep breath. "What I want? I don't know. I care fer ye. I don't know how, exactly. I told ye it was complicated. Love? I don't know if I'm able anymore." He gestured at the snow rose in her hair. "Have ye learned th' language of flowers yet?"

She nodded, fingering the blood tipped edges, "Some. This means that you see me as an innocent, unconscious beauty that makes you happy? As a single rose, there are many interpretations. Some more hopeful than others."

"The combination of colours in a single bloom at this stage of open symbolizes... a burgeoning passion in a previously innocent relationship." His voice was softer even than usual. "Blood is life, and we shed it so many ways, for so many reasons. That is *my* blood, and is only the smallest part of what I would give for ye."

"I don't want anyone to bleed for me, Jonny."

"Why? Ye've already bled fer me."

She flushed, feeling a heat that months ago would have sent her into a downward spiral, trapped in a vision of being forged and remade. She did the safest thing, which was to ignore the question, shunting aside the memory of the fetid breath and bloody weight of the cú she had been nearly crushed by trying to protect him last December. "I don't want to force ye to something yer... not comfortable with or seekin'. If love comes, love comes. If you find me unworthy, I'll leave ye be and ask no more of ye. But if ye enjoy m' company I'll take what yer capable of givin' an' give ye all ye'll accept. I don't... know my way around relationships, havin' never known love, never expected it." She frowned slightly, choosing Skye's word deliberately, "So if ye want me t' stop moonin' over ye, I will."

He shook his head. "Ye can't help yer heart any more than I, mine. Nor would I ask ye to. But ye'll have to patient with me. I literally can't answer th' question... because to be wrong, here, might bring a lie."

She sighed. "All that I ask is if ye decide I cannot make ye happy that ye'll tell me, kindly I hope. And feel however I may, I promise ye I'll walk away. ...Once I'm assured 'tis yer will and not something acted upon ye," she added with a rueful smile.

He looked at her oddly. "I hope ye'll be more patient than that. I don't know if I can *be* happy. That wouldna be yer fault."

"I suppose I misused the word. If ye decide ye can't be with me... for other than my own protection," she stiffened, "'cause I'll not be left for that. Stupidest reason in th' history o' man t' leave a woman," she growled. "I meant," she continued, getting herself under control, "...if ye don't want me any more."

He stopped, turned her, brushing his fingers along her face. "I knew what ye meant, I think. I... just be patient with me, and forgivin'."

"I will," she assured him. "I just wanted to be sure I wasn't ...forcin' ye out of some twisted sense of obligation. Th' thought had occurred t' me, you know."

He looked down at that. "If I thought that was it, I'd run. Never again shall I be forced." He shivered, and not from the cold he never felt.

"Good. We understand one another then." She slipped her hand into his. "Because I don't ever want to be 'that woman'," she said emphatically.

He smiled at her, the fingertips of his free hand brushing her jaw as they drifted towards the nape of her neck. The promised kiss hung in the air with sweet tension, and then the moment was ripped away by a barking howl no more than a single street over. They looked up; An wildly as she could see nothing.

"That was..." she began.

"Aye," he answered hoarsely. He was looking around for an avenue of escape should they need it, listening for the howl, to determine if it was nearing or not. Gunshots answered his question.

"Where are we?" An asked suddenly as he took her hand and led her across the empty street. "I smell water."

"Aye. By th' lake."

"But... th' Tallows live three blocks from th' lake. 'Tisn't on m' route."

He continued to draw her after him and she shifted her grip on the shillelagh to one more suited for defence, trusting Jonny to lead her. "Well, ye wanted a walk. Straight home was too short," he answered, seeing what he needed and heading for it. He pulled a penny whistle out of his vest pocket, guiding her down the slight incline towards the lake. Aislynn clung to her right shoulder, shifting to her normal, small white dragon form, no longer caring who saw.

An looked behind them, beginning to see something or someone around the curve of the lakeside road. It moved like a pack of hounds, though they walked mostly upright. Jonny came to a stop near some trees and began to play his little melody. An could feel what he was doing: opening an emergency gateway, so she watched the approaching pack. The man called Hellhound was at the back of the pack and spurring them on, with something or someone she could not see slung over his shoulder. He was shooting behind him and fire was returned. He laughed as what turned out to be a woman on his shoulder screamed.

An started to move towards them, her shillelagh at the ready, when Jonny grabbed her arm and pulled her back. "We have ta..." she began.

He pulled her close. "Do nothing. There are eight o' them and two o' us. Even *Cipín* is no match for seven ghouls and one of Th' Dark Man's lieutenants."

Gunfire rang out again, a stray shot striking a tree not fifty yards from where they stood. One of the lead ghouls noticed them, pointed them out, and half the group surged in their direction, the rest peeled off to take on those pursuing them.

An frowned as Hellhound pointed at them and began to run. His hand was oddly contorted. There was the report of a pistol and something bit into her shoulder even as Jonny seized her and threw both of them through the doorway he had made between two bent trees. The portal slammed shut behind them, but they had no time to rest as Aislynn hissed a warning. They whirled, went back to back, An holding *Cipín* across her body and Jonny drawing a pair of Francesca axes.

They were in the middle of a thawing field that, from the look of it, had never seen a plough. There were random stones and hillocks and the occasional barren tree. The sky was overcast and grey. Jonny paled. This was a battlefield, and a familiar one, and they were not alone in it. A small squad of men were combing the field intently, one of them on horseback, with two wolves serving as trackers, and all of them wore Yankee Blue ...And they had been seen. A word from the commander and they charged, only one of the wolves launching for them. The other remained on whatever trail she'd found.

An stepped out to Jonny's side, confident there was nothing behind them for miles and prepared to fight, in spite of the wet pain in her left shoulder. She kept that side between her and Jonny and set for the charge. The wolf leapt for An, trying to take down the weakest of the two and found himself dazed for his trouble. She followed the knob with a solid strike to the front leg and shattered the bone.

Jonny handled the two infantrymen with their bayoneted rifles. They were fairly easy to deflect with the dual axes, and their companions' muskets missed wildly. He caught one barrel in the crook of an axehead and yanked him into his neighbour, staving in the side of his head with the up-swung back end of the second axe before chopping downward and taking his arm at the collar.

Aislynn leapt from An's shoulder and flew, screeching, into the face of the lone horse, spewing a stream of frost that blinded it, causing it to rear. The rider found his hands full just trying to stay mounted. The second wolf suddenly screamed from where she had been sniffing and the one trying to crawl away from An looked over at the she-wolf. His companion had gone down in a spray of gore and something was rising from the ground drenched in her blood. An met the next soldier with the shillelagh tip first, letting him impale himself, then guided his momentum and slung him off the stick onto the already defeated wolf. Aislynn continued to harry the horse until it finally tore off across the field in a random direction. From somewhere nearby a raven took off and An glanced over that way.

On a low rise was a man on a horse in a duster and cowboy hat, watching the exchange. The raven had launched from his shoulder. As Jonny took down the last of the small squad, the horseman tipped his hat to them and rode off in the opposite direction the raven had gone, riding hell-bent for leather.

"That is not good," Jonny heaved. He was breathing heavy and not just from recent exertions. "We have to get out of here, quickly."

"Aye," came a gruff voice from a tussock a few yards away. "Yon raven'll be goin' fer makar. Lucky us, Cowboy's ridin' on a mission or this'd've gone def'ernt."

They looked for the source of the voice and saw a small, roughly built dwarf rising from the carcass of the she-wolf whose head he appeared to have bitten off. He had been dipping his hat in the blood of her belly. Dripping, he pulled it onto his head and An's heart sank. He was a *fear dearg*, one of the red-dressed pranksters who invited themselves in and doled out luck according to how they were treated. Though by this one's actions he was most likely the more dangerous Scottish redcap.

"If ye kin summon back th' door ye burst through, we kin be on ahr way." He glared at them with beady little black eyes from beneath beetled brows. "Ah were headed oot yon door when ye slammed it shut," he growled.

Jonny took a breath, making himself think. "Ye didn't want out that door any how."

"Chased were yen?"

"Aye. The Dark's men. Hellhound and a pack o' ghouls."

"Fryin' pans an' fires," he shrugged. "Kin ye open anither door or noo?"

Aislynn looped back from where she had been chasing off the horse and dove into the tall grasses just as Jonny's hand went to his pocket in a panic. She flew up carrying his penny whistle.

"Thank ye, ma'am," he said, taking it and began looking around at the treeless field. "Only trouble be, I am in need of a door to make a door."

"Hmm," the redcap mumbled. "Any kinda o' door? E'en one that ain't be a proper one?"

"Aye."

The dwarf walked around a large boulder next to the body of the wolf and pointed. "Tha' dew?"

Jonny walked over, looked down and laughed, that high, near hysterical laugh of the relieved under extreme stress. "Aye."

An drifted over, wincing as Aislynn landed on her bad shoulder. Jonny played his little melody, rapid-fire as he heard the cawing of a murder of crows in the distance.

He held out his hand to her. "All right, Alice," he said. "'Tis down th' rabbit hole with ye."

She looked down and saw that the door was a hole in the ground through which she could see a green field. She accepted his hand and, holding tight to Cipín, hopped in. It was disconcerting to say the least: falling down and then landing what was essentially sideways. She rolled out of the way and made room for Jonny and the fear dearg, who seemed friendly enough, though she knew that could change at any moment. She looked up as they came falling out of a dark, dirty hole in the sky a few yards above the lush meadow they were in. The moment they were through, Jonny reached up, grabbed a trailing root and pulled, effectively zipping the door shut behind them.

An looked around. They were seated in a pleasant meadow, green fields and flowers as far as the eye could see, to the edge of a white birch wood about a half league off. There were white horses grazing near that wood who regarded them carefully, but continued to graze. It was peaceful here.

The dwarf grunted in appreciation, "Huh, borderlands o' Amalthea's realm. Noice."

The name rang a bell with An, on multiple levels, but she couldn't pin it down.

Jonny came over, held out his hand to help her up and saw the blood painting her white blouse and went to his knees beside her instead. Aislynn began fussing over her immediately. An yelped when he lightly began to probe the wound. He checked the back of her shoulder and groaned.

"What?" she asked, biting back tears, holding her left arm tightly against her body. With the adrenaline of the battle finally subsided, the joint began aggressively making her aware of the damage.

"The ball's still in. I can't... do anythin' here."

She looked up at him, saw a line of blood across his temple and lightly brushed it away, discovered the gash beneath it. "Yer not so hale yerself. Help me up," she said, offering him her good arm.

Reluctantly, he brought her to her feet, being as gentle as he could. As she reached out for Cipín, she swept her eyes across him, taking in the varied light cuts he had acrued. Nothing was serious, or at least it wasn't any more. She looked over at the redcap. "Have ye a name, fear dearg?" she asked him.

He looked her over, from her very prim and proper attire to her no-nonsense, 'I know what I'm doing' manner. He grunted. "Call me Tam."

"Very well, Tam. I am An Ceobhrán O'Keefe, this be Jonny Sorrow and m' companion is Aislynn. Am I to be taking it ye'd like out o' th' Queen's service?"

"That'd be why they were huntin' me, aye."

"Well, might be there is a place we can take ye, but ye'll have to be on your best. There are some as might take exception to what ye are before they get to know ye. But we will take ye to someone who'll tell ye all th' rules and let ye make yer mind to stay or go."

His little black eyes watched her warily. "An' it'll be yer misty arse what gets us t' this faeryland?"

Before Jonny could do more than raise his eyebrow at the remark, An had lifted Cipín and turned in a direction parallel to the wood.

"Aye, it would. Follow me," she said and began walking.

2

By the time they had reached the right trod and the right gate, An was feeling weak. She had enough self control not to show it, but it was all she could do to keep moving down the path to the road, and from the road to the manor. The moment they emerged from the rath, Aislynn launched, flying ahead with a warning.

They had gotten only a couple hundred yards from the rath when she stopped in the middle of the unpaved carriage road. Jonny had his arm around her, holding her up and now she sank against him, letting him take her full weight. Someone came galloping up the road towards them and Tam crouched, braced for a fight, though he kept his eyes on his escort, not trusting their lack of concern.

The centaur, Coach and Four, did not slow down until he was almost upon them, and even then he was reaching behind him for the arm of the person mounted on his bare back and slung her forward onto the ground in front of him. Liberty landed neatly on her feet and ran forward as Jonny slowly lowered to the road, cradling An.

"What happened?" she demanded as she began to look An over.

"Th' shoulder," he informed her. "She took one o' Hellhound's bullets. 'Tis still in her."

"Aw, shite," she mumbled. "No tellin' what th' devil it's been up ta in there."

Coach stood over them and clicked on a flashlight, shining it down on the patient.

An gasped as Liberty touched her arm, checking the wound. "I couldn't see th' gun," she moaned, shaking her head.

Liberty paused. "At all?"

"Hand ...empty. I'm... cold."

"Lost a lot of blood," Coach commented.

"Damn it, I know," Liberty snapped.

"I did what I could without closing th' wound," Jonny said softly. There was pain in his voice, too.

"When?" An gasped, never having noticed the light layer of frost he'd coated her shoulder with. Perhaps that was why it hadn't start really hurting until they left Faery.

Liberty made some lightning calculations. "It'll be fine, Jonny, but I'll need yar help, an' ya can't be human fer it. I'll need yer beak, I've no tools with me."

Jonny made a face, but obediently and carefully lay An down. Before he shifted to the large white raven, he reached into An's little bag at her hip and pulled out her flask. He helped her to drink some, then he took a swallow himself before handing it to Liberty to pour on the wound. He looked over his shoulder, "Tam, ye'll be needed t' keep her still. Just do what Liberty tells ye, aye?"

The redcap grumbled, still not trusting the situation, but came forward as Jonny grew smaller and whiter, sprouting feathers. Tam placed his hands where Liberty told him, applying the necessary pressure to keep her flat. Coach stood over them, changed the angle of the light so that no one's head was in the way and Jonny could see what he was doing.

Liberty smiled down at An. "This is gonna hurt like th' devil, luv."

An gave a dry little laugh. "Already does."

Without any other warning, Liberty poured a liberal amount of the whiskey onto the wound and An bowed up, screaming. The raven's bill went into the wound in the wake of the whiskey and fished out the small pellet as swiftly as he could. It slipped once, forcing him to snatch at it. An kicked in response to the pain, unable to help herself or move the upper half of her body under the weight of the redcap. Aislynn landed quickly as An went limp and grabbed the hem of her skirt, pulling it back down into a more modest position before An could become aware of the slip.

Jonny changed immediately to man and placed his hand over her wound, stilling the blood flow with his frosty touch. An looked up at his face, saw her blood on his lips and cheeks and slipped momentarily from consciousness.

When she came to, she was still on the ground with the three of them hovering around her. Jonny's cold hand was still over her wound, but Liberty's were on both Jonny and Tam and she could see the magic flowing from her to the other two. It stretched across the gap like vines bursting into flower in that breach. She could feel similar threads wrapping over her, feel the tiny tendrils crawling through and sewing up the holes. She was breathing easier, feeling the strength returning to her limbs. She managed to slip her fingers into her pocket and snag her handkerchief, reached up and weakly wiped her blood from Jonny's mouth.

He opened his eyes, looking down at her and smiled, covering her hand with his and taking the kerchief. "Welcome back, Ceobhránach."

He cleaned his face, wiping his forehead as well. An noticed he was rather pale under all the blood.

"There any whiskey left?"

He chuckled, "Aye," handed her the flask and helped her to sit up. She drank gratefully, deeper than usual. She offered Aislynn a taste, but the dragon on her knee shook her head.

"Later," she answered in her preferred Irish.

An nodded and closed the flask, putting it away. She looked at the condition of her blouse, bright red and torn. Even her dusty blue vest was stained vermilion, though the bullet had missed it by a quarter inch. "Trick will be getting inta th' cottage without Skye findin' out," she groaned.

Liberty let out an apologetic laugh. "Not goin' t' be possible. He's at th' house fillin' Da in on th' deal with Hellhound."

An breathed in relief. "Good, then I can get home an' changed without his bein' th' wiser."

"Sorry, luv. Yer wanted at th' manor fer debriefin'."

An frowned and Jonny explained. "Ye need t' tell th' chief what happened."

"Can't ye do that?"

He gestured at Tam. "Technically, yer th' one brought him out. Yer responsibility."

"And Skye already knows ya've been hurt," Liberty added.

"What?"

"*My fault,*" Aislynn admitted, hiding part of her face behind An's knee. "*I needed a healer for you. He was there. He's... mad.*"

"Aye, an' he'll not be placated until he sees ya. So, up ye go."

Liberty moved back to allow Jonny to draw An to her feet. She was still a little unsteady.

"Oh, why is the wood spinnin'?" she moaned.

"Ya lost a lot o' blood, love," Liberty answered. "Th' wounds are healed, but that'll be a mite slower. Ya'll be right as rain in an hour but best ya ride back ta th' manor." She looked up at the roan centaur, "that is if Coach doesn't mind?"

He spread his hands. "If I can deign to carry the queen to the side of a patient in dire need, I can carry this misty little slip back to the chief at her request."

An looked up at the tall centaur's back and stifled a panic response. "I'll walk if it be all th' same. Thank ye kind though fer th' offer. I... I don't ride," she managed, desperate not to insult Coach but just as eager not to be put on his back with no one to hold her there. She had a flash of being on a horse once when she was very little, with someone she thought was her father or a brother, on an enormous plough horse. The memory was pleasant though it left her with a panicked feeling and she could not piece together why.

Coach twitched, flicking his tail against his flank and shrugged. "It is fine. If you would like me to gallop ahead and let them know you are coming, my queen?" he asked.

Liberty nodded and Coach trotted off.

Jonny slipped his arm around An and helped her to walk down the road. Tam followed along behind Liberty, still wary.

By the time they got to the house, An was feeling stronger, and needed less support from Jonny. Still, she was almost overrun by Skye as he charged out across the veranda. He took in the blood and tattered cloth and she could see the rage ticking in the back of his brain. He reached for her to pick her up and she dodged, giving his calf a swift strike with the shillelagh. He danced back.

"I'm not an invalid, ye Highland lummox!" she snapped, knowing it would derail him. "I've walked this far on m' own. I dinna let Jonny carry me, what makes ye think I'll let you?"

"Ah'm yer...."

The polished wooden knob appeared four inches from his nose, threatening him. He shut his mouth and moved out of her way. Behind Liberty, Tam chuckled, mumbled a comment about her spunk and Skye looked around her at him. His eyes went wide. Before he could even decide how to react to the redcap, Cipín cracked across his other calf. He jumped, glaring at An.

"Leave it be and get th' bloody door," she growled.

An rarely swore or used such language, so it threw him off again. He found it better to just do as she asked and went to get the door as Jonny guided her up the steps. Once they were inside, he fell in behind the redcap to keep an eye on him. Besides, if she had her Irish this far up, she was mostly all right.

They did not need Liberty guiding them to figure out that the 'debriefing' was going on in the living room. She let Jonny lead her into the rather crowded room and set her on one end of the couch. She was not going to settle back, fearing to get blood on the upholstery, but Jonny stood behind her with his hand on her good shoulder and pulled her back, making her relax. Liberty returned to what had apparently been her seat before she had left with Coach.

Ian was standing in front of the cold television, half pacing. Roulet was perched on the back of Liberty's chair and Skye was standing next to it. Mikey was in one corner, leaning on what An could only surmise was a bookshelf based on the two slim volumes she could see just behind his head. She made a note to herself to ask Ian later if he knew they were magical. The room was crowded with people she could and could not see and a number of them smelled of gunpowder and blood and recent combat.

Tam stopped just inside the door and Ian glanced over at him, then at Jonny and An. "Why don't we get yer tale, afore we go any farther?"

An glanced up at Jonny, not knowing which of them should speak. He came to the rescue. "I take it ye heard Hellhound paid us a visit?"

Ian nodded, his arms folded across his chest. "Aye. Not word fer word, but as folk could remember."

Jonny grimaced and began to emotionlessly recite Hellhound's rap. Several in the room behind them reacted badly. Even Martha gasped as she entered with a large carafe of fresh coffee. She placed it on the small table and slipped out again, apron crushed in her hands. Someone began serving it out to those who wanted more.

When things had settled, Jonny continued. "I were walking Miss O'Keefe home hours later when we heard him howl uncomfortably close. I headed fer th' lake to a place I could make an escape door when they came around th' far edge. He had a pack of ghouls with him, seven I could see, and a woman over his shoulder. They noticed th' door I'd opened and headed our way. He shot at us, tryin', I think, to stop us goin' through and closin' it ahind us, lockin' him out. An was hit afore I could get her through. Wanted t' rescue th' woman, I expect," he said tenderly, the back of his fingers brushing her cheek. "We got away but ended up..."

An felt his fingers all but turn to ice against her skin, felt the faintest tremble and rescued him. "I think it were one of Her battlefields," she said softly, taking his hand in hers to warm it.

"I'twere," Tam grunted from the doorway, accepting, with some surprise and trepidation, the coffee he was being offered. Ian looked his way, but said nothing for the moment, turning back to the bard and the governess.

"There were a unit with two wolves an' a horseman. They were looking for our friend there, I believe," An said, indicating Tam, "but our appearance with no escape changed that. They came at us. We dispatched them with help from our new friend and looked for a way out. We saw..." she looked over at Tam, "what'd ye call him?"

"Cowboy."

This single word caused as much of a reaction as Hellhound's rap. Ian stiffened. "What'd he do, what'd he see?"

An shook her head. "He saw th' battle. I don't know how much. The mounted officer escaped, ran off when Aislynn terrorized his mount. Might be one of th' wolves survived, I don't know. But a raven flew off in one direction from Cowboy's shoulder and, after tippin' his hat to us, Cowboy rode off in another. Jonny opened another door as we began to hear an approaching unkindness."

"Murder," Jonny said flatly.

She looked up at him. "Ravens are..."

"An unkindness, aye," he answered tightly. "But crows, and thus makar flocks, are called a murder." He locked eyes with Ian. "Th' Hard-ridin' Cowboy was salutin' me. He knew me."

Ian nodded, politely said nothing.

"We... we went through another door," An continued when it became apparent Jonny would say no more. "It took us to th' borderlands of Amalthea," she said, remembering what Tam had called it. "Cipín led us home from there. Tam here," she indicated him, "was running from Her men. He agreed to come with us and talk with you."

Ian nodded to Tam, introduced himself. "I'm th' clan chieftain and th' Oak King o' th' Gryphon's Rest. Yeh an' I'll have our talk later. What we need ta discuss now is what th' devil is Hellhound up ta and what does it have ta do with Spetznakov."

"Why are ye connectin' the Russians with the Dark Man?" someone behind An asked.

"Because th' right bastards sent folk int' Depravity t'night and started trouble," Mikey snarled. "While th' bouncers were dealin' with th' mess, another guy hit th' cash register and dropped in about fifteen dime bags of cocaine after they swiped several hundred in cash. We got it before cops showed up, but... I'm going to have to put cameras on th' register and behind th' bar now."

"Not a bad idea all around," Ian said softly, looking pointedly at his daughter.

"So?" the unseen voice persisted.

"Timin', man," Liberty growled.

There came a quiet, mousy voice from the back corner and it took a moment before An realized it was Bethany. "I think I know why, uncle." There was a cold terror in her voice. "Well, why the Russians are attacking."

An heard her rise and carry something that made small creaking noises as she crossed the crowded room to her uncle. An watched Ian peer down at something held up to him. "Show that t' Jonny an' th' others."

Bethany brought what An now surmised was a laptop over and showed the screen to Jonny. Aislynn stood on her shoulder for a peek herself, glanced at the bard before she turned to Ian and said in a small voice, *"Aye, chieftain. That's th' lass th' Hound had."*

Ian groaned.

Skye looked at the screen and echoed Ian. It was an early police report about a kidnapped heiress, one Marina Sergovna Spetznakov. It was definitely her.

"All right," Ian began. "Skye, who was in yer group chasin' Hellhound?"

Skye immediately began naming them off. "Seamus, Harry, Peter... an' thon short fella ower thar," he said, pointing the man out.

Ian looked and frowned. "Davey, yeh'll sit this one out. Yeh're kinda wanted." Davey took the cue and left the room, heading out the back door. "Anyone see yeh?"

"Nae thon ah kin point tae an' say aye. Ah werenae wearin' m' kilt, so ah dinna stand oot sae much," Skye said.

"How many o' yeh shot?"

Peter spoke up. "Me an' Davey. We got the guns from our truck. They're clean."

"Oh good, you're already battening down the hatches," came a voice An had never heard from the door.

She turned, saw a tall, handsome man in his early 30's, who looked like he should have been a fireman instead of a lawyer wearing a sharp suit. There was nothing odd at all about him, except that she could see him.

"Bad sign when th' lawyer shows up without bein' called," Seamus groaned.

The man chuckled, "Yeah, well, news travels fast when a rival Mafia Don's daughter is kidnapped and fingers are pointed in your favourite client's direction." He crossed to Ian and, taking his hand, gave him a one armed hug. "Good to see you, Uncle. I've got Tisiphone on the alert in case there are any arrests, so she can jump on them as prosecutor. So, what have we got so far?"

Ian explained as the extra people filed out, making themselves scarce or going to help others prepare. Realizing she was not one of the ones told to stay, An rose, deciding she should not be here in bloody clothes when the police came. Ian's voice stopped her. "An, yeh were no where near this, understand?"

She nodded.

Skye started to take her arm to guide her home when Ian diverted him. "Skye, I'll need yeh ta stay an' work with Rowdy on alibis fer yeh an' th boys. Jonny, can I ask..."

Jonny nodded, was moving before he finished his sentence and led An from the room. He started to guide her out the front door when the phone in the front hall rang and Shannon bustled out to answer it. She listened for a moment then hung up and yelled towards the living room. "Chief! Th' police have entered th' Rest! They'll be up in five."

She took in An's blouse in one glance and immediately began to shoo them out the back door. "Get that way, ye two. Can't have them see her like this." She turned to Jonny, looking at his clothes,

"An' you could use a trip to th' bean nighe too. That vest'll be ruined an' ye don't."

Jonny thanked her and turned An around, led her out the back door and down the usual path to her house.

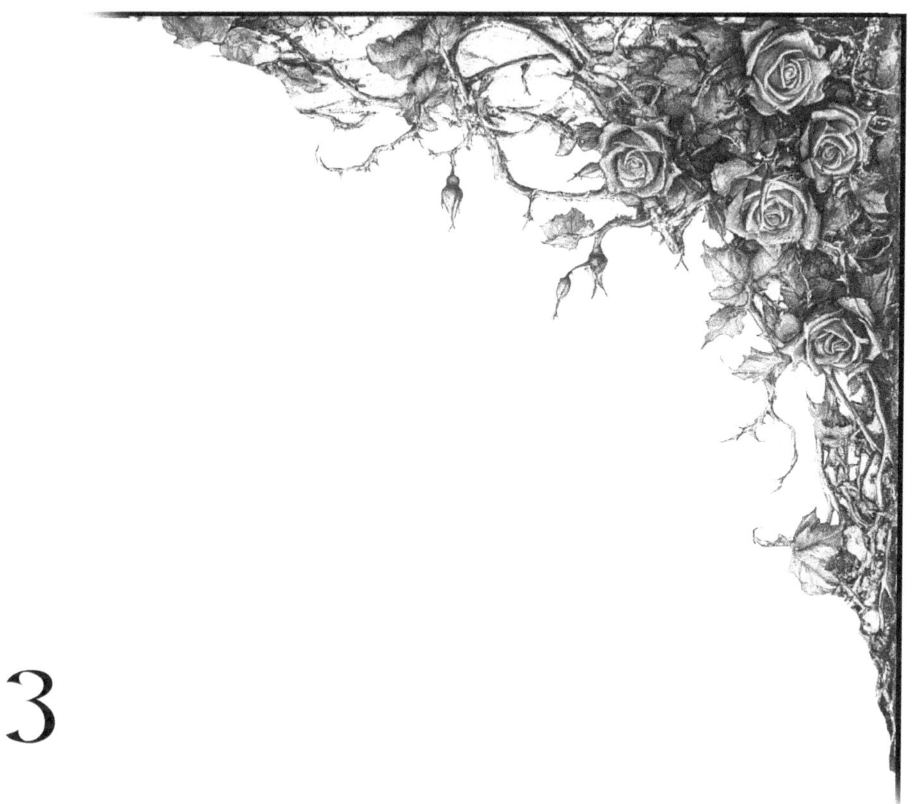

3

Over the following weeks, the missing heiress remained solidly in the news and prompted a great deal of focus on the clan's activities by the police. Those with influence in such places did what they could, and An noticed a great deal of frustration among her 'family active' friends. The Russians were making subtle moves and the O'Keefe's were hard pressed to do anything about them without calling undue attention to their own enterprises.

Even Jonny was behaving a little odd. If he showed up to Courtz at all, he was a little more belligerent than normal, short of temper and tense. He was even curt with the women who flocked around him any time he performed. And things had begun happening when he sang, his music was affecting his audiences. His rendition of "Pain Without Love" by Three Days Grace left the dance floor a very dangerous place and when he came to the table, he flinched when An touched his arm. He wouldn't touch the tea and didn't even bother with beer, just went straight for the hard stuff. He was dishevelled and unkempt. What little facial hair ever grew on his face had the look of patchy frost; but even that only managed to make him more ruggedly attractive, more dangerous-looking. Indeed, he was attracting the attention of a very different sort of woman. An said nothing, but she was not the only one who noticed.

Courtz was having a big St. Patrick's Day event later that week.

"Isn't that takin' th' drunken Irishman sterotype a bit far?" An frowned. "That we're turnin' a saint's feast day into a bar party? I wouldna call myself exactly Catholic anymore, but even I find that in poor taste."

Jonny raised a brow. "It sort o' became somethin' else entire, here in th' States. Have ye remembered th' Great Hunger?"

An paused. It had been a long time since she had tried to remember anything of her own past. Usually titbits were hard won, but this fragment slid to the fore with ease. "Not... not really. I vaguely remember my Granfer tellin' me about it, though. Somethin' about... almost..." The memory had slipped away just as blithely as it had arrived. She sighed. "It's gone. I only know we didn't emigrate."

Jonny did some quick mental calculations before shaking his head. "That's not much help. That were 1845, an' ye've said Prince Albert were already dead, which were 1861. Though it does narrow th' gap a hair or two, fer yer granfer t' have been alive t' remember it." He gave her a sad smile. "Gettin' closer. Providin' ye still care t' know?"

She gave a tiny nod. "It's no hardship if I never remember, but I'd like t' know one day." She sipped her tea. "But th' perversion o' th' holiday?"

"Rec ye th' conditions fer th' Irish in the States?" he asked.

She realized he did not mean whether she recalled having been there, but referred to the extensive historical research she had subjected herself to last year, trying desperately to catch up. "I remember Tamany Hall and the Know Nothing party in Boston. Violent times."

He nodded. "Th' modern celebration started in response t' all tha'. A way of displayin' Irish pride. Things just devolved from there. Nowaday, like Cinco De Mayo, it's just an excuse t' party."

She thought about that. "I think I might attend. Broaden my horizons."

"That might not be a good idea," Roulet said, sitting down at their table for a little breather from the DJ booth.

Before An could ask the question, Jonny explained. "Mortals take th' holiday... t' extremes. Ye'd be safer at th' Hedge Gate with real Irishmen."

Roulet nodded. "The wannabes get... stupid."

Jonny glanced over where Skye sat at the bar, occasionally watching their table. "Ye'd get propositioned and felt up and someone'd end up broken. Not good fer business."

"In fact," Roulet said, sipping her drink, "this year we're asking that there be no O'Keefe's here at all. Even Liberty'll be out at the Gate."

"Who'll be watching th' pub... club," An corrected herself, remembering the proper word.

"I will. I'm not known as an O'Keefe and it's as much mine as Liberty's. I'm going to see if Cass and Dukes are on duty that night and if they'll stop in once or twice. Just to see that all's on the up and up and make sure that things don't get... out of hand. Well, outside of the usual of course."

Suddenly, An shuddered.

Even Jonny frowned as he looked at her.

"What was that?" Roulet asked.

An thought a moment on how best to answer. It felt like the twinges she got from lies, but it had crept all over her like a swarm of insects. She looked around her, but could see very little beyond her table at the moment. "I don't know ...yet." She set her hand on Cipín where she rest against the table. "Excuse me. I'll be back."

She rose and began to slowly wend her way through the crowd. She walked as if on her way to the bathrooms, but did not find what she was looking for. She went on ahead to the ladies' anyway and washed her hands. When she felt sufficient time had passed, she and Aislynn headed back, though she did not go to her table. She wandered towards the front room, where the pool tables and dart boards were. She didn't make it all the way when the crawling feeling happened again. She turned around, looking every bit the lost blind girl. She caught a glimpse of a server coming out of the game room, weaving in between the mortals with an empty tray.

Of all the people who worked here, only Silhouette and Tori were visible to her. This server was therefore new. She stared at him without moving, letting her eyes follow him but not her head. He was not one of the touched and he did not look like Elizabeth and Sean did. Nor did he resonate the way the ghoul pack that Hellhound had led. This was something new. She moved in his direction without appearing to intend to, tripped over a chair left out, getting Cipín tangled in the legs.

The server was near enough, but did not move to help her, though another patron did. As the server brushed by she felt as if ants were crawling all over her body, radiating out from that contact. An did not realize she had visibly reacted until the man helping her chuckled and said, "Felt like someone just walked over your grave, huh?"

She turned towards his voice, a blank look on her face. "Huh? Oh, aye. Thank ye. Aislynn, will ye guide me to the bar?" she asked the small monkey on her shoulder.

The man let go of her uncertainly, moving the chair back in under the table. "You sure you can make it? I'd be glad to lead you," he said. There was something in his voice that An could not identify. "I'll even buy you a drink."

She blushed, smiling. "I have one at m' table, thank ye kind. I... have friends waiting for me. I just got turned around coming back from ...the ladies."

"Oh. If you're sure. You change your mind... have the bartender tell Charlie." She could tell from his voice that he was grinning hopefully.

"I... I'll do that... if I change my mind." She turned slowly, stopping when the 'monkey' tapped her shoulder and began to walk purposefully forward, using Cipín to avoid people and Aislynn to tell her when she was at the end of the bar. From there she knew the way and followed her normal, precise path.

When she finally sank into her seat, Roulet was smiling. "What?" An asked, still embarrassed.

"You're blushing. What happened?"

Jonny was regarding her without fully looking at her and An became even more uncomfortable. "Someone just... well, someone left a out chair and a gentleman helped me."

"That all?" There was an edge to Jonny's voice that did not seem warranted, though there was amusement as well.

"No," she felt her cheeks flaming. "He... offered to buy me a drink."

Roulet stopped suppressing her giggle. "He was hitting on you."

"He didn't touch me," An insisted hotly. "Accept my arm to help untangle me."

Roulet just laughed. "It's an expression. It means he was flirting."

"What'd ye find out?" Jonny asked shortly, mercifully sparing An further embarrassment.

"One of th' servers is a walkin' lie," she said flatly.

"What?" Roulet stumbled, shifting emotional tracks. "Which one?"

"Th' new one."

Roulet looked around the club, taking note of all the servers. "There aren't any 'new' ones. Everybody on the floor has been here for at least four months. Most of them longer than that."

An shook her head. "Then something is new about one of them. I can see him."

Both of them turned to look at her. "Which one?" Roulet asked, her eyes starting to spark.

"A little taller than I, about Jonny's build. Blonde, I think. He was over by the bar last I saw."

Roulet looked around, found the man in question and then turned back to Jonny, exchanging a meaningful look with him. "An, that's Dustin. He's worked here for over a year."

"He is a walkin' lie, and he is not like us in that way. We look different than we are in many ways but do not set off my ...lie detector... in this manner. When he brushed by me I felt as if my skin were crawling."

"An illusion?" Roulet asked Jonny.

"Anything is possible. You sure he was not one o' th' taken?" he asked, drinking the whiskey in his hand.

"What I am seein' is not ...it's like a coat. That's th' best I can explain."

There was silence for a moment as Roulet considered what to do. "I have an idea." She pulled out her phone and began pushing buttons.

An noticed Silhouette, behind the bar, suddenly grab his pocket and pull something out of it, look at it and frown. Then he shrugged and put it away. A few minutes later, 'Dustin' came back to the bar and Sil took care of his orders. Even from this distance, An could tell the feline bartender was flirting. She watched 'Dustin' stiffen up, though he visibly laughed and said something back before moving away with his drinks. Sil then pulled out his phone and typed something.

Roulet picked hers up and frowned.

"What?" An asked, sipping her tea.

Aislynn was paying attention as she broke off a piece of biscuit and dipped it in her teacup.

"Sil knows that Dustin is... less than receptive to..." Roulet paused, trying to find a way of saying it politely.

"He's politely tolerant of others but violently heterosexual," Jonny supplied.

"Oh." An looked back at Roulet. "And?"

"Well, I had Sil hit on him. He knows better. He implied to Dustin that they had a less than platonic relationship, and asked if he wanted to spend the weekend again. Which they've never done. Instead of telling him off, Dustin... put him off, gave an excuse and said maybe another time." She set the phone down. "That isn't Dustin."

Jonny nodded, shifted to Irish, *"I'll see where he goes tonight."*

Roulet sighed, began texting again. *"I'll let Liberty know."*

An did not stay much longer after that, went home through the upstairs door.

St. Patrick's day was in the middle of the week, so An had to make arrangements with the Tallows. She worked for George and Sharon Tallow as a governess to their very special daughter, Elizabeth. The girl was eleven and magically active. Her family was unaware of exactly what made their daughter special or have so many problems at school, which was why they were so pleased when a mysterious benefactor (read: Ian O'Keefe) paid for a live-in governess to help their daughter with her problems. They still did not understand the whole situation, but they could not complain about the results. Their daughter got in less trouble in school and her grades were up. As far as they were concerned, the blind governess was Mary Poppins and Nanny McPhee all rolled into one prim and proper package.

Elizabeth herself was pleased as punch with the arrangement. An was teaching her so much more than she learned in school, helping her to understand a great deal the school wasn't explaining well. She was also learning special things that no school taught and most would consider absolute nonsense: old wives' tales and faery stories from all over the world, as well as cautionary tales and legends dealing with supernatural creatures of all kinds ...and the truths behind them. An exposed her to literature of a much more diverse nature than public schools, read to her in her sweet Irish lilt, had the girl read her while she worked her lace with her crochet hook. An had also been secretly taking her to lessons with a real magician, who taught her how to focus the latent power that brooded beneath her rather turbulent surface.

An's real job was to protect her from those things which would attempt to steal her or drain her power from her. As a power child from a non-legacy family, i.e., no one in the family even remotely clued in, she was particularly vulnerable and An had already had to fend off numerous attacks until the locals got the message. There hadn't been an attempt on her in several months. Still, An kept what Sean called the 'remote' with her at all times. It was a small figure of a garden gnome she kept in her pocket that was keyed to the various other gnomes hidden throughout the Tallow's yard, all of which were enchanted with guardian wards to alert An to intruders. With it, An worried less.

Thursday afternoon, she dined with the Tallows, tolerating Sharon's meatloaf surprise, and telling Elizabeth not to sulk. Sharon made a small concession in spite of it being a school night, and promised to rent a movie that Elizabeth had been wanting to see for some time. With the promise of getting to stay up late with popcorn and a banana split before bed, Elizabeth did her best imitation of her mother and turned to her governess. "In that case, Miss O'Keefe, you may go."

This caused her father to burst out laughing and her mother to frown, and, though An was equally amused, she did not show it.

"Thank you, Miss Tallow. I trust you will have all of your homework finished prior to the film," she said, her accent decidedly more British than Irish at the moment.

Elizabeth groaned. "Yes, ma'am."

When they were alone upstairs, as An was getting ready, Elizabeth began an entirely different conversation. "Everything all right?" she asked, watching her governess carefully as she brushed out her hair.

"Aye, why do ye ask?" She eyed the girl in the mirror as she pulled up one side of her hair over her ear and held her snow rose to it, asking it to hold it back for her. The rose wove itself in obediently, only scratching her a little with its thorns.

"Well, ...I'm worried. It's one of *those* holidays, where everybody gets drunk and you've... not been to one in this century," she added quietly. She had learned some time ago that her governess was well over a hundred years old, for all she looked like a young woman in her early twenties. She had served a full century and a half as a governess for the three children of the Seelie King.

"I'm not goin' t' Courtz," she said, referring to the nightclub owned by her friends and neighbours, Liberty and Roulet, the place she ate every Wednesday and Friday night. "I'm goin' t' th' Hedge Gate, t' celebrate with my own kind in a manner to which I am quite accustomed. While in my country and day we merely went to church, I am no stranger to pub holidays. Admittedly, it has been a while, but I won't be among complete strangers."

"Well… I'm just worried about weird stuff," she shrugged, a gesture she knew An hated.

An fidgeted with the uncomfortably short skirt of the forest green dress she wore this evening. Elizabeth had helped her pick it out, assuring her that green, and not blue, was the color of the day. The skirt came to just below her knee, a half a foot shorter than she liked, and flared out a little with the help of a ruffled petticoat. The neckline swept in a wide V to the tops of her shoulders and had sleeves that were little more than a three inch wide band extending across the bodice. The silver pendant of two entwined figures glittered on her chest, their abstract toes resting just at the beginning of her modest cleavage.

She took the diamond flower broach from a box on her dressing table and pinned it on the band over her right breast. She wore it whenever she dressed up. It was worth a fortune, of which she had no idea. The sentimental value of it was far greater to her. It, like the snow rose, had been a gift, though this one had been from the Lion Prince who had played her 'faery godmother' for a single night the previous Yule.

She ran her hands along the fine gold embroidery on the edges of the bodice. The brownie who lived in her house had done lovely work enhancing the originally rather plain frock, making the whole thing visible to An in the process. She looked herself over in the mirror and frowned. She looked nice, but worried she was… too improper. Elizabeth handed her the low heeled shoes they had bought to go with the dress.

"You look beautiful," the girl said. "And modest," she added. "You'll probably be in the longest skirt there. And it's a party. You said yourself, lower necklines and bare shoulders are perfectly acceptable for that."

An sighed, sat and slipped the shoes over her stockinged feet. "Thank ye, luv."

Elizabeth grinned. "Jonny's gonna fall all over himself."

An's eyes flicked up to the child's face. Though there were no pupils in the pits of fog that served her for eyes, Elizabeth had the uncanny ability to know when An was looking at her and to read her intent. "That, young lady, is a step too far."

"Sorry. But... you are going to stun him."

An huffed, slipping on the other shoe. "I want him stunned, I'll use Cipín," she said.

It took Elizabeth a second. Then she laughed. "I promise, I won't call unless something happens. But you got to fill me in tomorrow."

An had the girl walk her to the door. She regretted the need to be seen leaving the house. Normally she took the short-cut in her closet which led to her cottage, or from there to Courtz' upstairs if that was she was going. But tonight the Tallows knew she was leaving and had to see her go. Which meant any marauder lurking outside would know too. When the girl closed the door behind her and locked it, An made a show of pulling out a large skeleton key and slipping it into the very modern lock, which it shouldn't have fit. Twisting it activated a magical lock which only she or the members of the household could open. Mr. and Mrs. Tallow would never notice the door had been locked other than mundanely.

Slipping the key into her pocket, An walked down the street, using Cipín as a tap-stick to guide her. The doorman at Courtz let her in without a question. She went straight for the back staircase, neatly avoiding the thin, early crowd. The sound system was playing a Dropkick Murphy's song at near full blast, and the dance floor was in use. Silhouette was at the bar, pouring a series of coloured drinks, which surprised An that she could see. The man was apparently truly magic with alcohol.

He flashed her a smile and winked, sliding the drinks across the bar in front of him. An cast her gaze around the club once, looking for signs of Dustin and did not see him at all. With that, she climbed the stairs and closed the upper door behind her. She crossed the empty private lounge carefully, following her magic gaze to the only door she could see. Humming a brief little melody, she opened the door not into the bedroom that mundanely lay on the other side, but into her cheery little Irish cottage at the Rest.

Aislynn was waiting for her there, her scales brightly polished and a gold ribbon around her slender throat with a fresh shamrock tucked in the bow. An stroked her between her wings, scratching that hard to reach spot she loved to have rubbed. She laughed as the petty drake trilled and arched her back like a cat. "Ye look lovely, my dear," she said.

"And you look positively edible," the dragon grinned.

An frowned, certain there was something outside the obvious in that comment and just blushed on principle. "Is it too much? Or too little? Risque?" she asked, turning.

"Ye look like yer ready for dancing, and any fool what doesn't take ye fer a spin is just that, a fool." Aislynn jumped to her shoulder and wrapped her tail around An's throat loosely, letting the pearly white scales dangle like a choker. *"When ye are,"* she said.

An set her bag down on the table. Tonight she wouldn't need it, so planned to leave it here, but first, she pulled something from it. She had acquired a small bottle of Irish whiskey and now set it on the table with a pair of meringues she had picked up that afternoon. She brushed her fingers across the table and thought about it, telling the house that they were for the brownie. With that, she collected her shawl and carried Aislynn out the front door, began to walk down the pavement to the pub.

It was just twilight as she arrived, her favourite time of day, and she paused outside the Hedge Gate doors to enjoy it a little. Several people passed her, some greeting her by name as they went by. Finally, she went in.

The bar was packed. There was a band on the stage playing "Who Put The Overalls In Mrs. Murphy's Chowder," and more than half the patrons were singing madly along. She could hear the stomping of feet on the hardwood floor that told her the dancing was in full swing.

She found her way over to an empty place at the end of the bar. She poked Skye in the ribs as she slipped up behind him, perching on a stool as he jumped and turned the other way. He scowled, then grinned broadly and pulled her into a hug. She laughed as Aislynn tried to launch out of the way and got her tail caught between them.

Skye apologized, ordering her a shot of whiskey in apology. Aislynn stuck her nose in the air and looked away from him, pretending to be reluctant to be mollified. When he pulled a small platinum chain bracelet out of his jerkin's pocket and offered it to her, she lit up, flapping her opalescent wings in pleasure and slipping her new treasure around her neck. It must have been sized for an infant, as it only hung a little loose against her chest.

Skye laughed as she hopped onto the bar and sat up, prim and proper, to sip her alcohol, calling out in Gaelic for the bartender to bring a cracker and cheese plate. If the bartender was disturbed or surprised by the little dragon ordering food in clear Irish, he did not show it and put in the order before bringing over a double of Irish Mist in a chilled glass for An.

She looked around, seeing a great number of the touched and hearing a few mundanes that she knew. Harry and Peter were not far off down the bar, bickering as usual. Billy Younger was on the stage singing, his voice ringing out like the strings of the harp he once had been. She smiled. "Nice turnout. Bit crowded though. Courtz was no where near this full."

"Early yet," someone on Skye's left said. "The Irish-fer-a-day don't come out in force 'til the parade's over. They'll get rowdier than we will though. *They* can't handle their alcohol. Though there might be a brawl or two here afore the night's old."

An looked around Skye's broad chest to the person sitting beside him. He was an odd man, a little soft at the edges. His hair was lanky and uneven, in spite of a clear attempt to do something with it, and his skin was unevenly coloured. After a second she realized it was because he was put together from several individuals. This was the patchwork man she had seen Raven with, but never actually met. "Ye must be Patches," she said, leaning around Skye. She held out her hand. "I'm An Ceobhrán O'Keefe." She indicated the dragon, "and this is my friend Aislynn."

Aislynn gave him what could only have been the draconic equivalent of a curtsey.

He laughed, an easy, soft sound. "Yes, I'm Patches. Pleased to meet you both. Your brother Skye's mentioned you a couple times."

Without even looking, An swung, backhanding Skye across his bare bicep. He pulled back, his face stunned. "Whit th' bloody blue blazes wa' thon fer?" he yelped.

"Talkin' about me," she quipped, still smiling at Patches.

"T'were all guid," he complained, rubbing his sore arm.

Patches chuckled. "He was bragging about you. Something about a swampling with one strike?"

"Ooooo," Aislynn said, her eyes wide over the shot glass, doing a fair imitation of Elizabeth's 'you're in trouble' sing-song and taking perverted delight in it.

"Next thing I know t'will be seven in one blow," she said tightly.

Skye stood taller, "When ya actually manage seven in ane blow o' anythin', yer damn skippy! Ah'll bella' it fra th' fuckin' belltower!"

She swatted him again, turning to thank the bartender for the plate of various cheeses and stone ground crackers he set in front of them.

"An' that?" he growled.

"Language."

The evening wore on slowly. There was plenty of drinking, though very few people got so drunk they were sick or stupid. There was food a plenty and singing and dancing. Several young men of the Rest, most mortal, asked An to dance and, feeling festive, she accepted. The dances were all spirited and well suited to the country steps she knew from her youth, and perfect for crowded dance floors.

After a couple of sets, she came back to the bar for a bit of refreshment, laughing as Aislynn did a little jig on the bar. Fox came in, threw himself on a stool and ordered an 'Irish Carbomb', which caused An some consternation until she realized it was a drink. He slammed it back and was ordering another when he wrinkled his nose at something. "Do you smell that?" he said, looking over at Skye and An, frowned. "No, I suppose you wouldn't."

"What's it smell like?" An asked.

He thought a moment. "...Unicorn," he decided. He turned, looking towards the door. There was a young man standing there, looking a little lost in very fine clothing, the sort one expects of a faery tale prince out among the people. His hair fell to his shoulders in silky waves of rich brown and his eyes were a noticeable blue. He was slight of build and wiry, with a rapier at his side.

An caught his reflection in the mirror over the bar and turned, looked him over. He was pure touched and made to be attractive, to put one at ease.

Ian came from the game room suddenly, his face getting more beak-like as he followed his nose, his hair starting to have the look of crest feathers standing on end. As folk scrambled out of Ian's way, the new man took a step back, not quite going defensive but striking a pose that could fall into violence at any second.

"I seek succour," he said. "This was the only place with people and... if we cannot find it here we'll leave with no trouble. Unless you make it," he added. His eyes flickered, lightning fast, over the patrons of the bar, picking out the more dangerous ones.

The band screeched to a halt as a second man stepped in behind the first and the tension thickened instantly. Skye's sword fell into his hand and Ian's lip curled even as he growled, "Makar."

The person behind the prince stood like a man, but did not look much like one. His head was that of a crow, as were the wings on his back and the talons that served him for hands. His naked chest was feathered at the shoulders but blended down to inky black fur which ran all the way to his panther tail and hind legs. He was naked and freshly cut up.

Before anyone could make a move towards him, the prince jumped in front of him, rapier out and opening a circle around them. It was then that An noticed there was blood on his otherwise pristine white shirt.

"No one approaches him," he threatened. "He is with me." His attention went to Ian as the man shifted a little more in front of him. Beyond Ian, Fox burst into flame, and several others began to change.

"Shit," the makar squawked, "I told you I smelled griffin, that this was a bad idea."

"That is why I told you to wait outside," the first said tightly. He addressed Ian carefully. "Tell me now, sirrah, if we are to parley or leave. I've been through a squeak of hell with this man and will not allow him to be harmed now."

Ian stopped, held up his hands, ordering people back.

Skye cracked his knuckles, but obediently let go of his sword, confident that the moment he needed it, the claymore would be in his hand even as he swung it.

"Speak yer piece. Who are yeh and whence come yeh?" Ian asked.

The prince straightened a little, lowered the point of his sword. "I am William...." He looked genuinely surprised that he could not remember his last name. "William of... I am terribly sorry, but I seem to have forgotten. I... have been released from Amalthea's service and seek refuge, at least for a short time. My friend Mak here saved me from an ambush and the two of us have fought our way here through a great deal. Seeing you are what you are, I can understand your reluctance with his form, but I assure you, he is not one of Them any longer."

Ian looked from William to Mak, addressed the makar. "Why'd yeh leave Her?" he asked flatly.

Mak looked sullen, his beady black eyes taking everything in, as if fearing attack in spite of the stand off. "She took my rider away."

An felt Skye tense as he stepped in front of her. "Ah've on'y known ane makar as ever had a rider. Come tae parley wi' th' King, she did. Would ya ha' been thon makar?"

He shifted uncomfortably. The bones of his neck gave a series of sickening pops. "That would have been my rider, yeah. But the mount were not me," he said bitterly. "I don't want to be there if I can't be with her; don't want to watch her with him. So I left." He turned his head to regard Skye with one eye. "You look familiar."

Skye cracked his own neck. "Ah shood," he ground, his highland accent thickening.

Mak seemed to wilt, head shrinking down into his neck feathers. "You're the one She was mad about. The one the challenge was for. Many died because you weren't there." He watched Skye stiffen, seemed pleased. He added with a shrug, "She put them back together again… and took them apart again…"

William redirected the conversation away from this most dangerous of topics. "So, may we abide or must we fly on?"

"Stand down, all o' yeh. Peter," Ian said to the young man who appeared at his elbow at the summons, "get th' sidebar cleared out."

An heard him scurry off to obey.

"If yeh two will follow me, I give yeh my oath no harm will come to yeh an' yeh abide by Hospitality this night," he raised his voice so that it could be heard by everybody. There was murmuring in the wake of the announcement, but people began to move off.

On the stage, Billy got the band to start playing again, called An over to sing something with him. In interest of distraction and keeping the peace, An agreed, allowing the people in her path to the stage to help her along.

Liberty came over to Skye, dragging him onto the dance floor to get him to take his eyes off where the trio had gone. It took a little bit of time before he could focus on her, but eventually he managed.

An sang a few songs before she begged off and went back to the bar for a nip of honey whiskey. A white raven flew in as a couple slipped out the front door. It landed on the bar next to Aislynn, startling the person beside her. Aislynn looked up at him with some concern, frowned and handed him her shot glass. Jonny took it in his bill and tipped it up, managing to get most of it down his gullet. "Ian," he croaked, dropping the glass onto the bar.

An shook her head. "Sequestered with two fresh out."

The bird nodded, looked at the plate of fruit, cheese cubes and meat rolls in front of them and glanced up at An in askance.

Concerned as to why he did not change back into a man yet, An nodded, taking up a rolled slice of salami and breaking it into bite sized pieces for him. She found it a little odd, but fed him, casually looking him over for signs of injury which might explain his reluctance to change. She saw nothing, not the tiniest flick of red on his snow white plumage. When she reached out to stroke his breast feathers, he hopped back, giving her a warning eye. She pulled back, but showed none of the hurt she felt. She called the bartender over and ordered him a pint, which he drank as a bird drinks and croaked an understandable 'thank ye' to the bartender.

Finally, Ian came out of the back room and cleared his throat. Everyone turned and fell silent. "Until such time as I have reason to declare otherwise, William and Mak will be accorded Hospitality here at th' Rest. Yeh will treat them wit'out prejudice, and if yeh can't... avoid them politely."

There were murmurs of acceptance and grumbles of rude things said about the makar, but everything bustled back to relative normal. An was a little startled when the raven jumped off the bar in front of her and changed back into a man as Ian approached. She was even more concerned by his human state. His hair was braided but looked as if he'd slept in it for near a week, and slept badly; his shirt was missing a button on one sleeve and flapped open at his wrist; his jeans were wrinkled, torn and dirty and his soft leather boots crusted with mud.

Ian saw him and came over, gesturing for the bartender who brought him a Jameson's without asking what he wanted. "What'd yeh learn or need this be private? Th' sidebar… isna an option at th' moment," he said pointedly, not explaining.

Jonny shook his head, taking his pint in hand. "It is as we suspected," he said, his lilt light and airy compared to Ian's heavy Cork. "Th' man's got a glamour on him t' make him look like Dustin. Wears it like a coat. He works directly for Spetznakov and I've reason t' believe he's done somethin' unsavoury t' th' lad. He's livin' in his home and no sign o' th' real."

"Any idea where he got this 'coat'?" Ian asked, drinking half his whiskey in one swig.

Jonny shook his head. "Only thing that is clear is that he got it from Spetznakov. And there is more magic to be had, from th' way he was talking. Mysterious benefactor."

"I don't like this," Ian growled.

"Neither I," Jonny sighed, drinking deep of his Guinness. "There's something smacking familiar about a lot of things but I can't see th' picture clear. What about… th' other?" he asked, glancing up at Ian.

Ian shook his head. "Nothin'. I'm sorry."

An watched his arm twitch and his jaw tighten. "Ye took a shipment yesterday. I know ye did. I heard them complainin'," Jonny said, his voice tight.

Ian reached out, started to set his hand on Jonny's shoulder and pulled back when the man flinched. "I'twere contaminated. Dangerously. Bastards laced it wit' PCP. It wouldn't end well. Don't worry, I got O'Roarke coming in from Boston wit' some relief."

Jonny relaxed a little, became less belligerent at least. "When?"

"Some time t'night."

Jonny nodded, finished his pint and ordered something a good deal stronger, took the sweetest morsel from the plate and popped it in his mouth.

"O'Roarke," Fox asked from nearby, slamming back another carbomb. "That Kitty's boy, Aiden? Got taken by the Dark Man six years ago?"

Ian nodded. "He's really good at carrying t'ings no one'll ever find."

An frowned. "Kitty an O'Keefe?" she asked.

"Aye," Ian said. "She were."

"But… ye said those of th' blood were protected, couldn't be taken. Were he tricked?"

Ian scowled. "No. Th' devil found th' loophole, an' Kitty dinna realize why it be so important that I acknowledge each an' every child born ta one o' th' blood. Like Liberty, he dinna bear th' O'Keefe name or blessin', so was fair game, and oh so deliciously temptin' a morsel," he snarled.

"We got him back," Fox said.

"And how many have we not?" Ian snapped.

Jonny slammed back the clear liquid he had been given and headed for the stage. He borrowed an acoustic guitar from one of the band and did not bother with the microphone. An followed his progress, leaning back against the bar to watch. The melody was familiar-ish, like many good traditional songs, but the words she had never heard before. He seemed oblivious to his audience as he sang, his voice full of pain and self loathing.

> Born long ago and far away,
> Like every faerie story starts,
> I had a childhood wild and gay
> And learned full well a minstrel's arts.
>
> One Day, in May, when nearly full
> Had blossomed manhood in my heart,
> A-strolling on th' green was I,
> And practising my parts.
>
> When I was spied by wanton eyes,
> And heard by wanton ears,
> And lured by wanton laughter
> Into slavery, for years.
>
> I saw her there, across th' glen
> Her lips were red as blood

Her skin was white as winter snow,
Her hair a ruby flood.

Her beauty burned me like a brand,
Her eyes were red as fire,
Th' smile that danced upon those lips
Inflamed me with desire.

I stared, amazed, and followed her
Down twisted paths into th' wood,
And never once looked I behind,
And never knew I should.

She stopped, I stopped, at th' edge
Of thicker thickets, bearing thorn,
A mighty barrier of hedge
With stalwart gates of bone and horn.

Said she,"Whilst come along with me?
O sweetest bonny boy e'er born?"
And helpless said my lips for me,
"I will." And I was torn.

Her laughter led th' way for me,
Th' stalwart gates swung wide,
And crossing thus, from east to west,
we reached th' other side.

Th' gates clanged shut, Then clicked th' lock,
And I, inside, was trapped,
I noticed not, for shame, in truth,
Her beauty held me rapt.

When her pavilion we did reach,
Upon th' meadow side,
I never looked around th' tent,
To see what it might hide.

I sang, I played; she laughed and danced,
We made love in th' shade,
With every word, and every touch,
My own heart I betrayed.

For back there, in th' village
A girl for me did wait,
We were to have been married.
We'd even set th' date.

When she was sated, as was I,
She raised her mocking eyes,
And said, "I need a dirge singer."
And that was my demise.

From my eyes th' scales fell
I saw th' meadow clear,
A shattered, battered battlefield
Of blood, sweat, death, and fear.

Her fingers snapped, and I was grabbed
Strong arms did hold me down,
She kissed me, long and hard again
Upon that blood-soaked ground.

With every moment of that kiss,
I lived another life,
Another span of tragedy,
Of sorrow, pain, and strife.

At length, when she released me,
My memories were filled,
A thousand lifetimes' tragedy,
They lie inside me still.

> And worst of all, and first of all
> In all those memories fell and grim
> I'd lost th' face of my true love,
> Betrayed by wanton whim.
>
> From all that teeming reverie
> Of memories of pain,
> I could not sort my own recall,
> Or even reck my name.
>
> I stood, a sad smile on my lips,
> And reached out for my harp,
> And wrung from it a single note
> So sweet, so mournful, and so sharp
>
> All stood amazed, and at me gazed
> And listened with their hearts
> I played my sorrowed agony
> With all my bardic arts.
>
> I sang "Th' Minstrel Boy" for her
> Till tears came to her eyes
> And all her host began to weep,
> Th' air filled with their cries.
>
> And then, like that most famous bard
> I broke my harp across my knee
> And said, my smile sad and hard
> "I'll never sing aught more for thee."

Done, he dropped from the stage without preamble and out of An's sight in the mortal crowd.

She tried to find him again. Her heart was hurting for him. She wiped the tears from her eyes and noted she was not the only one. A mortal next to her, an older woman by the voice, commented softly to her friend. "Wonder what's gotten inta him. He hasn't sung that one in years. Och, but it always makes me cry."

An's hand went to the pendant around her neck and tried harder to find him. She knew something wasn't quite right, but couldn't put her finger on exactly what. Aislynn helped by launching herself into the rafters, getting a bird's-eye view for her. Shortly, she dropped down to her shoulder and pointed towards a table in the back corner. An took up Cipín and headed in that direction.

When she got there she slowed, saw that Jonny was sitting across the table from Mak and the tension in the air was palpable.

"I remember you," Mak was saying.

"Many do. Is it just heard of me ye have, or've ye *seen* me?" There was a barely concealed hostility in his voice, but it did not seem aimed at Mak directly.

"I don't remember. Not sure. I know She still has the harp you broke. No matter what She does, She can't fix it. She's mad about you."

"Mad?" he asked, arching one eyebrow. "So many meanings, one little word."

"Crazy, angry; She's all of them. Hates you, loves you. But She's like that with everybody who dares to leave Her or want more." His voice dropped and he looked away. "Probably hates *me* now."

"Not altogether a bad thing," Jonny said, with more gentleness than before. "More dangerous, aye. But Her love is hard."

"Her love kills," An said softly. Mak looked up at her and she suppressed a shudder. Jonny did not turn his head completely, managed not to flinch as she reached out and tucked in a stray lock of white hair that was sticking out at an odd angle. She kept her touch light, coming into contact with him as little as she could as he seemed to want to avoid her right now.

Just as she was thinking in the back of her mind that she should stop acting the moon-struck calf and walk away, he reached out and took her hand, drew her closer to the table. "This is An Ceobhrán O'Keefe," he said. "Our governess, and her petty drake, Aislynn," he added when Aislynn puffed up.

Mak reached a clawed hand across to her. "Pleased," he said politely. "I... don't remember my name. Will calls me Mak, but I know that isn't my name."

She accepted the handshake, keeping control of her natural aversion to his kind. He was only what She had made of him, she told herself.

He looked over at Sorrow. "I... don't remember yours either," he said sheepishly.

"Jonny Sorrow," he said, extending his own hand.

An was distracted for the tiniest second by little stab of a lie off to her right and glanced over to see William kissing the hand of a mortal woman, telling her she was a marvellous dancer. Finding it harmless, she was just turning back when Jonny kicked back from the table with a bellow of agony. He fell to the floor clutching his temples and thrashing. An dodged as one boot kicked out, striking a chair instead and shattering the leg.

Aislynn jumped for the rafters with a shriek and An fell to her knees beside him and tried to hold him down, to keep him from hurting himself further. He was flailing too much, too strong for her. The second time his skull cracked against the floor she grabbed a handful of his hair and pulled his head into her lap, holding it there, yelling for Liberty. Let him beat his head as he would, he would do nothing more than bruise her, which was preferable to bashing his brains out.

People had jumped back immediately, giving him room. William was there, trying to gain control of his legs and then Skye, grabbing him by the arms and pinning him to the floor. Liberty was right behind him, extending her magic, trying to heal whatever it was. The seizure did not stop, and the harder Skye and William pressed his flesh the more he screamed.

"Yer hurtin' him!" An yelled.

"Better than he hurt himself!" Skye snarled. "I' yar gonnae dae sommat, love, dae it quick!"

"There's nothin' t' heal!" Liberty cried.

"Back off!" came Ian's bellow. William jumped back as one wing swept in his direction and Ian took his place, straddling

Jonny's legs and sitting on them. He grabbed hold of the bard's right arm and pulled it taut, ripping the sleeve up his arm to expose the underside of his tanned skin, marked by the tracery of a thousand tiny, white scars. There were other marks there, on either side of his elbow, a red tracing along the veins. An was confused.

"Skye: tourniquet," Ian ordered.

With a frown on his face, Skye reached over and grabbed the upper part of Jonny's arm and squeezed, cutting off the circulation.

Someone An could see but did not know stepped up. He was a shadowy-skinned man who knelt next to the stretched arm, laid a flat black box open on the floor. He held his hand in the air, inspecting something small which he flicked with a finger. Satisfied, he separated his thumb and first two fingers, laid the thing to the inside of Jonny's elbow and slid it against it, pressing downward and bringing his fingers slowly together.

Just that quickly, Jonny stopped thrashing. He went slowly limp at the pace of whatever it was slipping into his veins. An could see his vein bulging a little, even as Skye let off the pressure on the arm. She loosened her grip in his hair, settled him a little more comfortably in her lap. He sighed, slipping from agony to unconsciousness that easily. She brushed her fingers gently across his forehead, moving aside his hair. The strands felt snow-damp to her fingers.

Ian stood, gestured for Skye to move, then bent and picked Jonny up as easily as if he were a doll, carried him to the snug. An rose to follow, confused and determined to know what was going on. She looked at Mak who had shrunk back against the wall as if afraid everyone was going to turn on him now and tear him apart. William was dealing with him. Their eyes met, neither really understanding what they saw there. She turned and followed Ian.

She had gotten as far as the door to the game room when Skye grabbed her arm and pulled her back.

"Ah dinnae want ya seein' him anymar," he said flatly, ready to brave her anger.

"And why is that?" she asked curtly.

"He's a fuckin' drug addict, is why!"

"There'll be an explanation. Did ye not see th' pain he was in? Ian wouldna give him sommat dangerous. Th' clan don't deal in th' dangerous shite," she said. Her choice of words should have warned him.

"Thon IS th' dangerous shite!" he snarled, tightening his grip. "He's on th' nod, An. Chasin' th' dragon. However ya want tae say it. Thon there were heroin. Ah've seen what it kin dae tae a body and ah don' want ya near thon."

She set her teeth. "There'll be an explanation, Skye."

"An' it won' matter. This be a matter o' yer safety an' integrity an' ah'll nae allow it. It's dangerous, an' it makes him dangerous. Ah've suspected sommat an' been willin' t' overlook, but this.... Na. Ah'm puttin' m' foot doon. He'll nae drag ya wit' him inta thon pig's walla."

Her hand cracked across his face, her shillelagh trapped in the hand whose arm he had a death grip on. He reeled, seeing stars for a moment. "Yer gonna let go m' arm, Skye O'Keefe, an' let me go t' him. I'll get m' own explanation an' come t' my own decision." His hand tightened instead of loosening. "An' ye don't I'll drop Cipín on yer foot, iron first."

He let go, watched her go to the closed door and enter without even bothering to knock. His rage was boiling, threatening to wipe every sane thought from his head. He shouted at the closed door, "Mrs. McNeil hits harder!"

That having failed to satisfy him, he turned and put his fist through the wall.

Mikey stepped up at that point, helped him to pull himself free from the plaster and broken wood. "That's it, boyo, you an' me: out back."

"Whit fer?" he growled, inspecting his fist, beginning to feel like a lout.

"T' have this out on somethin' ye can't break."

"An' whit'd thon be?"

"Me."

An slipped silently into the room, closing the door softly behind her. Ian looked up from where he sat on a large chair directly across from the door. Like the rest of the pub, the furniture here was invisible to her, but she got the feeling it was a small room, intended to be quiet and intimate. In fact, the moment the door closed she could no longer hear the music and noise of the celebration resuming outside it.

She drifted to where Jonny hung suspended just off the floor and sank to the carpet beside him. She ran her fingers along his brow, brushing away the snow. His temperature was elevated slightly, making him feel almost normal. Something she was beginning to associate with fever in him. Her fingers ran down his arm to the fresh track marks blending into the tracery of white. It was almost as if the Northerner had intended it to compliment Her artwork all along. She continued to his wrist, checking his pulse. It was strong but irregular, and his breathing deep and slow. She laced her fingers in his and just sat with him, forgetting Ian was even there.

Ian let her sit there, waiting on her. Finally she turned to him, still not letting go of Jonny's hand. "Will you explain? Or needs I wait fer him to come out o' this?"

Ian tipped his head ever so slightly over his steepled fingers. "That could be a while. Ask. If I feel it too sensitive, I'll let yeh know."

"Ye told me th' family works hard t' keep this out o' town, why then do ye give it to him? Cause this is no' th' first. I saw a box just like that go inta his vest Christmas eve."

"Fair question," Ian nodded. "We do. That's stuff I don' tolerate on ma streets. Jonny's a special case." He faced her determined stare, unfazed. "He tell yeh what he goes t'rough every moment?"

"The pain? Aye. What She did t' him," she glanced at the arm she was leaning against, ran her free fingers over a flower shaped scar where the bone had been broken and poked through, then re-healed. "It's constant."

"It defies medicine modern and magical to stop. In th' beginnin' i'twere just regular pain killers. But they didn't work long.

Eventually i'twere morphine. Now heroin, an' next... I don' know what we'll do."

She was comforted by Ian's near emotionless delivery, felt confident enough to ask a few more questions. "How often?"

"That yeh'll have ta ask him. I don't rightly know. I know how much I give him."

"How dangerous is it?"

His voice was steady, with none of his usual warmth, "It could kill him an' he takes too much. I do my best ta make sure what he gets is clean. I have every bit I confiscate tested. Normally, I let th' dealers off with a warnin' when they're caught at it. If it comes up impure or tampered wit' ...I break t'ings."

She felt a shiver run up her spine at the coldness in his voice. "And these last, what put the... CPC in it?"

"PCP," he corrected gently. "It's a powerful hallucinogen. Too much can kill ye quick an' messy, make ye... too strong an' violent an' out o' control. Mix that with a drug most commonly injected wit'out th' user bein' aware an' ye have a recipe for disaster."

"Ye killed him," she said.

"Pumped him full o' his own shite an' watched him writhe. Left him an' his junk fer Cass an' Dukes. One o' th' reasons I test everythin'."

She did not flinch. She tried to picture the dealer's death, thought of Jonny going through that and found the original image satisfying. "Skye..." she shut up, not wanting to validate his suggestion by asking if it were a possibility.

"Skye's afraid of yeh bein' associated wit' this?"

She nodded, resting her head against Jonny's shoulder.

"I'll deal wit' Skye. Provided yeh still want ta pursue this course?" he asked, one brow arched. He shook his head. "Yeh don't have ta answer that. 'Tis yer choice. But yeh should know everyt'in' afore yeh do that. I'll... make sure he gives yeh th' option."

"What about Jonny... tonight?"

"I can take him up to th' manor, or he can stay here. He should be comfortable enough." Ian finally moved in the chair, leaning forward. "I'll have someone stay with him."

She shook her head. "I'll.... He watched fer me that awful night. 'Tis the least I can do."

Ian said nothing, just watched her sitting on the floor next to the unconscious bard. "I'm of th' understandin' yer th' one called attention to th' impostor at Courtz."

She looked back up at him. He was resting his arms on his spread knees, fingers still steepled, watching her intently with his eagle eyes.

"Aye." Her voice sounded smaller to her somehow.

"Thank yeh. But I fear I may have ta call on yer sight in th' near future. Fer other things. Some o' them dangerous. Are yeh willin'?"

She nodded. "I'll do m' part to keep us safe, uncle. Fear ye not on that account. Yer my king, whatever the season; m' chief. Ye ask, an' it be in m' power, I'll do. Unta death need be."

He sat back. "There'll hopefully be no need fer that. I'll not send yeh wit'out due escort an' protection. I hope what I'm fearin' isna true an' I won't hav'ta utilize yeh. But I've learned never ta put much stock in hopes. That's like trusting a boat made o' clouds an' victory ta take yeh down th' Boyne."

He rose with a great deal of popping bone. He stretched and groaned, satisfied. "I'll leave yeh be then. Other business t' attend. O'Roarke has other things fer me than just Jonny's anodyne. I'll send in things t' yer comfort. Send Aislynn ifn' yeh have need. None will disturb yeh."

She thanked him in a soft voice and watched him go. He paused to place a hand on her shoulder and squeezed it before opening the door. The room filled with an assault of pub noise and fell quiet again just as quick. The silence was almost as painful as the noise had been.

She turned her body to face the sleeping Bard, getting more comfortable on the floor, leaning against the couch. She slipped her hand back into his, keeping her fingers where she could monitor what she needed to and watched him sleep, wishing she knew the dreaming as he did, to be able to help him. Instead, she sang. She began with "Red is the Rose", and moved on to "Súil a Rún" and the "Green Fields of France". She sang everything she knew, and some she didn't know she remembered, sweet Tuatha lullabyes. Aislynn curled up in her lap and fell asleep listening.

An was not aware of when she had taken down her hair, holding the rose in her free hand and gently stroking the razor's edge of the petals. The sharp was unconsciously comforting. At some point she fell asleep, her head on their clasped hands.

The room was dim when she woke, feeling a hand stroking her head. Her lap felt cold, as did her cheek, though for entirely different reasons. Her lap was an absence. Her cheek was... a cold hand. The fingers at her temple suddenly made sense and she lifted her head, trying to focus in the darkness. She felt her hair flow off his body where it had been carefully spread. She blinked.

Jonny was awake and watching her. His smile was weak as she sat up, his body languid on the couch.

"How do ye feel?"

"Half here," he said softly. "Tolerable." He stroked her hair, spreading it out again and she realized he must have been playing with it for a while now.

"Can ye eat a bite? Need a drink? I... don't know th' protocols fer... this," she said, her voice getting quieter.

"Nothin' fer ye to fret about. Or slice yer fingers to ribbons o'er." He slipped his hand from hers and reached down, taking the rose from her other hand and setting it aside, drawing it up and showing her the little red lines of blood that criss-crossed the tips of her fingers. Her thumb was a mess. Almost as soon as she noticed it, the cuts frosted over and healed. "Ye need be careful with tha'. An' ye needn't have stayed."

"I... wanted t' be sure. Has it... ever been this bad?"

He nodded. "Once. Th' first time I tried t' quit. I'm... not like other addicts, Ceobhránach. I don't chase th' dragon fer th' high or th' euphoria. That's a side effect, let's me judge my needs. I take it fer surcease o' pain."

"I know. I've been told."

He frowned, brushed aside the curtain of her hair so he could see her face. "What all ye been told?"

"That this is th' only thing what works and may not for much longer. An' that... it could kill ye... yer not careful."

He watched her, waiting. When she did not continue he prompted, "And?"

She blushed and looked away. "It has been suggested it can make ye dangerous t' me."

He turned her face to meet his eyes. "I'm no more dangerous than I was a few months ago when ye took th' brunt of a cú hound who'd have mauled me unsuspectin' when we kissed beneath that oak. Or when we warred on th' dance floor, a highwayman combatin' th' Snow Queen and I ...kissed ye 'neath th' mistletoe," he chuckled, remembering the force of that kiss and her response. "No more dangerous than a season ago when ye lay on m' bed like a Briar Rose and we fought that dream curse upon th' road. I'll hurt ye, aye, but not fer that. Not over that. That's not what ye should fear of me."

"Then what?" she found herself asking, getting caught up in the dreamy tone of his voice.

He traced the contours of her face with calloused fingertips. She could smell toasted tobacco and whiskey and snow and frozen earth and sighed, closed her eyes and leaning into the caress. "That," he whispered. "Losin' yer heart to an unfaithful bastard like m'self."

She opened her eyes just as his lips met hers and she melted into him, what protest she had dying between their lips. Her desire welled up inside her, threatening to smother her or make her float away. It couldn't quite make up its mind which. She clung to him, wanting to drown in the kiss but not trusting herself at all. Tears rose to her eyes, filling her with a desperate sadness she could not explain.

The moment was broken by a tiny voice clearing its throat from the back of the couch. They looked up, saw the bright opal eyes of the petty drake regarding them in the dimness. An frowned, trying to get her head to focus.

"Aye?" she asked.

"Perhaps we should take him to some place like a home," she suggested slyly, as if not at all aware of what she had interrupted.

An shifted, immediately felt pain in her legs. They had gone numb from the way she had been sitting and moving flooded them with needles. She gave a small cry of surprise and pain, reaching down and using her hands to stretch them out.

"And there's another good reason," Aislynn said snidely.

"She might be right," Jonny said ruefully. "Hardly appropriate or comfortable for you."

She stopped rubbing her legs to glare up at him. "For me? Aye, I've seen your idea o' personal comfort. Penance more like."

He merely shrugged. "What need have I of comfort when breathing hurts?"

She groaned. "Now's not th' time t' have that particular argument." She resumed trying to get her circulation going again. "Where do ye want?" she asked him.

He leaned back against the couch, having tried in vain to get himself up. "I'm in no condition to get to mine," he sighed.

"An' I don't know th' way," she said. "'Tis too far a walk anyhow e'en if Cipín would get me there. I suppose I can step inta th' bar an' get some help t' get ye up to th' manor.... Ian's said he'd provide a bed."

"Darlin', there's no one out there."

"What?" she replied. She rolled to her knees and made her legs cooperate. It felt like she was walking on peglegs, but she made it to the door and opened it, found the room beyond dark. "Where is.... What time is it?"

"I've no idea, but Aislynn and I've been... talkin'. Th' party wound down hours ago, far earlier than its wont. She said something happened. Th' Russians, she thought."

"At th' Rest?" An gasped, turning. "There'd have been alarms, I'd have..."

"Heard nothing," he said. "Room's soundproofed. For various reasons. And no, t'weren't here. Likely Spetznakov learned from our doppelgänger that every bloody O'Keefe were goin' t' be here and decided th' time were ripe." His voice dripped with anger at himself, "If I'd not been in so much bloody pain I'd hav' lingered nearer th' winda an' found out what they were up ta."

"Let th' O'Keefe decide whether ye've failed him," she growled with a smile, closed the door.

He raised an eyebrow at that. "I'm afraid I'm not goin' t' be much good fer anythin' for a bit. Any walkin' past that doorframe is goin' t' be a chore. An' I don' think ye kin manage me much farther than that."

She turned and looked at the solid oak, her eyes narrowed. "Leave that t' me, *a chroí*. I have my way ye'll not need t' go much farther than yon door." She blushed the moment she said it, refusing to turn around. Behind her he seemed surprised at first, then smiled.

He watched as she worked the magic on the door, humming a familiar melody under her breath, singing to the pale wood. A moment later she pulled it wide. It opened into a warm and cosy room with a merry fire in the grate. There was a little table set up before the fire with a small meal on it. Jonny's eyebrow went up. "Yer home's brownie works fast," he breathed, forcing himself to rise from the couch.

An ran to him, catching hold just before he fell back, helped him into the cottage. She settled him into one of the chairs, made sure he was stable before she walked away from him.

"I don't really want food," he breathed.

"Ye need som'thin'," she said, going into the door beside the fireplace to get her brush.

He looked down at the two plates, saw different things on each of them. His was lighter fare, just enough to stabilize him without making him sick. He picked at it. Once the first bite was in, he realized it had been some time since he had eaten and ate a little more. He was careful though. He insisted An sit and eat with him, ate a little more as an excuse to get her to comply.

"I want to do something with that raven's nest of yer hair," she complained, though she ate.

"I think 'tis a shower I'll be wantin' afore that," he said with a tired smile.

She was about to mention she hadn't one when the table informed her that it would be hot and ready when he wanted it. And to take off her shoes, it added.

An blushed. In all her haste to take care of him, she had forgotten. She slipped her shoes off under the table, telling the house her stockinged feet would have to suffice. The house was satisfied, having more direct contact with her to communicate. "I... th' shower is in th' other room an' waitin' for ye."

He smiled at her blush, mistaking its cause. "I think I kin make that on m' own. Though I've no..."

"Clothes too," she interrupted as the house informed her. "Apparently ye left something at th' laundry."

"Yer brownie raided th' bean nighe?" he chuckled. "Brave lass."

An relayed the house's comment. "It were yours any way."

When they had eaten enough, she helped him as far as the bathroom door and turned away, blushing as he closed it behind him. "Let me know if he has trouble," she told the house. "I may not be much help but I'm better than nothin'."

Hurriedly,, she changed her clothes into something more modest and comfortable, putting away her jewel and her rose. She put the dress back in the wardrobe and closed it, felt suddenly self-conscious as she heard the water shut off. She stepped back into the other room hoping to find a couch or a second bed, and found the fireplace cold and nothing before it but her usual wing-back chair. She heard something in her room and rushed back in to see Jonny clinging to the door-frame of the bathroom in a pair of loose black trousers and a kilt shirt he had not even bothered to tuck in.

She slipped under his arm and helped him to the bed. He rolled onto it and seemed to stop breathing as he sank into the softness of it. He was just out of her reach and she scrambled up to check him. Her fingers fluttered to his throat under his ear, checking for a pulse and he breathed in again.

He blinked up at her. "Ye sleep on clouds, Ceobhránach," he sighed.

She popped him for the scare he had given her. "No, I just don't sleep on a slab o' ice wi' only a few furs to pad it." She started to get back off the bed and he rolled onto his stomach with surprising speed, grabbing her wrist. She gasped, her heart falling into places she was not entirely sure were proper.

His eyes seemed to stare through her to her soul, as if reading every impure thought trying to form in the back of her mind and she blushed. "I don't usually bother with th' furs," he said.

She let loose all the tension she had suddenly built up. She laughed. "Yer a regular Cistercian, ye are, Jonny."

His eyebrow went up. "I'm no monk, lass."

She blushed more furiously. "So I'm aware."

"An' I'd be careful smackin' a man other than yer brother like that," he added, something else smouldering in his eye.

"Why's that?" she breathed, still very aware of his hand on her wrist.

"Some'd take it as foreplay."

She frowned. "And that word'd mean...?" she prompted.

This time it was Jonny who didn't know what to make of the situation. His grip became loose, more tender, the calloused fingertips softly stroking the underside of her wrist. "It's... little things... intended t' arouse th' other party, t' get them... interested," he said, his eyes filling in the blanks.

She squeaked and flushed, pulling back so quickly she slid off the bed and nearly fell on the floor. She caught herself before she took the tumble. He just smiled at her from the bed. "Though I assure ye, Ceobhránach, I don't have it in me t'night. And I'll not touch ye in that way until ye ask. So please, come t' bed. I... if ye kin stand it... countenance it... I need..."

She did not make him finish.

He was laying on top of the covers, so she went to the chest at the foot of the bed and drew out a quilt which she lay over him before slipping in between the sheets. He pulled her to him, laying one arm over her and resting his cheek at the crook of her shoulder, the sheets and the bedspread between them.

"By th' way," he said softly, "ye were a right vision in tha' dress."

She smiled shyly, remembering what certain people had said when she had put it on.

She lay there, tense for several minutes, terribly frightened by the situation and not understanding why. It felt... natural, comfortable, and perhaps that was what she was afraid of, that it was too easy a trap to give in to. She let her hand go to his now unbound hair, and found herself singing softly until his breathing fell back into the deep and easy draw of sleep. Her last thoughts were to the house, to wake her if anything changed in him. Only then did she surrender to the call of dreaming.

4

The next morning An woke to find herself in the same position she had gone to sleep, but alone save for the dragon curled up in the hollow between her neck and her shoulder. Even as the thought formed in her mind, the house informed her that Jonny had flown away only a little while ago. The quilt was folded neatly on the foot of the bed and the bedroom window was open. He had seemed stable enough.

She felt bereft in his absence, could not help but wonder what it would have been like to wake up next to him.

She dismissed that thought almost violently and got out of bed, slipped into the shower. It felt good but she found she still preferred her claw foot bathtub. Drying off and going back into the bedroom, Aislynn was still curled up asleep where she had left her. An dressed and headed into the kitchen. A modest breakfast sat waiting for her and she got down one of the two books the Princess had sent her months ago.

One was a slim volume on the care and feeding of petty drakes, the information in which was accurate enough according to Aislynn, though the delivery was highly demeaning. *"As if we were pets,"* she had snorted. It had come in handy so far and An now knew not to even offer her vegetables, though fruits were perfectly acceptable. She ate just about everything else, including precious metals, as Ian had told her. They did not eat worked metal, though, preferring to admire those and guard them though they were very much not 'stuff dragons' as Aislynn put it. They were 'people dragons'. Once they attached they were viciously protective.

The second book was a large botany volume that was too large for the box and had been delivered to her through other means. She guessed brownie connections or goblin mail. The book was vaguely familiar to her. She was certain she had read it once, and was equally certain it was one of those things which had faded to make room for other things. There were a great deal of interesting passages about a variety of different plants and their properties to be found in faery. There was a single page marked with a flat yellow ribbon which covered vamprick roses.

Once they were established, they were almost impossible to kill. They were often used to protect castles with captive or sleeping maidens. There were ways around them, and they were apparently trainable so long as you kept them properly fed. Liberty had recommended feeder mice, which she had learned she could buy at pet stores. It had worked so far. The roses were a lovely golden yellow with deep red singeing and the bush had become a little larger and healthier looking. She was still not sure about it yet.

This morning, over breakfast, she was perusing the section on garden plants, making a list of things she might want to buy from the goblin market to plant in the garden. It felt odd to her that gardening had become a hobby as opposed to the means of feeding oneself that it had been in her youth. So much had changed in a century.

Aislynn came in as An was on the phone with the Tallows, landed on the table. The petty drake stretched like a small winged cat before curling up around her morning tea and dipping a biscotti in her cup, crunching away as she slowly woke up.

It had taken a little careful manoeuvring, as An did not lie as a rule. Apparently, as far as George was concerned, the town had gone insane the night before. Several businesses had been hit by what had looked on the surface like drunken pranks but the press was beginning to believe it to be part of a mob war. He had been concerned for her this morning when he read the paper. An assured him she was fine, that she was at her uncle's and had ended up watching over a friend who had… overindulged after too long a dry spell. It was a shade of the truth. She begged his pardon but she would like to stay out here through the weekend if it was all right by him.

George acquiesced once he was assured she was in a safe place. He told her not to worry about Elizabeth today. Sharon was staying home from work and the school was closed due to some rather destructive vandalism. A neighbouring business had caught fire in the minor riots and the clean up was causing a hazard at the school. He rang off with a sour comment on what the world was coming to and An put the phone into an apron pocket.

Since Aislynn was still eating, An took her own dishes to the sink and took pleasure in washing them for herself for once. When the petty drake was done and had flown her teacup to the sink, the pair of them went out into the garden.

An had a habit of humming or singing to herself as she worked outside, so this morning she was singing merrily away as she was digging up faery lilies and crocuses which were sprouting up in the middle of the lawn and transplanting them to appropriate beds along the edge of the house. She had been singing "Red Is The Rose". She moved on to one of the new songs Jonny had sent her the lyrics for and suddenly the house told her to sing the other one again.

She looked up. "What?"

It asked for the rose song, and told her to watch the vamprick. She looked across the garden to the wall and began singing the chorus, softly at first. To her shock, the bush, which had been twitching, grew still. She stopped singing and it moved again, began scratching at the wall. When she sang, it stopped.

Getting an idea, she pulled her phone from her pocket, telling it to call Skye.

"Aye?" There was a mild strain in his voice she could not place.

"Are ye in a class or doin' anything at th' mo'?" she asked him, not taking her eyes off the rose.

"Nae. Why?"

"Come over for a minute. I'm runnin' an experiment an'... I need a guinea pig."

"Whit!?"

"Just come over. I'm in th' garden," she snapped, hanging up, keeping her eye on the rose bush.

When Skye stepped out of his front door he looked over, saw where she was standing and came around. He stepped up next to her and stared warily at the rosebush. There was clearly something else he wanted to say or talk about but was gauging if this was the time or not. "Whit are ye up tae? An' why am ah havin' flashbacks o' Little Shop O' Horrors?"

"Little what?" she asked, taking her eyes off the rose for the first time.

He sighed. "It's a film aboot a killer plant frae outer space. Ya'll have tae... listen tae it ane o' these days."

She heaved a sigh of her own. "No, I just have t' mention it t' Elizabeth one afternoon. She does something with th' television box that lets me see what everyone else does. I don't understand how she does it. It lasts longer now than it did. At any rate, step closer to th' rose, slowly."

He looked at her as if she were daft, scowled when he realized she was serious. He narrowed his eyes. "This payback fer last nicht?"

She shook her head impatiently. "I want vengeance, I'll take it more direct."

He took a step towards it, edging within a foot of it and reached out, snatching his hand back just in time as a cane lurched for him.

"Nao whit?" he growled, trying to glare at her and still keep a wary eye on the damned flower.

"Sing "Red is th' Rose"."

He turned to stare at her, deeply shocked and jumped as the rose took another swipe at him, catching only the bottom hem of his kilt. "Are ya daft, woman?"

"Just hum it if ye can't sing it," she snapped. "But sing it and approach."

He took a deep breath, trying to control his temper and faced the bush. He would have sworn the blossoms were staring at him, salivating, waiting for him to make a mistake. He began humming, less than effectively, but he continued until he was satisfied he had it recognizable, if not exactly right, and took a step closer. The bush did not move. He got within inches of the main branch, singing. He smiled, touched the lip of one flower before stepping back. So long as he sang, the roses let him be.

There was a strange, buzzing shout of triumph from among the lilies lower in the garden. Aislynn crept closer, keeping An between her and the rose. *"Still don't trust th' damned thing,"* she snapped. *"But th' pixies are happy."*

"Why would that be?" Skye asked.

"Cause now they can get near it and use it to protect th' garden."

Both An and Skye frowned, looking down at her. *"What dae they need tae protect th' garden from?"* Skye asked.

Aislynn shook her head in disbelief. *"Oh, lots of things. They've already run off a couple boggarts and a púca who tried to move in. One of which was just spying. So, yeah, having a little extra security around here would not go amiss. And if that thing will let th' pixies near if they sing..."* she gave a little flap of her wings which was as close to a shrug as she got.

An put her hands on her hips. "Wait, I've had someone trying to spy on me? Who?"

Aislynn only flapped her wings in another shrug and stalked off through the grass after a mole cricket she'd just seen. *"No idea. They didn't question it."*

Skye frowned. "Ah've a guid guess."

An watched him, reading his expression. He had a *really* good idea, but was not likely to tell her. She sighed and approached the rosebush, deliberately not singing. The roses tilted towards her, hesitated, but did not attack.

"Apparently they ken th' hand whit feeds 'em."

"I think I unconsciously taught them th' song," she said in answer, delicately stroking the blushing petals. "I was humming it when I was trying t' find out what th' devil it was needing."

"Whitever, it worked," he said. "Question is, kin th' house keep it from attackin'?"

"I don't think so. There's no communication between them. Th' house told me it reacted to my song, but it couldn't tell me what th' rose wanted or I'd have fed it mice afore this."

"Ah wonder how ye'll ken 'tis feedin' time."

An gave a quiet little laugh. "When th' blooms are mostly yellow. Red means fed."

"Ah'll keep thon in mind."

"We'll have t' warn Liberty. And th' twins," she smiled, pleased.

This brought Skye up short. "Speakin' o' th' wench," he began. "Kin ah... ha'e a word?" he asked, rubbing the back of his neck.

She regarded him carefully. He was nervous and uncertain, so this may not have anything to do with what Ian had said he would talk to him about. She nodded her head towards the back door. "Ye had lunch?" she asked, taking note of the hour.

He shook his head. "A spot would be grand."

An warned the house through the lawn and called to Aislynn. She got a lifted wing in response. Apparently, she was stalking something. An led Skye back into the house, leaving the top half of the door open for Aislynn and the pleasant breeze. Coming into the kitchen, An found a loaf of bread on the counter with several thick slices off it, and all the workings for a serious sandwich laid out. She told Skye to help himself and washed her hands.

By the time Aislynn came in to make her own little snack, the pair of them were at the table eating. An let Skye eat first, not plying him with questions yet. When he was down to snacking on the crisps she had found in the pantry, she made light conversation. "So... last night?"

"All hell," he said. "Th' impostor telt th' Russian thon there weren't tae be any O'Keefe's in town, sae he had his people slip intae th' parties all ower and wreckin' havoc. However, there *were* O'Keefe people all ower. People associated but nae known tae be?" An nodded, understanding. "Got us word an' we managed tae contain most o' th' damage." He chuckled. "Fire fichters were a wee shocked tae get tae a fire call an' find O'Keefe's already there wi' hoses an' putting th' matter tae richts. Normal they'd complain, but it freed them up fer other fires. T'were several."

"I hope ye weren't worried about me," she said.

He eyed her, answering her question of whether Ian had talked to him already. "A mite, but ye were here an' safe, an' he in nae condition... Other thin's loomed."

When he finished his crisps and sat back drinking the rootbeer she had found in the fridge, he finally broached the subject he had come to discuss. "Ah... ah've come tae a decision. Ah jest don' know how tae approach it."

"About what?"

He leaned his elbow on the table, as uncomfortable talking to An about it as he would be dealing with whatever it regarded. Finally, he pulled something out of the pocket of his jerkin and Aislynn's head came up as he placed it on the table between them. An frowned, set her hand over the place where the table had disappeared. It was a small velveteen box. She fumbled with it, figured out how it opened and flipped the lid up. She felt around inside it carefully and found a ring. It felt like a cladaigh ring with a gemstone where the heart should be.

"Does this mean what I think?" she asked.

"Aye."

She looked shyly up at him over the box lid. "I'm terribly sorry, Skye. I dinna mean ta lead ye on like this. I... I have t' say no." She watched his face collapse, then the brow crease in confusion, then blacken at her devilment. He snatched the box back as she laughed. "Had ye there fer a moment. This is fer Liberty, aye?"

"Aye, ya pest. Nao how dae ah dae it?"

An sipped at her drink. "Ye clear this with her da?"

He groaned. "That's where ah need a leg up. Liberty ah kin handle."

She chuckled. "I hope so. Yer in fer a lifetime o' trouble an' ye can't."

"Be serious fer a breath, ya pain in th' arse."

She thought about it. "The only way I can see is t' just take him aside an' tell him. Show him th' ring. He's just a man fer all he's a gryphon and a king."

"Worse, he's *my* king," he groaned. "Am I reachin'?" he asked, begging for reassurance.

She laughed. "Yer bitin' off a bit more'n ye kin chew, I think. But Ian'll be easy. He likes ye."

"Fer nao," he exclaimed, letting out a breath explosively. "If he don' approve..."

"He'd've said sommat afore now, I assure ye. Ye've spent some time with him. He ever say anythin' to ye t' give ye th' impression this would aught but please him?"

Skye thought back, remembering numerous occasions where Ian had warned him how to handle An. If he turned those conversations around, it gave him a little hope. But men were strange about their daughters; held them to different standards. He sighed. "Nae," he admitted. "Ah'm jest..."

She reached out and set her hand on his. "Listen. How ye approach him, how ye behave when ye ask is a test in and of itself. Ye come across weak and he'll find ye unsuitable fer sure. Respectful nerves are one thing, but ye got to let him know ye mean t' have yer way. Blessin's bein' preferred o'course."

He took a deep breath, nodded. It made sense. He drank the rest of the root beer, set the bottle down and regarded her carefully, wondering if he dared to broach the other thing that was bothering him right now.

She saw him watching her and scowled, reading his face and thus his mind. She grabbed their plates and stood. "Don't go there, *daor deartháir*," she warned, going to the sink.

"Ya know ah worry."

"Don't say ye have m' best interests at heart. I've heard that lie afore. It excuses a great deal o' abuse."

The comment bit him and he started to say something when she set her hands on the edge of the sink and sighed. "I'm sorry about that. I don't mean to imply... But ...I've wrestled with this problem already a great deal and... I've decided, same as you, to just see where th' road goes. I'm old Irish, Skye. Livin' with a man with a drinkin' problem's nothing new."

"Yer father?" he asked, wondering what she had remembered.

She shook her head. "Nay. But friends, neighbours I think. Mothers used t' teach their daughters how t' handle it, how t' decide if it were worth it, stayin'."

"He's no a drunk," Skye said quietly.

"No. He's a man in physical pain whose medicine is dangerous, who needs lookin' after." She turned to face him, leaning back against the sink. "He's been without fer some time now, since th' Spetznakov woman was taken. He hasn't gone crazy tryin' t' 'get his fix'. I believe that is the current vernacular?"

"Ya ken modern drugs then, an' whit they can dae tae a body? Yet ye dinnase understand whit were happenin' tae him?"

An made a gesture with her hand. "I know what they've told Elizabeth in school. Th' warnin's. Th' particular drugs I don't know. I was a country lass, Skye. Our only vices were pipes, gamblin' an' alcohol. And two o' those weren't considered a vice. Laudanum we couldn't afford enough of fer it t' become an issue." She was silent a moment or two. "I don't know what th' future holds. It may be that I'm chasin' a false hope but... I'll follow th' road where it lead."

"An' it be a deid end?" he asked.

"I'll turn aside and find another. There are roads an' there are roads."

"Yer too trustin', An."

She smiled ruefully, "Yer too suspicious, Skye." With that she turned and walked back out into the garden.

An spent Saturday helping Liberty and the others decorate for the Ostara rites the next day. There were garlands of flowers to make and objects to wrap in the glamoured streamers which were now the bright colours of wildflowers. When the witch came out of the house with her basket on her arm, An went over to her, offered her one of the small asters she had been weaving into wreaths.

The witch smiled, tucking it into her kerchief. "Vhat can Baba do for you, dearie?"

An relaxed, glad she had apparently caught the witch on a good day. She had been warned that she was unpredictable, but that if she called you dearie or *tovarish* you were ok for that encounter. "Well, ye said ye go to th' goblin markets often, and I've a list of things... I'd like t' get seeds. Might I go with ye? Or could ye at least tell me what's a fair price?"

She frowned, squinting up at An. "You ever been to goblin market?"

An shook her head. "While mortal I was not so much th' fool, and in service... I weren't one of those who took care of such things. I know they can be dangerous, but I also know they're th' only place t' get certain things."

She nodded, held out her hand. "Leest."

An fetched it from her pocket. The old woman held it really close to her face, then at arms length, adjusting it back and forth until she had the gist of what she was reading. Her eyes widened. "Ye've soil an' garden space to handle thees? Some uf thees... they take... fey space."

An blushed lightly. "I believe I do. The bottom of my garden is a hollow, I think. A really small one, mind, but I get cross-over vegetation. I have a vamprick rose on one wall. What I can't manage, I'm sure the pixies'll..."

The old woman's eyes lit up with avarice. She grabbed An's arm in one ancient claw, drew her aside by the veranda, out of the way of the people bustling to and fro. "I kent farm thees kind of soil. I get too near for too long - I call bad attentions. Is how I marked Her territory in place was station. But I have nid of herbs only grow in thees," she said waving the paper. "You grow for me, tend, harvest: I get you what you nid."

An was wary of the woman's eagerness. "What kind of herbs? I don't want to grow anything will upset my pixies or harm my garden."

She shook her head. "Nyet deat'wid, promise. Is seemple stuff, for potion, some normal stuff work better grown in fey soil: Rampion, rape, some special cabbages..."

An knew the old woman was not lying, but that there was much she was not saying. She laughed softly. "So long as ye tell me which I shouldna use for myself, an' th' pixies don' complain, I'll make th' trade."

The old lady cackled happily. Someone walking nearby looked up at that sound and, disturbed, gave the pair of them a wider berth. "You say you haf vamprick rose, eh?" she grinned, began walking, pulling An along with her.

"Aye, I do."

"You got trained yit?"

An looked the savvy old bird over. "Mayhap I should have just asked you about th' thing."

She shrugged. "Mebbe."

"I've gotten it to not attack when I want. Been feedin' it. Don't know if that counts as trained."

She nodded. "Close enough. Let blossoms go to heeps," she advised. "Vhen ripe, feed to those you vant it leave be. Kip it fed." She thought a moment. "Is vhite or yellow?"

"Base yellow," An answered.

The old woman nodded again, confirming suspicions. "Is better for you. Vhite... cold beetches. Yellow more friendly, more loyal. It like you, it always like you. Though it hate you..." she cackled. "Vould not mind cutting if you can get. Now, have to go. Baking lots for tomorrows."

An let her go and pondered the conversation. She had to wonder if she had just made a deal with the devil. Still, it was good to have a witch on your side, even if she was occasionally wicked.

Ostara dawned clear and cool but quickly warmed up. As far as An was concerned, it did not bode well for the temperatures in the coming months. She headed out to the manor fairly early, right after she heard the bells of the parish church signalling the end of mass.

She wore a green sundress with a sheer, long sleeved blouse beneath it. The high, ruffled collar was held closed by the diamond flower pin. She had conceded to the season and modern style and worn sandals. It was a little easier now that she had gotten used to walking barefoot around her house. Her snow rose was in her hair, twining up the braid artfully at the nape of her neck. She felt like Spring.

There were tables all over the green with baskets of boiled eggs in the middle of them, and kids of all ages and many adults taking turns at decorating. There were hundreds of them. An smiled at the eager noises and avoided the tables. She moved towards the veranda, where she liked to sit and watch and listen. There were pockets of lowered voices here and there, unintelligible over the sound of the bandstand getting set up for later. This was Irish country. It was not possible to get together without music of some sort being played and dancing being done any more than you could escape the inevitable alcohol.

One of the young men in the band began playing "Easter Parade" on his violin, apparently teasing a young lady with an elaborate 'Easter Bonnet', and was rewarded with a sound scolding and a slapped arm and the laughter of his buddies. An could tell, however, from the sound of their voices, that there would be more to that pair later in the season. Maybe even at Bealtaine.

An sat in a rocking chair, working on her lace in the light March breeze and enjoyed the afternoon. Aislynn took advantage of the chance to fly around like a mad thing, chasing children and small animals alike to the delight of everyone involved.

She had been there about an hour when she heard a familiar voice cutting through the air as it came around the side of the house from the carriage-house. "Well, he's certainly not *you*," she was saying.

The words themselves did not affect her so much as the laughter of the man with her did. "Thank God fer that," Jonny was saying. "World can't handle two o' me. Hell, it can't handle th' one o' me."

As they passed by, An saw Serephina walking arm in arm with Jonny and he seemed to be enjoying her company. An continued to crochet, ignoring it and trying not to let it bother her at all. Serephina looked up as they walked by, caught An's glance and smiled wickedly. She leaned into Jonny's ear, kissing the edge of it even as she whispered something which made him laugh again. She turned him down the path in front of the veranda steps, walking away from the house and slipped her hand into Jonny's back pocket.

An refused to let the woman see this affect her in the least, looked down at her thread and the tangle she had made of the rosette. She began pulling the thread, unravelling it. Aislynn landed on the back of the chair, causing it to rock further back than she meant and apologized. She sounded absolutely giddy. An glanced over her shoulder at the little dragon. "Are ye drunk?" she snapped, not meaning to. She got hold of herself quick as Aislynn sobered. "Sorry. I'm..."

"Who's got your twang in a twingle?"

An growled, looking out across the grounds where she could just see Serephina being physically inappropriate for public with Jonny over by one of the decorating tables. *"Th' angel who isn't,"* she said, alluding to the meaning of the woman's name.

Aislynn followed her gaze, scowled herself, muttered something unkind. *"She's doing it deliberately, you know that, right?"*

"I do," An sighed, dropping the unfinished rosette into her bag and pulling out her notebook and a pen. She stared for a moment at the blank page even as she glamoured it so she could see what was written there. She flipped a few pages more until she found one that was really blank and began to write. She just let the words flow. It wasn't perfect, she knew, not precise in rhythm or rhyme scheme, but it said more of what she was feeling.

Her
That woman
Claws like a harpy, clinging
Dog
In the manger
Doesn't want him, wringing
His heart for all it's worth
Grinding his trust into stony earth
Wanting only his pain
My pain
Seeing them
Together
On his arm
Where I should...

No
Where I *want*
To sit like a lark, I'd be singing
Fly
Nevermore
From that place, I'd be straying

He deserves more
Faithful
But if I fight
Am I better
Or worse
Than all her scheming
But I'll not cry
    ...where she can see me

She closed the book and put it away. She would work on it later. Or not. She'd had it out on paper and that might be enough for the time being. She felt a little drained as she got up, leaving her bag where it was. It would get back to her house one way or another. The book remained in the little bag she always had slung at her hip, with her flask.

As she stepped off the veranda with intent to wander a little, she heard some louder voices being raised in less than friendly ribbing. By the time she found her way near the argument, Ian had stepped in to take a hand.

"What th' devil is yer complaint, Charlie?" he growled.

Normally, he allowed folk to fight matters out if it were to come to blows, knowing things would be fine again after. But there was something about this argument that reeked of the Raigne incident.

"THAT," Charlie shouted, pointing towards Mak who was meekly tagging along behind William as if afraid of everybody. The man speaking was one of the treants, though he was more a hamadryad as one found them in the Gryphon's King's territory. "That filthy, stinking makar! It fouls our ground walking on it!"

Ian's voice was calm, but even An could feel the tempest just below the surface waiting for an opportunity to explode. For the moment, it was on a short leash. "How so?"

The leaves in the man's hair rustled as he used his whole body to express his frustration. "You know what they are, what they do! How can you ask that question, Ian? You of all people! They're vicious, treacherous, ravening beasts! They're mindless! We can't trust him not to see... oh, Pawz for instance," he shouted, pointing out a small raccoon girl hiding behind Fox, "and decide 'oh look, a bickie!'!"

Ian gave a small, controlled chuckle, his voice dangerously quiet. "There are times I have that problem myself. She is small, and very bite-sized."

"But you are different. We know you won't..."

"An' did we know Baba wasn't here ta turn us inta toads and eat our children?" Ian interrupted.

Someone in the back of the crowd said, loud enough to be heard, "We still aren't sure about that."

Several people laughed and even Ian did not argue the point. "Or that Matt'ew wouldn't go on a rampage," he waved his hand towards the troll who was standing at the back, "or Foxfire wouldn't lure th' unwary off back ta Sawgrass; or hell, that Raven wasn't here ta gain our sympathy and learn our secrets and run off back to 'mother' ta betray us all?" Charlie began to shrink a little. "Or Magdalena? Th' Dark Man's torturer." Ian took a step closer to him, looming. "Yeh tellin' me yer still afraid she'll take yeh home one night and show yeh her 'play room'?"

The man was decidedly uncomfortable now. Ian stepped back and began pacing the circle that had surrounded them. "Isna' a one o' us ain't done sommat we regret fer Them. Not even I. But when yeh left there, each of yeh were given a chance ta swear th' oath. A chance t' redeem yerself. Each and every one o' th' taken what reside here or once resided here were given that chance; were fergiven what yeh did fer Them."

He drew himself up. "I ha'e given him th' same courtesy I gave th' rest o' yeh. I've told him what happens to betrayers; what happened t' Raigne. He knows th' price. But he can't redeem himself if yeh don't give him th' chance. An' until he begins t' feel less o' what he is and more o' what he was afore he'll not be able to even have a human head, hands." He stopped in front of Pawz, looking down at the young woman with raccoon ears sprouting from her dark brown hair and the dark patches around her eyes. "How long had yeh been livin' in our wood afore yeh even realized yeh could *be* human?"

Her voice was small. "Three years... or so. Three winters for sure."

He bent nearer, softening his voice. "And what'd it take fer yeh ta gain this pretty, human face?"

She smiled shyly. "Someone human to play with me."

He stood, turned back to the hamadryad. "Yeh see, Charlie? He has ta be given a chance. I don't expect everyone ta like him or want ta deal wit' him. I'm asking those what can, do what they can, and those what have issues avoid him. But we can't pick an' choose who we help." He turned, aimed a hand at An. "Hell, yeh t'ink our fair governess woulda brought home a bloody redcap an' she didna t'ink he was genuinely done wit' what he was made ta do?"

An blushed.

A man to her left growled at that. "Ya, well, I've a bone t' pick regardin' yon redcap," he snapped.

Ian turned, held up his hand to the man with a tiny nod as soon as he identified him. He turned back to Charlie MacAver. "So, are we done wit' this fer now? If ye have a proper grievance, a *specific* grievance, yeh can see me an' we'll revisit th' issue."

Charlie threw up his limbs. "I'll abide… for now," he said and stepped back into the crowd.

Ian turned back to the other man, pinched the bridge of his nose and sighed. "Well, I might as well make this an open court. State yer case, Michael. Wait, where is Tam?"

The crowd shuffled aside like so much wheat as a small animal crawls through it, and spilled the dwarf out into the circle. Ian turned back to Michael. "Go on."

"Ever since he got here, I've been havin' issues in the south pasture. The sheep are terrified, Daisy can't control them and two have broken limbs in the damned holes he's dug."

Ian turned to Tam. "Holes?"

The redcap shrugged. "Ah hit rock ah couldna work around. So, ah started a new one."

"But why dig th' pasture up in th' first place?"

"Ah like holes… ye seid ah could set up hoosekeepin'."

Ian took a deep breath and let it out slowly. "Michael, t'ank yeh fer bringin' it to my attention. Tam, I take it pastures remind yeh o' battlefields?"

"Aye. Feels natural."

"Then we can take up a portion o' one o' th' less used pastures, one wit' less bedrock, an' put up wards t' keep th' sheep at a comfortable distance. They won' take fright an' ye kin hav' yer battlefield view."

Michael nodded this was acceptable and tugged his hat brim in salute.

Tam nodded as well. "Thank ye. Th' blighters were keepin' me awake, bleatin' all th' bloody toime. Though..." he took off his hat, ran it through his hands, regarding it thoughtfully. "Ah doan ken... how much o' tradition rules me now... but ah'd no like t' find oot th' hard way th' connection twixt me cap an' me life. Any chance ah kin work th' slaughterhouse?"

"We don't butcher often, just certain times o' th' year, but in yer case I think we can hold a few back fer more regular sources. We'll work on' that."

The redcap put his cap back on and nodded his thanks, slipping back into the crowd.

Ian sighed, turned to regard the circled citizens. "Any one else have a grievance? I'd like t' get this over wit' so's we can get back t' th' fun stuff, like watchin' th' kids at sack races."

To An's surprise, Skye stepped forth, arms crossed over his massive chest. He was dressed in trousers and his jerkin. "Aye, ah have a grievance."

He looked angry.

Ian looked at him, frowned. Then there was a wary spark in his eye and he stepped back, sweeping his arm out to tell him to proceed.

Skye turned, "Liberty Merribelle O'Keefe! Get ower here! Ah've a bone ta pick."

Stunned, Liberty untangled herself from Roulet across the circle and stepped forward. Even An was confused. Aislynn whispered in her ear, *"What is he doing?"*

"I havn't th' slightest," she whispered.

The same whisper seemed to be circulating the crowd as Liberty stopped in front of him, her floral print sundress fluttering slightly in the breeze and the crown of flowers in full bloom. She looked up at him, concerned, hurt and confused.

"Since th' day ah set eyes on ya, ya been a royal pain in my arse," he began. "Ya've hounded me, dragged me hither an' yon, used me fer a pack horse, a fencing dummy an' a general jack of all.

Ah'm tired o' yar teasin', a' goin' home wi' ma kilt in a twist cause ya got me so workit up ah can't think straight, sideways or upside yon. Ah'm afraid t' offend m' chief by retaliatin' ar start a clan war cause ah lost m' temper an' shouted back at ya. Ah'm tired o'it, ya hear me?"

Liberty looked on the verge of tears, covered her face to control them so she did not see Skye drop to one knee and pull something from his pocket.

Aislynn snickered softly. *"Och, he is so going to get slapped for this."*

He went on, reaching up to take one hand. "So, here's whit ah propose t' do aboot it. We take th' whole matter in-hoose. Just ya an' me. Husband an' wife?" She was looking down at the ring now on her finger, stunned. "Whit say ya? Will ya marry me?"

Tears running freely, she threw herself in his arms, kissing him. He stood as she came at him, lifting her off the ground in a kiss 'to curl her toes' as she had once put it.

Aislynn slumped a little. "Humph, *I was certain she'd hit him for that,*" she said, disappointed.

Finally Skye set her on her feet as she said yes, beaming like the moon. That was when her hand flew out and cracked loudly across his cheek. Even Ian winced, though he was grinning. It was Skye's turn to look stunned.

Aislynn grinned, sitting up. *"There it is!"*

Liberty began to lay into him, punctuating her points with little slaps to whatever she could reach, though she was half-laughing as she chewed him out in rapid fire Irish. He put up his hands to protect himself, but grinning. He looked over at Ian for help.

The chief threw a small blanket at him.

It landed on his head and made Liberty back off for a moment. Skye pulled it down and looked at it, then at Ian. "Whit this fer?"

Ian laughed. "Yeh made yer bed, lad. Thought a blanket were th' least I could do."

This brought everyone to tears, they were laughing to hard.

Liberty turned, glared at her father, marched up and slapped him as well.

His hand flew to his cheek, hiding the bright red patch there. "What th' devil was tha' fer, woman?"

"Collaboratin'!"

This set off a fresh round of laughter as Ian couldn't argue the point. Instead, he looked over towards the decorating tables and frowned as he began shooing people off. "Oi! I still see several hundred naked eggs over yon! Those tables won't have food on 'em until every last shell has a fresh coat o' *somethin'*!"

This caused a scramble, as people who hadn't intended to decorate suddenly became eager to do so. An was jostled a bit, but held her ground, chuckling to herself. She had to admit, she felt a little better now.

Later she watched as Liberty and Ian went through the Ostara rites, making the offerings and blessing the seeds and flocks for the coming growing season. She wandered after that, taking delight in the laughter of the children even though she could not see them. She also took note of the pairings that were beginning to occur. Raven and Patches slipped off into the lover's maze, which was at least a foot or so taller than it had been when An had last been in there. Not to mention was now faintly visible to her. Liberty and Skye were snuggling openly, and An had to wonder how she had missed it getting so serious. She worried a little about Roulet, but didn't when she saw how happy the gypsy girl was for her friend. Even Solitaire was beginning to feel the itch of Spring, as An watched her getting very friendly with Ian. She wished her luck with that and headed over to where the music was being played and took a seat to listen, not feeling much like dancing.

Aislynn, however, felt very much like dancing and launched into the air to engage in wild aerials with the butterflies and the occasional bird who flew through the area. An smiled, enjoyed watching her play.

Eventually Jonny took the stage, beginning with a rousing dance number on his fiddle. Even An could not avoid being dragged onto the floor with that. Young Harry had seen her foot tapping and drew her out with him. She was flush and laughing when the song ended and she sat back down. Jonny took up his guitar and sang a few songs with different paces, all of them in keeping with the Spring theme of the day.

Later, Billy Younger got up with him and they sang a duet, with Jonny getting off the stage after that, letting him take over. He came over with a beer in hand, sat beside An.

"Evenin', Ceobhránach," he said, a soft smile on his lips.

"Evenin', Jonny," she said. "I've never heard that last," she said by way of conversation.

"Jethro Tull. He's after yer time, though old fer this one. Well worth a listen. I'll get ye copies."

She nodded her thanks, turned to watch Aislynn playing a hopscotch game with the dancers, trying to hop from head to head without using her wings.

"Looks like Aislynn's gotten inta th' whiskey early," he said softly.

"She's sober as far as I know."

"Must be Spring then."

An glanced off towards the lover's maze where a young taken woman was drifting out with someone cuddled up against herr and looking happily dishevelled. "Aye, let us blame it on Spring."

Then she smelled a familiar, sickly sweet and powdery scent. She made herself not react in the slightest to Serephina as the woman came up behind them and draped herself over Jonny's shoulders. An was mollified a little by the slightly stiff reaction Jonny gave her. She interpreted it as his finding the action in bad taste in front of her, but she was just guessing and she knew it.

"I have to go, darling. It's getting late, and I have calls to make," she purred, kissing his neck. "You coming by tonight?"

Jonny sighed. "Aye," he answered. It sounded reluctant to An, but maybe that's because she wanted it to be.

Serephina laughed, soft, low and seductive, running her manicured nails along his collarbone under his shirt. "I'll see you then. We can go out for breakfast. ...or lunch, whatever we get to."

As she walked away, she gave An a look that left no doubt that all of that had been strictly for her benefit.

An turned back to look at the dancers and realized Jonny was observing her.

"She's..." he began.

"Everything ye said ye didn't want at th' Masque," she finished for him.

"A special case," he said.

An turned slowly to look at him. "Is she?" She regarded him a moment before saying, "Tell me how I'm supposed t' feel, Jonny? Am I supposed t' fight that? Let her rub it in, flaunt ye? ...What does she mean to ye?"

He registered the hurt in her eyes and drank the last swallow of his beer, setting the bottle on the seat next to him. He stood, held out his hand to her. "Come, walk with me."

She hesitated, the hurt of so many things still fresh.

"'Tis just twilight," he lured. "Yer favourite time o'day. We'll walk down by th' river."

Reluctant, but wanting answers, she accepted, setting her hand in his and taking up Cipín. Aislynn flew up, started to land when Jonny shook his head.

"An' ye don't mind, Aislynn, I'd like a private word? Ye kin follow if ye don' trust but...."

Aislynn hovered in the air a moment, looked from one to the other, then sighed and flapped off.

"I'll never hear th' end o' that," An said softly, letting Jonny lead her away from the crowd and towards the light wood where the small river ran.

She could feel the coming night in the air; hear the softening of sound and the change of singers in the world chorus. Crickets and other insects began to hum and the birds were winding down. Off to their left an owl called. She could feel the rising mist coming off the water as they neared it, and see parts of it, at least around her feet.

They were down by one of the streams, she could hear it running over the rocks, when he stopped, leaned back against a tree. She stepped closer to the water, bent, reaching out a blind hand and dipped it into the current, relishing the silky feeling of the cold flow over her skin. She waited for him to speak.

Eventually, he did.

"We were... over There together. She managed to escape. ...An' then she came back for me. Got me out, but herself caught again in th' bargain. She put herself through hell fer me. When she got back out... there's a great deal between us. And magic," he added with a sigh. "It's... not a healthy relationship."

An listened, stepping one sandalled foot in the shallows, felt a minnow dart over her toes. Her heart was sinking. This was not something she could or would fight.

"When we're together... every touch is pain, fer both of us, wringing memories out of us, oft-times violently."

"So why do ye? Touch?"

There was silence. She did not look up at him, did not want him to see her face until she knew how she felt about all of this.

"Because we can't help it. Because we're gluttons fer punishment. Because... it beats th' hell out o' th' alternative an' we need at least one person who understands."

"Do ye want to see her again?" An thought her voice was small when she said it.

There was a pause. "I promised her I'd come tonight," he said pointedly.

"I meant ever," she corrected, looking up at the sky. "Tonight is foregone."

"I don't know if I'm ready t' break that habit yet."

She nodded. "I'll let it be then. Though you ever decide ye want t' be free o' that..."

He shook his head. "I don't know that's possible. There's magic involved. Th' only way t' be free of her... is to love someone as much as I ever loved her."

An looked over. "She used magic on ye? And ye still want that?"

"It's complicated, I told ye. 'Tis somethin' She gave her. She just makes sure I never get close enough to another to have a chance."

"Ye ever decide… ye even *think* ye want t' try t' be free o' her. Say th' word. That one I'll happily scratch the eyes out o'er ye."

He chuckled, "Ye'd have better luck with yon shillelagh."

"Didn't say I'd kill her. Though she give me reason… who knows."

He grew serious again. "I can give ye no promise o' fidelity."

"Men have strong needs," she said emotionlessly. It was a fact to her, and not something to stress over.

"And women don't?" he countered, lighting a cigarette. "That's an unfair double standard."

"'Tis life," she said with a tip of her head. "I've never lain with a man afore, Jonny, and I don't intend to begin as a wanton."

He chuckled. "Yer a right contradiction, Ceobhránach. Victorian sensibilities and Celtic morals."

She stood, taking a step further into the stream, the mists curling around her. They seemed to be pouring from beneath her skirts, obscuring her ankles and sandalled feet. "I am what I am."

He focused on her a moment, watching her and the mists and the way they reacted to her. "I kin see why they called ye *Bean an Ceobhrán*," he mused. She looked over her shoulder at him. "Ye know, ye concentrate, there might be sommat ye can do with that mist."

"Explain." She stood, her body half-turned towards him, a few tendrils of hair having escaped their braided prison fluttered at her brow and across one foggy eye. She was completely unaware of the vision she presented.

He took a long drag on his cigarette, savouring the image for the moment. He blew out a long, thin stream of smoke. "No tellin'. Call it, thicken it, disappear in it. Hell, try hard enough ye might e'en become it. There are those what can."

She thought back to the first fight at Elizabeth's, when she had killed the swampling. There had been a smokeling on the fence. "Ye think?"

He shrugged. "Anythin's possible. We still develop and evolve. What we left them as is malleable sometimes. We can become more, even as in some ways we become less. Some things we can't change," he added ruefully, tracing a thin scar on the side of his hand, "however much we want to. But others... ye can always add on. Things can be bought at th' market, bargained for with Them. Not recommended either choice. Sometimes they just happen."

She thought about it. Tried to gather the mist to her, calling it, willing it to coalesce around her. She laughed as she began to see it thickening. "Is it thinnin' out elsewhere or just thickening around me?" she asked.

"Ye can't tell?"

"I see what's around me, what I've touched I guess." She turned, her skirt flaring a little and seeming to float in the fog.

Jonny watched and smoked, propping one foot up against the tree behind him, crossing one arm over his chest to brace his smoking hand. "I told ye it liked ye."

She looked up at him. "But does it..."

"It thickens. What lies across th' stream, at th' outlying edges crawls toward ye, but more grows behind it."

She turned in a slow circle, her arms out, gathering the mist up to her and willing it to be a part of her, playing with it. She was childlike, caught up in the wonder of a first snow, and Jonny watched her. Even the smoke of his cigarette wandered in her direction, though not as eagerly. He noticed she was becoming a little misty at the edges. One white brow arched. He rolled out his cherry, grinding it with his heel, field-stripping his cigarette and slipped it into his pocket.

"Ceobhránach," he called. She looked over at him, startled, as if she had forgotten he was there, and snapped back to solid. "'Tis time to go. ...Unless ye've more questions?"

She stood still a moment, thinking. She shook her head and stepped out of the stream. "I don't think so." She looked around, seeing nothing but feeling the hour with her whole being. "And ye have a... tryst. I'll not keep ye. Cipín can see me home an' ye want to go on," she said, holding out her hand for the shillelagh that waited for her on the bank.

He shook his head, taking the hand himself, drawing her over the slightly steeper embankment where she had ended up. "An' what kind o' cad d'ye think me, that I would do such an ungallant thing?"

"Well," she answered, Cipín slipping into her other hand, "ye keep tellin' me what a terrible person ye are, and I keep waitin' fer evidence…"

He pulled her close, his nearness suddenly a very different kind of threat. There was something in his eyes that was changed, something very subtle and it sent a delicious thrill throughout her entire being. "Ye mean like th' kind o' man who'd cause ye t' faint under th' mistletoe from one taken kiss?"

She was nearly breathless, but managed, her eyes locked on his. "Ye had no way o' knowin' I'd react that way."

His smile was wicked. "Oh, I had some idea. I intended an extreme reaction." His finger traced the line of her jaw, delighting in the catch of her breath it caused. "Though fainting was unexpected. It pleased me."

His hold on her was firm as the fingers wandered down her throat to her collar.

"Ye… ye apologized fer that…"

"Oh, bein' sorry after dosena mean I didn' do it apurpose."

He was going to kiss her.

"Ye… ye shouldn't go to one woman's bed with th' kiss of another on yer lips."

He was closer, his hand slipping behind her neck. "An' ye think she wouldn't do th' same t' you, were th' shoe on th' other foot?"

She had been caught up in the intensity and the touch and seduction she knew this was, but this gave her one last toehold on sanity. She leaned in, setting her forehead gently to his chin, preventing the kiss. "But I am not like her," she said, and stepped back, out of his embrace.

He let her go, seemed a little stunned by her reaction. His eyes followed her as Cipín began to lead her homeward.

She walked away from him, regretting the action, knowing it was best. She could only imagine what that kiss would have been like, and if she would ever have another like it. He was not often in one of these moods and it… honestly, it thrilled her. It was not what had attracted her interest; that had been his kindness, tenderness and concern. The perfect gentleman... well, not perfect. This was just another aspect of this man she was coming to love. Though, if she were honest with herself, which she could tell she wasn't being, it was too late for that. She did love him, or Skye's warnings would have carried more weight, and she would not have allowed a great many things to which he had already subjected her. ...Or called him a chroí not that long past.

She felt him come up behind her before she saw him. He came up on her off side, away from Cipín, and set her hand on his arm and took her quietly home.

5

The next week, during the day while Elizabeth was in school, Roulet and Liberty dragged An out and all over town with wedding plans. Both Liberty and Skye had agreed on Bealtaine, which was a little over a month away, leaving very little time. They were going to be married first in a Catholic rite at the Cathedral in the city, with a second, more intimate, slightly more pagan ritual at the Rest that afternoon which would satisfy the rites of the season as well. This meant she would need two dresses; which required *days* of shopping.

An did not have enough lace made for an entire wedding gown, but she had enough for a veil. "Would ye be terribly upset if ah gave ye yer present afore th' weddin'? Well, one o' em?"

Liberty eyed her as they sat at a table at an outdoor café they were fond of. "Why would ya need ta?"

"Well... I... that is if ye want to, I'll understand an ye don't. I kin save it fer a proper dress fer someone else...."

"Spit it out, woman!" Liberty growled, her smile broad.

Roulet giggled, watching the people as they passed.

"Lace," she blurted. "Yer veil. If ye want it… I'd like to make yer veil."

Liberty looked stunned. "Ya wan… that'll take a span o' time…"

An shook her head. "I have pieces enough for a veil. Th' brownie and I'll only have t' put it together an' edge it. …If ye want it."

"Oh course I want it!" she exclaimed. She pulled out the wedding dress book that she had been using to narrow her choice down to and began crossing out those she did not think would look good with Irish lace.

Roulet watched her. "You know, you could always go to Dublin for a dress," she suggested.

Liberty stopped, stared at her as if she could not believe the words coming out of her mouth. "I… I can't believe I dinna think o' that. Da's a door to Cork. 'Tis a few hours ta Dublin."

"Well, I can't go today," An said. "That'll be a whole day affair and I'd have to make arrangements. I've got to get back t' th' Tallows' afore three."

"Oh, I'd have ta make arrangements anywho," she said, with a wave of her hand. "See if ya can get Wednesday and Thursday off, we'll make a whole day o' it, an' get ya fitted fer a bridesmaid gown."

"Best be after Easter, then. Perhaps Monday and Tuesday?" An suggested.

"Might work."

"What about the other girls?" Roulet asked, watching something down the road.

"I can have measurements sent and dresses ordered. Tha two o' ya an' yar sister I'll want fitted proper. Asides, ya'll have t' help me pick it out."

An smiled, sipping her tea. "I'm not familiar with all this pageantry. I'm more familiar with country weddin's, where ye had a maid o' honour and a flower girl, maybe a bridesmaid or two an' ye had sisters."

"Gypsy weddings are wild," Roulet mused, her attention still caught by something.

An turned, looking where she was. "I imagine," she mused. "Very colourful." Finally her eye caught what had stolen Roulet's attention. There was a man, wavering in and out of visibility as ordinary people passed in front and behind him. He was standing in front of a shop window, tilting his head in strange, catlike ways. He reached up to touch his mouth, stroking his whiskers. His face was a hybrid of man and tiger, though more of man at the moment, and around his neck was a studded leather collar. He moved like a beaten cat, but his white ears were going forward in curiosity. None of the people moving around him seemed to notice anything odd about him, so An figured he either had something about him that allowed him to appear human to the mundane eye or she was just seeing what he really was.

"The tiger man?" An asked softly. "Aye, I see him."

Roulet tore her eyes off him and looked at her, even as Liberty looked around, trying to see what they were talking about. "Tiger? He's one of us?"

"Th' one staring at his reflection in th' window as if he's never seen it... or never seen it quite like this? Aye. He's a white tiger. I thought he was known," An said.

Roulet was up from the table and moving away, "I thought that's what I was seeing." She headed down the pavement towards him, and An and Liberty watched as she cautiously approached.

Liberty shook her head. "Never seen him, but that's not surprisin'. A lot don't come through th' Rest, or come from other places, other gates. There are several other of th' Fair Folk who's realms don't connect anywhere near ours. We've a few, but th' Dark for instance," she said, deliberately not saying his full title, "most of his would escape through th' city. There's a bog somewhere ta th' south where a lot o' Sawgrass's people pop up. Also where a lotta them get taken. A lot o' th' City Folk don't find th' Rest comfortable. Some flock there ta escape anything resembling where they came from."

"Do you get many from Amalthea?" An asked, remembering William and his makar friend.

She shook her head. "Very rarely. She's... different. Only one o' th' seelie who take."

An sipped her tea as she watched Roulet charming the tiger, trying to think back what she had heard of Amalthea from her Service. She knew she should know that name. Finally, something Fox had said clicked it, "Unicorn. She's th' Lady of th' Unicorns." Liberty nodded. "So th' white horses we saw in her border-march weren't horses but unicorns. Interestin'. If I remember correctly, she only takes those who are lost or damaged, to heal them."

Liberty smiled, watching her friend walking away with the tiger after looking back once and waving that it was all right. "Aye. Th' otter girl, Jasmine?"

An nodded, remembering her from the Winter Masque.

"Her parents went off a bridge with her in th' car. It was a terrible accident, happened last year. There were th' parents and a four year old in th' back seat. Th' authorities think th' child was dislodged and floated down th' river out th' open window. Her grave is empty. She *would* have died, had Amalthea not snatched her up and changed her, brought her to her own realm. Likely ta help with th' tragic loss of her parents, th' violence o' th' wreck, and partly ta help prevent a fear of water, which would explain why she made her an otter. When their minds are healed and they are, so she thinks, capable of returning ta th' world, she sends them on. Jasmine's lucky she came out our door. Mean well, however much, They sometimes do more harm than good. If we hadn't taken her in... Child's supposed ta be four years old and dead, and here she is alive and all of fourteen."

"Surely William is a different case. He's an adult."

Liberty shook her head. "Maybe, depends on when he left. What he knew o' th' world before it broke him. Either way he'll not be our problem long." She waved a waiter over for the check.

"Oh? He taking Mak elsewhere?" she asked, a little hopefully.

"No. He's likely going ta Boston with cousin O'Roarke after he helps Da with Hellhound."

"We need it," An said. In the few days since Ostara, there had been numerous little incidents all around town.

"Aye," she said, accepting something from what An assumed was the waiter and looked it over, placed some money in the folder and handed it back. "Come on, we've got an hour left afore I have ta get ya back and there's a florist just down th' way I want ta check out."

"What about Roulet?" An asked, grabbing Cipín and getting up.

"She'll either catch up or meet me at Courtz later."

With that, the two of them walked the opposite way down the pavement.

Easter dawned with more than a few surprises. An had gone out to take milk and honey to the pixies and found a delicate, gold filigree egg hidden in the lilies. When she picked it up she discovered that it was an actual egg, just the gilding was magical.

Aislynn found one balanced in the crevice of her favourite perch. She had to describe hers for An. It was a bluish-white pearl with real silvering that made it look like scales. She sniffed it, frowned, then crunched into it, shell and all, began grinning immediately. The lacing was real silver and the inside was a honey cream confection she pronounced heavenly.

An managed to coax the gold off of hers without breaking it, and had the sweetest, most savoury boiled egg for breakfast, and a gold filigree one for her shelves.

When she took out her boots, An got a warning before putting her foot inside. Reaching in with her hand, she pulled out a third egg. This one was a swirl of colour that could not seem to make up its mind which set of colours they were going to remain. She was warned to open it outside. Curious, she set her boot down and opened the cottage door, stepping down into the grass and cracked it in two. From within the small shell burst forth a swarm of butterflies all made of flower petals. They fluttered into the air and about the garden, began sipping at everything in bloom. One even settled on the snow rose in An's hair for a moment. As it fanned it's orchid petal wings open and closed, they felt velvet soft against her cheek and smelled like the most fragrant orchid she had ever encountered in Faerie.

She laughed as it fluttered away, not finding what it wanted from the artificial blossom. Leaving Aislynn to play with them, she headed back inside to get her shoes on and took the magial door that opened to the closet of her garret room in the attic of the Tallows' home. Just as she closed the closet behind her, she heard a shriek from Elizabeth's room and rushed to the second floor.

As she threw the bedroom door open, she saw Elizabeth sitting on the floor with two halves of a kaleidoscope egg in her hands and in front of her was a tiny brass rabbit, hopping around on her carpet. It was mechanical, but very lifelike and adorable. An scowled down at her. "What is the meaning of that awful shriek? Were you trying to give my heart a jolt?"

Elizabeth looked up at her, sheepish at first, but then caught sight of something that made her laugh instead. "Looks like the Easter Bunny got you too!"

"What are you talking about?" she said, trying to remain stern. Elizabeth pointed and An's hand went to her hair. A tiny buttercupfly was crawling across the wrapped braid. It climbed onto An's finger when she brushed it and she held it in front of her. She smiled, crossed the room and bent, placing her finger in front of Elizabeth's face. The buttercupfly crawled onto the girl's nose, causing her to giggle.

"I didn't know the Easter Bunny was real," she said, wrinkling her nose as the buttercupfly tickled.

"I'm not entirely sure this wasn't done by th' brownies," she said, her accent relaxing to her normal lilt. "We decorated an awful lot of eggs last week and there is a large clan o' them living at th' Rest. But put your rabbit away and lets go downstairs. I'm sure your mother has breakfast ready."

It turned out that Ian had a door, not just to Cork, but to Dublin proper. Liberty, An and the twins made a full day of it, starting with breakfast at The Kingfisher. By eleven, they had visited three bridal shops and only had two possibilities for the wedding dress and one option for the bridesmaids. They were walking down the pavement, thinking about lunch when something across the street caught An's eye.

A shop door opened and someone was let out by a little old lady that An could clearly see. The lady waved and wished luck to the invisible person as they walked away from her carrying a barely visible dress bag. She tugged Liberty's sleeve and asked Aislynn if the street was safe to cross. When the dragon gave the all clear, she began to cross the road. The others hurried to catch up.

"Where are ya goin', luv?" Liberty asked.

"T' get yer weddin' dress," she said.

"There? Why there?" she asked, warily, aware something was up.

An reached out and felt for the door handle. She looked back over her shoulder at her friend and smiled. "Cause I saw th' shopkeeper." With that she went in and the others, looking at each other with surprise, hope and excitement, followed.

The lady An had seen was shorter than she, white-haired and well-aged. She had to be in her eighties, but looked to be around fifty. She was well-dressed but not fancy, the simple clothes one would expect a shopkeeper in a village to wear, her white sweater open and held by two pretty little ceramic flowers on clips with a chain between them. She turned her merry blue eyes on them and smiled.

"Evenin', ladies," she chirruped. Her eyes set on An's determined face and then on the monkey on her shoulder, which was very much not a monkey, and something changed in her demeanour. She went from the typical 'how can I help you?' to sincere welcome and genuinely pleased to see them. "And where are ye fine folks from?" she asked, but there was something secretive and knowing in her tone and eye.

"Florida, by way o' Cork," Liberty said, catching hint of something, but still not certain what it was.

Solitaire smiled, "My sister and I by way of Paris."

The old lady looked at An and her dragon again, expectantly.

"Originally I'm from County Clare, I think. No, of that I'm certain."

"And late..."

An smiled, equally secretive, "*In service t' th' King below Tara.*"

She took a deep breath and her wrinkled old face relaxed with joy. "Would you fine ladies like to meet my dressmaker?"

There was the sound of something dropped off to the left and the lady chuckled. "Mavis, watch the front for me?"

"Yes, Ma'am," came the shocked reply.

"Don't mind her. Nobody ever gets to meet the dressmaker," she chuckled, leading them through a floral curtain into the back. "Not no way, not no how," she laughed at her own joke. Liberty and the twins laughed with her, but An did not get the reference and just smiled politely. "Even Mavis hasn't met her. So, I'm Deirdre Moffett, proprietress. And you?"

Liberty introduced herself and her party and the name O'Keefe made Miss Moffett smile. "And the petty drake?" she asked, unlocking a small door in the back of the store room.

"*Aislynn, an' it please th' Weaver's Daughter,*" Aislynn said, introducing herself primly. This made the old woman smile even more as she threw open the door.

The twins' jaws dropped.

"I kin see why no one gets ta see th' dressmaker," Liberty smiled.

The centre of the large room was dominated by an enormous web which filled the rafters but only touched the lower floor in a few places. Descending from said rafters was a spider the size of an elephant. Her abdomen was a shiny blue-black with ripples of green when the light struck it right. Her legs were long and slender, infinitely graceful. Instead of the typical spider's head, she had a human torso, with black-skinned arms that were as delicate-seeming as her other eight limbs. Her face was a little angular, slightly elongated and sloped gently back into a mane of silky hair that was a fair match for the carapace of her abdomen. When she smiled, she showed a mouth full of very sharp little teeth, but in spite of all this, she was disturbingly beautiful.

"Actually, I'm the dressmaker," Miss Moffett said. "Arachne is the weaver. Aren't ye, mother?"

As Arachne set her last leg down on the floor, she spread her arms and sank into a dainty and graceful curtsey. "Pleased," she said. Her voice was delicate and her words spoken with deliberate care, as if she did not trust her mouth to say them right. "Welcome to our shop." She studied them a moment with her swirling, dark eyes, which, while there were only two of them, looked very much like spider's eyes. "Ahh, I see why Deirdre brought you into the back to meet me. You are like us. Welcome again."

"Would ye ladies like a bite of lunch?" Deirdre offered.

Liberty readily accepted, though the twins were somewhat reluctant. Their fears were soothed by the sight of a perfectly ordinary table with a pot of Dublin Coddle in the centre. Deirdre told them to pull up chairs while she got more bowls. The twins looked around the workroom until they found a few extra chairs that look like that hadn't been used in a long while. Arachne settled down just off to the side as her daughter began to ladle out bowls of the thick Irish stew, serving Aislynn in a ramekin.

Once everyone had food, Deirdre sat down and initiated conversation. "So, been out long?"

The twins nodded. "At least eight years," Roulet answered.

"I've been out about two," said Liberty. "I escaped from th' Sky King. I found m' Da quite by accident as he an' a group were comin' out from rescuin' m' cousin from th' Northerner."

"Brave of him," Arachne replied.

She chuckled. "Oh, ya don' know me da. He's th' Gryphon o' the O'Keefes."

Deirdre nodded, looked up at her mother as she dipped a thick slice of fresh soda bread in her coddle. "He's the O'Keefe of the American O'Keefes, mother. Ye remember hearing about him?"

She looked thoughtful a moment, then smiled, taking care to keep her mouth closed as she did. "Ah yes, I remember now. Has a place over in County Cork. You will have to forgive me. I don't get out much. This is as human as I get."

"I'm sorry to hear that," An said.

Arachne shrugged with a hand, "It is what it is. When th' Gnome Queen makes you into something, you tend to stay that something. But I am a homebody anyway. And you, blind one with eyes of fog which see more than you let on?"

An smiled shyly. "I... was governess to th' Gryphon King's three children."

Arachne looked down at her daughter and the two of them exchanged glances. "Go on," she prompted.

"Nothing much to tell. Though I suspect you two have a very interesting tale. One worthy of a Nursery Rhyme at th' very least. I would love t' hear th' truth of it," she said, deflecting the conversation deftly off of herself.

Arachne smiled but said nothing, resumed eating. Her daughter sipped her tea and cleared her throat. "Nothing quite so... romantic, I think is th' word I'm looking for? Somehow mother got herself taken by th' Gnome Queen."

"Still can't remember quite how that happened," she mused, annoyed.

"I were only eight, but she was frantic t' get back t' me. Well, the Queen thought she'd have a bit o' fun, and let my mother go to me. There I were, sittin' on a hillock, eating a shepherdess's dinner of curds and bread when down she comes from a tree branch, this gigantic spider, no where near that big of course," she said, pointing up at her mother.

"That came later," Arachne injected.

"I did what came natural. I ran screaming." She gave a rueful chuckle. "Damn near ended up some boglin's dinner but some elves were out hunting, took pity on me and brought me home. I was taught th' dressmaker's trade and took to it like a duck t' water. When I was fair grown, they sent me home."

"What the Queen did not know," began Arachne, "well, maybe she did know, but she thought it would only torment me, was that I would slip into her chambers and use her scrying tools to watch my daughter. When I saw her leaving, I began looking for a way to escape. When one of the tunnels collapsed and I was sent to use my webs to shore it up, I took the chance and fled. Luckily, I ran into a bridge troll who arranged for a letter to be delivered to my daughter while I hid under the bridge. I explained things to her before I revealed myself."

"It was a shock," Deirdre said, mopping the last juices from her bowl with the bread. "But I got over it. We opened this place. That was... fifty years ago? While mother hasn't aged a day... I have," she shrugged, began collecting the empty bowls.

"Now," Arachne said, reaching over her daughter's head and setting her bowl in the sink. "Which of you is the bride?"

The twins both pointed at Liberty. She laughed. "That'd be me."

"Lovely. How much time do we have?"

"Bealtaine."

"Oh my. You don't have much time, do you? Waited until the last minute or..."

"He sprung it on me a week ago. We've both decided Bealtaine's right."

Deirdre nodded. "Can't say as I disagree. Wonderfully auspicious time to begin a new life. So... have ye something in mind?"

"Well," Liberty began, waved An to pull out the lace pieces she had brought with her. "I had some ideas, but had to scrap them. An here is makin' ma veil."

An laid several of the crocheted flowers and leaves on the now cleared table. "All I've to do is put them together."

Deirdre sighed wistfully. "Traditional Irish lace. Don't see it much by hand any more."

Arachne bent and picked up one of the pieces. "You have glamoured this?"

An nodded. "'Tis the only way I can see it. I'm blind to aught but magic."

The spider nodded. "And you wish a dress to match this?"

"If ya can," Liberty answered.

Arachne seemed to be getting an idea. "Have you enough of these to make a few embellishments for the dress? I can't match these myself. If I make something it will look different and throw the whole ascetic off."

"Not at the moment, but between my brownie and I we can have enough, if yer thinkin' of edgin' and hems."

She looked startled. "You have a brownie? Well then, this will be done in no time. Can't use one myself. They seem to be afraid of me... that and I never leave the workroom." She took a sketchbook off a high shelf nearby and began sketching immediately. Moments later she set the finished drawing on the table in front of them and moved across the room, over shelves and work tables, to fetch a bolt of cloth. This she also set in front of them.

"Here. I am thinking something simple." Her hands sketched the air over Liberty's body as she described the dress in more detail. "An angled, sweeping neckline to frame this marvellous figure, belled skirt, a hint of a train..."

"It will have ta be cathedral length, I'm afraid," Liberty interrupted.

Arachne paused, seemed disappointed. "Cathedral wedding? Hmm. I can work with it. It'll be a little shorter than proper, but so beautiful no one will think twice about it. Sheer sleeves for coolness with the lace edgings here, here and here," she said, tapping the wrists, the neckline and the waist. "Of course the hem, but here," she traced a wide triangle with her front legs from about Liberty's knees to the floor, "will be a central motif of Irish lace to match the veil, with a diamond cut-out just like it on the train. Think you can manage that in one month?"

An smiled. "Make sure I have th' measurements for each piece and aye, we'll have it. And a week t' spare. My brownie lass will be glad of something serious t' do. 'Til now we've been using this for idle hands. She'll like this work."

Liberty fingered the fabric that Arachne had set down. It looked thick and heavy, and on the surface, looked and felt like silk peachskin. In reality, it felt lighter than air and blissfully cool to the touch. "What is this?" she asked. "I can't say I've ever felt anything like it."

An reached over and fingered the snow white fabric. She smiled. "I have." She flicked her eyes in Arachne's direction. "Spider silk. At this weight, ye could likely run through briars and not tear it."

The spider-woman smiled proudly. "Hoist four grown men with a strip of it and never fear it breaking. Spun and wove it myself."

"I am flattered and honoured," Liberty breathed. "This is going ta be beautiful."

An stroked Liberty's arm lightly with the back of her fingers. "Yer goin' t' be beautiful," she corrected.

This time, it was Liberty's turn to blush. She wiped a tear from her eye and turned back to Deirdre. "Would ya mayhap be able ta dress my bridesmaids, too?"

She glanced over the sketch. "Maybe as I might. How many ye need?"

"Six and a flower girl."

Arachne nodded. "The Kennerly dresses."

The twins stopped oooing over the fabric and looked up.

Liberty looked confused. "Kennerly?"

"The weddin' got derailed three weeks before the date, got pushed back, moved forward, pushed back, then the dress wouldn't suit and therefore they needed eight brand new dresses in new style and colour."

"Bridezilla?" Solitaire chuckled.

"Mamazilla," Deirdre countered. She waved her hand in the air dismissively. "These dresses are the perfect style, will flatter these three at least, I don't know from the other three, not seeing them. And it'll flow with the wedding dress. What colour will ye be wanting them?"

"I've an emerald in mind, but... if th' dresses are already made..."

Deirdre smiled and patted her hand in a grandmotherly way. "Magic dear. Gold trim, I take it?"

Liberty laughed, "Silver actually."

The four women submitted to being measured within an inch of everything, and An was handed a glamoured page with the exact measurements for the lace pieces needed. Before they left, Arachne came up to her and gave her an oiled silk bag. "Here, use this to assemble the lace."

An peeked inside and smiled.

"You'll need..."

"I have some colt's foot oil at home, thank ye."

The spider smiled, a surprisingly warm expression. "You've used spider silk before."

"Aye. Threadwork were one o' th' things I taught th' Princess. I miss workin' with it. Thank ye. This will be th' perfect framework."

The ladies took their leave, waving to poor Mavis who stared after them, flabbergasted and thoroughly jealous.

When they finally came out the door upstairs at Courtz, it was very late. Liberty led the way downstairs and was surprised to see the place nearly empty and the staff beginning their closing routines. She looked at her watch and sighed. "I totally fergot th' time difference."

Tori saw her and headed immediately over with some paperwork.

Liberty groaned, "An, ya might as well have a seat at th' bar. I'll drive ye home when we're done. It's a little late fer walkin'."

An laughed quietly, "May as well take th' upstairs door t' th' cottage if it's late enough fer closin' time. Not like th' Tallows would hear me come in. But I'll bide fer a moment."

She found her way to a barstool and smiled as Silhouette held up a finger for her to wait with a mischievous light in his eyes. She watched him mime the act of selecting and pouring in the air above the bar, though she knew he was actually doing what he seemed to only be pretending to do. Slowly, a drink began to materialize in front of him and An watched in wonder. "What ye do with alcohol, Sil, is nothin' short o' magic, ye know that?"

He smiled. "Natural talent," he purred.

"No, magic," she insisted. She pointed at the glass. "I can see that."

He seemed genuinely surprised. "Well, fancy that. Here," he said, sliding a highball glass in front of her. "I call it the Morning Dew."

The drink was a dark amber at the bottom, lightening to a clear gold at the surface and gave off a faint mist. She sipped, found it mostly a honey whiskey base with a faint hint of sour in the finish. She set the glass down and rolled the liquid over her tongue a moment before swallowing.

He leaned on the bar, watching her intently.

"I declare this concoction ...a keeper."

He beamed, and a ripple of pleasure ran visibly down his skin. Of course, An saw sleek black fur instead of the white skin everyone else saw. She laughed, gave his hand a pat as he pulled back to begin closing down and cleaning up and left her to drink it.

She watched her friends in the mirror behind Sil. Roulet was at the DJ booth, fiddling with something and her sister was on the floor dancing to what music was still playing. An was relieved as Solitaire seemed better than she had been. The wedding was good for her, though An had feared it would well up regrets and other unspoken emotions from Henry's death. It seemed to be having just the opposite effect. Liberty was at a table at the corner of the dance floor looking over some paperwork with Tori. A shadow moved across the wall on the far side of all of them, on a side of the room An had never wandered into. She looked back down at her drink, taking another sip and then looked back up, suddenly realizing that what she had seen did not belong.

"Sil?" she asked softly.

"Yes, ma' petit?"

"How many customers are left?"

He glanced around the bar. "I think the last one just walked out." There was something in the way she played with the rim of her glass and the nervous way Aislynn looked around that told him something was afoot. "Why?"

She pitched her voice just a little higher, searching the mirror for the shadow. "Liberty, *luv,*" she said in Irish, even as she pulled her phone out of her pocket and set it on the bar next to her, resting her hand on it. "*Ye should get the mundanes in the back. We have... untoward company and this might get a little messy.*" Under her fingers, the phone began doing what she asked it to do: texting Skye.

Liberty looked up, frowned, looking around before catching An's eyes through the mirror. Tori got up without another word and crossed to someone out on the floor, wiping tables and pushing chairs in by the sound. Within a minute she was heading up the stairs and holding the door open for unseen people.

Just before the door closed on the last person, An found the shadow again. This time it was behind the bar, halfway up the shelves of bottles. She had an image press into her brain of Peter Pan's runaway shadow. That was exactly what this looked like. The shadow turned to look up the stairs, then down at An and a very audible, very Slavic curse came from it, followed by a shout of "*Teper'! Napadite na nih!*"

Everything exploded at that. Sil followed the tilt of An's face to the shadow man and twisted, his body shifting to that of a large, sleek panther. He jumped, snagging the thing in his teeth and dragging it down, even as the man solidified enough to pull out a wicked knife and attempt to stab him. An reached over the bar with the shillelagh and cracked the shadow's wrist with the iron tip, disarming him. At that same moment, several invisible men rushed out of the bathroom and into the main room. Once they were clear of the bathroom hall, An caught a glimpse of one she could see remaining behind, fiddling with the door.

Silhouette looked like he had the shadowling handled. Roulet was wholly electrified and using her staff to full effect. Solitaire was still dancing, though An realized it was a dodging dance with the high kicks doing more than just showing off her legs. Liberty had backed in among the tables, snatching up the heavy glass candle globes and hurling them with frightening accuracy at the mortal thugs

An ran for the hall. Halfway there something invisible grabbed her, chuckled in Russian. She tossed Cipín up through her hand, holding it further down the shaft and rapped whoever it was on the head with it, even as Aislynn dropped onto his hand to sink claws and teeth savagely. He cursed and let go. The shadowling yelled something in Russian: an instruction. The man left off and she could hear his footsteps going up the stairs as she reached the man at the bathroom door, swinging her shillelagh.

She was certain she had broken his jaw, as he collapsed backwards, pulling the now fully visible door open as he did. She was too late. Immediately, the stench of hot tar and broken asphalt and smog and rot assaulted her senses. A wave of heat washed over her through that door so intense it stole her breath for a moment. As she reeled, she caught sight of a dark city street and a pack of walking corpses staggering her way. She rushed to slam the door closed, but the pale man on the floor grabbed her ankle and bit. She screamed as fangs sank in. It felt like a snakebite. Before she could turn to strike him, the door was pushed further open and she was thrown against the back wall, the fangs torn from her ankle.

The upstairs door came open and a highland yell ripped through the club. Striking wildly as it was the only thing she could do in the close quarters, she kicked and swung, throwing herself against the bathroom door and forced it closed. She spared a single hand to touch it, begging it to close and stay that way. It obeyed and she stabbed downward with the shillelagh's iron tip into the vampire on the floor. He exploded in a shower of glittery ashes as the iron pierced his flesh and carried the wood through his still heart.

She turned to face the three shambling corpses who remained to attack her. Some were fresher than others, but they all had teeth and sharpened, jagged nails that tried to grab for her. Aislynn breathed a spray of frost at them and An drove them back, using shortened swings and stabs in the narrow space. As she stepped out of the corridor, finally able to take a full swing, she threw her whole weight into it. Catching a corpse just under the ear, sent the head sailing across the room sans body, which stumbled about for a moment before it finally collapsed.

Skye saw the head go flying and bellowed "FORE!" in a joking warning. He, himself, used the claymore to it's fullest, mowing down the zombies like a field of hay with broad sweeps of the blade. It was not on fire at the moment, a rather wise precaution under the circumstances, but still deadly.

There were other people from the Rest here as well, including Lafayette who had come out of the kitchen with a cleaver. Liberty had pulled a pair of water pistols from somewhere, filled with something that sizzled when it struck the undead things. When the last zombie was in pieces and the mortals were subdued, everyone took a moment to assess the situation. Silhouette was human again, wiping an inky, black substance off his face and hands. Skye was checking on Liberty, not that he needed to, and Solitaire was physically sitting on someone An could not see. Roulet was zipping into every nook and cranny of the club, making sure they were alone.

The woman An had seen talking to Cass that one night was there, in a camouflage bikini top and low slung jeans and bending over someone that An was slowly beginning to see a little. She took a guess that she was healing the man. A young man with blue hair and a very wolf-like face was trying to calm Lafayette down as he hacked away at one of the now inert zombie corpses.

Liberty took a single moment in Skye's arms to allow her anger wash over her and the adrenaline to ease out of her system. Then she pulled away, looking around to assess the damage and then took charge. "All right. Serenity, that lot still breathin'?"

"Yes, ma'am," she called, tying something to the man's hands as he slowly began to fade from An's view, the magic done.

"Good. We've got a golden opportunity here ta stick it to those Russian bastards! I need a door ta somewhere. We've got ta get rid o' th' zombies an' then I'm callin' Dukes ta come deal with th' mortal ninnies."

An went back down the hallway, checked the door. She could still see it. "Liberty, th' door they came from is still active."

"Really, now?" She looked over at Skye. "You and Kyle make sure there aren't more waitin' t' come through. If there aren't, we'll chuck 'em all out th' door they came in."

Skye nodded and gestured the wolf-man to him. They both joined An in the hall and allowed her to open the door for them. Everyone was braced for trouble. There was nothing there, just a deserted alley in the worst kind of city, stinking to high heaven of putrid flesh and rotting trash. At the end of the alley they could occasionally see the odd passer-by furtively hurrying past, but nothing to worry them.

An closed the door again and the others began collecting the bodies, piling them up in the hall next to the bathroom door. When they had them all, or thought they did, An opened the door again and held it as they began chucking the pieces into the alley. An was about to close it when Skye remembered something and ran out into the club. There was the sound of shifting tables and a few curses from the Scot, then he returned holding a zombie head with a large round dent on one side. He beamed down at her with pride.

Silhouette came up, dragging an unnaturally dark-skinned man with Russian prison tattoos all up and down his arms and several on his face. At the door he picked up the body and threw it into the dumpster next to the pile of zombie parts. He saw the look Skye and Kyle were giving him and scowled. "*You* want to explain to the cops why he looks like a jungle cat mauled him?"

Kyle shook his head vigorously and backed off. Skye just dropped his head and sighed, looked over at An. "Kin ya shut it doon?"

She nodded, closing the door and stroking the painted wood. After a few seconds' conversation, she frowned and stepped back. "Oh, really now? I disagree." With that she lifted the shillelagh and gave the door three hard raps with the iron tip, one at each hinge and one by the handle. It immediately vanished from her sight. She turned, saw the three men staring at her with widened eyes. "What?" she snapped. "It said 'no'."

"On that note," Kyle said, "I'm going home. I should have been in bed hours ago." He made his escape rather swiftly.

Silhouette bowed out gracefully, "I've got an unexplainable mess behind the bar."

Skye just looked at her. Finally, "Yer hoose ken how violent ya kin get when an object tells ya nae?"

She fixed him with a withering look and he immediately danced out of reach.

They returned to the main room. Tori and the others had apparently come down when Kyle had gone up. Everyone was gathered at the end of the bar, away from the site of the fighting, leaving evidence as it lay. Sil had the foresight to go and mop up the places where the juicier zombies had oozed. When he was done, he poured everyone a round of drinks.

"So, how did ya know we needed ya an' t' bring help?" Liberty asked her husband after downing her first shot.

Skye grinned. "Got a text message." He glanced down the bar at the three mortals sitting with Tori and added for their benefit, "good thing we weren't far. We were at th' dojo an' lost track o' time."

An felt the twinge of the almost-lie but said nothing.

They had just started the second round when Cass and Dukes arrived. This time An got an actual introduction, instead of just noting them from afar. She watched Serenity flush with pleasure at the sight of them. Casper Torres, aka Cass, was of mixed Hispanic origin, tall and ruggedly handsome. He had light brown eyes that first danced, then darkened at the sight of the buxom blond in camo. Paul Dukes was shorter, more wiry and far more surly. He had light brown, tightly curling hair and dark brown eyes that quickly revealed his suspicious nature.

"So, what is it this time, Miss O'Keefe?" he sighed. "More 'planted drugs'?"

Liberty kept her temper in check, though it was difficult. "No, actually. Those assholes," she said, pointing to the dance floor where they had laid out the four Russian mortals they had subdued and tied up.

Cass walked a little farther down, checked them out and whistled. "Might have them, Paul. This time we might have them!"

Paul growled, pulling out his notepad. "We'll see if shit adds up to squat first. Go ahead, Miss O'Keefe, what happened?"

"I'll start over here," Cass said, drawing aside one of the servers and began to ask him questions.

Paul drew Liberty a little ways away and took her statement, and between the two of them, got the statements of all present. There were a few discrepancies, but nothing unexpected. The story was that the Russians had come to the club, waited 'til near closing, then hid in the bathroom before attacking. An had already called her ride, which was Skye. Serenity claimed to have been staying with Roulet upstairs and had come down when Skye had arrived through the back door and gone to the upper floor, thinking that's where An was waiting for him. One of the Russians trying to kick down a door alerted him to the trouble and the two of them had gone downstairs to deal with matters. As far as anyone was able to tell, it wasn't a straight out robbery as none of them had made any demands; just came in swinging bats and fists aiming to break things and heads.

When Paul made a quiet comment to Liberty about the mess being a little more than just the four on the floor, she had whispered back, "There were. Zombies, but ya'll not be wantin' that in yar report."

An paid attention while they waited for the crime scene people to come and verify that everything happened as they claimed and the captives were cuffed and taken out. Pictures were taken of bruises and minor cuts that the defenders had sustained. Silhouette claimed to have just hidden behind the bar. Cass seemed impressed by Solitaire's story, and when she demonstrated a high kick at Skye's head, stopping a few centimetres from his ear, he fully believed that she had taken on one of the men herself. There was no explaining the electrical marks on them, so Roulet kept her mouth shut, claiming to have used an old broom handle on hers, though she was quick to talk up An's dealing with the one who had tried to grab her. This of course, made her blush.

When everything was said and done, and the mortals had been allowed to go home and the Russians were carted off, the detectives sat down at the bar and just breathed. There were no other people present but the taken and the two detectives, so everything relaxed. Both men accepted coffees.

"So, you gonna tell us what *really* happened here?" Paul asked.

Skye and An looked at him in surprise but Liberty chuckled softly. "S'ok, they know a lot. Not everything, mind, but more than they should."

"About a lot of ugly things," Paul sneered.

"You sure you want to know?" Roulet asked.

Cass, Serenity snuggled up to him, shrugged. "Makes it easier to explain off the weird, knowing what might crop up. Anything in all that the tech boys are going to have an aneurysm over?"

Liberty shrugged, "Zombie gore?" she suggested.

"Inky icky?" Silhouette added.

Paul scowled.

Liberty smiled and filled them in on what had really happened. "We got rid o' th' bodies. Hopefully ya'll never end up where they are. It's not a pretty place. Though technically on'y one o' em were alive afore we tore 'em up."

"What ah want tae ken," Skye said, "is what Taken were doin' wi' th' Russian dobbers o'er yon? An' how'd they open a door t' th' Dark City?"

Liberty frowned. "Questions fer Da. If ya gentlemen are done with us?"

Paul downed the last of his coffee and set the mug on the bar. "Yeah, we need to get this report in anyway... what we can write of it. Those Russians could be out by morning, so... I'd up your security around here."

"I intend ta. Thank ya," Liberty said and saw the two of them to the door.

They finished closing the place down and headed upstairs, letting Liberty open the door first and filed into the Manor. There was a light on in the east wing, telling them that Ian was up and in his office. Skye took An's arm to guide her, knowing the sudden shifts of place sometimes threw her off.

Lafayette and Serenity both begged off, heading out the front door to their respective homes. When the rest of them got into the office, there was just not enough seating for everyone, so Silhouette shifted to cat form and curled up on the floor. Liberty perched on Skye's lap.

Ian rubbed the last vestiges of sleep from his eyes and sighed. Explanations were repeated. By the time they were done, Ian was lighting his fourth cigarette and pouring his third Jameson. He sat quiet for several minutes, thinking, and no one bothered him. Skye lit a cigarette of his own and Solitaire poured herself a scotch.

Finally, "An, yeh know that thing I said I dinna want ta ask o' yeh, but might?"

She nodded.

"Well, I have ta ask."

Skye looked from An to Ian, suspicious. "And what moight tha' be?"

"He's asked me t' use m' sight," she said curtly, without looking at him.

"This'd be so much faster and safer if yeh could fly. Then I'd just send yeh out wit' Jonny."

This comment did not make Skye any happier.

"Tomorrow, whilst Elizabeth's in school, I'll have Sean pick yeh up. Drive yeh around town, see what yeh kin see. Should be safe enough. I'll decide then if there need be more."

"What about Courtz?" Roulet asked. "Dukes said they could be out on bail by morning. Surely they'll retaliate. Try something else?"

He nodded. "Well, from what yeh said, and what th' Russians likely know, none o' th' staff saw anything, so they should be fine. At least not targets fer silencing. An, yeh'll not be walkin' anywhere outside th' Rest 'til this is done. Not e'en wit' Jonny. He can't save yeh from a bullet fired from a rooftop. Don't worry about Elizabeth. I'll be discussin' some extra precautions with Sean fer her, in case they know what yeh do. Liberty, yeh an' yer beau are glued t'gether from here out."

She looked indignant. "I can handle ma damn self! Asides, there still be wedding stuff ta arrange, fittin's, an' I'll not have him see one stitch o' that dress…"

He held up a hand, cutting her off. "When yer out o' th' country 'tis a different matter, idn'it? Yer at th' Rest, do as yeh please. No leavin' if yeh can help it. That goes fer yeh two as well," he said, pointing at the twins. "Hell, goes fer everyone!"

"Fine by me," Solitaire shrugged, refilled Ian's drink and sat in his lap.

"Who'll take care of Courtz?" Roulet protested.

"Yeh will, and Liberty. Yeh'll just not be seen comin' or goin'. And Skye'll be workin' security, along wit' whatever other goons I kin rustle up. Also, I've someone arriving tomorra who's going to rig yeh up a security system ta rival Fort Knox. Not an inch o' floor space isn't goin' ta be filmed."

"What about us, and the things we occasionally do?" An asked. "Are we going to be handicapped if this happens again because we can't shift," she said, aiming her hand in Sil's direction, "or be thought to be able to see anything, or use a sword?"

He grinned. "Oh, Willy assures me this is special equipment. He calls it th' NOO: Nothin' Out o' th' Ordinary. Don't ask me how it works, just that dear little An could probably see enough o' it ta work it. If yeh don't want somethin' endin' up on th' final tape …what th' police get… it don't. Yeh kin see it on th' equipment if yeh like, but it don't download that way."

Silence filled the room while people drank or smoked. Then Liberty had a horrible thought. "Ma weddin'!"

"What about it?" her father asked, suddenly worried by the look on her face.

"We're still havin' it," Skye insisted, holding her more firmly on his lap.

"Aye, but no. We've posted th' banns, at th' church. It's all over th' society pages. Invitations have gone out already!"

"So?" Ian frowned.

"So Spetznakov likely knows!" she growled. "What if he tries ta …ruin my weddin'!" She was furious at the very notion.

Ian laughed at that, which only got his daughter more worked up and Skye had a hard time holding on to her. "Oh, I think th' potatah-drinkin' bastard'll have his hands full that mornin'."

Even Sil's ears went up at this, quite literally.

Liberty stopped squirming. "What ha' ya done?"

"Nothin' yet, just put a bug in th' ears o' a cousin or two, let Aiden do what he does best... set a few things in motion... nothin' fer yeh ta fret over until it's done. Not'in' is goin' ta interfere with either ceremony." That last was said in a tone both cold and flat that was chilling to hear. There was finality to it.

No one dared ask him to clarify.

6

The next morning, An watched Elizabeth catch the bus from the girl's bedroom window. She saw nothing at all on the street but her and a white raven nesting in the tree. Elizabeth waved just before the bus pulled up in front of her to let An know what was going on. She had been quietly warned to be more alert. An heard the bus pulling away and started to move from the window when she saw the raven leave the tree and fly in her direction. He landed on the window sill and peered up at her.

"Up for this?" Jonny croaked.

"No," An sighed. "But there is no choice, is there? Th' thing must be done and I'm th' only one what can."

"Illusions are lies."

She nodded.

"Courtz. Sean," he said. With that he flew off and An closed the window. She hated this thing called screens. She understood the benefits of keeping bugs out of the house, especially in this mosquito infested part of the world, but she had longed to reach out and stroke those white feathers and couldn't.

She went down to make sure the doors were locked and then headed upstairs to her garret. She thought about Courtz as she opened the door and found herself stepping into the upstairs lounge of the club from one of the small bedrooms that were up there. She took a moment to get her bearings. It was always a little disorienting when she went from a mundane place to a mundane place via these doors, not being able to see. With Aislynn giving her verbal guidance and Cipín keeping her aware of the ground ahead of her, she turned left instead of right, down the back stairs and out the kitchen door. The white raven sat on the loading dock rail waiting for her.

She smiled at seeing him, and he hopped to her other shoulder, opposite Aislynn. His weight was comforting. Sean was waiting below, leaning up against something she could not see, and smoking. He stubbed out his cigarette and flicked it deftly into the trash bin. He opened the car door for her, held his hand out for hers. Jonny butted his head against her cheek before he leapt into the air. An let Sean hand her into the vehicle and fastened her safety belt.

Aislynn, in interest of being less recognizable, changed into a small, white terrier and perched primly in An's lap.

It soon became fairly obvious to her that Sean was following Jonny, using some magical means to keep track of him. He led them through several neighbourhoods and, while Aislynn assured her there were plenty of people and Sean stated a good number of them were Russian, An saw none of them. At least, until they got to the edges of the inner city.

Jonny had landed on a tall building, maybe eight stories according to Aislynn. An could barely see him. It was a tenement of some sort, and while An could not see the building as a whole, she could see four of the windows on the upper story and the man sitting out front by the door. Just being near the building seemed to put a great deal of weight on her heart and body, as if the brick structure itself were pressing down on her.

An asked Sean to describe the doorman while he was stopped at the nearby traffic light. He described a man of muscular build, average appearance but rough, dangerous looking. What An saw was a large man made of a black, tarry substance with flecks of white and cracks throughout. He had reflective yellow lines serving for tattoos going up his arms and the eyes which followed the car were rusty round discs of metal with the word 'Metro' stamped on them. She shivered, told Sean what she saw.

They drove on when the light turned and traffic moved, scouting out a few other places. While she saw a glimpse or two of something in the shadows near the building, there was nothing else until downtown itself. These few were innocuous: a wasp woman coming out of a sub-shop, a well-dressed spaniel doing a little window-shopping, a nun (who was visible for entirely different reasons) strolling down the street talking animatedly with someone, and Serephina coming out of the cathedral. An frowned, asked what building that was and was not pleased with the answer.

"Ye think she's in league?" Aislynn growled, her paws on the window sill, glaring at the woman.

"Not with that one, likely," An answered, though not entirely convinced.

"See something?" Sean asked.

She shook her head. "Nothing here of import. People we know." Her fingers touched the open face of her watch and she frowned. "Is it really that late?"

Sean looked at his own wrist. "I'd better get ye home then. I didn't realize m'self."

"Someone on watch for th' bus?" An asked, a sudden fear gripping her belly.

He seemed to be thinking, or using whatever magic he possessed. An couldn't see it, but she could feel it. After a minute he said, "Yes, someone is ...now."

"Thank ye."

"My fault. I expected t' be back by now. I didn't make provision. Hell, we didn't even stop fer lunch."

As they drove, Sean put Ian on speaker phone and they gave a report of what they'd found. When An described the door man, he sighed. "Asphalt elemental. Dark Man fer certain then. An' yeh could see th' windows?"

"Aye. He's something on them. They're magical."

"Explains why Jonny couldn't see in them th' other night. We'll have t' keep tabs on 'em other ways. I'll let yeh know when I need yeh again. It'll be soon. Go home. If yeh got to go out, use yer door."

"Aye, chief," she sighed.

At that point, they were pulling up to Courtz and Sean got out, gave An his arm to guide her back upstairs. An went through the door quickly, heading downstairs to Elizabeth's room to let the watcher know they could leave.

Jonny was sitting on a lower branch of the neighbour's massive oak which hung down over the Tallows' yard. He was watching the house and the street at the same time with his dark eyes. He looked in her direction when she drew up the window, bobbed his white head at her and flew off. She felt a little disappointed, but controlled herself, closing the window and locking it back. As she left the room to go downstairs, planning on making Elizabeth's tea, she heard something from the girl's study that caught her attention.

An unfamiliar voice, hesitant, spoke. "...This is... this is the lady Amalthea. We seek audience with King Haggard."

Her heart stopped for a breath. Even Aislynn, who had been headed to the kitchen, flew back up and hung by her front claws on the bannister. "*I... smell no one,*" she frowned. "*Just th' kid. ...And popcorn.*"

An moved towards the study door, slowly opened it. Elizabeth was sitting at her desk, leaned back in her chair and munching on a bowl of popcorn, staring at the desktop. The voices were coming from there.

She looked up, smiled. When she noticed how pale her governess had gone, she sat up, reached over to what An now understood was her laptop and paused the voices. "You ok?" she asked. "Did things ...go badly?"

She shook her head. "Found out some uncomfortable things, but.... What are you doing?"

"Watching a movie?" Elizabeth said, unsure of An's mood at the moment and still a little worried by her reaction. Aislynn had landed on the desk and was looking at the screen.

"And homework is done?" An had the presence of mind to ask.

Elizabeth smiled. "This *is* homework. I have to watch *The Last Unicorn* and then read the book by Peter S. Beagle and write an essay comparing the two and explaining possible reasons for the changes. 'Do you think the changes made the story clearer, or changed the author's intent,' kinda thing."

"*The Last Unicorn*?"

"Are you ok? You're all white."

"I... am learning something I did not conceive possible."

"Would you like to watch it with me? I can start it over."

As much as An hated these things, she agreed, pulling her rocking chair over so that she could watch comfortably while she worked on her lace. Elizabeth did something to the screen that allowed An to see the film and started it over.

When it was done, she continued to rock quietly, absorbing what she had just seen. Memories of the Unicorn Lady began to filter through and nothing in the film contradicted it. She knew there was a Gentry called Haggard, who was also the Old Man of the Sea, and the Man in the Carrion Coat, and, occasionally, Lir. There was an old Celtic deity called Lir or Ler who was the sea, and the father of Manannán mac Lir who became the god of the sea. But, she supposed, the mythology of this story could be strong enough to influence the Gentry, and he could be this story's Lir too. Which hinted at more connection between The Old Man and the Lady than she had previously known. She had certainly heard of the Red Bull.

She had been present once when someone had come to the King, called him Néit before they had been shushed and reprimanded. An paused, she had not remembered that name before, but she knew it belonged to the Gryphon King, and she kept it close to her heart, encased in silence. There had to be a reason he had not wanted his old name known, and she would keep that secret with her last breath. But the messenger had come with news of a bridal party, a royal cousin who had been coming to wed a member of the Gryphon's court to seal some political arrangement. They had been riding along a beach, the bride upon a unicorn mount, when the Red Bull had beset them, driving the mount into the sea with the hapless bride still clinging to the saddle. It had trampled everything in its path. The Bull was unstoppable.

At the moment she could not remember how that tale had worked out. "You have the book?" she said at last.

"Yes, ma'am," Elizabeth said, holding it up.

"After dinner, I want you to read it to me. You have a few days for this assignment, aye?"

"Aye. Not due 'til next Tuesday."

"Good. Your mother has dinner ready, I expect, and will need ye to set th' table. Go on." She shooed the girl off and remained in her chair, rocking slowly and finishing the rose she held in her hand. "What do you think?" she asked Aislynn.

"I think form follows function. Or Life and Art, one of those sayings. Maybe this Beagle guy was one of the taken, or knew one who told him what he remembered. Maybe he made parts of it up and that just made the fair folk more what he said they were. Kinda like with Peter Pan and Hook, though Barrie got that one all twisted."

"Anything is possible."

By Friday, An was going a little stir-crazy.

When she smelled the unholy stench of broccoli, spinach and tofu steaming together in the oven, she took pity on poor George and Elizabeth and wandered into the kitchen. She had a quiet word with the oven who happily turned up the heat and dried out the casserole to an inedible crust by the time Sharon had come to check on it.

George was delighted to declare dinner a disaster and decided they were going out. An noticed that Sharon was the only one upset by the 'casserole catastrophe'. He took them for Chinese and they was a small issue at the door over the monkey. George was quick to site the state's laws, chapter and verse, regarding service animals and the hostess backed down.

Of course this had only served to draw attention to her, and the few other children and even some of the adults kept looking and giggling. This only made Aislynn ham it up, though she remained perfectly behaved.

When the Tallows were momentarily distracted, Aislynn whispered in her ear. *"After this, we're goin' t' Courtz. I need a dram."*

An smiled, started to bring the matter up to George, but he'd had an idea of his own. "There is this new creamery a few blocks from the house. I thought we'd stop for ice cream on the way home. What do you think?"

Elizabeth was excited by this idea, and Sharon relented. They drove almost home, parked the car in a lot down the street and walked down the pavement amid the crowded night-life of this part of town. Sharon proclaimed it a very 'artsy' community.

"I had no idea we had a place like this so close to the house. We never drive this way."

Most of the shops Sharon found interesting were closed at this hour, but there were several places still open, including an art house, a small theatre, the creamery, a coffee house and a nightclub. The last George had commented on because the line to get in stretched half the block.

"Place must be jumpin'," he laughed.

Something about where they were struck An as familiar even before Aislynn tapped her to warn her. "Would that club happen t' be Courtz?"

"It would," Sharon answered, reading the sign. "Oh, they have Karaoke! George, we really ought to do a date night one Friday and go."

George seemed less enthusiastic about that idea, but did not shoot it down entirely. He held the door to the ice cream shop open for the ladies and as An entered, she suddenly oriented herself by the sounds around her. The location of the club and the thump of the music as the doors opened, the squeal of someone's brakes as they came to a stop at the light on the corner where An had nearly been run over. This doorway... had once led to a dark road which eventually had taken her to Jonny's little faery hide-away. She blushed as she entered, reaching out for Elizabeth's shoulder in the crowded little parlour.

It was one of those places where they mixed the ice cream to order, and An let Aislynn whisper what ingredients she wanted and ordered just a small scoop of it in a mini waffle bowl. They sat as a family and ate their desserts. Elizabeth giggled as Aislynn helped herself to most of 'An's' ice cream with one of the little sample spoons and then ate the bowl. An merely nibbled. Passing the door again, remembering where it had once led, had put her in a mooning mood and she found herself longing to see him again. They had not had the opportunity to exchange more than a few words since Ostara, not even at the big Easter Egg Hunt the Sunday that followed it. "If it's all right by you, Mr. Tallow, I'd like t' go down t' Courtz myself tonight. Don't worry about gettin' me home. I've walked home many a night."

Sharon sipped her coke. "That where you go?" An nodded. "Nice place?"

She gave a small gesture with her hand. "I like it. I know th' owners, so ye need not fear fer me safety."

George was still clearly uncertain. "I don't feel right just leaving you here."

"Well, if ye insist I come home with ye, I'll just walk back," she said softly.

He relented. "If you're sure."

"I am."

She waited until they were done and ready to go before parting company. She was aware that George was watching her as she tapped her way down the pavement towards the crowd she could hear and the bouncer she could see. "Evenin', deartháir," she called cheerfully.

Skye turned, startled, then beamed, pulled her into a big hug. Then he scowled. "Whit th' divil ya doin' walkin' aboot?"

"Not alone," she smiled after he was done crushing her. "Kindly wave t' poor Mr. Tallow so he'll take his family home and stop worryin'?"

Skye looked up, saw the family near the end of the block and waved, gave the man a thumbs up. He was rewarded by a look of surprise and relief, and the man turned his family towards the car. Elizabeth waved at him.

"Afore ye start fussin', I had no reasonable means o' tellin' him 'no, I couldna go out t' dinner with th' family'. Only by happenstance that ice cream parlour opened at th' end there. Now, ye gonna let me in, or make a blind girl with a possible target on her back stand in line?" she growled in Irish, though she was smiling.

He sighed and moved to open the door for her, waving dismissively at someone just inside. "Ah'll talk at ya later when ah'm spell't frae th' door."

As she went inside she heard "Why'd you let *her* in?" echoing through the people near the head of the line. She grinned when he snarled back, "Cuz she's nicer than yoo!"

Once inside, though the music was loud and the sounds of billiards and darts surrounded her, she felt more relaxed. Aislynn guided her by taps to the shoulder to the door to the main club and she headed for her usual table, stopped when she saw that it was occupied. Jonny she had hoped and expected to see. Serephina, not so much. Instead, she diverted to the bar to order a drink for herself and Aislynn.

Silhouette smiled apologetically as she found a hole at the crowded bar. "Sorry if your table's taken. Busy night like tonight it was bound to happen. What'll it be?"

She gave him a rueful smile. "Were it normal folk it wouldn't matter."

Aislynn hissed an unkind word in Irish which made Sil start.

"Serephina," An explained. "I'll have a double of that morning dew ye made me, and a shot o' Tennessee Honey on the side."

He nodded, whipped up her drinks and slid them over to her. "Why's it so busy?" she asked, taking a sip and letting Aislynn sip hers.

"Got a local band coming in." He glanced at his watch, "Should be in in about thirty. They set up this afternoon. Liberty was lucky to get them. That's why there's a door-charge tonight. She's donating the cover."

She suddenly realized what Skye had been waving at. He had signalled the person collecting the cover to pass her through. "She didn't tell me."

"Last minute. They're kinda up and coming, and when she ran into the drummer at the Rest..." he shrugged, grinning.

"He's one of us?"

He just winked in response.

Tori swept by, using her hip to bump Sil out of her way. "Two of your specials- other end of the bar. I can't make those." He grunted and headed down bar and Tori gestured her head towards An's regular table as she poured a handful of pint mugs. "You might want to go rescue him. She's on a tear tonight. The Ice Queen's been ordering frosted mint vodkas, and by the third one, she gets vicious if you cross her."

"How many's she had?"

"Just delivered the third. Either way, I think you can handle her better than Jonny. Though he seems to be standing up to her tonight," she said with a surprised shake of her head.

An thanked her and took her drink, letting Aislynn carry her own and carefully began to make her way to her usual table. More than once, Aislynn had to let loose a monkey shriek to get people's attention and make them move. As she neared the table, An could hear Serephina laying into him.

"...counting on you for this, Jonny. You're the only thing that makes these farces tolerable."

"Then why do ye do it?" he snapped. "Go through man after man..."

"Girl after girl?" she countered.

An stopped a table or so away. Not because she wanted to listen, but because her path was blocked again.

"I don't marry them, Serephina."

"No. You seduce them, fuck them and walk away. You break hearts, Jonny. I make a few older men happy and let them take care of me before they die."

"They seduce themselves," he snarled in self defence. "I make them no promises."

"Typical bard," she spat, saying it as if 'bard' was a dirty word.

Jonny actually laughed at that, a dry and ironic sound. "Yer not gettin' what ye want this time, m' dear."

"You *have* to play at my wedding!"

His voice was cold. "Hold it some other day."

"I want May first. He wants May first...."

An managed to get a little closer, sighed as she was stalled again and drank about half of her whiskey as she waited.

"He wants what you want," he snapped. "We both know ye only want Bealtaine t' screw with Liberty. And I've already promised her the day."

"So the O'Keefe's lesbian daughter finds herself a man and the world drops everything for her? You sleep with her too? Does she mean more to you than I do?" she cried, loud enough to be heard almost to the bar even over the music and the crowd. There were still some karaoke going on, killing time and keeping the audience happy while they waited for the main act of the night.

She heard Jonny stand. She stifled a yelp as someone stepped on her foot.

"Ye'll have t' change th' date or find another singer. I'll not break my word. Not even for you."

As he pushed his way through the crowd, away from the table, Serephina called after him, attempting one last time. "You'll come by tonight and we can talk about this more rationally?"

Someone on the dance floor backed into An, propelling her forward just as Jonny had slipped between the two large men blocking her approach to the table. They collided, Jonny reaching out in time to keep her from getting hurt and half-looked over his shoulder at Serephina.

"No," he said, in a voice that would brook no argument. He took An's now empty glass from her and reached behind him, setting it on the nearest table, occupied or not. He then took her hand and used his own body to shield her from the press as he navigated the crowd to a more open location. It wasn't much better.

He turned, bent to her ear, whispered. "Sing with me?"

"Anytime," she breathed.

"Ye know "Jar o' Hearts"?"

She ran it through her mind quickly. "I think so."

He pulled her up to the stage steps, paused to have a word with Roulet in her little booth. She nodded, and as soon as the person currently singing was done, he led An up onto the stage, stopping her in front of one microphone before taking his place at the other.

Once the music began, An did indeed recall it from the music he had been sending her. It was one she had liked very much. She found the words poignant and the melody beautiful. They sang it as a duet, a vocal back and forth even though she was more support for him in this. Her voice was haunting and full of pain, uplifting; his: sharp and determined, his clear tenor cutting.

His eyes drifted across the room, singling out certain people, mostly the beautiful. Serenity, at the bar, blushed a little when he stared over-long at her, tore her eyes away and concentrated on her drink. Even William was singled out, though he did not back down. Eventually, his gaze fell on Serephina, sitting at their table in her designer dress and diamond drop earrings, frost forming on the tall, narrow glass in her hand, fury in her icy blue eyes.

When they were done, the audience was wild, even though more than one person was feeling the sting of the words. Jonny seemed to drink in the adulation for a moment, maybe even hating himself for it. He turned to collect An, slipping his arm around her waist as he guided her off the stage and back into the press of humanity. Aislynn looked down at the arm, glared but said nothing, wrapping her tail around An's neck.

Jonny headed to the bar, steering her to the end where there were less people. He turned to watch Serephina storming out, pushing when she was blocked.

He looked up at the stairs, down at An, then began to lead her to the lounge. Still reeling from the very intimate action of his arm around her waist, she flowed with him unresisting, thin mist spilling down the steps in her wake.

Once the door was closed behind them, he let go, leaning back against it. The sudden silence was nearly deafening. She rest against the wall, watching him, waiting for the ringing to stop. Aislynn had already checked for people up here, launched herself into the air and gone to the liquor cabinet around the corner.

Jonny finally opened his eyes, looked down at her, reached out with a cold finger and traced her jaw tenderly. "I am sorry about that."

"Which that?" she asked, breathless and trying not to show it. There were many reasons for it.

"Using ye, takin'... liberties... especially fer th' purpose..."

Aislynn was back, hovering in mid-air, an empty shot glass in her clawed fist and fury on her scaled face. *"Damned right you ought to be sorry! You're doing exactly what she said ye do! And I won't have it,"* she growled.

Jonny winced. "Ye heard that?"

An blushed. "A bit. Not like I had a choice. I was comin' t' rescue ye and found myself in a press. I couldn't go forward or back, so.... 'Tisn't like she was bein' discrete."

He chuckled humorlessly. "That she weren't." He held out his hand. When An slipped hers into it, Aislynn let out an exasperated snort and flew back to the cabinet to fill her glass. Jonny ignored the outburst politely, lead An further into the room and set her on the couch. "Ye want anythin'?"

"Is there aught o' th' honey? I sort o' had mine spilled."

"Ye and yer whiskey candy," he chuckled. "Aye, I see some Tennessee." He poured both of them a healthy measure and returned. He smiled softly, breathed on the belly of the glass and An watched frost appear, and the tumbler become visible. She returned his smile and let him set the glass in her hand, sipping the now deliciously cool liquor.

He sat beside her, stretching out and propping his feet up on the table in front of them. He held his glass to hers. "Sláinte," he sighed.

"Sláinte," she echoed, tapping his glass with hers.

They sipped quietly. Aislynn returned, landing on the back of the couch between them, drinking her own.

"Not so much th' teetot'ller ye used t' be," he observed quietly.

She tipped her head slightly in acknowledgement. "Aye, well... I'd never had it before. Then I had need and low and behold I have a tolerance," she said with mocking surprise.

"Fancy that, ye bein' Irish an' all," he smiled.

She laughed softly. She sipped, sobered. "I'm sorry for what I overheard. ...She's no business dressin' ye down in public like that."

He snorted. "Hardly public. A crowded bar, pre-concert?"

"She really trying t' ruin Liberty's wedding by having her own th' same day?"

"Aye," he said into his glass.

"Why? Doesn't she realize no one at th' Rest's even goin' t' show up at hers? Savin' ye maybe? Th' women hate her."

He tipped his head with a bitter smile. "Ah well, she did that t' herself. And aye, she knows. They're not who she's tryin' t' draw off. Her newest victim is a society man. She holds th' weddin' th' same day and she'll force a good bit o' th' formal weddin' guests t' make a choice. She even tried t' get th' Cathedral, but Liberty'd already made those arrangements."

"That's what she was doin' there on Tuesday," she mused.

He nodded. "Again, I'm sorry fer draggin' ye inta this fight. She's goin' ta... try t' make yer life hell fer this," he said regretfully.

She tipped her head for a shrug as she sipped. "There's not much she can do t' me. I don't swim in th' same waters she does."

"I hope yer right. She requires thick skin to handle."

"I've noticed."

He reached into his vest and pulled out a cigarette, looked over at her, "Ye mind?"

"*Aye,*" Aislynn said, at the same time that An said, "No."

She glared at the dragon who went back to her whiskey, sulking.

"It smells different than m' father's pipe, but... what ye smoke is not unpleasant. ...I must say I like it better before it's lit," she said with a quiet laugh. "I can't explain. Th' toasted tobacco...."

"Smells like home?" he offered, lighting it up and drawing the smoke in.

"Maybe. I don't remember much o' that. I've remembered a name... something I dreamed, but... I don't remember if it were mine. I didn't like it much, but I don't rightly know if that's cause o' th' name or who it belonged ta."

"It'll come or it won't," he said. "Ye kin try t' force it if ye like. We can explore yer dreams, but... that's a risky road if it's not close."

She shook her head. "Not necessary. I'll let ye know an' I change my mind."

He nodded. "Will ye be wantin' t' go down fer th' concert? I should a thought o' that afore I swept ye up here but ...I needed breathin' space."

She smiled. "Not really. I... don't like th' press. I didn't know there was to be one, truthful. My bein' here is pure happen-stance."

Aislynn cleared her throat and arched a brow ridge.

She blushed a little. "All right, not *pure*. Th' bein' out is all my fault, but not where we ended up. Sharon was makin' somethin' that smelled..."

"*Like soured milk, old curds and wet, dirty laundry,*" Aislynn quipped, making a face. "*I don't know if pigs would eat it.*"

Jonny chuckled.

"So I convinced th' oven to make even Sharon think it inedible. George took us all out for Chinese and ice cream after. We were just down th' row," she blushed a little more when she said that, remembering her thoughts at the time.

There was something in his eye, "That new place on th' corner?"

She could feel the heat rising in her cheeks, convinced he was remembering too. "Aye. I didn't feel like goin' home, honest. We were right here, so I came. And Aislynn wanted a dram."

"I'm glad."

Some of the words Serephina said crossed her mind suddenly. Her blush began to fade as she wondered if she fit into that category. It didn't help that Jonny was watching her. She was brought out of her reverie by his cold finger brushing her cheek, drawing back her hair, running it over the blade-sharp ice petals of the blooded snow rose over her ear. "Yer not like th' women she was referrin' ta. And I've told ye I'd hurt ye."

She made herself look at him, watching his face, drinking in the beautiful, elven lines of his jaw and the high bones of his cheeks. "Do they mean anythin' to ye, these girls who 'seduce themselves'?"

He looked away, staring into the depths of his glass. "I barely remember their faces once they're gone. Unless I see them again. I promise them nothing." In the tightening line of his jaw she thought she saw self-loathing there.

"Ye've promised me nothing." Her voice was soft, almost a caress.

"That's not entirely true, now is it?" he said ruefully, draining the last of the liquor and setting the glass aside. He drew in a long draw of smoke, let it mix in his mouth with the whiskey before swallowing both. "I promised I'd bring ye pain," he said to the ceiling.

An could not explain why that statement made her whole body quiver. She should have shivered in fear, not reeled in minute joy. But the meaning in those words had their impact below the surface. He had promised *them* nothing. *She*, he had warned. In some way or another, he cared. Unless... "Do ye warn th' women o' th' Rest? Th' taken?"

He chuckled, tipped his head. "I am smart enough to avoid th' women of th' Rest. Somethin' about foulin' one's nest. As fer th' taken... many o' them have their own problems. I've been chased once or twice. It came to naught. I was too cold. Or too broken," he added with a light snort. He concentrated on his cigarette. "There is no explanation for ye," he said, watching the smoke curl into the air.

She wasn't sure how he meant that. Whether he had no explanation to give her, or if there was no explaining *her*. Even Aislynn looked at him funny.

A few hours had passed when Skye finally found her. He had gotten off door duty when the concert had started and shifted to floor. Once the concert begun, he'd evicted at least two people for harassing other patrons, but it was mostly uneventful. He had been surprised to find a group of mortals at An's usual table, hadn't seen her anywhere. When Sil told him she'd gone upstairs, he half expected to find out she'd gone home. He had not expected to find her sitting on the couch with Jonny, learning new music. He listened to the sweet trill of her voice as it wavered through a series of notes in perfect compliment to Jonny's base-line melody.

An opened her eyes and looked at him, smiled.

"Ye've a knack fer wanderin' harmony, Ceobhránach," Jonny said. He looked up and nodded to the Highlander. "Ev'nin, Skye."

Skye was a little stiff, but polite, nodded back. "Jonny." He turned to An. "Ah half thought ya'd gahn home."

She shook her head. "Not ready. And th' crush downstairs was too much."

Skye took a deep breath. "Ya may want tae gae soon tho'. Concert's aboot done. Th' band'll be retreatin' up here shortly an' 'tis loike ta get crowded. Unless ya've a mind ta meet them?"

Her fingers went to her watch. She was shocked at the time. "No, I think I should be gettin' home. I've things needin' done t'morrow." She stood, turned to Jonny. "Thank ye. I've enjoyed this. I can't say as I've ever..."

"Worked on music afore?" he smiled, standing and putting out his cigarette.

"Aye. Well, good night to ye both."

Aislynn leapt lightly to her shoulder, gave Jonny a half glare, still not liking him but unable to complain really about his behaviour the last few hours.

Jonny took her hand and guided her around the coffee table, placed a light kiss on the back of it before he let it go.

She blushed lightly, used Cipín to find her path to the door. She looked back, her hand on the knob, and glared at Skye. "And daor deartháir," she said with a smile that was full of warning. "I know what yer thinkin'. Don't." With that she slipped through the portal into her cottage.

For a moment Skye stared at the closed door, trying to control himself. He turned to face Jonny, who was just standing there, watching him warily. They stared for a few minutes. There were things Skye wanted to say and so much he didn't trust himself to. Finally he settled for, "Ya hurt her..."

Jonny arched an eyebrow at that. "I've already promised her I would," he said quietly. He watched that send the Scot's mind reeling as he reassessed his footing.

Skye's jaw tightened. "Physically. Ya hurt her physically then, an' ah'll break ya in half." Jonny started to nod but the Highlander wasn't done. He leaned forward just a hair. "Ya git her killed or taken... Ah'll *kill* ya."

Their eyes met for just a moment more, then Jonny said, taking a breath, "Fair enough."

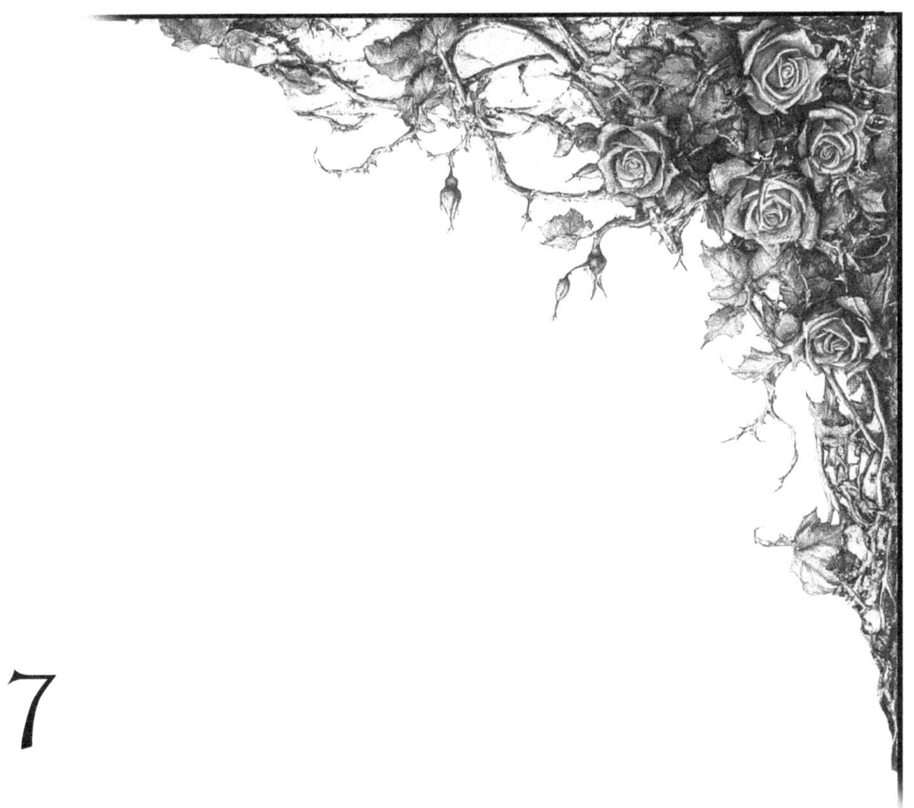

7

An was in the garden the following Sunday tending to the roses. The vampricks had spread several feet further down the wall and remained a rich, vibrant red with bright yellow roots so long as she brought them two or three mice a week. They were filling the garden with a lovely fragrance that mingled well with the now blooming wisteria climbing the front wall of the cottage and around her bedroom window, and the other flowers that were blooming lower down in the garden.

She was putting down a little fertilizer on the blackberries when Aislynn, who was lazing on the bottom half of the Dutch door in the sun, looked into the house, then out at An. *"Th' chief needs us up at th' manor,"* she called. *"Said it's time."*

An sighed, taking off her garden gloves as she stood. She entered the house, setting them on the kitchen counter. She wasn't really surprised when she found her boots waiting beside the kitchen table. Once she was presentable, she and headed out the back door. Also on the table were bits of lace leaves and flowers lain out in a sweeping triangular pattern. She looked it over, made a few adjustments as if working on a jigsaw puzzle, picked out a different rose motif for the centre, then put the other one back. Then, on inspiration, she gathered several into a bouquet arrangement which satisfied her more.

"Do me a favour, dear," she addressed the brownie she knew very well could hear her. "See which would look better, tiny pearls on the flowers or the crystal drops on the webbing? I'll trust your judgement either way."

With that she slipped into her boots, collected her shillelagh and left through the back garden gate. Stepping out, she told the house not to expect her for supper, and as she turned to close the gate, she noticed cuttings of the vamprick planted on both sides of the wicket. They were already about a foot tall and putting forth new, dark red leaves.

Aislynn landed on her shoulder as she stared at them and chuckled. "*Pixies have gone hog wild with those things. They're referring t' them as th' watchdogs.*"

An smiled. "Glad my garden is well-tended and protected," she said, as much to the pixies as to Aislynn, and turned to walk up the path to the manor.

She had just passed the rath when she heard a loud crashing through the under-brush on the opposite side of the road from the faery fort's entrance and her grip on the shillelagh shifted. She was startled by a large raccoon dropping from the tree and becoming a girl just before she hit the ground a few feet away from An. Luckily, An realized she was no threat before she actually struck her. The girl seemed to be in a panic.

"Calm down, Pawz. What's wrong?" An asked, treating her as she would any panicked child, even though she knew she was no child.

"Dead girl in the river," she gasped. "But I don't think she's dead, but she has to be, but I can't pull her out to find out for sure."

Aislynn leapt into the air and flew in the direction Pawz had come and An took the young woman by the hand and told her, "Lead me. Mayhap between the two of us..."

Pawz nodded and began pulling her through the forest toward the distant sound of running water. It only took a few minutes, but An knew those minutes could matter a great deal. They had just emerged on the river bank, Pawz looking up and down frantically when An laid eyes on something further down river at the same time Pawz shouted and pointed. Aislynn had already found the girl, landed on her and sat on her back, front claws buried in her hair trying to hold the face out of the water.

An waded in, never minding her boots at this point and, with Pawz' help, managed to snag an arm and a leg of the face-down, floating body and roll it onto its back. Luckily for all of them, the woman had gotten caught on something unseen on the riverbed and had been unable to float farther away. The fabric of her dark shirt tore as they pulled. As soon as An seemed to have the pulling out in hand, Aislynn launched straight up and flew like a bullet to the manor to get others.

It was a struggle, but between the two of them, they got the body completely out of the water and dragged her up onto the mossy bank. An took note of the blue lips and bloodless skin and set her hand to the pale throat, not expecting even a thready pulse. She jumped back as the eyes snapped open, a glassy, dead blue. They blinked, then the woman began coughing, rolled over and expelled a fair amount of river water.

Pawz shifted back to raccoon and climbed the nearest tree, leaving An on the shore with the 'corpse'. She set her hand on the woman's shoulder, supporting her, kept her from rolling back into the water. An let her do what she had to do, struggling for breath. The woman looked around fearfully as she wiped her mouth on the soaked sleeve of her dark sweater. "Fresh water," she gasped. "Not the sea. Where...."

"Haggard," the raccoon chirped from her perch, gulping.

The woman spun, her long, dark hair hitting An in the face and across the chest. She pulled back, seemed startled to see An there.

"You..." Suddenly she squinted and moved closer, looking at An's eyes. "You don't ... that's not... Haggardish. You're not from the Sea."

An gave her a comforting smile as she wiped a streak of water from her cheek. "No. Gryphon King. You are not There any longer. Do ye remember who ye are, and how ye got away?"

"O...Ophelia. And... I was thrown away."

An frowned. "Ophelia. Beautiful and appropriate." She introduced herself and Pawz, who had come down the tree to peered over An's shoulder at the very drowned girl. "Now, ye were thrown away? Doesn't sound like th' Old Man."

She shook her head, sending a rain of water everywhere. She stopped, apologized and gathered her hair, wringing it out. "Wasn't him. Unicorn. He sent me to steal something from her. She caught me and threw me out of her realm. I hit water that wasn't salt and.... That's all I remember."

"Well, we'll get ye squared away. Yer in a safe place now. Welcome t' th' Gryphon's Rest. There are a lot of normal people here, but they're family and know about th' weirdness. There are a lot of people like us here, too, were taken or served willin'."

She frowned at that. "Who would ever serve willing? What idiot goes to that? Unless they didn't know what they were getting? I know that happens."

An took a slow breath, trying to soothe her by remaining calm. "Ye said ye were in Amalthea's realm, tryin' t' steal sommat. Can ye think o' no reason anyone would want t' serve her, t' live in that place? There are some for whom remainin' in this world is neither desirable, bearable or safe."

The woman did not look convinced but she did seem a little mollified. Anything she was going to say was interrupted by the arrival of the gryphon on the far bank. Ian had circled over and chosen to drop onto the other shore, to give a chance to be seen at a 'safe distance' before coming closer and possibly frightening her. Ophelia looked ready to take flight or panic, but An set a hand on her shoulder, keeping her voice low and soft and sursurrating. "'Tis all right. That is Ian O'Keefe, the gryphon of the O'Keefe's. He owns the land yer on, and protects those who live here. He's a clan chief."

"He safe?" she coughed.

An smiled. "No, he isn't safe. But you will be when yer near him."

She thought a moment, then nodded. "Ok."

An turned to Ian and signalled him that it was all right and he leapt over the river, barely needing to open his wings to clear it. Once on their side of the bank, he changed back into a man, crouched near them. He held out his hand as An affected proper introductions. Ophelia took it tentatively.

"Has An explained things?"

"A little," she almost whispered. The woman was either painfully shy or still disoriented and frightened, quite possibly both. "You're the chief and you protect people like me. This is your home and I am safe here."

"Good enough fer now."

"Is there an outlet to the sea near?" she asked, terror in her drowned eyes as she searched his.

He shook his head. "No. Not near. There is a city within easy enough reach, an' docks there, but from here... no, he can't reach yeh."

She relaxed completely then. Ian stood, held out his hands to help both women to their feet. "Well, if yeh ladies don't mind a short flight, we'll get yeh both ta th' manor and inta sommat dry."

When they were standing, he stepped back and took off the broad belt from his waist. He re-buckled it at its largest and slipped it around his neck. Shifting once more into the gryphon, he shook himself to settle it, giving the women something to hold on to.

At that moment An envied Ophelia just a little for the trousers she was wearing. Once Ophelia was mounted, An blushed furiously as she got on behind her, glad she had chosen a wider skirt that morning than the narrower ones she had been wearing of late. If she had not been working in the garden, she might not have. Pawz scrambled up, still a raccoon, and crawled into An's vest for safety. An grabbed hold of Ophelia who seized the belt with both hands when she felt the leonine muscles beneath her bunch and ripple as the wings spread and he leapt into the air.

It was a frightening ride for An who could see very little of what lay below them. There were small things she could glimpse: her cottage, the rath, a dilapidated little hut deeper in the wood. The flight was thankfully short and it seemed only a minute of skimming over trees before she could see people scattered on the green in front of what had to be the veranda.

The landing was as smooth as take off and An quickly slid off his back, aware that her skirts had flown up almost past her knees. Ophelia was more graceful getting down. Pawz wiggled out of An's vest and shifted herself.

Immediately, Liberty and Roulet stepped forward to help her as Ian changed back to man. However, the moment Roulet noticed they were dripping wet, she took a step back. "I'd better wait 'til you're dry."

Ophelia looked at her oddly. "But... I've never been dry. It's how she caught me. The water."

Liberty looked back at Roulet then at Ophelia. "We'll see. We'll certainly try. Ya'll be amazed how much o' what ya were There is less concrete here."

Ian drew An back as she started to follow them. "I need yeh ta go with Shannon," he said. "She'll get yeh dry an' changed, then I need yeh in ma office. We're waitin' on yeh."

She nodded as Shannon dropped a large towel around her and began patting her dry. She let the older woman lead her upstairs to the first bedroom. It was not the one she'd used when she was here last, but it would suffice to get her dry and changed. She could see her own clothes laid out in the air, presumably on the bed and smiled. The brownies definitely worked together no matter where they actually lived. It further confirmed that her own was likely a younger member of the main family's.

She began to peel out of her wet garments the moment she heard the door close. Shannon helped her where she needed it. "Sorry about the water on the floor," An said, hearing the wet plop of her now heavy skirt as it hit the wooden boards. She stepped out of it and bent to collect it, but Shannon shooed her hands away.

"Dry," she ordered, pressing another towel into her hands.

An obeyed, moving to her clothes and changed. As she picked up her blouse, she noted that it was one of her summer ones: short sleeve, light cotton, a neckline that stopped just above the entwined dancing figures of her faery token. She looked down at the luminous white metal and diamond flower in her hand. She had worn it everyday since the night the Princess had given it to her for the Winter Masque. It glittered on her palm. Reluctantly, knowing it the wiser course, she handed it to Shannon with the rest of her clothes, then picked up the last article which she did not recognize at all.

It was a vest like many of her others,, but this one was more angular. Instead of providing a squared, corset-esque frame for her body, it ran down into a deep V with a swallow-tailed hem. It was a faded, earthy brown and felt like suede to the touch. When she put it on, it fit her body like a glove, completely eliminating the need for the modern bras that Liberty and Roulet had gotten for her, which was the way she liked it, support without the straps. She could move in it in ways one couldn't with a corset but there was something about it which, while not pressing upon her as a lie, was not what it seemed to be.

She had no time to ask about it when a pair of brogues were dropped in front of her and Cipín was pressed into her hand. She slipped into the shoes and Shannon was ushering her downstairs. Any mystery was cleared up when she set foot in the crowded office and Ian exclaimed, "Oh, good, yeh gave her th' armour. Thank yeh, Shannon."

The door closed behind An and she took note of who else was in the room. Skye stood closer to the door, leaning against the wall by the desk. The blue wolf known as Kyle was on the couch with Roulet, though he was looking much more human than he had when she had last seen him. The person An did not know was sitting in the chair in front of the desk. He was a very nondescript individual, average height, average features, average colouration.

He could have been anybody, everybody. Around his neck was a pendant of a naked woman kneeling before a framed mirror. The figure held a piece of real mirror, and in it An could see the woman's reflection which revealed her to be skeletal. It was a very macabre piece.

The man stood when she turned to face him, offering her his chair. She thanked him politely, even as she regarded him, but did not move to sit just yet.

Ian watched the two regard each other, each trying to figure who the other was and why they were here. Finally he intervened. "An, this is Gem Rayburn. Gem... Miss O'Keefe here is yer spotter."

In that one sentence several things became apparent on the man's face at once. He had registered her connections. And then the fact that she was blind when Cipín swept out to tap the leg of the chair and her hand reached out to find it. Aislynn waited until she was seated before she hopped from the desk to her lap and curled up, happy to be petted.

Gem turned back to Ian, a little confused. "A blind spotter?"

"I am not entirely blind, sir," she said primly, looking at Ian... or seemed to be. "Not where it counts."

"She th' one whit's gonna tell ya if whit we see is whit's ta'be seen," Skye said, and An heard pride in his voice warring with his concern.

Gem thought this over, then nodded. "Very well. We may need more people, to be able to protect her."

"That's whit ah'm fahr," Skye grunted. A tiny throat cleared. "An' th' dragon."

Gem looked down at Aislynn. "I beg your pardon, Miss Aislynn," he said, clearly having been introduced before An had arrived. "But, you are such a tiny dragon. Your skills as a scout might serve us better."

She rolled her eyes, then her head to look up at him. "Do not discount me just because I am little, doppelgänger. Smaller things than I have wiped out nations."

He did not appear convinced but decided not to pursue the matter. He turned back to Ian. "Well, if this is all of us, we should be going then."

Ian sat up, folded his hands on the top of the desk. "This is yer mission: I need yeh ta go ta th' edges o' th' Dark City. Find out, if yeh can, if there is a connection between Spetznakov an' th' Pyramid. An, yer there ta alert them ta lies and illusions. Yeh feel somethin' or see somethin', let 'em know." He looked to Skye. "I want ta know what you see versus what she does, so she tells yeh, take note yerself."

"Aye, Chief."

"This is not an engagement," Ian warned. "Yer t' scout an' get out."

Skye nodded. "Ah get m'self killt afore th' weddin' an' Liberty'll murder me twoice."

An chuckled at that, rose. She was nervous, but ready. Ian stood, pulling out a ring of skeleton keys of various sizes and gestured for Skye to open the door.

She followed him out to the atrium, everyone filing out after them. At the door below the staircase, Ian pulled out a key and opened the door. An could see through it to the warehouse where they had been running triage the night Reggie, Ian's original heir, was killed.

Ian stepped aside. "Yeh should be able ta find a suitable gate relatively close. I don't need ta tell yeh ta be careful."

"Nae, sair," Skye said and stepped through.

Roulet stepped up, took An's arm and led her in. One by one, they gathered in the warehouse. Ian stood in the doorway. "I cannae leave th' door open, but when yeh need it, call." He grinned, "Though if An were ta ask it real nice it might open itself."

She blushed. "I don't know about all that, now."

Before anything else could be said or done he closed the door. She turned, not really certain who was leading this mission. Gem was halfway across the warehouse, opened a pedestrian's door while holding something small in his hand. An guessed it was a phone. Hers insisted that it could tell her where she was at any given time and guide her to anywhere else, but she preferred to rely on Cipín for that.

Finally Gem waved them over. "OK. I know where I am and I know a good door. It's not too far if you don't mind a little walk. It's a pleasant afternoon."

Skye let him lead the way, occasionally looking back to keep track of the rest of the party.

He led them about a mile down the street through a run-down neighbourhood to a park. An could smell a large amount of brackish water nearby, and a fishing dock. There were birds everywhere and An thought she heard crows, or a raven. She searched the trees, half hoping, but saw nothing. Saddened just a little, she leaned on Roulet for comfort as well as guidance.

After several minute's walk, they came to the base of a bridge. she was more than a little startled to be able to see the underside of it, but not the top. Then she saw the troll sleeping with his back to the wall. It made sense now. Bridges were 'tween places: neither land nor water, neither one shore or the other, neither inside nor outside... they made for powerful gateways. It suddenly dawned on An why Ian's doors were under the stairs. It was a symbolic 'tween itself.

"Hey, Matthew!" Gem called cheerfully.

The troll started awake, stood with surprising speed and began to swell in size until he realized what was standing in front of him. He shrank again, scratched his head. "Oh, hi, Gem. Hello, Skye, Roulet. Miss An," he added, tipping an non-existent hat. He squinted at Kyle. "Who're you?"

Roulet rescued him. "This is Kyle. The wolf Baba found under her house."

"Oh. I remember. Hi. Why are you guys here?"

"We're goin' intae th' City," Skye told him.

"Through *this* door?" Matthew grunted, jerking his thumb at the wall behind him. "Why would you want to do that?"

"Ian needs some scoutin' done."

Matthew scratched his head, sighed. "But this door?"

Skye looked back at Gem, arching an eyebrow in question. Gem consulted something in his hand. "Yes. This is the door we need."

Skye nodded to Matthew. "If ya donnae mind, Matt?" he gestured to the wall.

Matthew began to get bigger, seemed to take substance from the cinder-block and concrete of the underbridge until he was almost scraping his head on the arching ceiling. He bent and slipped his fingers between the stones where the wall and the pavement met, then lifted it as easily as hefting a garage door.

An was hit by the wave of heat and asphalt and the general city nastiness she had smelled that night at Courtz. She could see through the bridge wall now, into a similar area of town, though far more run-down. No sun shone on the other side of that stone, though that did nothing to alleviate the heat. An was already beginning to sweat. Aislynn buried herself in An's hair.

The moment they stepped through, the gate closed behind them. The moment the gate closed, An doubled over. The pain was intense, not quite as intense as burning, but still crushing. She felt the pressure on her whole body, against her heart, keeping her from getting enough breath to even scream.

Aislynn panicked. Roulet grabbed for her, tried to get her up. Other hands reached for her, but Skye barked out orders to back off and guard. He, Gem and Kyle formed a circle around her, taking watch posts in the middle of the street as Roulet tried to help.

An felt the tingling all over of electricity as Roulet tried to heal her of whatever was hurting her. It did nothing but prickle. A voice echoed in the back of her mind, a deep chuckling that made her hair stand on end.

How lovely. Visitors. What, you thought you could get in and I not know? You want the truth? Look around you. There is. No. Truth. Here.

The voice began laughing as she managed to draw in enough breath to throw her head back and scream, "LIES!"

The others heard the laughter. Gem tightened his grip on the gun in his hand. "Oh, this isn't good."

"Whar th' divil ahr we, Gem?" Skye growled, his claymore in his hand and flaming. "This dinnae look like th' manky suburbs tae me!"

"It's not," he confessed. He turned, trying to orient himself.

"An?" Skye called. "Whit th' divil?"

She managed a dry laugh, as she began shutting herself down magically. She had not known it was possible. But thinking how desperately she needed to not see the truth in a place built on lies with her fist locked in a death-grip on Cipín, the shillelagh promptly told her how. "The devil is in the details, Skye. He *is* the devil."

Flatterer.

They all heard that.

"Oh, this is not good," Gem whimpered, fidgeting. "Skye, we really should get moving."

An climbed to her feet, turned to face Roulet. The gypsy woman gasped, her mouth falling open as she met An's eyes. Her sockets were deep, empty voids through which she could occasionally see a wisp of smoke. What was worse, there was a solidness to that empty. An could barely see through them. It was as if she truly had cataracts.

Skye began to notice people stopping to watch, gathering in corners and doorways. "Then pick a direction, pal."

Gem looked around, saw a convenience store nearby and headed them that way.

Skye brought up the rear, keeping them covered from the cluster of individuals half a block up that were wearing gang colours of some kind and watching them with too much interest.

As they opened the door, the bell over it rang cheerfully and the gentleman behind the counter called out in an equally cheerful tone. "Good evening, how will you be robbing me tonight?"

Skye turned at the sound of his voice, pausing in the act of grabbing a pipe that was just lying conveniently by the door to brace it closed. The man behind the counter looked and sounded like a caricature of the foreign quickie-mart attendant. He could have been Indian or Middle-Eastern, though his cadence leaned more to the former.

"Sorry. Not tonight, Habib," Gem sighed. "I need information."

Habib seemed confused, more taken aback by the news that he *wasn't* being robbed than he should have been facing down armed robbers. "Um... OK? What... what...." He searched for what he wanted to say, then leaned forward to whisper, "What is it I am wanting to ask you if you are *not* robbing me?"

"'How can I help you?'" Kyle supplied.

The man beamed. "Oh yes! How is it I am helping you?"

"Information, Habib," Gem said. "And quick. Where are we? Where in the City are we?" he clarified.

The man frowned. "Downtown... well, just South. The Battery. Look down the road. You can see the bloody pyramid from here," he pointed.

Skye looked out the front window, saw a giant Aztec styled ziggarat rising even higher than the skyscrapers. This did not bode well at all. There was a sinking feeling in his gut.

"This is not the way," Habib complained. "You are not even supposed to be here. You are Uptown, clearly. Or Lab... not Battery. You are not even..."

Something clicked in An's head. She tightened her jaw and slid her grip down on the shillelagh. Without even looking at what was to her right, she swung Cipín out and shattered the glass of the refrigeration case beside her. The sudden cool felt delicious.

Habib held his hands out in her direction, emphatically pointing her out to Gem. "See! The lady knows how to treat the Habib! She understands the rules!" His tone immediately shifted to his initial, amiable attitude, completely at odds with his words. "Now, please do not hurt me. Just take the money and go."

An stepped forward, flipped the shillelagh around so that the iron end was aimed outward like a fencing sabre. She pointed it at his chest, kept moving forward until she came up against the counter and his back was against the cigarette case. "You know things. You will talk," she snapped. Her accent shifting to a clipped British which brooked no disobedience. Even Gem took a step back, eyes wide. "Hellhound. There was a woman he kidnapped, brought here. Who and why?"

Skye thought the man's eyes were going to pop out of his head. He chuckled with pride, continued watching the street, but keeping an eye on the cracked anti-theft mirror in the corner above him.

The man's hands were as high as they could go as he gulped, staring at the iron tip less than an inch from his purple, Hawaiian print shirt. "Hellhound is not a kidnapper. He is in collection and extortion. The girl was payment. Her father traded her for power. Standard contract," he shrugged.

"Where is she now?" Kyle asked.

"At the pyramid. In His bed. Where all the new ones are going until He decides what they should be. ...The pretty ones, anyway."

Kyle punched a gumball machine beside him, shattering the glass and sending the candy cascading across the floor.

"Get it oot yar fool heid, Kyle," Skye snapped. "We're not goin' after her. In fact, we're leavin' nao." Skye moved away from the door and approached the counter. "Ah ken ya have a back door."

Habib just pointed, yelped as the movement brought the fabric of his shirt against the end of the shillelagh and it began to smoulder. He sucked in his gut.

Skye followed his finger, stepped through the curtain into a tiny and very dirty back room with just a safe and a well-used chair. There were rolls of duct tape, both used and new scattered on the floor. There was the occasional splatter of blood and brain matter, and the requisite exit. As he stepped back into the main of the store, gangers had gathered at the front, trying the door.

"Look, lady. Either be putting down the weapon or be putting me out of my misery. Because I am thinking you kill me with that and I get to stay dead, escape this hell. Not even become walking dead. ...On second thought, kill me, please."

"Kyle! Leave tha' damned thing alone! Oot th' back door, th' lot o' ya!"

He left off trying to right the candy machine and followed Gem into the back. An remained where she was, eyes locked on the terrified clerk. Aislynn was trying to get her to move, but she was not listening.

"An!" Skye barked, "Leave th' man his loife an' get a move on! We're gettin' oot o' this hell."

Roulet gave her elbow a light jolt and An turned to look at her, snapping out of whatever it was she had slipped into. She lowered the weapon and the clerk began to breath again. "You can't get out!" he said. "You are Downtown, sahib. Too far in to be getting out now!"

"An' tha' be whar yer wrong." He reached over and took An's arm, pulling her in front of him to cover her from the shotgun now aimed at the glass door. He guided her into the back just as it fired and Habib's protest was cut off, along with half his torso.

Roulet shifted to lightning and zipped to the front window, waited until the hand reached in the broken glass to remove the obstruction and touched the metal. She grabbed the pipe and held on, keeping him locked, muscles contracted and unable to let go, until his friends tried to pull him off and got shocked themselves for their trouble. Satisfied, she zipped out the back door just before it closed behind her friends.

In the alley behind the store, Gem and Kyle had already dispatched three zombies and Skye had Gem leading them out of there. There wasn't much light in the alley, but they were able to thread their way through a series of them until they came out on another block several streets down, or so they thought. "This city is huge!" Kyle exclaimed. "How is it you happened to know that one clerk?"

Gem furtively poked his head out of the alley, checking the street. There were only a few streetwalkers out here, giving them catcalls and comments worthy of New York construction workers. "I don't. They're all Habib. That's all they're there for, to be robbed."

"Hell of a life," Roulet quipped.

"It's not life. It's purgatory," An said flatly.

Astute, came the dark voice again. **Wrong, but astute. I might have to keep you. ...Separate you from that stick first.**

An's grip on Cipín got tighter.

They turned down another street and Gem swore. Skye saw what he was looking at and let loose a single, very long, vehement word. "Cuntybuggeryfucktoleybumshite!"

Just down the road was the pyramid, looming larger than ever.

An stopped. "That's th' end o' this," she snapped. She asked Cipín to get her home. The shillelagh gave her the sense of it being about time. An pointed off to the left and started walking. "This way."

"HEY!" Gem cried, panicking.

"Folla her!" Skye ordered, giving him a shove in her direction. "Keep her covered!"

Roulet zipped in front of her and just in time. The alley An had walked into had a pack of stray dogs rooting through the trash. The moment they saw her, they shifted into mangy looking wolfmen and attempted to jump her. Roulet zapped the first one and he fell into a puddle in whimpering heap. An stepped up and swung with no reservation at the second, knocking him back into Kyle who had shifted into wolf form, and then stabbed the second. Gem's bullet missed its target because An had impaled him, but ricocheted off a dumpster to nick a fourth who had been hiding to ambush them.

As An stalked past the now cowering fourth wolfman, Kyle tried to get ahead of her. "Miss O'Keefe, let me..."

"Dinnae get in 'er way, laddie," Skye warned "Yon pain in th' arse has her Irish up. Ya'll jest get trammelled ya get in 'er way."

Confused, he dropped back, but remained close enough to do something if something needed doing.

Several streets later, An changed direction, listening when the shillelagh said that way was no longer safe. They were beginning to pick up an entourage. Every once in a while, something that was watching them, or following, would make an attempt, only to be mown down fairly quickly. An rounded a corner and a vampire, sparkling in the lamplight, stepped out, trying to intimidate or seduce her, she wasn't sure which. She pointed the shillelagh at his chest and he ran.

"Yar reputation precedes ya, yar majesty," Skye taunted. He knew it would make her angry. He also knew he needed her to stay angry, at least for a little while longer. It didn't look like they were getting anywhere, doubling back and going in circles as it seemed they were, but he could tell there was progress. Every time he looked back at the pyramid, it was a little farther away.

Things began attacking more frequently now and in greater numbers. Everyone was busy dispatching undead. There were other types of vampires, ones which did not sparkle, held a great deal more threat and menace, but they shied back from the shillelagh. There was even a Jiangshi, hopping about in its tattered shroud, so hungry, oh so hungry, seeking meat.

It was mostly zombies swarming them, though someone tried sniping Roulet from a building. She was pure lightning at that point, so the bullet skipped across the pavement and merely nicked An's ankle. She ignored it and kept going. They waded down another street, sidestepping a car bomb, when the zombies suddenly scattered.

"That is never good," Gem said.

"What do you mean?" Kyle exclaimed. "It's great. We've scared them off!"

"Not us," Roulet said, looking up and over her shoulder as a wyvern sailed into the steel canyon and landed on Skye. Gem was knocked flying by a wing-stroke. Roulet latched onto it, trying to stun it or electrocute it or something but it seemed to have little effect. An parried the stinger tail with Cipín as it tried to stab her while its toothy maw fenced with Skye's claymore.

With a warning shriek that sounded like it came from a creature twelve times her size, Aislynn launched from An's shoulder, actually tearing her blouse and raking her with her back claws. She flew at the wyvern, all claws extended, and breathed a cone of dagger-like icicles at it. The thing screamed, rolling off of Skye to defend itself. It tried to fly off to escape, but one wing was now trapped in a block of ice. Aislynn continued to breathe ice at it, pinning it to the asphalt which was melting the ice just a little slower than Aislynn could freeze it. Skye got to his feet as Kyle was hacking at the tail, and brought his flaming claymore down upon its neck, severing it.

An started to step forward, Cipín raised to shatter the frozen wing when Cipín informed her that they needed to go two streets down and to the left immediately. She pulled back. "Go, now!" she shouted, and began to move in the direction she had been told. The others followed quickly. Aislynn flew along beside her, looking skyward frequently, her breath trailing visibly from her nostrils in the hot, muggy air.

As An made the required left turn, they came upon what looked like a gang war. They dodged down the pavement, trying to keep derelict cars between them and the gunfight. An followed Cipín's guidance, making a sharp turn down an alley when she was told. This alley, unlike the others, was a dead end.

Roulet zapped to the end of it, checking it out, reappeared next to An. "No way out. You sure?"

"Gem," An said. "You have to open it."

He hustled to the front, going to the wall and began looking for the door.

Everyone was safe in the alley, watched a group of gangbangers run past, completely ignoring the back street. As natives, they would know it led nowhere. Bullets chipped the brick on the wall above their heads as members of the rival gang fired wildly.

Finally, Gem got the door open. Roulet zipped through, followed by Aislynn and An. Kyle was at the end of the alley, ready just in case someone tried to come in and stop them. Skye yelled at him to get through the door.

Just then, someone ran past the alley mouth and was shot down. They dropped something that landed with a with high pitched 'tink'. It rolled into the shadows near Kyle's feet as he began to turn. Not thinking about what he was doing at all, he grabbed the neck of the red glass bottle, ran down the alley and jumped through the doorway.

Skye grabbed Gem and hurled them both through the door as a hail of bullets ripped through the air above their heads. It slammed shut behind him.

Skye rolled to his feet, ready for any trouble, but a cop car zipped past, followed by a second. Gem started laughing, rolled onto his back, stared up at the sliver of a moon he could see through the clouds. Kyle was hunched over his prize, making sure he hadn't broken it.

An was leaning against a wall, panic on her face. Aislynn was dangling from her vest, tail around her neck, front claws holding An's jaw, looking into her eyes. There was still nothing in there but wisps, though the void was no longer solid. There was just nothing there. Roulet got herself under control, moved to check An.

"Are you all right?"

"Nothing," she choked.

"Nothing what?"

"I see... nothing."

Roulet looked over at Skye.

"*Turn it back on,*" Aislynn hissed.

"I'm tryin', luv," An responded tightly. "'Tis on... as far as I can tell. Tell me a lie."

"I think I'm in my backyard. I'm going to start the barbecue," Gem said from the ground, then rolled to his feet.

An felt the pressure, the magic confirming that he was lying even if his words did make it obvious. "No. It's on. The Sight..." She didn't finish.

There was a roar of rage and Skye was charging Gem, fist cocked. Gem backed up swiftly, hitting the wall full force, winding himself. The fist landed on the brick close enough to his ear that he was cut by a flying chip of masonry.

Skye stood there, his fist planted centimetres deep in the old brick, his eyes blazing and his teeth bare inches from the man's face. "Whit th' hell wis thon, ya manky glaikit knobdobber?!" he roared. "Droppin' ahr jauries smack inna Down-bloody-Town!? He tole ya th' mawkit bordermarch! Th' suburbs! Out skirts!"

"I...." Gem looked panicked, trying to face down the raging Highlander, decipher what he'd yelled and still figure out what had gone wrong. "It was a door I knew. I figured a strong door would give us a better chance of getting in. I was sure it'd be the same kind of neighbourhood!"

Kyle had gone to the entrance of the alley, drawn by a car driving by sharing its music with the world at large. The music had been mariachi. "Um, guys... we're not in Florida."

"What makes you think that?" Roulet asked, torn between helping her friend and calming Skye down.

"The signs are in Spanish?"

"Could be Miami," she suggested, whipping out her phone, and using her GPS to locate where they were. "*Merde!*" she exclaimed. "We're in Cancun!"

"Mexico?" Skye exclaimed.

"I'm calling Ian," Roulet said, fumbling to find the right app.

Skye pushed himself off the wall, taking a step back before he hurt the man. "Ah'll dae it. Ya see tae An." He pulled out his own phone and stepped away to make the call.

Roulet cupped An's face. "You'll be all right."

An huffed, "Ye don't really believe that. ...Any more than I do." She reached up, ran her hands through her hair, leaving Cipín resting against her hip. She found the rose and drew it out, cupping its sharp, comforting petals in her hand.

"It may just take some time for that to rebound," she suggested. "Do we even know what happened to them?"

"What happened when we got in?" Gem asked. "You folded up like a marionette with cut strings."

An turned her empty eyes towards him. They had been a little disturbing before. They were unnerving now. "I know I'm in th' presence of lies by pressure, Mr. Rayburn. It pushes. Dangerous lies or lies that affect things I care deeply about affect m' heart. Th' outskirts ...I'd have been achy but fine. A lie here, a lie there, ...I deal with it every night I go t' Courtz, every night I deal with large numbers o' people: th' little white lies, th' shades of truth, th' lies meant t' save face and feelin's. Ye took me inta th' heart o' Lie Central. I was crushed."

"I thought he said you could see lies, not feel them."

She laughed, a hard sound. "I see magic. What I see over There is not what you see. Some things are more vivid t' me, brighter th' stronger they are. I don' see th' illusions. Which makes little sense t' me," she snapped, thinking about it. "If I see only th' magic I should see th' illusion but not what it hides...."

"Maybe it ties in with the lie thing?" Kyle suggested.

"Mebbe. Then again, I don't see what a magic does, just that it's there. I have t' touch it an' ask fer that."

Gem thought about it. "So, you were blinded the moment you came through the door?"

She shook her head. "No. The moment the gate closed. Everything was a dark and darker haze."

"But..." he frowned. "You were running, making turns... reacting to... Hell, *I* stumbled once or twice and I could see!"

"Cipín. I've learned t' just do what she tells me. T'were a matter o' faith."

"So, all the doubling back and changing direction..."

"Were th' exact path we had t' take to get out o' th' Battery. Once out o' th' Battery Proper she led us t' th' nearest gate."

Skye sounded a little calmer as he closed the phone and came over. "Well, ah need ya tae ask her ag'in. Th' Chief seid tae ask her tae guide ya tae th' Rest. They're op'nin' a door here somewhere. He seid she'll foind it."

"I need a moment first, though."

He nodded.

"Did anyone else hear the voice?" Kyle asked.

An pulled her flask from her bag and started to take a sip, stopped, sniffed it. There was something oily about it. She held it blindly out. "Dump it."

Roulet took it, reluctant to obey. She took a sniff and then was more than happy to pour it out. "Yes, we heard Him, Kyle," she answered.

Skye looked around. From the look on everyone's face they had, too.

"He said th' same thing to all of us, I expect," An said. "Relatively."

"I doubt it," Kyle muttered.

"What'd he say to you?" Roulet asked.

"That I wasn't ready for him yet. He had to work on my family first."

"Ouch," Gem said. "He told me the Doc missed my expertise."

Roulet shrugged. "Said I had the seeds, but wasn't as ripe as my sister. I was too slippery." She looked to An, called her name softly.

"He said... I was astute. And that he might have to find a way to keep me, after he separated me from Cipín."

"Kipeen?" Kyle asked.

She held up her shillelagh in answer. She turned her face up to her brother, hoping to see some glimmer of his face bleeding through the darkness. "Skye?" she asked, her voice husky.

He didn't answer at first. But he could not stare into those black voids and hold out on her. "He were gonna tae take ya, alla ya. Ah tole him he couldna. Some o' ya were O'Keefe an' aff-limits. He seid..." he stopped, more than a little disturbed. An's hand on his arm brought him around. "He seid 'Enterin' here is consent, but... Ah can't take ya. Yer a'ready claimed. But ya'll make a guid bargainin' chip'."

"You're an O'Keefe," Roulet shrugged. "Of course he said..."

"Nae," he snapped, whipping his head around to look at her. He made himself calm down before saying anything more. "Nae. Thon were no whit he meant. Ah know thon shor as ah breathe. Whit he actually meant... ah kin only guess. Th' Northerner mebbe."

"Why?" An asked softly.

"Th' duel?" he suggested. "Ah doan know. An, ya ready tae walk? Ah'd like a pint somewhere 'tis safe tae drink th' bleedin' water."

An slipped her arm around his, clinging to him, once more lost in the dark and liking the feeling less than she had when she had first lost her eyes to chimera venom. She rubbed her cheek against Aislynn, taking comfort in her trilling purr. Her left hand held Cipín to her chest, and her right cradled the singed and wilted petals of the ice rose.

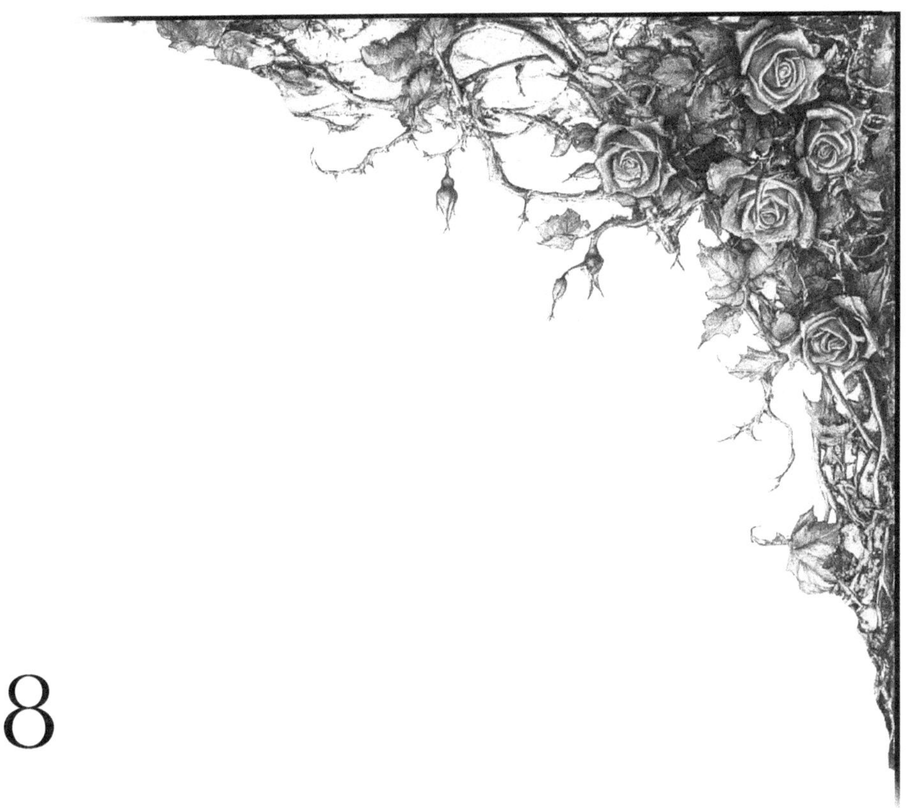

8

It was nearly dawn when Roulet escorted An home after a thorough debriefing with Ian. Skye and Gem had remained behind and An did not envy the man at all. Even blind she could tell her brother was in high temper. Ian had not been pleased when he learned where they had gone, and the information An had gotten from the Habib had only served to make him angrier. Thankfully the yelling did not start until they were almost out of the East Wing, though they could still hear it in the atrium.

Ian had looked An over, understood nothing. Liberty had checked her thoroughly, could not heal what was not a wound; though she had put the rose back in An's hair and healed the thin cuts that webbed her hand. Ian had sent for the witch. Baba had poked and prodded, even stuck a bony finger into the empty sockets, tickled what little mist lingered in the back, and then pronounced there was little to be done but wait, but she would 'look into the matter meanwhile'. There had been nothing left to do but go home and Roulet was already going that way.

They said nothing the entire walk, both too wrung out for conversation. They got to the bottom of the garden gate and An could hear the soft sound of harp strings. As Roulet opened the gate for her, she could hear the shin-high roses scrabbling to make a grab for them, but unable to reach. Aislynn leapt immediately from her shoulder and flew towards the cottage, leaving Roulet to lead An under the overhanging limbs of her orchard and over the little bridge that crossed her stream. The scent of crushed thyme rose pleasantly in the warm night air and eased some of the ache in An's head brought on by the stink of asphalt and tire rubber. She looked around, saw nothing but dark and wisps of smoke.

The music ended abruptly. Roulet said nothing but led her about halfway to the herb patch and stopped. She held An's hand out and set it in someone else's. She instantly knew it was Jonny's by the chill. Roulet kissed her cheek. "I'll leave you two alone. My sister's worried sick."

An nodded helplessly, so confused about so many things that she couldn't keep a stray thought in her head. Why was Jonny here? How had he known? Why didn't he seem to understand what was going on if he had known to be here? What was she going to do now? Suddenly she was sinking in his arms and weeping without really knowing the reason.

He eased them down onto the lawn, holding her in what was left of the moonlight; Let her cry herself out. He didn't ask what was wrong. He had seen her eyes, ...and the rose. It was singed and wilted, the blood blackened and the edges shrivelled. What few leaves it had possessed had crumbled away.

The sky was starting to grey when she took a final, deep breath and tilted her head to look up at him, trying desperately for a glimpse in the dark. She felt a soft cloth wiping her face and almost started crying again, but this time she maintained her composure. She heard Aislynn on the kitchen door, moved to stand and Jonny helped her up. Still, he asked her nothing.

She was a little startled when she entered the house. She couldn't use Cipín as she was meant to be, not wanting to touch the floor with the iron. Aislynn took her and flew the shillelagh to her stand. An put her hand out in front of her, knowing there should be something in her way between the kitchen and the fire she could feel across the room. She heard a chair scrape lightly across the hard, polished wooden floor, and then the little table by her living room chair. She felt no one else in the house and Jonny was next to her. From the grip he had on her arm, she understood he was a little surprised himself.

Then she was sinking into her wing-backed chair in front of a blazing fire and Jonny was at her feet slipping off her brogues. She heard him sink into another chair, felt as well as heard the idle plucking of harp strings as he waited her out. An just sat there for a while, drinking in the dry warmth of the fire, so different from the sticky heat of the City. She heard a rooster from somewhere and reached up to where Aislynn was curled up on the back of her chair and stroked her between the wings.

"Will ye be a love an' go get Elizabeth up fer school? Have her tell her mother I had a family emergency or that ...I am having problems with my eyes and had to see someone about it. Neither are really lies. Just..."

Aislynn nuzzled her fingers in answer and flew to the door, opening it only just enough to get through.

An pressed her forehead against the high side of her chair, facing Jonny but not looking up at him. Her hair fell across her eyes, hiding her blackened sockets. "I... don't know where to begin," she whispered.

"Anywhere is fine," he said. A melody began to emerge from the strings, soft and soothing.

"How... did... Why'd ye come?" she asked, finally decided which question she wanted answered first.

He was silent for a few measures, then, "I am a bard, Ceobhránach. I know how t' find out things that happen here, what concern th' Rest."

"Then ye know what happened?" she asked, a little relieved she would not have to speak of it.

"No. I know ye went ...Beyond. Into Their places. And I know Ian sent ye, no more. I'd know what yer comfortable tellin'."

She nodded, it was only fair. She'd asked him painful questions herself and he had answered them. "I... We were only supposed t' go t' th' suburbs..." she began, telling him everything she remembered.

"It was horrible. That voice was cold and dark and..." she shivered. "I can't explain it. But there was a horrible pressure in my sockets, like I had something in them too big fer th' holes. And then there were that poor clerk. I... I would have used th' iron on him. I wasn't just doin' what was expected t' get what we needed, I... wanted t'... I was angry in a way I've never been before. It was a cold anger, not my usual temper. And when we were attacked later... I was efficient, vicious. Anger was all that drove me out of there. Could that have sommat t' do with why..." her fingers drifted to her eyes.

Jonny's voice was snowfall soft when he spoke. "Th' Master o' th' Dark City is different from all th' others. Only he among Them can lie. I've never been to that place m'self, so I could not tell ye much, but I have smelled it on those who have ascended from that hell, spoken to them. You are patient and kind. Ye were still patient, but yer anger overrode yer kindness, even though to have struck him down might have been a kindness. He is good at blindness... of all kinds."

"And th' gift th' King gave me? He kin just take that away? Or merely suppress it? Did he put something in to replace what he took? He said he might have to keep me. Did he do something? I'm an O'Keefe, he can't take me without consent, but did he do something to give him th' ammunition he'd need to make me give it?" She stood, began pacing in front of the fire, knowing she was ranting and not caring. Jonny watched the furniture move quietly out of her way. "There was something in my sockets for a while there, I know it. Did he replace my eyes with somethin' he kin use..."

She screamed in frustration. "Death would be preferable to this... not knowing! To harming those I love... I'm afraid I've even compromised you.... What has he done t' me?"

"He's made ye afraid. That's what he does," he said simply.

She stopped pacing, turned towards his voice. "And my eyes? Can he use them now? Use me?"

Jonny hesitated, sighed. He set aside the harp and stepped to her, setting his hands on her upper arms. "I don't know for sure, Ceobhránach, ...but I doubt it. What was done was superficial. Ye weren't there long."

She searched the darkness for the source of his voice. "Is there any way to be sure?" she pleaded. "It was so hot there... suffocating. I felt like parts of me were burnin' away on a peat fire."

He had no words of comfort to offer her, so he just gathered her in his arms and held her, a cool pillar against the hot, sweltering dark that still lingered in her mind. He began to sing softly, crooning some ancient lullaby to calm her. She slipped her arms inside his vest and just held on, fighting the sobs that wanted to return.

Aislynn returned quietly, closing the door softly. She looked at Jonny and An, heaved a tight sigh, then nodded her head towards the bedroom and flew in that direction.

He nodded and, without asking permission, lifted An up in his arms and carried her into the bedroom. The petty drake was pulling back the covers on the bed. He set her down on the backless chair at her dressing table, began to untangle the rose from the hastily twisted knot she had twined it in. He turned it over in his hand, frowned as he examined the damage before setting it on the dressing table and picking up the silver, boar bristle brush.

She just sat there, let him brush out her tangled locks and braid the dry strands. Even though she was not the one touching her hair, she could tell it had lost its lustre, was brittle.

An forced herself to shut down, to be lulled by the strokes of the brush and the feeling of his hands in her hair. There was an intimacy there that both thrilled and frightened her. In just a few weeks, Liberty would be marrying her brother, two lives joined.

Even Roulet had Sori, that white tiger she had rescued in town. That was something she would never have, never expected to once she lost her family and her home. Perhaps it was time to accept what she *could* have.

Almost too soon he was reaching past her to set the brush on the dressing table. He set his cool hands on her shoulders and whispered by her ear. "Soft though it might be, sleeping in yer armour isn't advisable."

"My armour?" she asked, not knowing what he was talking about. He turned her to face him, ran two fingers down the edge of the vest's suede neckline, slipping them in behind the latch and with a flick of his thumb unfastened the first one.

Aislynn jumped from the foot of the bed to her shoulder, hissing at him. He took a step back. She hung by her tail from An's neck and started to undo the rest of them until An realized what he had meant and began to unfasten the vest herself. "I... I'd forgotten he said it were armour. Forgot I was wearin' it, truth be told."

Jonny's voice was halfway to the door when she stood, turned towards the window as she slipped the vest from her shoulders. "Can ye make it t' bed on yer own?" he asked.

She stopped, thinking, wondering if she dared. She shook her head at first, telling herself no, then realized how he might take it and nodded quickly. "Aye. I can manage, thank ye." She reached out with her hand and found the brass knob of the bedpost, drew herself to it, felt the nightdress neatly laid out.

She heard his footsteps leave the room, the door close softly behind him. She all but tore the clothes from her body, still smelling the taint of the City on them. On impulse, she felt her way to the bathroom door, felt it open before she reached for it. The house tried to press images into her mind as it always had, but nothing visual translated. Instead, it guided her by sensation and sound. Inside the small chamber, An found a steaming shower running and stepped gratefully into it. Wet hair meant her pillow would be wet, but she didn't care right now. All she wanted was the smell of the City gone.

She remained in the water until she could no longer stand to breathe the steam. She took the towel Aislynn handed her and dried herself, pressed her braid dry the best she could and slipped into her night dress. As she stepped out of the bathroom into the bedroom, she heard the soft strains of a harp from the other room. She smiled as she felt for, found and climbed into the bed. The last thing she was really aware of was the citrusy-sweet smell of the vamprick roses outside the window and Aislynn's trilling as she curled up in the crook of her neck.

When An woke much later that afternoon, she was dazzled by the sunlight coming through the window. The light hurt. She rolled over, putting her arm over her eyes. She then sat up immediately, realizing that she had been able to see the light ...well, the white spread upon which it was reflecting. Aislynn tumbled end over end from An's shoulder where she'd been curled, and unrolled herself, stretching her wings against the covers and her neck and tail out until they popped. *"He's gone,"* she huffed, mistaking the reason for her reaction.

An reached over and picked the little dragon up, held her to her face. "What do ye see?" she exclaimed excitedly.

Aislynn frowned, a little startled at being grabbed. She stopped flapping her wings and snaked her head out, peering deep into one eye and then the next. *"Fog! Not much. But more than yesterday."*

An set her down, sighing in relief. "Well, I can certainly see more than last night."

"Maybe it was one of those 'until dawn' things?" Aislynn shrugged, began preening herself.

"Maybe." An got up, went to the dressing table and looked for herself. There wasn't much there, but she could see the wisps of the little Prince's gift beginning to return. She sank onto the chair, began to take down her braid. That was when she remembered who had put it up for her. She blushed, decided to just twist the braid up with the rose.

When she laid eyes on the rose, she gave a tiny squeak of horror. The flower had seen better days. It had not melted, as one would have expected, but looked like someone had made an attempt to dry it. The stem was a little shorter than it had begun and there were no leaves left. Even the razor edges were dulled.

Aislynn landed on the back of the mirror, debating on whether or not to tell An something, finally deciding that she could not stand to see her upset about it. *"It looks better than this mornin'. It looked burnt."*

An gathered the braid up at the nape of her neck and set the rose to it, asking it to twine itself. She had to help it a little, but it held. She was just pulling on a vest when she felt the knock at the closet door. It was Elizabeth. She picked up her watch, and was startled to notice what time it was. She told the house to let her in, rushed to finish getting dressed. She stepped out of the bedroom to meet the girl who looked her over critically.

"You look OK. Mostly. But what's wrong with your eyes?" she asked, effecting one of her teacher's own mannerisms.

An smiled. "Nothing that won't heal, I'm beginning to understand. I went somewhere I shouldn't have."

"So, the 'appointment' I told Mom you had this morning went well?" she asked pointedly.

She had to admire the girl's ingenuity. "You may tell her that, aye. As much as I abhor lyin'."

Elizabeth shrugged. "You gotta do what you gotta do."

An nodded, sighing. "Aye. Well, let's get ye to yer lessons."

They went next door and Elizabeth went straight to Sean. Skye, however, had decided that An would not be at practice herself today. He took her upstairs, offered her tea. She was surprised that he had gone to the trouble. It was a simple service, just a pot of a fragrant brew and a box of Walker's, but it was pleasant.

She let him pour her a cup of tea, taking a more sturdy mug for himself, and nibbled delicately on one of the biscuits before she confronted him. "All right then, formalities are out of th' way. Spit it out."

"Spit whit oot?"

"Whate'er's botherin' ye! Ye always want t' work my skills. And here ye've laid out tea, so it must be important or terrible news."

"Nae terrible…" he grunted, having run through the gamut of emotions from rage and indignation to resignation. "An' no news, neither. Ah jest… wanted tae know hoo ya were doin'?"

"Well, I can see th' dragon on my shoulder and th' sword on yer back this afternoon. That answer yer question?"

"Sort o'," he said, surly. "Yar eyes're still…"

"But getting better," she insisted softly. "It may take time."

"Ya sure?"

"Nothin' is ever sure."

He sighed. "Ah wanted tae tak ya home, but…"

"Did ye leave anythin' of Gem fer Ian to dress down?" she asked over the rim of her teacup.

"A wee," he grumbled. "He were as mad as ah were, but thinks th' strength o' th' gate we used got attention, an' th' Dark Man micht've shifted us farther in. Still don't know if thare be anythin' we kin dae fer th' lass. Ah hated leavin' 'er thare…"

"We could not have gotten her out," she said firmly, setting down her cup. "Don't even begin thinkin' we could've. It were too easy we got that information."

"Ya obeyed th' rules…" he began.

"It were more than that and ye know it, Skye. I lost control. But that doesn't change th' fact that he wanted us t' know. Wanted us t' try t' rescue her. We wouldna succeeded and would've ended up where he could manipulate us inta his power."

Skye knew she was right. It didn't change how powerless he felt and that made him angry.

"We can't let him win. Ian now knows what we're dealin' with. That's important. I'll be right as rain soon enough," she added, trying to convince herself that it was not a lie. "Now, I appreciate th' attempt. Yer learnin' diplomacy. But, there are a few things I'd like t' get done t'day and I've slept most of it away. Unless ye'd like t' go with me t' th' witch, I'd best be off."

"Why're ya…" he frowned.

"T' let her know my *sight's* back. And t' take some herbs I've harvested fer her."

Skye handed her the second, unopened sleeve of the cookies from inside the red box. "Here, give 'er these. 'Tisn't much but...."

"Thoughts count," she nodded, accepting them. She paused to kiss his cheek before she took her leave. "I'll be fine. Ye've trained me better than ye think."

Skye saw her to the door, watched her tap her way to her own gate and go in. He sighed, looked across her lawn to the house on the far side. Determined to beat this wistful feeling, he went back into the Mead Hall and pulled out several of the practice dummies and began hacking them to bits.

An woke up the next few nights panicked and in a sweat. The nightmares were intense and pushed just the right buttons to cause the maximum effect with the minimum of effort. There were no visuals at all. Every one began in darkness and ended with the bright light of the dawn streaming through her window. It was what she heard and felt in that darkness that frightened her. She would wake bruised and scraped as if she really had been running from the terrors in her sleep and fallen on real, broken pavement.

These were just nightmares, real nightmares, not like the dream trap she had been subjected to last year. But still, even though they lessened a little each night, even as her eyes slowly began to return to their normal, mist-filled voids and her rose unwilted, she knew she had to do something or she would be in no condition at all come the wedding.

The week before Bealtane, they went back to Moffett's to bring the finished lace and get the final fittings done. The bridesmaid's dresses were brought home and An's hung on the back of the wardrobe door, an emerald reminder. Liberty was understandably nervous, but An knew there was more there than pre-wedding jitters. She was worried about the Russians and what her father was up to. An did what she could to comfort her, but she knew it was only a temporary measure. Liberty had railed about how her father was shutting her out of things at the moment, and how much it pissed her off, for all it gave her genuine deniability. The fact that she was going to need plausible deniability at all made her even more anxious about what was planned.

The Friday before the wedding, An went to Courtz as usual. She had finally decided to talk to Jonny about the nightmares, before the effects became too obvious. It was not like the last time, where she was exhausted and losing herself. She was just run-down and sore. Liberty was no where to be seen and Roulet was in her little booth up and behind the stage, managing the music. An went straight to her usual table.

Thankfully, it was empty, though there was a good crowd tonight. A waitress appeared shortly at her elbow, rattling off the specials of the night. She ordered a plate of the salmon and her usual pot of tea, and a Morning Dew from Sil while she waited. The waitress bustled off.

An looked around the club. Serenity was at the bar, snuggled up to Detective Torres as he ate. Not far from him was Skye, watching the whole club from a seat at the end. William was on the stage, singing "Barbara Allen", of all things. It was bad enough the term 'sweet William' had already suggested itself around him, but that he had actually said that phrase himself made it worse. She would never be able to think of him in any other terms. Not far from him, at the edge of the dance floor, was Mak, looking surprisingly human.

When the waitress arrived, she set An's drink down in front of her, slid it against her hand so she would know where it was, and set a bottle in front of the seat to her left. "I didn't..." An began.

Then came Jonny's feather-soft voice, "Thank ye, Daphne."

An could hear the flutter of the poor thing's hands as she clutched the tray to her, and breathed, "Any time, Jonny."

She sipped her whiskey until the girl left. "Evenin', a chroí," she said softly.

There was a slight twitch of his lips at that, "Evenin'." He looked her over as William finished on stage, reached over to brush a lock of hair behind her ear. "Ye look worn, Ceobhránach," he said softly.

"I am. Was wantin' t' discuss it with ye, an' ye had th' time."

"I've a bit. T'night at least. Stag party's t'morra," he said picking up his beer.

"I know," she nodded. "Th' hen party's then, too. I'd not wanted t' wait this long t' ask but... findin' ye's no easy thing."

He lifted his fingers from the bottle in a gesture of 'ah well', lifted his cigarette from the ashtray and moved it away from An's side of the table. "What were ye needin'?" he asked casually, moving his bottle as Daphne came back with the tea service and An's supper. He called the waitress closer to him, slipped her something papery and quietly ordered a light supper of his own.

She waited until Daphne had gone before she spoke. "I'm havin' nightmares again. Not th' same ones. It's not like from th' ring. But they're not goin' away fast enough, and if I don't get some decent sleep soon, I'll be back where I were last year and vulnerable t' all sorts o' mischief."

"We can't have that," he replied with a slight smile, taking another pull from his beer.

She blushed a little, getting the feeling there was a secondary meaning from the way he'd said it. She fixed herself a cup of tea, offered Jonny one, which he turned down. Aislynn poured herself some in the espresso cup she had been provided with, and helped herself to a few choice morsels from An's plate.

Jonny's sandwich arrived at the same time as Mak, though from a different direction. Mak pulled out a chair and sat down without permission or preamble. He gave a brief nod to An, but his eyes were on Jonny. He lit up a cigarette and blew out a long column of smoke. "So what's this about?" he asked just as An was thinking how rude he was.

She noticed he wasn't quite as cowed as he had been lately. Aislynn resisted the urge to hiss at him and shifted herself over so that she was between him and An, chewing savagely on a chunk of fish.

Jonny took another pull from his bottle of Nut Brown before he answered, watching the once-makar. "Yer a hard man ta find."

"Yeah, well, I've been avoiding you," he admitted. "What's this about?" he added, tossing down something that sounded like waded paper.

"'Tis about who ye are, lad. Yer name fer starters."

This caught Mak's attention. He cocked his head in a very crow-like manner, and even though his nose was aimed more at An, she knew he was seeing Jonny more. "How would you know?"

Jonny tore a bite from his sandwich, ate and swallowed before he answered. "Yer name was Caleb. And I can't say as ye were much of a nice boy at th' time."

An stared, her food forgotten on her fork, suspended halfway to her plate. Aislynn looked from her to Jonny to Mak and then back at the fork. Her neck snaked out and she took the bite for herself.

Mak shuddered, the truth settling over him like a hot blanket on a cold night. "Caleb," he echoed. "I remember... nothing. But it ...feels like it fits."

"A'course it fits. 'Tis yer's. And so're th' memories I got with it," Jonny growled.

"When..." An asked.

"When I touched him that night at th' pub," he explained, not taking his eyes from Mak. "It's never happened before. All th' memories I have She gave me when She took me. I've never gotten new ones." He turned back to Mak, "An' yer's... yer's are particularly nasty. We talk to th' delver, ye kin have 'em back."

"Um..." Mak... Caleb, began. "I'll have to think about that."

An stared at him now. "Why would ye not want yer memories?"

"Well, like he said, they're not nice. And... I'm not sure I want someone called a 'delver' to go poking in my noggin."

It was an excuse, An could tell. But it was also, mildly, the truth.

"Gem is a memory delver. He collects, sorts, catalogues memories. He's assured me 'tis an easy process, once we've sussed out which are yers. 'Tis more dangerous for me than ye. Ye'll be wantin' th' whole package." Jonny went back to his supper.

Caleb was clearly thinking it over. "Maybe. I'll... have to ... think about it."

"Don't take too long," Jonny said, setting his beer down more forcefully than he perhaps had intended. "Ye'll want them before they get muddled back in wit' th' rest."

Caleb nodded, getting up and leaving the table.

An turned to Jonny. "Been almost a month, it has. Why'd ye take so long tellin' him?"

"Like he said, he's been avoidin' me. Like as he felt some guilt fer that night. It happened when we shook hands. 'Tis what triggered th' fit. It was just one more thing on top of th' others... I couldn't handle it. Truthfully, I still can't. It's eatin' at me inside. Increasin' my need." He picked up his sandwich, stared at it and dropped it back on his plate. "I'm tryin' less more often, but I don't think it's workin'," he added softly.

She set her hand on his arm, felt the slightly distended vein. She ran her fingers along the inside and found she could almost read it like Braille. There were more there than last time. She sighed, finished her dinner.

"Aye," he breathed, picking up his sandwich again. "We'll try workin' on it tonight if ye like. This time ye get t' sleep in yer own bed," he smiled wryly, returning to their original conversation with ease.

"We won't need th' wardin'...?"

He shook his head, washing down the bite with a healthy swig of beer. "I don't anticipate a fight." For some reason what he said amused him as she watched the tops of his cheeks turn a little darker. Whatever mirth he had enjoyed was shattered by the sudden appearance of Serephina at the table.

She sat down next to Jonny without even a nod to An or a by-your-leave. "It's not too late to change your mind," she said. "I managed to get..."

He cut her off. "Aye, it is." He did not even look at her, but continued to eat his food as if its nutrition was the most important thought on his mind, though An knew just moments ago he had been forcing himself to eat.

The woman just glared at him. She waited until he was done and had no more excuses. "You'll not even come as my guest?"

He eyed her over his now empty beer bottle, decided he was ready for tea and poured himself a cup. He did not offer Serephina any. "Will be kinda hard seein' as I'm performin' across town at more meanin'ful nuptials."

"Then come to the reception," she cajoled. "Surely you're not playing that, too?"

"Aye. I am. That's th' Bealtaine ritual, Serephina. Ye know that."

"Aye, I do," she snapped, then became more irritated because she had fallen into his speech patterns. She tried a different tactic, smiled, running her fingers along his arm. "I remember a few Bealtaine eves spent in the fields making wild, passionate love under the open sky. ...Ancient fertility rites."

"Aye, well, ye'll be performin' them with yer new husband this year, won't ye," he said, taking a sip of his tea. He arched an eyebrow at the appearance of An's flask at his elbow. With silent thanks he opened it, tipping some of the contents into his cup.

This seemed to anger her even more. "It's not the same, and you know it." She closed her eyes, drank down about half the contents of the tall glass in her hand, got herself back under control. "I'll be back in the country on the fourteenth. He has a business conference the fifteenth through the twentieth." She reached into her clutch and pulled out a small card, pressing it into his hand with a seductive smile. "I will be all alone in that big... empty... house," she said, applying all her wiles. She leaned forward, flashing her cleavage at him. The way her arms rested pushed them more outward, straining the elasticity of her top.

An saw the magic as she began trying to work it. It clung to her hand where she touched Jonny, wafted off her skin like heat waves off a summer road. His eyes were starting to glaze, and she could feel the tension in his leg beside hers under the table. She had to do something. She reached blindly for the teapot, her hand flailing with a great deal less than her usual grace. She felt the cold touch of the empty beer bottle and nudged it, knocking it in Serephina's direction.

As it fell, Jonny's free hand caught it deftly and swiftly before any damage could be done. Aislynn was quicker though, realizing that An would never have been so clumsy and in that instant also reacted to help, deliberately stepping on An's saucer, flipping her teacup so that it spilled, the hot liquid cascading towards Serephina.

She jerked back as the tea splashed her half-bare chest and the magic was ruined. She glared at An and the monkey, acknowledging their existence for the first time. "Interfering little..." she hissed. She stopped at the shift in the way Jonny looked at her, patiently waiting for her to finish. His brown eyes were cold and hard. She swallowed. "My blouse is ruined," she said unconvincingly.

"I'm sure yer new husband can afford to buy ye a new one."

"A whole one even," An added, ineffectively attempting to mop up the spill with her napkin. She was more concerned with Jonny's sleeve than the table.

"Come see me when I get back," she smiled, still trying to cajole him, to salvage something from the encounter.

"I don't think so, Serephina," he said. "Not this time. Ye'll be a married woman, and I won't help ye cuckold this one."

An watched her fair face darken, the blue eyes turn to ice.

"How is this any different than the last?"

Jonny shrugged. "I don't know. He's not an old man deludin' himself into thinkin' he's desirable? He actually has something to offer th' world aside from his bank account? Maybe I'm actually growing morals, I don't know. Maybe I'm tired o' bein' used."

She reached for his hand, clasping it with both of hers. "Tonight then. One last night..."

"I have an appointment fer t'night." He freed himself and stood, reached for An's hand. "Ye've overstayed yer welcome at th' lady's table." Uncertain, An placed her hand in his and let him draw her to her feet. "An and I are goin' out on th' dance floor fer a bit. Ye'd best not be here when we return."

She scowled, was about to say something scathing when he leaned in to her, his breath cold on her bare neck as he said softly, "And I ever find out ye tried that trick on me again, I'll rip yer heart out and feed it t' m'feathered brethren." He turned back to An, smiling pleasantly, though his eyes still betrayed his anger. "Ceobhránach?"

An bobbed a shallow curtsey, flushing with a multitude of emotions.

"Aislynn," he added, looking down at the little monkey. "*Would ye please stay here and make sure th' harpy leaves in a timely manner?*"

Aislynn nodded, and turned to glare at Serephina, grinning toothily, her tiny arms crossed over her furry chest.

An found herself swept into Jonny's arms and onto the dance floor. It was an upbeat, modern song, not badly sung, but the rhythms were such that more traditional dance moves still worked. An had been introduced to the simple ballroom styles before the Masque last year and knew most of the steps. He was easy to follow.

"So, am I t' take it…"

"I'm done wit' her," he said flatly. "Did she…?"

"She tried."

"And I damned near facilitated it," he growled at himself over the bottle and his reflexes. "Thank ye. Again."

"Not necessary," she blushed, looked away.

He tipped her chin with a finger to face him. "Don't let me near her again, an' ye can help it."

She smiled. "Am I t' understand that as permission t' scratch her eyes out o'er ye?"

"Well, I'm hopin' it won't come t' that, but were it to… ye'll need sommat a mite stronger."

"Cipín?" she asked, wide eyed.

"Bit much," he quipped.

"Skye then," she decided.

Jonny spun her, laughing, "I think he'd be just as apt to turn on me."

An shook her head. "Oh no. He's afraid o' Cipín, ye see."

"And rightly so."

An was feeling positively giddy at the moment.

"So, I know ye'll have yer hands full Sunday mornin' with th' bride and all, and gettin' ready yerself, but... might I impose on ye? I'll be needin' sommat done with m' hair and as ye've already pointed out," he grinned, "I'm hopeless at it beyond just gettin' it out o' th' way."

She laughed. "Aye. How would ye like it? Simple or complex?"

"Appropriate."

Her eyes flashed, the mists within them flickering like flames in the dark pits. "I'll see what I can do."

The song over, they clapped for the singer and Jonny started to head back to their table. He took note that, while Serephina had left it, she was still lingering nearby, watching the pair of them with venom in her eyes. An felt the sudden stiffness in his arm and looked up, tried to see what had caused the change. Before she managed, he was drawing her towards the bar, leaving her at an empty place two or three seats down from Skye. "I'll be back," he said, running his fingers along her jaw, brushing stray strands of her honeyed-amber locks back behind her ear. "I've one last thing t' do. Then, if ye'd like, we can go and deal with these nightmares o' yers."

She nodded, her breath caught by his touch. "Aye," she breathed.

He crossed to Roulet's booth, had a word with her. Within a moment he was on stage and the regulars of the club were turning with eager anticipation. When the white-haired bard took the mike, it was always good. An heard the sighs of a nearby group. "Think he could go for a girl like me?" a young woman was asking.

"Babydoll," the guy next to her said with a snort, "he's too pretty to like girls."

"Wishful thinking, Dominick," another friend laughed. "I've only ever seen him with women. Mostly with that blind girl. You know, the one with the monkey?"

Then Jonny's voice was coming out over the speakers followed by a strong American country rhythm, though the song was really anything but. Someone next to An began tapping out the beat on the bartop. "All right! "Country Song"!" he exclaimed, began singing along with the chorus.

The Seether song had a pleasant rhythm, but it was deceptive. His eyes were locked on Serephina's icy blues and he was telling her to 'say what you want, but you're not goin' to win this time', and to 'get your sickness off me'. From the look of things, she wasn't taking his message well.

An was beginning to rather enjoy herself when something down bar from her caught her attention. It was 'Sweet William' talking with Mak ...Caleb. "So, are you going to take him up on it?"

"Hell, no!" Caleb exclaimed. "What do I want the baggage for?"

"What about Jonny?"

Caleb snorted, "The guy's used to it."

An felt the heat rising on her cheeks as she felt her way over to them. It was a little harder to do without Cipín. "So ye don't care who ye hurt, so long as you don't suffer more than ye haf ta?" she snapped.

He jumped. His friend set a hand on his shoulder to calm him. "I think you do not understand what we're talking about, miss," William began.

"Oh, I know more than ye what this is about. This is about memories of his he's willing t' let fester inside Jonny. Memories that are rightfully *his* burden!" she growled, pointing at Caleb.

Caleb sounded surly when he snapped, "So? That guy's got thousands of lives wrapped up inside his head. He's used to it. What's one more?"

It was all An could do not to slap him. "Th' straw what broke th' camel's back, is what i'tis!" she hissed. "One more pebble in a jar already over full is enough t' tip it over an' break th' whole! Ye thought o' that, ye selfish bastard?" She felt hands on her arms, ignored them. "D'ye give a thought to th' others affected by it? And ye wonder why folk at th' Rest treat ye like a pariah? 'Tis 'cause th' outside's just a reflection of what yer tryin' t' hide!"

The hands were pulling her back, steering her towards the stairs. She turned in them, looking up to find herself facing Skye. She started to lay into him when he said softly. "Richt or wrong, no' here."

She clamped her mouth shut, noticed Jonny coming up behind him with Aislynn and Cipín in his hands and turned, going upstairs on her own. She stood in the centre of the lounge, holding her arms, angry with herself for losing her temper. Jonny just stood there behind her, Aislynn on his shoulder and Cipín in hand, watching her. She turned, found it hard to meet his eyes. Aislynn was a dragon again, giving her a wide-eyed look of 'what bit you?'

"I'm sorry," she whispered, holding her hand out for the shillelagh. "I'm... just glad I left her at the table. Not sure I could have restrained myself."

"What'd he say that got yer Irish up?" he asked softly, letting the stick go and watching as it sailed to her hand.

"That he's no intention o' gettin' his memory back from ye. His exact words were, 'he's used to it. What's one more'?"

Jonny stiffened. "One too many," he whispered.

"And that's what I told him."

He cocked an eyebrow. "That's not all ye told him from th' look of things."

Skye opened the door, saw they were still here and came in. "Ah'm sorry, An, but... ya left me nae choice."

"Did ye hear what he said?"

"Aye, ah did... after..."

She held up her hand to forestall the lecture he was about to deliver. "I know, it dinna excuse what I did, but... damn that man! I..." she stopped pacing suddenly, just before her shin came in contact with the coffee table. "Wait... ye think... could it be His influence makin' me lose m' temper so quick?" she breathed, horrified by the very idea.

Jonny spread his hands. "Anythin' lies within th' realm of possibility. Was that somethin' ye'd have done before?"

She thought about that, deflated. "I can't honestly say. I handled Serephina with more calm to say the least."

"And more deftly, though a bit more stickily," he said, a smile in his eye as he plucked at his tea-stained sleeve.

She melted, surrendering to the tired and the ache and the frustration. "Maybe 'tis th' fatigue speakin'."

"Gie home then," Skye said. "Rest. Won't be a whole lot o' thon after t'nicht," he chuckled.

She nodded, watched as Aislynn flew down the hall to the door, opening it for them. She held out her hand to Jonny. He took it, lead her towards the cottage door. He turned, caught the scowl on Skye's face and paused, letting An go on ahead of him. "She's still havin' nightmares from th' Dark City," he explained. "She's asked me t' help. Don't fret. I'll be in next room."

Skye's entire manner was tight, but he nodded, and there was a world of threat in that gesture. He didn't like it, but Jonny was the best dreamwalker the Rest had. Better than Roulet. As the door closed behind them and Skye was alone in the upstairs room he let loose a roar of frustration, unleashing everything he didn't dare to say or do to the empty room. It made him feel a little better. He turned and headed back downstairs, hoping someone would act up enough to warrant his cracking a few heads. With his luck, no one would.

9

Morning dawned with An having slept better than she had in weeks. There had been no nightmares that she could recall. She did not remember seeing much of anything, as she had on previous nights, only this time all she could hear was soothing music and the sound of raven wings. Any time she began to smell asphalt or burnt rubber it would immediately be covered by the rich fragrance of the roses someone had put on her bedside table.

She was not surprised to find Jonny gone, nor that he had not stayed for breakfast. She was surprised, however, by the appearance of a black raven on her open kitchen door as she sat eating her own porridge while Aislynn crunched on an apple.

"Raven?" she called.

Taking that as an invite, the girl launched from the door to the floor, changing mid-air. She looked frantic, was all but in tears. "It told on me! I still love Her, I do, but... I love him, too, just... differently!" she sobbed.

An pushed aside her bowl and took the girl into her arms, held her until she calmed down. "Now," she said, drying her tears on her apron, "tell me what th' devil yer talkin' about."

Raven pulled a letter from her pocket. "This! It was in my mailbox this morning. Goblin post probably."

Aislynn handed the girl a tissue as An opened the letter and read what it said. It was not pretty. In short, the Northerner told her daughter that she'd had her fun slumming with her little 'ragdoll' but that now it was time to come home and stop mucking about. Marriage was out of the question. She forbade the union, and if Raven insisted on trying to go through with it, Her cú would have a new chew-toy.

Raven was heartbroken. An let her cry for a little while longer, told her that she would try to think of something.

"If I could find a way to do it without Her knowing maybe, She couldn't stop us," she sniffled. "But the minute I make plans, She'll know."

An brushed her hair out of her face and smiled. "I will think o' something. Just... forget about it fer tonight and tomorrow. We have Liberty to think about, and then th' rite. We can't let anything spoil tomorrow, not th' Russians, not th' Northerner. All right?"

Raven nodded, sniffing deeply and getting her emotions under control. She looked into An's eyes, took courage from the swirling banks of mist within them. "Your eyes are almost back to normal," she said, smiling through her grief. "I'll... I'll worry about it later. Wait 'til they've left on their honeymoon, then maybe the O'Keefe can help."

"That's a good idea. Wait 'til after Bealtaine."

The girl flew off just as quickly as she had come and An sat back down at the table, staring at her cold porridge and thinking. Then the idea hit her and she turned to Aislynn. "Willin' t' do me a favour, luv?"

Aislynn grinned.

Several hours later, Patches came into the Hedge Gate pub with Aislynn on his shoulder. Ian and some of the other men were there, getting things ready for Skye's stag party.

Harry frowned at the dragon. "Oi, technically that be a hen and not allowed!" he called. "Unless yer th' entertainment?" he added teasingly.

"In a way I am," she primped, grinning.

This brought everyone to a halt.

Patches laughed. "Here's what going on: I need some help. I know that all of this is for Skye and Liberty and we don't want to take anything away from that special day. *However* ...I'm finding out my future mother-in-law is going to stop my own nuptials one way or another. And Raven's ring kinda tattles. Sooo, An's got an idea and I've got a plan, but I'll need help."

"What's th' plan?" Ian asked.

"We have to elope. I know she'll say yes, so I don't have to ask her. I just have to not tell her that's what we're doing until she's in the church and I've got the ring out and the priest is running his mouth."

Ian laughed. "Yeh have ta do it th' old way." He looked over the gathered men. "Lads, I think we'll be organizin' an old fashioned raid t'night."

This was met with a great deal of enthusiasm. "Patches, yeh choose yer second, th' one yeh'll take ta th' church wit yeh ta make sure yeh make it. Once yer on holy ground there'll be nothin' She kin do. Yeh just make sure Father Thomas knows ta be ready. Niall, make sure yer son, Timothy, 's here t'night. We'll send him ta warn th' Father when we launch th' raid. Aislynn, will yeh be willin' ta play spy?"

She grinned. "Aye!"

"Let them get th' presents out th' way. When they're gettin' ta th' rest o' it, come warn us. Then we'll have ourselves a wee bit o' fun an' carry off a bride or two."

"And one what doesn't know she is yet!" Seamus laughed.

Skye had to admit, he felt a good deal less nervous with a pint or two in him. Nothing seemed out of the ordinary except that there wasn't a skirt in sight. Lafayette had produced a huge cake in the shape of a cast iron frying pan, since Skye had made frequent jokes about Liberty's aim with one. Seamus came up with a fresh pint, asked Skye if he wanted to play pool.

Skye shook his head. "No' here ah ain't!" he exclaimed.

"An' what's wrong wit' *my* pool tables?" Ian roared.

"No' yer bloody pool table ah've a problem wi'. It's whar they're at. Every time ah gae in thon bloody room ah get slapped!"

This caused a roar of laughter and Ian came over, stepped in and made a great deal of showing him there wasn't a woman in sight. Skye grinned, a little embarrassed, and entered the room. Ian began racking up the balls. As Skye went to select a cue, he heard sniggering just off the 'sidebar' room. He turned, was suddenly confronted by Peter in a curly blonde wig.

"Whit th' divil...?" he began. Then Peter slapped him. Skye's hand went to his face and he scowled.

"Can't break with tradition, now can we?" Peter laughed and tore off running.

Skye charged after him, roaring like a madman, even though he wasn't half as angry as he made out to be. Spying a half-eaten piece of cake abandoned at the end of the bar, Skye snatched it up. "Oi, Petricia!"

Harry saw what was up, and that his cousin had no clue, yelled, "Peter!"

He turned, looking over his shoulder, and got a face full of frosting and cake.

People were rolling on the floor laughing. Harry came over with a bucket. "Here, let me help ye wash yer face, Petey," he laughed and tossed the half-bucket worth of water on him.

George and Mikey started pulling back tables and rescuing chairs as the two cousins were suddenly in a furious tumble, punching and kicking and cussing.

Skye sagged against the bar, he was laughing so hard. Ian came of out the room with a pool cue. "Are we goin' t' play or what?"

"Aye, sair," he wheezed, trying to catch his breath. He followed Ian back into the game room. "This is a perfect nicht, sair," he sighed, lining up to break. "Truth be telt, ah wis worried ye'd drag me t' Depravity or some other strip club."

Ian shook his head. "Not safe t'night. Be th' perfect time ta kidnap th' groom, wouldn't it? As it is, we've one or two parties wi' a Highland lookalike out trollin' th' bars, includin' Depravity. We'll see an' they take th' bait."

Skye stepped back and let Ian shoot. "Ah loike this much better. Tho' ah confess confusion at th' box o' rags by th' doar."

Ian grinned, tapped the cue ball to sink three balls in a row. "That's fer later." There was a clatter against the lights hanging over the table and a small, pearly white dragon hung down from the fixture by her tail. She gave him the thumbs up. "Or now," he chuckled, dropping the cue on the table.

Skye frowned, uncertain what was going on.

"We'll finish th' game later," Ian assured him, setting his arm over his shoulders and guiding him into the main room of the pub. "Gentlemen!" Everyone stopped what they were doing and looked up. Jonny set his fiddle down mid-note, Billy stepped off the stage and even Peter and Harry let go of each other and got off the floor. At a signal from Ian, whiskey shots and strips of black cloth were passed around.

Ian lifted his shot and everyone with a free hand did the same. "All right, lads. This is ta th' bastard who thinks he's good enough ta be ma son-in-law."

"To th' poor bastard who thinks he can handle yer daughter!" Mikey shouted back. Everyone laughed.

"This is fer our daughters and our sisters, may they find men twice as capable an' half as ornery," he continued. "This is fer tomorra's bride ...and fer tonight's," he added, looking pointedly at Patches who nodded. "'Cause yeh see, Skye," he said, pulling the Highlander closer, "we're revivin' an old tradition tonight, 'cause there's need. Yeh've won yer fair maiden. Yer's is gonna walk down that aisle of her own free, and ain't a damn thin' yeh can do t' get out o' it now."

More laughter and cat calls of 'sucker' and 'he's right done for!'

"But this lad here," he said, pointing out Patches. "He's goin' ta have ta steal his. Oh, *she's* right willin'. It's her mama what says it's not gonna happen, and are yeh gonna let that stand in 'is way?"

Skye began to get into it. "Hell, nae!" he crowed.

"Well then, lads. We're goin' on an old fashioned 'cattle raid'. On'y th' object a'n't be cows but hens." Skye frowned as he was handed a black cloth with eyeholes in it by little Timothy. "And, if we're blessed, more'n' one o' us louts'll get lucky t'night!"

This was greeted with a roar of sláinte and everyone slammed back their shots.

Aislynn landed on Timothy's shoulder as he handed out the last of the masks, reminding him of his other job. The two of them disappeared into the night. Aislynn followed him to the church before doubling back to the manor to watch the fun.

The ladies, An included, were unsuspecting. They were set up in the back parlour, a rarely used, but sizeable room opposite the kitchen that had French doors opening onto the veranda. Some of the women were out on the porch itself, the party being quite large enough to need the extra room. All of the presents lay open on the tables and they were in the midst of a party game. Liberty was blindfolded and had a small garland in her hand. She was trying to find and catch someone in a bridal version of blind man's bluff. The ladies were giggling and dodging, teasing her while trying not to be caught by the garland.

It was hard for that many men to be absolutely quiet, but the ladies were making more than enough noise to provide cover. Some of them had crept through the house. Someone gave the signal and they swarmed the rails and ran up the steps. It became instant bedlam.

Liberty was jostled, and tore off the blindfold when someone near her screamed, found herself staring at a broad chest. She looked up, saw a familiar grin beneath a highwayman's mask just seconds before she ended up over his shoulder and was hauled off.

Raven had hung back during the game, using her smaller stature to avoid getting tagged. Patches had slipped in through the side door from the house and when the attack came, Raven turned to run deeper into the house, ahead of the others. He intercepted and snatched her up, covering her mouth and whispering, "Don't shift," into her ear even as he felt her starting to sprout feathers.

At the sound of his voice she stopped, confused, but allowed him to drag her through the house to the front door where Ian was waiting in gryphon form. Patches swung her onto his back and clambered up behind her, holding on as Ian wasted no time getting into the air.

Someone of Ian's human build grabbed Roulet from behind, found himself shocked for his trouble and tossed her off to someone else. "I think this one's yours, mate," he called, charging after Solitaire. She was much easier to catch.

Roulet didn't know whether to be insulted or not, and shocked who had hold of her on principal. He just laughed and exclaimed in an atrocious French accent, "Spicé!"

She spun in his arms, startled. "Lafayette?"

"'Allo, my leetle bonbon!"

She laughed, zapping him again for good measure.

Next to them, one of the women grabbed and ripped off the mask of her bandit. "LIAM!" she cried and began beating him about the head and shoulders with the mask and whatever else came to hand. He let her go and ran off, laughing, with her hot on his heels.

Solitaire was scooped up without any further ceremony by the man who had tossed her sister and was hauled off into the hedge maze. She only put up a token resistance.

An had been just inside the door, trying to stay out of the way of the garland game when the whole thing had begun. When she had seen the first of the men coming over the rail, she frowned, then realized what was happening. She heard a few men coming in through the front, catching up with the women trying to escape through the house. An darted into the kitchen to hide from the worst of it.

She found herself laughing softly. This had to have been what Aislynn had been up to all afternoon. She had heard of these things, but never actually seen one. They stemmed from older days than hers. Leave it to Ian to twist her idea into something that was itself a diversion.

When most of the noise had moved outside or upstairs, she slipped quietly out the kitchen door. There was still a great deal of activity on the veranda, so An opted for the front door, hoping that way would be clear. She set Cipín at the baseboard on her right and slid her ahead to find any obstacles. She didn't expect any, but it was habit; so she was more than a little confused when the shillelagh met resistance.

She turned to look, not really expecting to see anything, and reached out to feel what it might be. What she touched was coarse fabric, wool perhaps and had give to it. The second she realized it was a man in a cloak it was too late. Even as she shifted her grip and turned to run, the cloak fell away and a gloved hand was on her wrist, keeping her from using the shillelagh. The masked man bore her back against the wall, pinning her there with his body and kissed her with a fierce intensity that left her unable to breathe. Before she could catch her breath, the shillelagh was in his hand and she was over his shoulder being hauled unceremoniously out the back door into the night.

No one stopped them. Everyone was busy in their own chase, and no one was seriously fighting back. The sounds that filled the night were squeals of delight and shouts of indignation more than anything. Her captor did not stop until they were well within the woods, where he set her down, pressed back against a spreading oak. He kissed her again. There was less force this time, but just as much passion.

She was confused at first. The lips were warm, but the kiss was the same. Her hand came up, touched the cheek beneath the fabric and smiled. It was cool. She untied the cloth, pulling his hair free of it. His kisses became more insistent, deeper. She gave a tiny whimper as she clung to him, her mind going everywhere at once and no where at all. She wasn't even sure her feet were still on the ground.

He broke off the kiss with effort, pressing his forehead to the tree beside her, his cool breath on her neck sending chills down her spine. "I warned ye. Someone I once was were a highwayman." His hand rest over her heart, just above her breast, but oh so close. Her breath was ragged, her heart racing, every part of her alight and keenly aware of every inch of him. "He's been wond'rin'... what'd it'd be like t' steal ye away."

She set her hand upon his, terrified of her own daring. She tilted her head away from him, exposing more of her pale golden throat to him. "Ye... ye can't steal... what's freely given."

His head came up, looked into her eyes, seeking those signs that would have been there in a normal woman: the dilated pupils and slight glaze to the eyes. The mists were swirling fast, though, and her skin was flush. He could feel her heart-rate beneath his hand. There was a scent in the air, different than her normal, faintly honeyed, fragrance. It told him other things. "Don't..." he tried to say. "Ye don't... I... can't promise control..."

He pulled back, intending to step away from the temptation. An made up her mind in the space of a heartbeat, reached out, locking her fingers in his hair and pulled him into a kiss of her own, drawing him back to her. His hands braced himself against the tree, their lips the only point of contact. He moaned against her mouth. "An..." He was trying to warn her. "Ye don't know..."

She took his face in her hands, looked deep into his eyes. "I do. I'm... truthfully I'm terrified, aye, but... I refuse... *refuse* t' live a life full o' regret, wantin' what'll never be mine. I'm not fool enough t' think I can have what they have. And if I've learned nothin' in th' last century, it's t' take what I can get. If this is how it has t' be t' have ye...."

He shook his head. "It isn't... We don't have to... I don't require that of ye."

She gave a frustrated laugh, "But I want it. I want all ye'll give me, a chroí, all and more. I'll be satisfied with what ye'll grant. I'll not *ask* fer more. But what ye'll give I'll drink like th' drowned."

Her voice was husky. She tried to keep the desperation out of it, wasn't sure she succeeded. "If ye don't want that kind of relationship..." she choked. "If ye don't want..."

"*Wantin'* isn't th' issue!" he gasped, tearing his gaze from hers.

Her voice was small and soft, prepared for heartbreak. "Then what?"

"Takin' advantage of a hundred year old virgin in a moment o' passion and havin' her regret."

It was her turn to tilt his chin to look at her. There was a soft smile on her dusky rose lips. "I'm a bit older than that, thank ye kind."

He started to say that this was not the time for humour, but her thumb slipped up to cover his lip, feather light. "And i'tisn't a choice made in th' heat o' passion. I've been... considerin' it fer ...a while now. Tryin' to make up my mind. ...If I dared." She searched his eyes for answers she knew she'd never find. "Yer th' one keeps tellin' me I'm an old Celt and should act like it. Well, if I remember aright, chastity isn't actually a virtue. I'd be a woman known if yer willin' to be th' man t' make me one."

The offer hung between them like the first snowflake of the season. She held her breath, terrified he'd take it and desperate that he not refuse. He was searching for something, strength, weakness perhaps. She couldn't be sure. His lips slowly met hers.

This kiss was different. Not just because it was soft and slow, full of fear and hesitation. It was searching, probing, promising. She opened her mouth to him when he asked, still breathless, still certain of being ultimately rejected. When the tip of her tongue met his, it was decided. His hands left the tree, gathered her up in his arms and carried her home.

Aislynn sat in the tree branch above them, sighed as she watched the pair of them go. It was not what she wanted. She didn't like him enough, not for her. But it was what An wanted. She had just made that perfectly clear. She sighed again, dropped from the branch to Cipín, left behind in the heat of the moment. She picked up the shillelagh and flew slowly back to the cottage, giving the pair time to make it in, hoping they wouldn't stop in the front room.

10

The morning of the wedding An awoke to the smell of breakfast and roses. There was a warm breeze coming in through the open window and something soft caressing her cheek. She stretched languidly and realized several things at once. One: that she was naked beneath the sheets for perhaps the first time in her life. Two: that she was not alone in the bed.

She blinked, memories of the night before flooding through her mind and suffusing her body with a warm blissfulness. Jonny was laying on his stomach on top of the coverlet stroking her cheek with a dark red rose. She smiled, blushing a little, sinking deeper beneath the coverlet, fully conscious of her nudity. "Mornin'," she breathed.

He arched an eyebrow, though there was a twinkle in his eye. "Regrets?"

She tipped her head at him with a little frown. "I believe last night was supposed to be an attempt to avoid regrets?"

"Did it work?"

"I don't know yet, do I? Though I have none at th' moment, nor do I expect them. Why do ye ask?"

He rolled onto his side, his head propped up on his hand, drawing the rose down the length of her hidden body. His hair was splayed out over his naked chest, but he was wearing a pair of black pants. "Well, I do believe yer th' first woman I've ever slept with what attempted t' hide her body from me th' next morn."

Her blush deepened. "Well, if ye see it all the time it tends t' lose its power."

He chuckled at that. "Not necessarily true. But not completely false, either. And as much as I'd like fer that glimpse of pale golden shoulder to incite hours of further debauchery... we've a wedding t' get to, ye've a bride to attend and a field of snow t' tame."

She blushed, mistaking it for a metaphor of a different sort. "Jonny!" she scolded.

He frowned, lifted a lock of his wild, white hair. She darkened further and he smiled teasingly. "Really, Ceobhránach, what were ye thinkin'?" He hauled himself from the bed, tossing the rose to her. "It seems I may have utterly corrupted our prim and uptight little school teacher," he grinned.

He headed lazily towards the door. She threw a pillow at him, missed, having not calculated for the weight. He looked back, saw her sitting up holding the covers in front of her and got a glimpse of long creamy back. He groaned and dragged himself out of the room.

An threw herself back down against the pillows as the door closed, covered her smiling face with both hands. She could not believe the tigress she had become last night. She had seen the claw marks on his long, lightly tanned back, nicely red against the artful map of white scars that she remembered tracing most of, kissing a great many of... and a few other things. He had been an extremely patient lover, while giving the impression of being just as intensely eager.

An slipped out of bed, realizing a shower was in order. There would be many today with beastly noses who would ferret out a few things she would rather not have known. The water was hot and running when she went into the tiny bathroom and stepped under the flow, savouring the feel of it against her body. She found herself imagining what it would be like to be pressed against his body beneath that water and blushed all over again.

He had undressed her slowly but efficiently, kissing every inch of skin he exposed as he uncovered it, as if she were a sweet he was unwrapping that would spoil if he didn't taste it immediately. He had been slow at first, his fingers gentle but insistent and thorough. Not an inch of her remained untouched, unkissed. When he had taken her the first time she had been more than ready and he more than gentle. The pain went unnoticed as everything else exploded. Every time after that had been more eager, more hungry.

She turned the hot water off, hitting herself with a blast of well-cold water. She had to get herself under control. There was too much to be done today. Once she had regained her composure, she stepped out of the shower, drying herself off and putting her hair up in a simple twist while it dried.

When she stepped back into the bedroom, Aislynn was stretched out on the sill, watching the bees playing in the blossoms. An smiled. "Good mornin'," she said, taking down the emerald gown from the wardrobe door and slipping into it.

Aislynn's tail flicked, catlike, against the sill, but otherwise did not acknowledge the greeting. *"Bees are going to get a nasty surprise at th' vampricks,"* she muttered.

An let her be contrary. *"I seem to remember reading that they do not eat insects. No blood. They prefer to lure in birds after the bugs."*

The dragon humphed, remembering her own encounter with the vicious flora.

An drifted over to the window, stroking the dragon in all her favourite places. *"I still love ye. Though I know ye don't approve."*

"You want what you want," she said quietly. *"I understand desire. I just have to learn to share."*

"Well, ye can zip me up if ye like. I still need ye. He won't be around all th' time. I'm not so foolish as to expect that."

The dragon sat up on her hind quarters and An turned around. *"Don't you want* him *to?"* she asked even as she ran the zip up for her.

"A bit too domestic, don't ye think?"

The dragon hummed a bit, then nodded. *"Go. Th' brownie has breakfast ready an' ye'll be late ye don't hurry."*

An bustled into the other room to find Jonny at the table, dressed, sipping coffee. She was suddenly self-conscious of her bare feet but came over to the table, ate the slight breakfast that had been set for her. Jonny frowned at what little was on her plate. "That all ye eat?"

She smiled. "I think she understands it's about all I could stomach this morn. An' breakfast for me is not a heavy thing unless I'm workin' th' garden. Advantages of unspoken communication twixt myself an' m' house."

She hurriedly ate, taking note of his attire. His shirt was distinctly elven, with knotwork embroidered on the cuffs, the round collar and down the button placket. He wore a red velvet waistcoat, and a black, tailed coat was draped on the back of his chair. He had brushed his hair out and a variety of ties sat in a small dish beside his empty plate.

An was self-conscious at first, but began to get over it as she dressed his hair. She did not go for the elaborate court braids she had seen Lion wear, opting for the simpler, warrior braids along the side, providing a light cage, letting the bulk of his hair fall free. She left a single lock falling from his temple, 'artfully escaped'. The work calmed her.

"I honestly half-expected ye t' be gone this mornin'," she said as she worked.

"Well, I would have had t' come back t' get my hair attended," he said with a wry smile, teasing, "wouldn't I?"

"Still."

"And who's t' say I didn't leave and come back?"

"The house," she replied, giving one forming braid a light tug in response to his teasing.

He chuckled.

"But honestly, thank ye fer... bein' here t' get th' awkward over with."

"Awkward?" he asked. He knew what she meant. He was drawing her out and she knew it, but she let him anyway.

"Aye. Had th' first time I saw ye 'after' been in public I don't know how I'd've behaved. It would have been... awkward."

Aislynn landed on her shoulder with a spray of tiny white flowers in her claw. One by one, she broke them off and handed them to An, watching her weave them into the braid junctions. The end effect was surprisingly masculine and very elven.

"There," she said. "I think that'll do. I hope yer pleased."

He caught her hand, kissed it. "Yer goin' t' be late," he smiled.

She whimpered. "I don't leave this minute I may miss th' whole event," she sighed, pulling her fingers from his grip with difficulty, and not because he was holding them too tightly. Aislynn flew up with her slippers in hand as a car horn was heard from outside. She ran for the door, snatching up the shillelagh and the snow rose where it waited on the dressing bench. She slowed down at the gate, orienting herself by Roulet's body in the driver's seat. Solitaire was holding the front door for An.

"Hurry up, girlfriend!" Solitaire laughed. "We still got to get hair and make-up done!"

An climbed in beside Roulet and her twin slid in next to her. She glanced back as they pulled away from the cottage and thought she saw a white raven flying off.

The catherdral wedding was beautiful and stately. Liberty was a vision of perfection in her fey-made wedding gown with her Irish, cobweb-lace veil. Arachne and her daughter had outdone themselves. It was a little disconcerting for An to see at least two of the bridesmaid dresses standing empty behind her, but what she could see of the proceedings made up for what she couldn't.

Ian was splendid in his black formals with a green vest. Skye had opted for a formal kilt in Black Watch plaid, not having a clue what his true clan was and being persistently stubborn about that for some reason.

Jonny's voice filled the church, pure and pristine, as he sang her down the aisle to meet Skye. There were few dry eyes when the last note faded.

The reception was held in the Cathedral's banquet hall. A full luncheon was served and Lafayette had outdone himself with a cake as tall as the bride.

An took note that while Mikey had been Roulet's escort down the aisle as Best Man and Maid of Honour, he was spending a great deal of time with Solitaire after. The poor girl didn't seem to know what she wanted. She kept watching Ian, confused as to his behaviour. An got the feeling she was expecting him to chase her, which he was not likely to do.

Her observations of the wedding attendants was interrupted by Skye as he came over to her, pulling her out onto the dance floor while Liberty danced with her father.

"It were a beautiful ceremony," she smiled.

He shrugged. "T'were Catholic. Thon were fer her. Tonicht's fer me."

"As it should be."

He scrutinized her a moment. "An' hoo are ya this morn?"

"Good. I confess I was a little hurried this mornin', but I had no nightmares an that be what yer askin'."

"Whit Jonny did helped?" he asked, reluctant to have her say yes.

An managed to not blush, "Aye. It did."

"An' did he..." he began and felt her stiffen.

"He slept in th' other room when he did th' dreamin', thank ye very much, as if it were any o' yer business. And are *you* up t' th' task tonight?" she countered, getting angry. "I understand it'll be th' first time in a few years since this particular part o' th' rite's been enacted."

It was Skye's turn to blush. "Non'yer," he said tightly.

She smiled, gliding easily through the last steps of the dance. "Don't worry about me. I can handle myself," she said, sinking into a curtsey.

Before either of them could say anything more, Jonny was behind her, taking her by hand and waist and sweeping her off with a grin to Skye. He didn't have the opportunity to complain as Liberty pinched his butt and laughed when he spun on her, stealing him for another dance.

"Mikey were richt," he growled, pulling her close.

"About what?"

"Ah'm gonna hav' m' hands full wi' ya!"

Near the very end of the reception, An noticed the arrival of Cass and Dukes. They were at least dressed in nicer suits than their usual, though Cass's rust coloured coat did stand out a bit. They observed who was present before taking Ian aside for a brief conversation. An felt no lies from that quarter at all and Ian gestured to the group at large in an open 'feel free' manner.

Liberty noticed them and made her way over. They were polite enough to wish her well, though An got the impression Cass's were more genuine than his partner's. They availed themselves of coffee and Cass allowed Serenity to feed him a single bite of cake before they took their leave.

Roulet and Solitaire collected An to get her into position to throw a mix of millet, spelt and barley. Solitaire made a catty comment as the bells of the Cathedral rang out, "I'll bet Serephina's crowd was pretty thin this morning," she laughed.

"Serves her right," Roulet crowed, began cheering as the bridal couple ran the seeded gauntlet to the waiting limousine.

The Rest was a completely different creature from the stiffly formal morning wedding. The church flowers were of course reused, but it seemed as if the entire community had burst into bloom. Liberty changed out of her wedding gown at the manor and appeared to have *grown* a new one. This dress was much simpler and more comfortable, made entirely of trailing vines and flowers. Her crown was prominent on her brow and in full bloom, with vines of wedding bell flowers trailing down the back of her coppery hair.

An had changed into a short-sleeved sundress in a green, floral print and simple slippers. She felt very exposed, but was fully aware she fit in better this way, not to mention was cooler. She carried a light shawl with her to cover her arms and protect the concept of her modesty.

The twins however, had opted for something more traditional. Well, traditional for *them* for Bealtaine. They were in full belly dancing gear with deep fringes, ropes of bells and coined scarves and rang merrily everywhere they went.

A Maypole was put up and the young people enjoyed getting themselves in a tangle dancing around it. Liberty and Skye both oversaw the driving of the herds between the two bonfires once they had been lit. It was a little terrifying for An to hear the horses running through and not being able to see them. But she could see Coach as he led them, running with them back to pasture.

Alcohol flowed freely, and even some of the kids were allowed their first tastes of whatever their parents were drinking. The people of the Rest believed in the Old World ways of teaching responsibility from a young age. If it's not forbidden and instead carefully monitored as children, as teens they are less likely to overindulge or binge the moment they have the freedom to do so. What is not forbidden does not hold the same allure. Most made faces at the stuff and ran off without asking for any more.

An sat at one of the tables, sharing a plate with Aislynn and young Timothy, who was giving her all the gossip on Raven and Patches' secret wedding the night before.

Kyle approached. She looked up, smiled at him. He was looking more and more human every day. At the moment he only had a small amount of blue fur around his jaw and his ears only sloped back a little. He smiled sheepishly at her, and sat, listening as Timothy finished telling his story.

"Thank ye, Timmy," she smiled when he was done. "I was wond'rin' how that turned out. I am pleased. Why don't ye take my plate an' go get yerself some o' that custard cake ye were eyein' earlier? I'm sure yer mother wouldn't mind, seein' as ye've eaten a good chunk o' roast and potatoes."

He grinned. "Ok, Miss! An' if she stops me, I'll send her t' you!" he crowed and ran off.

An turned to the young wolf. "Now, what can I do fer ye, Kyle?"

He startled. "What makes you think I want something?"

"Ye have that look," she said casually, sipping her tea.

He sighed, set a red bottle of cut glass with gold embellishments in front of her. It had a golden cork etched with a very elaborate and very magical design. "Would you read this for me? Tell me how to get rid of her?"

"Her?"

He sighed again, reached up and pulled the stopper from the bottle. A column of gold-coloured smoke rose from the neck, smelling strongly of sex and incense and formed into a very beautiful, dusky-skinned woman. She seemed to be of vaguely middle-Eastern descent, with almond eyes the colour of tiger's eye stones, glinting gold at the centre with rich brown edges. Her wavy black hair was drawn up in an off-centre ponytail and she wore a cloth-of-gold harem outfit strung with chains among the bells and coins. And around her neck, resting between her ample cleavage hung a large, golden key studded with rhinestones. She had a gold earring hung with red jewels from which a chain ran to a matching nose ring.

As she formed and appeared, she clapped her hands together and bowed over them. "Yes, Master?"

He groaned, waved his hand up at her. "An, meet Leila. Leila, this is An. She's going to help us with our problem."

Leila sank immediately to a seat, her beautiful mouth frowning. "Dawg pleez!" she chuffed at Kyle. "The only problem we got is that I'm eager to provide you with wish fulfilment and you ain't makin' any wishes." The djinni was beginning to attract attention.

An rest her chin delicately on her hand. "Kin ye grant any kind of wish?"

Leila looked eager. "Yes! Please get him to make a wish!"

"Does he have a limit?"

She shook her head, her ponytail flailing wildly. "Oh no. So long as he owns the bottle, my services... all of them," she added, leaning the middle half of her body in his direction pointedly, "are his. But he won't take 'em!"

"Cause you can't grant me the wish I want!"

An looked to Kyle. "And what wish is that?"

"I want my family back. I've remembered them. I've even found them. But... there's this guy who looks like me, living my life! Sleeping with my wife!" he exclaimed.

An nodded. "That would be a changelin'. What they sometimes put in th' place of those they take."

He frowned. "I thought those were babies."

She shook her head. "Most often they are. But sometimes they do it with adults too. If takin' them would be noticed, or it serves their purposes to replace them."

"Oh. But... she can't give them back to me," he complained.

"You won't make any *reasonable* wishes," the djinni countered.

"What is a reasonable wish?" An asked.

"Anything. Fame, fortune, me..." she suggested.

An looked to Kyle. He submitted to being stared at for a moment before he grumbled, "I wish I had a ham sandwich."

"No, you don't," Leila growled. "Dawg, it don't work if you don't really want it."

The faint twinge An felt confirmed the request was a lie.

"Kyle..." she admonished.

He sighed. "Fine. I wish I had a beer."

Leila smiled, spun her ponytail dramatically and a beer appeared on the table in front of him. A little farther down, someone complained that his beer had just vanished from his hand.

"Ye couldn't have conjured him one from th' cooler?" An asked.

She shrugged. "It comes from where it comes. I summon. I don't create."

"I wish I had my son here. Right here, right now," he growled.

She grinned, spun her pony tail. Nothing happened. She frowned, tried again. Again, nothing. "You sure this is what you want?"

"YES!" he roared.

A few of the men who had been easing their way over, drawn by the scent of her, suddenly changed their minds and found other places to be.

An studied the djinni for several minutes. "Maybe now that yer not... where ye were... yer not as capable as ye were. Yer powers are dimmed. Ye weren't a real djinni anyway." An could tell she was one of the Taken. She had the same resonance that everyone here but Sean and Elizabeth had.

"Of course I am," she scowled.

"Kyle, where did ye get her?"

"I found the bottle when we were running from the Dark City." At that Leila shivered. "I think it's what that gang war was over. The group running... one of them was shot and dropped this. I grabbed it and ran through the door," he shrugged.

Leila nodded, her hair bobbing violently. "Yeah, happened a lot over there. Who ever owns the bottle owns the djinni and gets more power on the block. The Kinders stole me from Pig. For which I was eternally grateful," she shuddered with revulsion. "Pig was a... well, a pig. I get stolen a lot. It's almost a game."

"So, will you read the bottle and tell me how to free her?" Kyle whimpered. "I don't want to give her to anyone else and I can't have her around when I try to get my wife back. It would be real bad. And she's really hard to say no to."

An wrinkled her nose. "I kin tell."

She studied the bottle for a few minutes, held her fingers a few inches away. She could feel the power radiating off of it. "No. I'm not touchin' it."

Kyle wilted. "Why not?"

"One, I know where that came from. I've just gotten over what that devil did to me..."

"He is, you know," Leila said quietly.

An looked at her. "Who is what?"

"He. The Dark Man. He is the Devil."

An absorbed that. The woman was convinced of it, but whether that was truth or not remained to be seen. It was believable at the very least. "Any way. I'm not readin' anything what came from there what's *that* magical. That bottle is a trap."

"It is not! It's my home!" the djinni snapped.

"And what happens when yer in it and someone slams th' cork in?"

"I'm...." She stopped, sinking lower in the seat. "...trapped 'til they open it."

An pointed at the cork. "That is th' Seal of Solomon. It was created t' bind t' th' bottles th' lawless djinn who refused to submit to God's will. Effectively enslaving them."

"So we just break the seal?" Kyle asked, perking up.

"I don't think ye can. And I can't swear to what would happen if ye did. Ye'll have t' find someone more deeply versed in Arabic mythology. I just don't have the expertise. But my suggestion, fer th' moment," she added as he deflated again, "is to give her th' bottle."

She watched his ears actually twitch forward a little. "Just... that simple?"

An spread her hands. "Who owns the bottle owns the djinni, right? So who says she can't own herself?" The two of them looked from one to the other, excitement beginning to build. "Though I'd put that cork in a safe somewhere, so ye can't be trapped in again."

Leila jumped up, bowed deeply to An. "Mistress, you truly wield the wisdom of Solomon!"

An blushed. "Oh, I wouldn't go that far, now." She rose, collecting her shillelagh and Aislynn and picking up her cup. "Now if ye'll excuse me, I've a bride t' attend."

As she walked away she heard Kyle slide the bottle to Leila. "Here. Take it. You're free."

"Ask me for something! Anything," the djinni asked, excitedly, clutching the red glass to her ample chest.

Kyle held his breath. "Go make me a sandwich."

An paused, waiting to hear her response. The djinni crowed as she felt no urge to obey. "Make your own damned sandwich, dawg!" She devolved into happy laughter.

"Thank God," Kyle breathed.

An smiled and headed to where she had seen Roulet and Solitaire gathering with Liberty. They had the wedding veil. Twilight had fallen and the night was deepening. It was time for other rituals. Liberty and her entourage of women gathered on one side of the fires. The twins flanked her, and An walked just behind her carrying the veil. The procession collected females as it wended from the veranda to the centre of the two fires.

Ian had started a similar procession which came up from the other end and he stood there, Oak crown tall and leafy, in brown pants and his green denim shirt. Behind him were arrayed the men of the Rest. He stepped aside and Skye stepped up. He too, had changed from his wedding finery. Though he still wore his kilt, he had foregone a shirt for his leather jerkin and soft hide boots. He took Liberty's hand and Ian held up a silk cord.

"I stand here as father o' th' bride, chief o' th' groom and king ta all b'fore me. Wit' this cord," he said, laying it over their joined hands and began tying them together in such a way that, while they could not let go, they could change how they held each other, "I now bind these two in matrimony until such time as their choosing. And let no man nor woman nor gentry attempt ta cut it asunder."

A cheer went up as the bound hands were raised. An and Solitaire stepped back, allowing Roulet to step forth. She and Mikey each took one end of the veil and spread it between them, held it over the couple. When Liberty and Skye kissed, they let go, and wild, cheering, passionate music began. Together, the veil still covering both of them, they turned and Skye led his bride back the way he had come.

An did not follow, very deliberately. She avoided going between the two bonfires. She danced with the others around the fires sunwise, for the fertility of the fields and the Rest as a whole, but that was as far as she was willing to go.

As she dropped out of the dancing, she saw Ian off to the side, watching the dancers with a man she could see but had never met. He was a handsome rogue, wearing a black suit coat in spite of the heat, his dark hair slicked back and a ready smile on his face that somehow never seemed to reach his eyes. She came over, offered Ian her flask. "Uncle?" she said.

He grinned, accepting the whiskey and taking a healthy swig, drinking to her health. The other man lifted the pint in his hand and concurred.

"Newly found cousin or newly made?" the man asked Ian.

Ian laughed, handed An her flask back. "Aye, I do adopt a great many it seems." He introduced An to him. "This is Cullen Thomas O'Keefe m'nephew... some how..." he frowned, trying to figure out how it was possible. "Not sure how but he's *actually* m'nephew. I had him come down ta deal wit' th' Russians t'day."

He held out his hand to An, shaking it firmly. "I'll be staying a bit until we have this mess untangled." An noticed the Boston notes to his lighter lilt.

She frowned, looking up at Ian. "Ye needed outside help?"

He shrugged, grinning. "Not exactly outside, now is it, what bein' family and all? He an' his boys just weren't *local*, and I needed faces what weren't when ...some o' Spetznakov's assets were hit t'day."

"And hit hard," Cullen grinned. "Kinda difficult to prove arson when there's no accelerant."

"Or unnatural source..." Ian added. "Nothin' spread?" he asked.

Cullen shook his head, "Nah. We know our job, Uncle. My boys are experts. Now the one car that blew up was totally the Ruskies' fault. The fact that it wasn't the car they'd rigged..." he shrugged, laughing.

Ian sighed, but he was smiling. "Sometimes I wonder why I sent yeh Nort', ...and then yeh do sommat like this an' I remember."

Cullen laughed, clapping his uncle on the back. "Plausible deniability. And alibis."

"I'll drink ta that," Ian said, accepting a bottle of Jameson from someone wandering by.

An smiled and started to back away, but she had caught Cullen's attention again. "So, what do you do, little cousin?" he asked.

"I teach."

"Sean's new pupil," Ian supplied. "She may be blind, but she kin see what we need her ta see ta keep th' child safe."

"She's blind? Yer blind?" he asked, confused, taking a closer look at her eyes.

Ian saved him from being rude by cutting between them. "Pardon. I've a word fer ma son-in-law. And Cullen, watch out fer th' shillelagh. She's a governess. Be rude an' she'll no' hesitate ta remind yeh yer manners." He gave An a suggestive nod. "That's permission, in case yeh missed it, lass."

Cullen drew back at that with a frown. An just smiled at him, turned Cipín delicately in her hand, showing she knew how to use it without ever issuing a threat. "Huh," he mused, went back to his pint.

An turned to watch Ian approach the new couple, who were trying to find ways to manage eating with their hands tied. Ian reached up to his crown and broke something off, a twig with a leaf and an acorn on it. He hugged his daughter, gave her a kiss. When he embraced Skye, he whispered something which brought a look of confusion to the Highlander's face. When Ian walked away, An noticed the twig was entwined in Skye's hair.

Aislynn landed on her shoulder, holding a miniature pint and a chunk of pineapple on a kebab stick. "*He's tapped him his proxy,*" she supplied, nodding her head at Skye.

An looked at her. "An' ye would know how?"

She nibbled delicately at her food. "*I was there when he told Barry he was going ta. They've got a bed set up in th' fields, nice little bower. She's th' May Queen. Skye's just been tapped to proxy th' Oak King. They'll be plowin' fields later,*" she grinned. An blushed. "*Ought to be a good harvest this year. Barry said they haven't done this part of th' rite in at least forty years.*"

An frowned, suddenly remembering a conversation her first morning here which contradicted more recent information. "Wait, Gabriella indicated she'd slept with both kings, ritually speaking, when she was queen. How could this…"

Aislynn shook her head, swallowing. "*That were just regular Bealtaine stuff. This is a marriage rite. They haven't had a bridal pair in the fields in forever, crowned or otherwise. Ian's already married. Ain't likely t' do it again, even symbolically.*"

This was more news. An mused on it as she followed her ears towards the music. "I didn't know…"

"*She was taken centuries ago. But as she isn't dead and he's no idea where she is… he can't rightly take another wife, can he?*"

She shook her head. "How is it ye find all this out?"

"*I listen,*" the dragon shrugged. "*Fly on th' wall an' all,*" she grinned.

An was about to say something but found herself facing the princely William. He looked very sharp in his wedding finery. He bowed and offered her his hand. "May I have this dance, Miss An?" he asked.

Aislynn drank about half her Guinness and then leapt into the air, giving An a light push in the man's direction with her back feet as she did. An sighed and accepted his hand, curtseyed. He swept her onto the green among the dancers, easily following the bouncing, hopping steps of the reel.

Jonny was on the stage with Billy, both of them sawing hotly on a pair of fiddles, duelling, but making sweet music as they did. It was a long song that invigorated the dancers even as it threatened to exhaust them. A couple of the dancers collapsed in a tired tangle at the end, laughing even as they tried to catch their breath. One of the young men tried to catch something else and got himself slapped for his trouble. Deeming it worth it, he stole a kiss while he was at it and then ran off with her hot on his heels. From the sound of her voice, it was the same couple from the hen party: Liam and… An thought her name was Penny.

In the centre of the dance floor though, another number had slowly begun. Skye was looking down at Liberty and at their bound hands, trying to puzzle something out. An paused, got William to wait a moment though he was trying to get her to dance to the next song as well. She watched with a smile as Skye figured out whatever it was he needed to. He held up his free hand, waving the band to hold up. The music stopped and the dancers turned.

Skye cleared his throat. "Ladies an' Gentles an' th' no' sae much." This evoked a titter from the crowd. "Thank ye all fer comin' but, damn it! Ah'm takin' m' wife home!" he crowed. He lifted his bound arm even as he ducked under it, deftly drawing a startled Liberty over his shoulder into a fireman's carry and started to haul her off toward the manor, intent on the door to the Mead Hall.

Liberty squealed, then realized where he was going and began to kick and beat his back with her free hand. "Yer goin' th' wrong way!"

Aislynn flew up in front of them, hovered before his face and said something in Gaelic that An could not hear for the laughter around her. Flushing red, he turned, looked off in the direction Aislynn had pointed then began to trudge off between the fires towards the fields.

An laughed, let William sweep her into another dance as Jonny struck up the chords.

She danced with several people after that, most of them mortal. She had to turn down more than one request for an assignation, blushing more furiously with each consecutive offer. Eventually she ended up in Roulet's arms, dancing to a slower melody that allowed the dancers to catch their breath. "Are ye goin' t' ask me t' th' fields too?" she flushed.

"Why? You want me to?" she grinned. That caught An by surprise for a moment, then she laughed. "Sorry, pet, I've a date with Sori tonight. Though I wanted at least one dance with you before we slipped off."

"Is it something about me or just Bealtaine itself has ...offers comin'?" An asked, worried that people knew somehow.

Roulet pulled back a second, looked at An as if she were daft. She brushed the bulk of An's hair from her shoulder, letting it hang freely down her back, held out of her face only at the side where the ice rose gathered it up. "You really don't know, do you?"

"Know what?" An dared, regretting it the moment she asked, starting to blush in anticipation.

"You are beautiful, An. For at least half the guys here, you are a wet dream. The staid, up-tight school teacher. Prim, proper, modest. They all dream of what all that propriety might be hiding." An blushed in earnest, remembering just what that was. "They all want to be the reason you let your hair down. And here you are tonight ...with your hair down... in a sexy little dress and showing off not only your ankles but those shapely calves of yours..." She laughed as An fidgeted, missing her step as her words made her self-conscious. She pulled her close, hugging her even as they danced. "Face it, An baby, they're all hot for teacher."

"That and you blush like a new bride," Solitaire added, joining them. "Makes it all the hotter. And you can't see it, but babe, you are being *checked out.*"

An tried to escape, embarrassed. She turned and found her way blocked by Leila who had come up. "This one of *those* dances?" she asked, her smouldering eyes alight with desire.

Roulet grinned, reaching out to take the djinni's hand and her sister's and the three of them linked up, forming a circle around An. On the stage, Billy had taken note and stopped playing his fiddle. He turned and grabbed a bodhrán, began to beat out a rhythm to the swaying hips of the three dancers. Jonny set down his own fiddle and pulled out a pipe, began to play something more appropriate to the eastern style of the women's moves.

An looked up at that, glared at him,

Leila's gold harem pants solidified into a pair of long, dusky legs and a gold skirt with as many bells and coins and flying fringe as the two gypsies.

They loosened up their tight circle, though still teasing, swaying and shimmying in and out, spinning around her. The circle loosened up more, but never enough for An to escape, even though she tried.

They danced, reaching in towards her from time to time linking arms or hands across her body, ran teasing fingers along her arms, her neck, her back. They kept her turning in reaction to their movements until she was completely unaware she had become part of the performance. Something else was happening, too. There was something in the air beyond the concentration of potential sex and nag champa she could smell from the djinni. There was a honeyed, rose fragrance beginning to rise, mingling with the tingling of ozone and lilies and lavender. There was meadowsweet too, and elder. Everything blended with the smell of the fires into one swelling scent of pagan need.

An found her movements, while not so blatant as theirs, beginning to simulate some of them. She was dancing too, giving in to what she was feeling and actually enjoying it. Everything else fell away. She spun at their encouragement, letting her hair fly. The song ended abruptly with the three of them on their knees around her and bent back in graceful bows, one hand outstretched to the audience around them and one held up to her.

She stopped, her heart racing, her body flush and glistening with a light sheen of sweat, and pressed a hand to her heart. She looked down at the three women, bare bellies up on the ground around her. She looked beyond them and, though unable to gauge the reactions of the mortals, she read all she needed to on the faces of the Taken. It was a mix of shock and open lust, and a great deal of genuine appreciation. An caught a glimpse of Jonny's arched eyebrow and the ghost of a smile as he took his pipe from his lips, and panic set in. Before any of the three women had even straightened up, An slipped out from between them, snatched Cipín from where she waited by a table and darted into the crowd, anywhere so long as she got away.

The last thing she heard from behind her as the audience caught its breath and began applauding like a mad thing was Roulet's demand of Leila, "What the hell did you do?!"

An had no idea where she was going or why she was running. She could feel her own arousal with an intensity she could barely stand. She had never felt like this, not even last night. Oh, he had teased her body to similar heights, but this was different. There was no one here causing it, releasing it, and she was certainly not going to allow it free rein in public.

People saw the state she was in and moved out of her way. While she looked like she needed comfort, there was also something about her that denied approach. She smelled ozone, knew Roulet was near, and turned away from the smell. As the music began again and the dancing restarted with something more traditional, she heard the flap of dragon wings and the ozone faded. Then she was out past the fires and only emptiness lay before her. She paused, sensed most of the people were behind her, either enjoying the party, seeking a partner or seeking a place to take that partner.

She thought a moment. Most people would be avoiding the main field, that being where the bridal couple had officially retired to. She also didn't want the openness of the other fields, knowing from numerous rejected offers that they, too, would be occupied. The woods closest to the manor would be full, as would the maze. She could just have told Cipín to take her home, but the shillelagh would have taken her the most direct and safest route and, while physically safe, that route would be a mine field of lovers, which would only compound her problem. So she simply asked her to guide her away from people.

To the river, she thought suddenly. It was not a common haunt for trysts, and it eventually trickled around through the bottom of her own little orchard. Deciding it was the safest bet, she followed Cipín's guidance in that direction, not stopping until she heard the rushing water and nothing else.

She wandered up the bank, feeling her way through the trees carefully until she found a place she could rest; a tree broad enough to support her. She leaned back against it, closing her eyes, trying to get her body back under her own control. It wasn't listening. In fact, it seemed to be getting worse. This was torture.

She threw her head back against the tree, grabbing hold of the nearest branch, her breathing coming in ragged gasps. She heard a splash from a fish jumping nearby and it reminded her that it was only just May and the water would be terribly cold.

She pushed herself off from the tree, ready to plunge into the water, not knowing or caring at the moment how deep or fast it was here. There was the rush of feathers against her cheek and then a cold arm around her waist, pulling her back. She started to call Cipín to her when she was crushed against a cool chest and a strongly beating heart and the intoxicating fragrance of fresh snow and earth, and clung to him instead.

There was a rumble in his chest that took her a moment to decipher as quiet laughter. "Yer supposed to wait 'til I tell ye t' 'hie thee to a nunnery' afore ye throw yerself t' th' river."

She looked up at him, gasped as the sensations continued to get worse. "Oh God, not now!" Her fingers tightened on the fabric of his vest. "It... it... I can't take it any more."

The light died out of his eyes as he looked her over, concern taking precedence over mirth. He ran his hand lightly across her cheek, down her throat, over the taut fabric of her bodice and she moaned, biting it back. Instead of making matters worse, An was surprised to discover his touch, while not lessening it, made it bearable. It was the promise of something other than frustration. She began to relax into his caress.

Without another word, Jonny collected Cipín from the tree and swept An into his arms, carrying her further down the river, deeper into the woods. Intermittently he would kiss her, or some part of her, when the force of desire threatened to become too much again. After crossing the river via stepping stones and a fallen tree, he stopped, dropping the shillelagh out of the way and laid her down in a mossy hollow as the mists began to rise around them.

The sliver of a moon was beginning to peer down through the trees when An was finally able to stir. She opened her eyes, saw the bank of mist thick around them. Beside her head lay Cipín with her snow rose twined around it. It was looking less wilted now, more its original self. She was aware she was lying on a bed of thick, soft moss. Her head was pillowed upon an arm that was not hers, and a body, as naked as her own, lay wrapped around her. A blanket of snow was draped across her chest and arms and she was vaguely aware of her dress covering her legs.

As she stirred, the arm pulled her in tighter and a pair of cool lips pressed a soft, slow kiss to the arch of her shoulder. She moaned, melted back against him. He only nibbled a little, then she felt the slow, silky draw of his hair across her breast and rolled onto her back to look up at him. He lifted his head to peer down at her from beneath the curtain of white. She smiled, sighed languidly.

"I..." she breathed. "I'm not complainin' in th' slightest about what happened because of it. I want *that* in th' open right off."

"Mmhmm," he prompted, his lips brushing, feather light, against the ridge of her collarbone.

"But... what th' hell happened t' me? What'd that woman do?" She gasped as his fingers moved against a sensitive spot.

He chuckled, the sound vibrating against her already sensitive skin. "Apparently she pushed th' self-destruct button on a century an' a half of sexual repression."

She growled, not wanting him to stop but wanting to have answers. He paused, looked into her eyes and sighed, drawing back enough to have the conversation more comfortably while keeping her accessible. "She's a succubus, An. It's what she does."

An frowned. "I thought she were a djinni. She's subject t' th' seal..."

He nodded, his fingers lightly tracing unfathomable patterns across her belly. "Aye. But she is a succubus first an' foremost. She just happens to *look* like djinn. And because function follows form There... she *is* a djinni as well. What she *did*, and she feels terrible about, by th' by," he added, "was connect t' that part of Solitaire which is also succubus-like, an' used it to cast a net o'er th' four of ye. She thought that's what they were tryin; to do, awaken ye for th' Bealtaine rites. She just wanted to help. She were as shocked as they by yer reaction. But then, she had no *idea* what it was she'd be waking up in ye," he chuckled.

An tried to concentrate, to ignore the cool fingertips playing her bare skin like harp strings. "Would... it have affected me at all if we... hadn't... last night..." she squirmed.

He smiled, hummed again, knowing how the vibration affected her. "Likely it might'a been worse. You might'a had absolutely no idea what to do about it. I might'a had my hands full..."

She reached over and slapped the arm she could reach, "Tis incorrigible, is what ye are, Jonny," she snarled.

He groaned, which turned quickly into a growl, slipping out from behind her and pressing her deeper into the moss. "I am very encouragable, madam. Especially if ye do insist on hittin' me like that." His voice had grown husky, deep with threat.

She froze. He lowered his head to her throat, rumbled near her ear, holding most of his body up off of her. "Sometimes a man does like a bit of a fight."

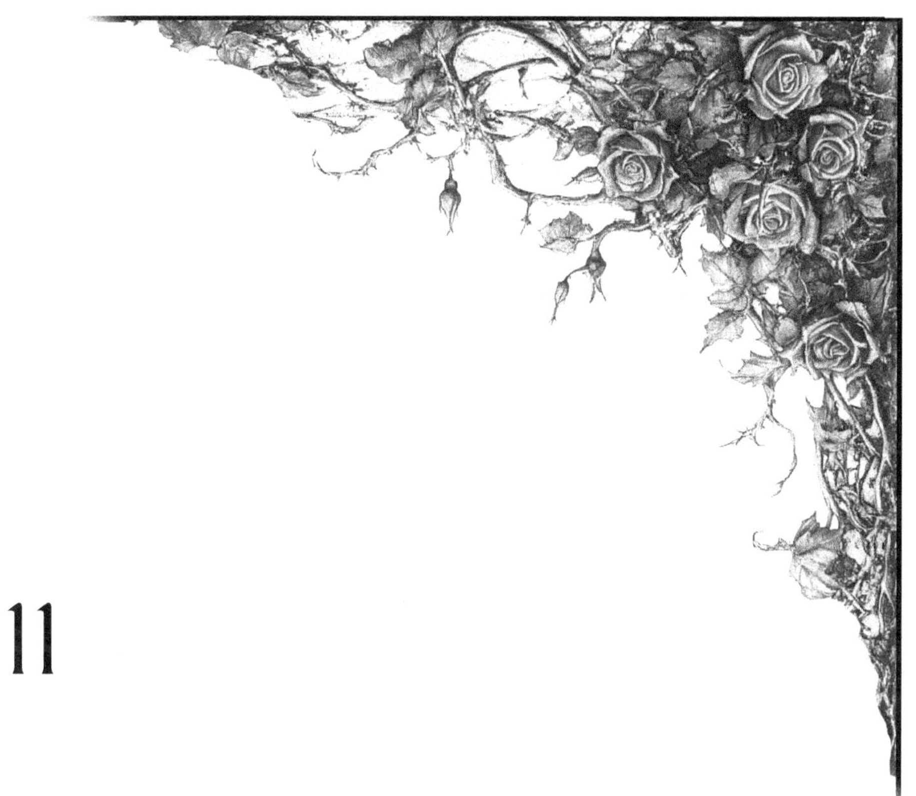

11

The events of Bealtaine had an interesting effect on the Rest as a whole. There were the expected pairings: Raven and Patches were inseparable, always being caught out in corners, cooing over each other; Liam and Penny posted their banns the day Liberty and Skye returned from their honeymoon. While pairings that had seemed fairly inevitable appeared to evaporate into thin air. Ian was showing no further interest in Solitaire, though he responded enough when she approached. The only person who seemed interesting in chasing her was Mikey, and he was pretty steadfast.

Prior, Serenity had been spending a great deal of time with Casper Torres, but lately she had been at the Hedge Gate more than Courtz, and a gentleman fresh from the Underdelve was captivated by her light. Leila was seen often with the twins, Roulet especially. Whenever she was not with Sori, Roulet was with Leila.

As An had told Aislynn, Jonny wasn't around all the time. He would disappear for days and then turn up on her window sill one night. Just as often she would wake as he flew out, leaving some flower or another on the sill. The Russians grew quiet in the wake of what was being called the May Day Massacres, even though only five people had died. Four of them had been at the hands of their own bomb. They lost a lot of their businesses though. The first two weeks of May saw a flurry of rather successful raids against the hard drug suppliers and dealers, and some of the loan sharks were convicted of racketeering and extortion. With only a few brawls and a drunk and disorderly to mar the O'Keefe's otherwise squeaky clean record.

Life returned to what passed for normal.

Elizabeth got out of school and An managed, with a little help from Ian and the lawyer, to convince the Tallows to take a well deserved second honeymoon cruise and to send Elizabeth out to the Rest for a few weeks of 'camp'. An had kept her mouth shut for most of the sales pitch, stoically not allowing her pain and shortness of breath to show. When they had asked her what she thought of the whole deal, An had to answer carefully.

"I have every confidence that your daughter will be safe and happy there and learn valuable skills and life lessons. And, I shall not be far away. There are children her own age whom she already knows."

In the end it was Elizabeth's begging that cinched it.

That Thursday night Skye drove the Tallows to the airport so that Elizabeth could say goodbye, and then promptly drove the two of them to the warehouse and into the waiting magical shortcut to the manor. Elizabeth was ecstatic, and so full of energy she was giving off bursts of random magical effects everywhere she went. Sean happily took over, taking her out for some magical exercises to get her back under control before letting her mix with the other kids also off for the summer. Elizabeth was set up in An's old room at the manor and Bethany and her little sister, Mary, were in the room next door, so she didn't mind being so far from her governess.

An watched her running off after her friends one afternoon while sitting on the Veranda with Ian and sighed. "I wish we could manage this fer a month instead of just a couple weeks. She needs this. Th' only kids on her block any where near her age are only interested in older boys and trouble."

He chuckled. "Oh... I've got plans," he said enigmatically. "They don't realize how badly they've needed this holiday. They've spent so much of themselves tryin' t' deal with Elizabeth's eccentricities... they've had no time fer themselves. Yeh've done them a wonder, An. Thank yeh."

She blushed. "Oh, glad t' help, t' be of some use. I think I'd have ...wasted away t' nothin' I didn't find somethin'."

"Yeh were startin' t' slip inta one o' them infernal Celtic black moods, aye," he laughed. "But we got yeh sorted."

"And ye?" she asked, turning the tables on him. "How are ye farin' yerself, uncail?"

He turned, watching something in the distance. "I'm farin'. My people are hale and hardy; my daughter's happily wed; my enemies, fer th' moment: cowed. My fields are planted and promisin' a surplus this year. My flocks quicken ev'n so... Life is good." He caught her looking at him, giving him that 'you know that's not what I mean' look. He sighed, granted her a half smile. "My happiness lies in them," he said, gesturing out to the Rest. He sat down on the rail, leaning back against a post, propping one foot up on the rail with him.

"Now what would ye say to me were I t' evade that question were ye th' one askin'?" she said, quirking an eyebrow.

He regarded her carefully. "That'd be a different matter, yeh see. In yer case I wouldn't be asking that question, ...not any more." She stiffened ever so slightly, but he caught it and laughed. "I kin smell yeh on 'im," he smiled, then sobered. "I'll tell yeh what yer brother'd tell yeh, only I'll be more politic. Be careful and sure of what yeh want and what yer willin' t' put up wit'."

She leaned on the rail, staring out over the green, finding wind-shredded remnants of glamoured Bealtaine decorations on the top of the bandstand and watching them lure birds for nesting material. "As folk keep reminding me, I'm a Celtic woman. He can take what lovers he likes and I can have mine. I hold no promise over him."

"But yeh want one," he said softly. She looked sharply at him. He held up his hand in surrender. "Yer a woman grown an' yeh know yer own mind. Jest be careful. So many ways this can go wrong."

She shrugged. "Then I'll move on and accept that I had something beautiful in my life for a while," she gave him a reassuring smile before stepping off the veranda and walking home.

Friday afternoon, An went to the Tallows' to check on the place. Everything seemed fine, though there was evidence that someone had tampered with some of the gnomes. Though it couldn't have been anything but mortal agency. Anything else and they would have gone off. In a summery mood, even though the heat was nigh awful, An went down to the shops by Courtz looking for interesting things for gifts.

One of the shops Elizabeth's mother had been so enamoured of had a selection of hand-made kites. She bought several of them with the aid of the shop-keeper who helped her feel out their edges without getting tangled in the works and described each one to her in vivid detail. She carried her bag full of kites down to the creamery, with rainbow ribbons fluttering from the bag. She got herself an ice cream to cool down and happily shared with her 'monkey'.

By the time An headed into Courtz, she was humming a tune that had been stuck in her head all day thanks to Elizabeth and her laptop movies. She saw Mikey and Skye playing a round of darts as she came through the game room. She stepped up to them. "Ye boys alone?"

"For the moment," Mikey laughed. "I'm just letting Skye kick my ass before I have to head down and open Depravity. How are ye this evening?"

"Oh, right fair enough," she hummed, stepping up to Skye and taking a dart from him. She found the toe line nicked into the floor with the tip of her shoe and turned slowly in place until Aislynn said to stop. She threw the dart, landing it just off centre, tossed them a little wave and headed into the main bar, still humming.

Skye just stood there, stunned, and not by her throw. "Did ya…" he stammered, looking at Mikey, then back after his sister. "Dae ya… know thon melody?"

It wasn't her usual. He and the girls had practically memorized 'Red Is The Rose' because of the vampricks, and An hummed it all the time. That wasn't 'Red Is the Rose'. He decided to follow her.

An went up to the bar and set her bag on it, smiling at the person she could hear setting up behind it. "Brad?" she asked.

The man chuckled. "Yes, Miss O'Keefe. Can I get you something? I'd offer you food but… Chef's in a tizzy today for some reason and I wouldn't call anything coming out of the kitchen edible."

She arched an eyebrow at that, "Hmm, just an Irish Mist then."

"Comin' up!"

She could hear the clinking of glass and continued humming. She felt Skye's presence before she saw him in the mirror. "Brother dear, be a love and put this upstairs fer me?"

He paused, scowling. He looked in the bag, taking it down from the bar. "What are ye singin'?"

"Am I not allowed t' learn new songs?"

"Thon's no' new. Thon's… familiar somehoo."

She tipped her head as she thanked Brad for her drink, taking a sip of the sweet, fiery liquor before she answered. "Just about everythin' is new t' me, Skye." She watched his lip tighten as he looked for a counter-argument. "It's something Elizabeth's been watchin' and it's stuck in my head. 'Tis soothin'."

"It soonds loike a love song," he accused.

She frowned, "And what's wrong with that? I found it pretty."

Brad hummed a couple of bars, supplied a piece of the lyric, "Yeah, I know that one, 'So This Is Love'. It's from Cinderella."

She lifted a finger from her glass at that. "That's it. She's been watchin' it on repeat last couple days. And ye know how she is… she finds somethin' she likes she just *has* to share it. Whether I understand it or no."

Skye found he couldn't argue with the explanation, but ...there was something more going on. Grumbling, he headed upstairs, opened the door to her cottage and set the bag on the floor inside. He paused before closing it back, addressed the room at large, "Ah dinnae suppose ya'd tell me whit's goan on?"

The house remained silent and dark. He growled. "Foine." And slammed the door.

When he came downstairs An was already at her usual table, having a conversation with Ophelia, the drowned girl they had pulled from the river. He sighed and walked away, heading for the front door to finish opening up.

Ophelia was almost painfully shy, and An had to admire the will it had taken the girl to come to the club. Raven had convinced her. As the club actually opened up and people began coming in, An managed to keep the poor girl calm in spite of being surrounded by strangers. While she remembered a little of her life before, at least she remembered being taken. What bothered her was the one thing she couldn't remember, her name and the face of the man she'd been standing on the docks waiting for.

Ophelia had just been married when her new husband had been shipped off to fight in the second World War. She had been standing on the docks, waiting for his ship to return when she was taken, pulled into the sea and locked in the soul cages, made into a drowned thing to serve His will until the day He had sent her to steal something from Amalthea. The poor girl still held out some hope that her husband was still alive, somewhere.

Eventually, they ordered food and drinks. An ordered a simple sandwich, but it tasted off, even though nothing in it was cooked. She could see the sandwich, as she could see most of the food that came out of that kitchen. She chalked it up to the chef being one of the Taken, just as she could see most of the drinks that Silhouette made. It made twisted sense then, that if the chef was off, so was the food.

An did not feel like singing, so did not bothering going up on stage; but she listened to those who did, and explained the practice to Ophelia.

Eventually Jonny came in. He looked like hell. His hair was in disarray, his jeans and t-shirt ripped and stained. There were sandals on his feet that had seen better days. He staggered onto the stage, only pausing long enough to tell Roulet what he wanted. He sang "Save Me" by Shinedown, his voice ragged as he pleaded for release from his addiction, but still beautiful.

Ophelia watched him, as entranced by his voice as half the audience. She frowned at his words though.

When he was done, he bowed his head for a moment, dropped the mike, and almost fell. He swayed, staggered with boneless grace, somehow, to the table, all but falling into the chair.

Concern flickered across her eyes, and she slid a cup of strong tea in front of him without looking over. Her hand brushed against the edge of his as if by accident and as she lifted her own tea to her lips she whispered to him, "I'd take them, an' ye let me."

Jonny sighed. "An' what do we replace them with? I'm just ventin' here."

"Might need to consider replacing them in any case," An said softly. She hesitated, slipped into Irish, "*I'd... offer m'self, but I don' think I'm a strong enough drug. Though I'd be willin't' try.*"

"What do you need them for?" Ophelia asked, her disapproval plain on her face.

Jonny sighed, and leaned forward, stripping off his t-shirt in a single languid motion, displaying a body covered with scars of every description: whips, blades, bullets. Most were obviously carefully and artistically placed. They did not detract from his appearance, but rather added to it. There were places where his bones had been broken and twisted up out of his skin to produce a flower-shaped scar on his flesh. The white on white scarring looked more like colourless tattoos than the detritus of battles and tortures past.

Ophelia gasped.

"This was done intentionally, so it would never completely heal. And that's just th' physical, innit? She signs Her work."

"She?" Ophelia swallowed.

"The Northerner," An said softly.

"Oh." Ophelia wavered, then stubbornly clung to her moral views on the matter. "Sometimes what you need them for goes away, but then your body has replaced the pain with the need for the pills. I'm fairly familiar with that concept," she said, taking a sip from a glass of straight vodka. "Sometimes you replace them with different pills or other addictions. Depends on what you need. Breaking yourself of the habit is of course the most admirable option, but I've never figured out how to do that. I've never resorted to... pills, though."

Jonny nodded, and pulled his shirt back on. "Aye. What I need them for *hasn't* gone away. And that's just th' physical. But I hate being dependent, so I sing about it."

She eyed him levelly. "If you really hate it, you could quit and find another way to deal with the pain. Bear in mind that I'm being a hypocrite by saying that," she sighed. "But it's an option. Weaning yourself off of your... addiction is the most painful part, and then comes learning to deal with your suffering. The emotional hurt is worse than the physical though," she added, staring into the bottom of her glass. "Either way, better a drunk than an addict."

An set her spoon down a little more loudly than she would have, trying to cover Ophelia's opinionated comment. "Ye want quit o' th' dragon, I'll nurse ye through it," she said. "But ye got t' want it. Ye want t' find a safer option. This... makes me worried."

Jonny slumped in his chair. "It still hurts. All the time. I don't think I'm strong enough to take the pain without help."

"Then let me help," she said.

Jonny snarled. "Aye, ye do help. But it's not *enough*. That's not yer fault, nor mine. It just *is*." He stood, and headed, swaying like a willow in the wind, for the front door. He stopped, seeing something in the crowd.

An excused herself from Ophelia, grabbing her shillelagh, and Aislynn hopped to her shoulder. She moved to follow Jonny, not trusting him to make it safely wherever he was going and saw what had caught his eye: Serephina, leaning against the back wall, drink in hand. She rolled off the wall like a boneless cat and slinked forward towards him, came up along side and leaned to his ear, her voice pitched so that An could hear. "I can make it stop hurting for a while. Make you forget..." she promised, her eyes locked on An and her smile was triumphant.

As much as An wanted those words to hurt, they rang true. She could, but at what cost?

Jonny seemed to be considering it. He turned to look at Serephina, caught An's reflection in the mirror: the tiny shake of her head, the minute signs she was debating interference, the pain on her face. He pulled away. "I said we're done, Sera," he growled in a low voice.

She seized his arm. "You can't handle this alone."

He pushed her off of him and turned, breezing past An with a swirl of cold air and a snowflake or two. He headed down the hall towards the kitchen and the back door. An paused long enough to give the hateful woman her most withering glare and turned to follow him.

As she came out onto the loading dock, he was just reaching the steps, stumbled. An reached out to catch him before he broke his neck and he shifted to raven form in her hands. She grabbed the rail in time to prevent her own fall as she overreached, watched him fly unsteadily away. She sank down to sit on the step, resting her head on her arm against the rail.

Just as she had decided to go back inside, perhaps to head home, a car peeled into the back lot and she could hear several men piling out. Three of them she could see. Mikey was dragging someone out of the back seat, Aiden moving to assist. Cullen climbed out of the driver's seat with something in his hand. Seeing An sitting there, he barked, "Go get my cousin!"

An jumped up, swiftly feeling her way to the door and down the hall. She stopped before she got to the main room of the club, hearing Liberty's voice in the kitchen reading Lafayette the riot act. She pushed the door open, found Liberty fairly quickly among the disaster of the half-magical kitchen. "Liberty, sorry t' interrupt but Cullen's headed upstairs with wounded."

"Oh fer FUCK's sake!" she shouted, throwing the saucer she had in her hand. Lafayette caught it. "You, go home! Yer worse than useless like this!" She turned to An as the small chef ripped off his jacket and threw down his toque. "Go tell Sil, he's either on kitchen duty tonight or th' kitchen's closed, his choice."

An nodded, continuing down the corridor to the noise of the main bar. Behind her, Liberty left the kitchen and went up the back stairs. Before she had even reached the door An heard a repeat of the epithet. From the end of the bar she saw Skye wince, knew he'd heard her.

Skye saw An and met her before she had gotten three steps from the hall. "Whoo pissed 'er aff?"

From the look on his face An knew he was worried it might have been him. "Yer off th' hook."

"Whoo's on?" he insisted as she moved around him to the bar.

"Sil," she called, waving the man to her. She noticed he still had his tail, twitching below the hem of his long apron. "Lafayette's been sent home. Ye feel like cookin', get in there. Otherwise, kitchen's closed t'night."

His blue eyes flashed. "I'd like to keep my tail attached to my ass, thank you. I'm not touching one copper pan in that kitchen." He turned back to Brad and Tori and the wait staff within hearing distance and bellowed, "Ladies and Gentlemen, due to unforeseen circumstances the kitchen is CLOSED. You can thank me later!"

"Ok, sae Lafayette," Skye surmised.

An headed up the stairs. "And Cullen. More Cullen right now."

Skye followed her.

The moment the door opened they were assaulted by the smell of wild-flowers and greenery and the sharp, coppery scent of blood. An took two steps into the room and stopped, found herself staring at Hellhound's head floating in the air in the middle of the room at about knee height.

Liberty stood up from the man on the couch, turned and saw the head. "Cullen, get that damned thing off my coffee table! Hell, get it out o' my BAR! What got inta yer fool head bringin' a head HERE?"

Skye had expected Cullen to wither in face of that assault and temper, but he stood up to her. "Yer father said if shite went south t' come here fer healin'! Ye were th' closest medic!" he roared back.

"But th' head? A HEAD, Cullen? I have *cops* what come here!"

"Fine! I'll take it and go! But ye'll have ta get th' boys home!"

Skye came to the rescue, marched down the hall to the door everyone seemed to use for everything and opened it on the manor hallway. He held it for him with mock gallantry.

Sullen, the man snatched the head from the table and went through the door. Aiden followed immediately behind. Skye slammed the door after him and Liberty put her hands to her temples.

"Skye, love, will ye fetch th' peroxide?"

He nodded, opening a door opposite the bedroom and pulling out an industrial sized brown jug full of the stuff, grabbed a rag and began cleaning the drips of blood Cullen had left behind.

Liberty turned to Mikey. "Now, will a cooler head be so kind t' tell me what th' bloody *fuck* happened?"

Mikey sank into a chair. "Somehow Cullen found out where Hellhound was going to be and set up an ambush. Bastard slipped the net. 'Course, he had those damned vampire things with him to help, but there were some Russians, too. One of 'em is what I can only describe as a Blackout."

"A shadowlin'?" Skye asked.

Mikey shook his head. "No. He were made to cause blackouts. He's like Elaroush and Roulet, electrical, except... he eats it, not makes it or becomes it. He drains the power of anything electrical. If he gets too much he can release the surplus but... otherwise he's just hard to hit. 'Cause even if ye hit him ye miss. They got up by Depravity and the bastard hit the club, drained us dry. Caused a panic and at least one of the girls broke a leg falling in the dark.

"I went out to see what the hell and ran into Cullen and his boys. I grabbed a few of mine and we chased him into that back corner between the megamart and that little strip mall. There's no outlet back there but up. Only trouble was there was plenty for the blackout to eat."

"That were when I did a stupid," groaned the voice of one of the Younger boys from the couch, Michael, An thought. "I'd wrestled one o' th' Russians into a retention pond earlier. Left th' bastard floatin'. I were soaked. Blackout were bloated so... I gave him a wee hug," he laughed, ended up coughing.

Liberty popped his shoulder. "Settle down an' let th' healin' work, ya ninny."

He oofed, wincing. "Yes, ma'am. We both got a hell o' a shock though."

"Might have to see if that Ophelia girl has any controls over water or if she's just a drowned," Mikey mumbled. "If we have to deal with that one, be helpful t' have water on our side."

"We'll have ta ask Da if we know anyone from Haggard who can. I don't think we've one at th' Rest current, but I know we did at one point," Liberty sighed. "I'd rather ye not pester Ophelia just yet."

"But I'm sneaky," came the quiet, sigh-like voice of Ophelia from behind Skye.

Everyone turned.

"That's... what I did for him. I can slip in places and out again. I often spied on his pirates... kept an eye on Hook."

"This would prefer a ranged attack, not up close, love," Liberty said. "Don't know what it'll do ta ya."

"I do, though, ...know what it'll do. I've been shocked before. If I'm watery, it just flows through. Locks me up, but then I can't let go," she shrugged. "And that serves the purpose. There was this thing called a floating freehold, whole group of the Taken who live on a ship. He's constantly at war with them, cause they're arrogant and don't pay tolls. They keep stealing His selkies. And there's the occasional Taken whaler... I've dealt with them too... I liked dealing with them." There was a gleam in her eye that was disturbing in so demure a woman. She was staring off into nothingness and there was a look of sadistic glee on her face. Just as suddenly she looked up, all mouse again. "So I can probably handle the blackout, and any other electrics. ...I just don't want to fight them near salt water."

"I think that can be arranged," Mikey said. "Thank ye."

Liberty took a deep breath, let Skye come up and wrap himself around her. "So explain t' me why I had a head on my coffee table?"

"I don't know." Mikey shrugged. "Cullen chopped it off, the rest of the idiots fled and we collected our wounded. Solitaire isn't at Depravity right now and you were closer than the warehouse. We had to do something or John-Michael would have died. We're just lucky it weren't a gunfight. Next one might be. I had no idea he had th' head with him. I was in the back seat with John-Michael."

There was a quiet tap on the door and Tori poked her head in. "Mrs. O'Keefe," she said, eyeing the people up here. "Um... those two cops are downstairs. They're asking for you."

"Oh for fuck's sake," Liberty snapped. Skye winced. That was three times in one night. "Is anything else going to go wrong tonight?"

The door pushed open past Tori and Dukes bulled his way in. "That all depends on how this next conversation goes."

Cass apologized to Tori who just sighed and left, closing the door behind her.

Everyone in the lounge froze. An was silently grateful that Cullen had left and Skye had at least cleaned away the blood up here.

"'Cause just imagine our surprise when we answer a call of shots fired over behind the megamart and find a whole mess of blood, a few shells, a dead homeless guy and a half drowned Russian in a retention pond. Now our Russian boy claims it was the O'Keefe's, but I got the homeless guy's buddies swearing Dracula killed him and that a shadow ate the electricity."

Liberty glared at Mikey. "Thought ye said weren't no gunfight?"

"A few potshots don' qualify fer a gunfight."

Cass drew himself up and took over, even though his partner was still giving off belligerent vibes. "The forensic guys are swearing up and down someone was decapitated, but we've got no head and no body and no drag marks or real footprints. Now, we've seen some really strange shit and not just tonight." He glanced over at An and Liberty, "Pardon my French." He looked down at his partner, then back up to the people arrayed around them. "We know what you guys are. You know we know. We even have some idea of what you do. We also know, there are worse things out there than you guys."

"How do you know?" Mikey growled.

Paul crossed his arms, glaring at Mikey as if he dared him to try something. "Friend of ours on the force. He was one of you. Had to take a leave of absence. He told us quite a bit."

"Jacob," Mikey sighed.

"Detective Duffy pulled our bacon out of the fire once or twice," Cass added. "By warning us that what we were dealing with wasn't what we thought we were dealing with." He held up his hand as Mikey started to say something else, cutting off Dukes' outburst too with the same hand. "I know you have criminal connections. I personally don't care. I've seen some of the shit you guys do and the city's better for it. Doesn't change that it's illegal. Doesn't mean we won't arrest your asses we catch you at it. *However*, there's some other shit goin' on in town that is particularly nasty and if we could have a heads up once in a while? Let us know so we can come up with a plausible explanation without having to ask for it?"

"Like tonight for instance," Paul growled. "Was there or was there not a decapitated body?"

"Not one you could take to your bosses," Mikey confessed. "And all that blood... it's going to pop confusing."

"Just great," Paul snarled, turning away.

"And the homeless guy?" Cass asked.

Mikey shrugged. "We weren't there for that. Likely it *was* a vampire. A couple of them got away."

At this Paul began cussing. An blushed, looked over at Cass. "If ye gentlemen have no need of me, I would like to go home."

Paul looked her over critically. "And where were you tonight? You involved in any of this?"

Skye started to bow up, his knuckles cracking. Liberty elbowed him lightly.

"Only in that I were here when they arrived," An answered as Skye backed down, gesturing to John-Michael and the others. "I've been here since they opened t'night, as has Skye. Ye can ask Brad downstairs."

Cass looked at Paul and shook his head. "I see no reason for those not involved to remain. Except you, Miss O'Keefe," he added, looking at Liberty.

"That's Mrs. O'Keefe," she corrected. "Ya were at my bloody weddin'!"

At this point, An took her leave, slipping to the bedroom door and opening it on her cottage, closing it quietly behind her. Her package had been put in the kitchen beside the pantry and An nodded, not sure yet what she was going to do with the kites. She slipped out of her shoes, setting them beside the bench and felt the house asking if she wanted anything: a bite to eat, something to drink? Her stomach growled at that, remembering she had not really eaten. "Just a boiled egg and a bun, if you please."

She took off her shoulder bag and hung it up, knowing by the time she got to the refrigerator what she had asked for would be waiting for her. She ate quietly, shared the bit of cheese that had been added with Aislynn. She told herself there was no point in worrying about the detectives. Ian would handle it. Surely this sort of thing had occurred in the past and there *was* something special about the two men.

It began raining as she dressed for bed. She sat at the dressing table brushing out her hair. Aislynn was on the bed, preening herself, when there came a light rapping on the window. An jumped, turned, prepared to throw her brush. A white raven was on her windowsill looking forlornly in at her. She dropped the brush and rushed to let him in. He flew in, landed awkwardly in front of the fire, shook most of the water from his feathered body before shifting to man.

She fetched a towel from the cabinet and draped it over him. He looked like hell. "What happened?" she asked, drying his face with the end of the towel. Aislynn flew to the mantle and sat there, watching.

"She was there," he breathed, shivering, though An did not think it from the cold. "In my hunting lodge."

She stored that titbit away for later, tried to focus on more important things. "Let's get ye warmed up and dry."

He gave a tired laugh. "I'm always cold, Ceobhránach."

"Aye, but cold and wet is another matter." She did not permit him to argue, began peeling him out of his wet clothes. His t-shirt was hopelessly torn and tangled in his hair so she just ripped it off of him. His jeans proved to be more of a fight. The two of them ended up in a confused heap on the floor, with nothing more than his fly undone and An caught in the web of his now sadly knotted hair.

The house suggested a hot bath and she agreed, began to patiently unwind the long white strands from where they had gotten wrapped around her buttons and her fingers. "If I thought you had any wherewithal at the moment," she accused, "I would say ye did this apurpose."

His breath was close as he answered, "What makes ye think I couldn't?"

"More a wouldn't," she responded, suppressing a shiver of delight at the nearness of his mouth to her neck. "Yer runnin' from one woman, why would ye then be all that eager for me?" She finally got them freed and helped him to his feet.

He stood over her, pulling her close. "If you have t' ask, Ceobhránach... I havna schooled ye well enough yet in yer charms."

She squealed as his hands began to wander. "All right, bath first!" She all but ordered his jeans to the floor.

He stood there a second, fully naked, staring at the puddle of denim at his feet. "Useful," he said somewhat drunkenly. He touched a cold fingertip to her nose. "Cheatin'."

"Aye," she snapped, getting a firm grip on her resolve, refusing to look down. She pointed to the open door. "Bath!"

He resisted.

"If yer still in th' mood after... then ye kin... we kin... just... go!"

He laughed as she blushed, pushed him into the front room where the claw foot tub waited, steaming in front of the fire. He obediently climbed into the water as she went to get what she would need to untangle his hair. When she turned, he had sunk completely under. She panicked, reached in and grabbed a handful of hair, pulling him up. He countered by pulling her in. She shrieked and Aislynn flew in, ready to attack something. She saw what was going on and sighed, going back into the bedroom to sulk, slamming the door behind her.

An began to scold him, trying to get back out of the tub without crushing something valuable. He kissed her to silence her. His hands were insistent and she realized that he needed this more than standard nursing, and gave in.

The water was still hot an hour later, when An was finally allowed to climb out and dry off. Jonny remained in the tub, sipping the doctored coffee that had appeared on the side table. Wearing a fresh nightdress, she knelt at the head of the tub, carefully combing the tangles and debris out of his snow white hair. He leaned back, resting his neck on the curved lip of the tub and let her.

"Do ye want to talk about it?" she asked after a while.

"No."

She heaved a tiny, quiet sigh, sitting on her disappointment and continued to run the comb through his hair, ignoring the mess her own was in.

"But I will," he finished. "I need ta... ta ask..." As her hand reached the top of his head, he reached back and gently took it, drawing her beside him so that he could see her to talk. She rest her arm on the edge of the tub, and her cheek against that, watching as he played with her fingers with his long, tanned ones. "Might I ...impose fer a few days?"

"As long as ye like," she smiled softly.

"Yer brother..."

"'Tis *my* house."

He nodded, sinking back, relieved.

"Ye've not told me why," she whispered.

"Serephina."

"I gathered."

He watched her for a moment. "This is a mistake, Ceobhránach. I shouldna've come here."

"Nonsense. My hospitality is as good as Ian's. Hell, my hospitality *is* Ian's." She let him brood a moment more before prompting, "What did she do?"

"Stalked me. I left Courtz and went home. Somehow she was there afore me."

"Ye didna likely fly straight," she said ruefully. "Ye were..."

"Nodding," he sighed. "Still am. Though 'tis wearing through..." His fingers tightened on hers, a little painfully. He did not notice and she did not let him. "She were in my house. On my bed. I told her t' get out and she accused me o' breakin' faith."

He slipped his fingers from hers, toyed with the they'd white marks left behind as if he had no clue how they had come there. "I told her she were th' one t' break that: after that first time, I told her she ever used th' magic on me again we were done. She did it anyway. I reminded her o' that. She flew into a rage and reminded me what she'd suffered fer me. She extolled everythin' She'd had done t' her 'cause she let herself get caught again t' give me th' chance fer escape."

An gave a quiet huff. "Well that'sna gonna work: usin' obligation on ye."

He stroked her hair, began idly working out the damp tangles that he had put in it. He smiled softly. "Aye. She flew into a rage. Broke..." he choked on the words.

Her eyes widened. "Yer harp?"

He breathed softly. "Thankfully, no. That were safe. 'Tis in the chest, and she can't open that. The others though... dinna fare so well."

"I'm sure we can repair them, or get ye new," she suggested.

"Not the point. She reacted as She taught her to: when denied, hurt them. I flew off. ...I'd just as soon not go back fer a while."

She lightly kissed his palm. "So long as ye need. An' no demands made."

"Yer too good fer a poor bastard like me."

She smiled. "That remains t' be seen. So far as I can tell yer th' only one interested who wants more than just t' find out what I'm like in bed."

He chuckled. "An' I'm th' only one who knows."

She kissed the fingertips. "And likely to remain so."

"Now that's hardly fair to you."

"My choice, now isna it?" She got off the floor, held up a towel.

He stood, took the towel from her and tossed it aside with a gleam in his eye.

Skye rose late. Liberty was already up and had left him breakfast and a note. She had gone up to the main house to confer with her father and Cullen and he really didn't want to get involved in that. Not right now. If he was there he might be tempted to punch Cullen's lights out and that would be disastrous. He dressed, wolfed down his breakfast and left the house, headed for the Mead Hall to get ready for the afternoon training sessions.

As he passed An's cottage, he noticed Aislynn in the front garden, hunting in the thick grass. He smiled and waved to her. She merely flicked her wing in his direction. This brought to mind that An had not been in for lessons in a bit. He stopped at the gate. "Oi, Aislynn, m' sister I' th' back garden?"

"Nope."

He frowned, reached over the gate and unlatched it, letting himself in. "Aff wit' Elizabet'?" he asked, becoming concerned. Her habit of the last few weeks had been tending to the garden in the mornings, then spending time with Elizabeth, especially Saturdays. After a rain like last night, she always had plenty to do outside.

"Nope." Aislynn pounced, managing to snag the mole she had been stalking. She carried it's squirming body around the side of the house to An's bedroom window where another vamprick was growing. She tossed the mole into the pale yellow blooms and watched them from a safe distance as they impaled the small creature and began to blush. Aislynn made a face, noticed Skye about to knock on the door. "*I wouldn't do that, were I you.*"

He paused. "Why th' hell no'? She ill?"

"No. She had a... late night," she offered, flying slowly back to the front garden and began checking the raspberry canes for bad bugs. She stopped to watch a ladybug crawling across a leaf.

"Sae did ah, and ah'm oop." He was beginning to get suspicious. There were any number of reasons she might be still abed and none of them boded well. She had only recently recovered from their trip to the Battery, maybe she was having a relapse. He stared at the door, then at the dragon. The dragon was unconcerned, bored even. And outwith the cottage. Skye's mind slipped into a place he didn't want it to go and began pounding on the door, bellowing her name.

An groaned. She tried to ignore the banging, not willing to have him ruin what had been a perfectly beautiful night. She looked over at Jonny, who seemed to be resting peacefully. She was not going to let Skye spoil that. Telling the house to muffle the sound, she slipped from the bed and grabbed the nightdress on the bedpost, pulling on her dressing gown as she closed the bedroom door behind her. She crossed the cottage, seized hold of the knob and pulled the door open, scowling at him. "What th' devil do ye want, Skye?"

"Ah..." he stopped, pulling back his hand, a little taken aback at the suddenness of the open door. Before he could change what he was going to say, she came out on the step and closed it behind her, and little things began to register. She was in her nightdress at ten am. Her hair was mussed, and not in the braid she usually slept in. And she was deliberately keeping him out of the house.

He leaned in, took a deep breath. He didn't notice anything striking; but then, he didn't have a beast's senses and he didn't smell anything recent or obvious on her like cologne, but that didn't mean nothing had happened. And he was suddenly very certain something had.

He glared, growled, "Ah'll kill 'im," tried to move past her.

She placed a hand on either side of the door frame and said very sternly, "Ye'll do no such thing."

"He took advantage o' ya, An," he began. "Jest loike Serephina seid he wo..."

An punched him. Hard. Skye's head rocked and, for a second, he saw stars.

"Never say that woman's name in m' presence again, not like that. An' fer th' record, if anyone took advantage o' anyone it were me. I pushed him when he were vulnerable."

He rubbed his jaw, realized the depth of her conviction by how hard she had hit him. "But ya were...."

"Savin' m'self fer what exactly?" she roared. "Marriage? Hah! That'll never happen, Skye. That's not fer th' like o' me. I've learned t' take what I can get." He stepped back as she came forward. "Don't I deserve a wee dram o' happiness? A modicum of pleasure to warm my otherwise cold life? 'Tis a new world, Skye, new rules! Well, I'm choosin' t' live my life by older ones than my own."

"But why him? He'll jest hurt ya."

"I know. He's warned me. But I don't care, Skye. He's th' only man what's ever made me want... that! Who saw something even I can't, something beyond th'... beyond wanting a 'tumble wi' teacher'! So, why can't I have that, Skye? Tell me!"

He was at a loss. He could not explain his mistrust, his dislike. He was grasping at straws. "Acause he's no' guid enouch fer ya! He's a womanizin' drug addict whoo'll only drag ye doon wi' him!"

"He's a man in need. And he actually wants me. For me. He's tried t' protect me, e'en from himself. He needs lookin' after."

He threw up his hands. "Why is it every woman thinks she's th' ane ta change a rotten man?"

"Liberty thought ye were worth somethin'," she snapped. He stopped as if he'd been slapped. "Aye, *some* women are drawn t' broken men, 'cause they see what they could be and want t' be th' one t' mend them: t' kiss th' frog and reveal th' prince. I've got no illusions left, Skye. I've got my hands full tryin' t' convince him he's worth lovin'. I don't want t' have t' fight ye, too."

As she approached him, her demeanour changed, became softer. He stopped backing away, though his jaw was tight as she cupped his face. "I were th' one who decided. I seduced him. I had to convince him I wouldn't regret it in th' mornin'."

"I'twere Bealtaine, weren't it?"

She laughed, dropped her hand. "The night before actual. If ye must know."

He flushed as he realized she had lost her virginity before he had. Then he darkened, remembering what had happened that night. "Whan we raided th' hen party."

"Aye. He carried me off and stole a kiss, nothing more. *I* pushed."

He turned away, held up his hand, not wanting to hear any more. An watched him walk away.

Aislynn peeked out from under the hem of her nightdress, and snorted, "*I warned him.*"

12

The next week was blissful for An. Life around the cottage was almost domestic perfection. Jonny wasn't always around, at least after that first day. He had things to do, as did she. Nor did they make love every night, which she understood and did not need. To be wrapped in his embrace was more than enough for her.

The second night he had gone back and rescued his harp. He also brought a guitar and one fiddle which was the least damaged and set about trying to repair them. That night had taken a lot of soothing, for there is no deeper way to hurt a bard than to ravage the instruments of his trade.

Much to Aislynn's frustration, An taught him how to bypass the roses and how to open the cottage door from anywhere.

Elizabeth was having the time of her life, riding horses, swimming, playing with kids roughly her own age, learning more magic than she had in the last year, now that they could work without time limits on more complex things. Sean helped her work on her own personal wards, ways of protecting herself. He also got her to help him with the wards that were on the Rest itself, showing her how they were made, how the faery magic blended with their own more hermetic methods, how to bolster or unravel it.

"For ye see," he told her, "knowin' how a thing can be unmade helps ye t' fix it so it can't be. If something is made to last, always check to see how it can be broken. Ye can see it if ye look right. Then, just keep an eye on the 'tails', those weak links. A'course, if it's something someone is going to try to undo, you could always weave in an alarm and leave a false weak point, just a little tail sticking out that they'll find if they look fer it, and if they pull it... boom! Alarms go off, trap closes, they're caught!"

Elizabeth had a long conversation with her parents over the phone near the end of her original two weeks. It seems they had an opportunity to do a little more travelling with a couple they had met and wanted to know if she was OK with it. Elizabeth had a hard time not crowing her joy and giggling. She told them she was fine, staying here was perfectly cool with everybody, that this was more of a family place than a camp anyway and they wanted her to stay the whole summer. That got tabled immediately. "We want to spend some time with you too, you know. Thought when we got back we might... sneak off to Orlando one weekend?"

"Uhhuh," she shook her head. "Tampa. I wanna try Busch Gardens."

George laughed. "Ok, kiddo, we'll talk about it."

When she got off the phone, she had gone to find her governess. It was only late afternoon, so she ran off down to the cottage. The gate opened for her. She giggled, stopped herself from thanking it. She ran up the path to the door and it too opened without asking. An was sitting in her chair before the fire, working on her lace and waved her over. There was a second chair Elizabeth had not remembered being there and she could not see who was in it from the door, but she could hear soft music coming from it. The cottage was blissfully cool in spite of the growing heat outside, cold enough for the fire to be needed. As she came around at An's urging, she saw that it was the white-haired bard tuning a newly repaired guitar.

She blushed a little and bobbed a curtsey. "Afternoon, Mr. Sorrow."

There was a glint in his eye as he nodded. "Miss Tallow," he said with equal formality.

An drew over a footstool for Elizabeth to sit. "What is it, love?" she asked. "Would ye like somethin'?"

She shook her golden head. "No, thank you. Supper's not long from now and Mrs. Shannon would be awful upset I spoil my appetite."

An noticed that the longer she remained here, the more an Irish lilt began to creep into her voice. "At least ye have more of one here," An sighed, pleased with the changes in the girl.

"'Tis all that healthful exercise," Jonny said softly.

"And th' magic," Elizabeth added. "Sean said the more I work, the more I need, though I'll need different things than when I'm just being active."

"Well, those are the things he's supposed t' be teachin' ye." An smiled. "But ye didn't run all the way out here an hour afore supper t' talk of that."

"No," she confessed, "I talked with dad today. They're... going somewhere with some new friends. I can stay another week or so."

"Ye don't seem too excited."

She sighed. "I am. I was... I love it here but... I hate that I can't tell them what I'm really doing here, that we have to ...trick them into letting me come. I want to show them what I can really do and..."

She leaned over and set her head on An's knee and An gently stroked her hair. "It's all right, poppet."

"Wantin' their approval is one thing, Elizabeth," Jonny said. "Their protection another. If they know and ye grow careless? Others not so receptive to what ye are find out? Their ignorance is a layer of protection not to be lightly thrown away."

"I know it's hard, my dear," An crooned. "But he's right. Maybe one day... but that day's a bit away." She looked over at him. "What say we have supper up at the manor tonight?" she asked him.

He tipped his head, half shrug, half agreement. "I'll be wantin' a word with th' chief in any case."

An put away her lace and rose, slipping into a pair of sandals waiting by the back door. Jonny slung the guitar on his back and the three of them walked down through the garden towards the wood with Aislynn riding Elizabeth's shoulders, tickling her with her tail.

Mid-summer was fast approaching and there was a great deal of speculation as to who was going to be the Holly King this year. No one seemed to know, but there were several who would not even involve themselves in the conversations. An found this significant and decided not to worry about it. That meant that a decision had been made and was just a secret for now. It should prove great fun come Mid-summer.

June brought another spate of unbearable weather, and An knew it was only going to get worse. She finally acquiesced to Liberty and Roulet's attempts to get her into cooler clothing, and added several short-sleeved sundresses to her wardrobe. They were still very modest and while shorter than she would have liked, they were as close as she was going to concede to the season.

While she spent more time at the Rest than she had been of late, and frequented the Hedge Gate, she still went to Courtz every Wednesday and Friday night. It was one such Wednesday night, not long after the Hellhound incident that Liberty came over to An's table, smiling.

An looked at her suspiciously as she just sat there, elbow on the table and one hand gracefully propping up her cheek. "What?"

"Nothin'," she chirped, trying to hide her glee.

An's eyes narrowed. "Liar," she fenced. "What are ye up to?"

Liberty gave her an expression of complete innocence. "I'm not th' one what's up t' sommat, I hear."

An's eyes swirled as her jaw tightened. "An' who might've been talkin'?"

Liberty relaxed, smiling, patted An's hand. "Oh, don't ya sweat, love, yar not gossip fodder yet. Th' little bird what I've been chattin' with needed a great deal o' calmin' t'other day."

She began to blush. "He told ye," she groaned.

"More like he ranted, and it's not like I'd'a given him much choice either way." She reached out and brushed a thumb over An's blushing cheek. "Ya've no worries, dear. I'm thrilled. Aye, there were safer choices," she conceded, drawing back and sipping the drink she had brought with her, "more steadfast. But there's nothin' like experience fer a girl's first, and he has plenty o' that, so I hear."

An blushed more furiously, studying the bottom of her own, nearly empty glass. "I've... no complaints."

"I'll just bet ya do." An looked up, frowning. Liberty grinned. "He's not around nearly enough."

That broke the tension and both women laughed. "He's gone back to his own place, aye. Though he still... noses about my garden once in a while."

Liberty nodded. "I thought I saw raven feathers about a bit more than usual. Explained why Skye was so out o' sorts."

"He still bent?" she winced.

Liberty sighed. "I got him calmed down. I had ta explain life ta th' lummox, but in th' end he realized he has no say in th' matter."

An laughed, "I'll bet that took some doin'."

"A wee bit," Liberty shrugged. "As long as he sees ya happy, he'll keep his nose out."

"I am content with what I kin get."

"We all should be so lucky."

An looked up. "Are ye not?"

"Oh, aye," she smiled. "*I* am. But a lot aren't." She glanced towards the bar, the gleam in her eye unkind. "What they have is never enough."

An turned to look, fearing Serephina had put in another appearance. But it was Serenity, snuggled up to a stone-like man sparking with electricity, kissing him and giggling as her hair started to stand on end. "I thought she were dating th' detective?"

"She is."

An glanced back, "Oh."

Liberty tore her eyes from the pair at the bar and set her hand on An's, gave them a squeeze. "I'm happy for ya. I really am, even if yar brother is too much of a Neandert'al ta be." An laughed. "Eventually, he will be too." She rose, gave An a kiss on her forehead and disappeared into the crowd to mingle.

She sat there for a bit, ordered a pot of tea when a waitress came over to check on her. After listening to two or three really bad poems, An got up and found her way to the stage herself. She was a little nervous at first, but she was getting used to it. The poem she intended to recite she knew by heart. She had written it not that long ago. Her fingers drifted to the the rose in her hair, took comfort from the cold and sharp. She cleared her throat and began, closing her eyes, unable to see most of her audience anyway.

> "ICE ROSES
> The rose
> As sharp as your love
> As biting
> Pleasure because of pain
> The softness of the razor edge
> Bringing forth precious blood
> Mine, yours
> What you will spill for me
> Theirs, ours
> The beauty and peace of the snow
> Pristine, perfect
> The flawed promise of future pain
> Roses die
> Love hurts
> Faith kills
> Still, we smell the flowers
> Chase our hearts
> Trust others
> We are warned."

The room was quiet as she stepped back from the microphone. Her voice had carried even without it, as haunting as her singing, touching different chords in different members of the audience. It wasn't until she had moved towards the stairs that the spell was broken and people applauded. Someone standing at the stage awaiting their turn took her hand and guided her down, whispered how beautiful her poem had been. She blushed, thanked him and slipped back to her table, following her normal route even though there was no doubt a faster way.

As she moved around a gentleman blocking her path, she saw Jonny sitting at the table. She felt the blush that had just begun to fade start to return as he held out her chair for her. As she took her seat, she felt for the tea she could smell and was surprised to find her cup already poured. She whispered a quiet thank you and sipped. He only smiled sadly at her, saying nothing.

They sat, watching the various poets and singers trying out their new material. Some of them were very good. Others... questionable. A few even recited classics. One trio of young women got up and did the witches from Macbeth, getting a surprisingly enthusiastic response for the crowd. About halfway through a young man's rather lewd comedy bit, An felt a horrible buzzing at her hip.

Her hand flew to her bag. She had no pockets in this dress, so had to rely on her little shoulder pouch. She pulled out her phone at first, then realized that was not what was buzzing. Jonny looked over at her panic, set down his ale. "*What is it?*" he asked softly.

"Elizabeth's," she breathed, staring at the ugly little gnome glowing in her palm. "Somethin's... I've got to..." she rose, tossing it into her bag and grabbing Cipín. Aislynn jumped to her shoulder, resisting the urge to just take flight across the bar. Before she had taken two steps, Jonny had her arm and was guiding her a different way, around people and to the staircase.

The house was dark as they stepped from her little closet into the rarely-used garret room. They crept to the attic door, pausing to listen. The house was silent as well. They opened the door and slipped on silent feet to the second floor where An went into to

Elizabeth's room. Crossing to the window, she looked around for something she could see. There was a man on the lawn, looking up at the house. Their eyes met and An felt something unpleasant roll down her spine. She tightened her grip on Cipín and turned from the window, moving past Jonny without a word and headed to the front door.

He did not try to stop her, merely shifting to Raven form and landing on her shoulder. Aislynn preferred a different approach, making herself into a small black cat and keeping to the shadows. An undid the locks on the front door and commanded the door to open itself. She let herself be seen standing there in the open frame, using every magical tool at her disposal to intimidate this dark stranger standing in the middle of the walk.

She just stood there, glaring, letting him take in whatever details he could. She called the mists to her, for the first time with intent, and seemed to float out onto the top step with it. She held Cipín in front of her in a loose grip, easily shifted to use whichever end she felt necessary. She felt the temperature around her drop, a light wind lifting the edges of her hair and noticed the frost beginning to creep down the rail.

The figure stood there, silent, measuring her. They were two Samurai on a one man bridge, eyeing each other to determine who would win the fight if it came to one. In the end it was the figure which spoke first. "Who are you, and why are you in this place?" His voice was soft, not oft used and carried the potential ability to force her answer.

"It is you who trespass," she said flatly, her accent clipped and formal, no trace of her soft Irish lilt. Her tone was hard.

There came the barest indication of a nod. "The house looked abandoned."

"It is not."

"So I see. And have you done something with the rightful residents?"

The question caught her off guard, but the only outward indication she gave was the tiniest shift of an eyebrow. "They remain the rightful residents. I remain their guardian."

He glanced aside, eyes flicking to one or two of the hidden gnomes. "Not your handiwork," he commented casually.

"No. But then I do not work alone. I will ask you once more, who you are and why you are here."

"My name is …well, I am going by Brink these days." Truth. "I am checking on a rumour."

"What rumour?"

He tilted his head, looked long and hard at the Raven on her shoulder and the cat skulking at the base of the steps. "Perhaps we can dispense with the theatrics, Miss Ó hAnnáin, and speak as four people with the same interest?"

The name made her stagger. There was nothing but truth in his words. There was no question the name was hers. She reeled back, found herself steadied by cold hands as Jonny shifted. "How…" she choked. "Do you know…"

He shrugged, relaxing his stance and lit up a cigarette. "I've read The Book. Sometimes I just remember." His eyebrow quirked up at Jonny, "And before you ask, no. That's… too muddy a puddle." There was something else in his eye as he looked the two of them over, but he said nothing about it. "So, can we discuss where the young lady who's supposed to live here is? And what we can do to improve these defences?"

An studied him. He looked like one of the Taken, but not. There was something else about him that, while it resonated like the magic of the fey, wasn't. Or it was just a purer form of it. "What… are ye," she breathed, and was immediately appalled by her rudeness.

He chuckled, shrugged out of his trench. A pair of palely grey wings stretched from his back, gave a few test flaps as they readjusted. "Ah, that feels better anyway. The name's Hafkiel. I'm an earthbound angel."

Jonny looked down at An, looking for her tiny nod that told him the man was telling the truth. "Per…perhaps we should retire t' th' back patio fer a chat," she managed.

The angel nodded, picking up his trench and slinging it over his shoulder as An managed the steps and led the way around back.

She lit the small mosquito candle on the patio table for a little light and gestured for Brink to take which seat pleased him. He chose a small bench. An sank into a chair and Aislynn immediately curled up around her neck.

"I apologize for shocking you, Miss..."

She held up her hand. "O'Keefe, please. I... whatever my name may have been... I am An Ceobhrán O'Keefe now. And true names are..."

"Power, yes," he nodded, understanding. "As I was saying, I had thought the house empty. It's not supposed to be."

"If she's yer charge, how is it ye don't know where she is?" Jonny asked softly, lighting his own cigarette, watching the angel suspiciously.

"She's not my only charge. Not the reason I'm down here, at least," he confessed. "That one I'm still looking for. I know he's out... but that's about it right now. I'm not always given... concise orders," he said with a rueful arch of his brows. "Or even complete ones. But I'd heard among the less savoury community that the power child here was gone. I come check it out and felt the vacuum."

"Vacuum?"

He nodded. "When something of strength resides in one place long enough, remove it and it leaves a vacuum. She's been gone long enough to leave one. So, where is she?"

"Safe," is all An would say. "And she'll be back. So ye can tell those reprobates she's still well guarded."

"Good," he chuckled. He glanced around. "Though I think I've seen enough of the magic here abouts to be able to find that particular mage. He and I will need to have a chat. This little one needs to stay in place. I don't know what part she is to play, but she's important later." He mused, studying the smoke curling from his cigarette as he thought. He seemed confused by his own information. He rose suddenly, looking off into the distance, flashed them an apologetic smile. "Sorry. Again."

In a blur of motion as much inward as upward, he was gone.

They sat there in silence, absorbing the event while Jonny finished his cigarette. There really wasn't anything either of them could say. Eventually, An led Jonny back into the house, closing it back up and locking the door.

As she felt her way across the room to the closet in her garret, Jonny remained standing on the threshold, and looked over the small room. "I think I see why ye prefer yer cottage."

She turned in the doorway, enchantingly back lit by the fire across the chamber. "Well, I was perfect content here before Danny built th' house. In my day this woulda been a palace. I didn't have t' share."

Aislynn went through the door, found herself a place to curl up, grumpy now. An stepped back into the attic room. "What, interested in findin' out how hard the bed is?" she asked, a hand on her hip. "I like m' clouds, thank ye."

He stepped closer, almost stalking her. "And th' missus doesna wonder why this room doesna feel lived in?"

"She doesn't come up here," she said softly as he closed the gap.

His voice was soft when he spoke again. "He's right though, I kin feel th' vacuum."

She drew him back into the cottage, out of the dead room and closed the closet door.

13

Midsummer struck An with more than oppressive heat. It hit her with a realization. This was effectively an anniversary for her and Skye. This was the day she had lost her eyes, and he had led her out of Faery and brought her here with the Red Queen's hounds at their heels. It felt like so much longer, and so much had happened since.

He was married and teaching fighting again. She was teaching another magical child and... well... had lost her heart and acted on it. Life was not perfect wedded bliss for her, but she had come to accept that was never to be hers. Her love was not often around, less so with this heat, and in other beds as often as her own as far as she knew and she had no problems with this. Well... it did not eat at her as it would have a more modern or possessive woman. She did not like it, would like it not to be, but would not argue for two major reasons. One, if she objected she would have been miserable and alone. Two, as far as she could tell he slept with few if any of the Taken save her, and no specific mortal with any regularity. For the moment, life was what she had time for.

She had not realized until she arrived at the green that bright Tuesday afternoon that she had missed all the activities the first time around. There were games of all kinds, from wrestling to horseshoes to fencing. Skye even had a caber toss going. The kites An had given out were being put to good use which reminded her sharply of Elizabeth's absence today. The girl had gotten her own kite and it had seen a good bit of flight while she had been here, but at the moment she was in Tampa enjoying herself. How her parents had gotten that much time off was only a surprise to George and Sharon. An knew how convincing Ian could be... and the people he knew.

While she could only see about a third of what she had missed the first time around, she was still able to enjoy it more. She wasn't fighting memory loss and adjusting to a strange place and lack of sight. This time when she sat to listen to the Bard, she understood his words on her own. Someone else apparently remembered the first event as well, as while she sat listening to Jonny teaching the young and fresh escaped through poetry, Bethany slipped up behind her and jokingly whispered in Gaelic, "*Need a translator*?"

She smiled, leaned back. "Has it been a year already?"

Bethany laughed and sat down next to her, giving Aislynn a scratch under the chin which set her trilling.

They listened to Jonny for a little while longer before walking off together, chatting about many things, Elizabeth included. An made a stop at the refreshments table and got a pint of ale, carrying it back to the bard circle. He had seen her coming, but not stopped his narrative. Beside him, a stump began to frost over, becoming visible to her. She returned his wry little smile, set the glass beside him and wandered off with Bethany.

"So, you going to be off on the sides with the rest of us non-com's tonight?" Beth asked.

An smiled. "I don't know... I'm thinkin' I might fight."

"Really? Not everyone on the field is going to be Touched."

An laughed. "Oh, I didn't say I was goin' t' *win*. I'll be fightin' on th' losing side anyway. But 'tis good practice. We have plenty of ordinary enemies." She then turned the conversation to more mundane topics, like Beth's schooling and what she planned to do once she graduated.

The two whiled away the hours pleasantly. Even Aislynn flew off eventually to play with the kites.

Foxfire arrived in time to light the bonfire, reporting that the hedges were up and the gathering safe.

Evening fell, the feast was served and An had more than a few helpers filling her plate. Aislynn primarily because she planned on helping herself to what was on it.

It was only an hour or so later when people began to gather by the fire, speculating on the coming battle. Liberty hung back with her husband and An left Bethany to stay near them.

"Ya might want tae gie aff wi' Beth an' t'others," Skye advised. "Battlelines are startin' tae be drawn."

She just arched an eyebrow at him. "I'm where I should be: attendin' m' Queen."

He stopped. "Ya ready fer a battle?"

"Aye. I noticed somethin' at Yule."

He frowned at that. "Wonder ya noticed anythin' after..." He yelped as Cipín clipped the back of his leg and Liberty's hand connected with the back of his head. "OI!"

"I noticed," she continued pointedly, "that once folk are taken down an' th' magic forces them t' switch sides... everyone becomes visible."

"All at once?" Skye perked up, trying to rub his calf and head at the same time.

"No. Not at first. But as th' magic bolsters them, one side getting weaker, th' other stronger... they kinda hove inta view like a ship out o' th' fog," she smiled.

"Ah, well, then. We'll keep ya tae th' back," Skye said. "Sae ya've time fer folk tae come visible afore they reach ya."

"Anyone know who the Holly King is?" Roulet asked, coming up, her metal staff in hand. "A lot of people are milling around not knowing which side they're gonna start on."

"Fickle lot," Skye grumbled. He immediately ducked when it looked like he might get popped again.

The same question was echoing across the field. Ian stood aside, waiting patiently with his core defenders around him. Skye began to set up the Queen's defences, drawing her to the back of the field and making sure she was surrounded. He had just finished giving his orders, hefting the wooden claymore he had to use, when there was a rustling from the far side of the field. The crowd parted from the back, leaving open a wide path, though no one strode forth down it to confront Ian. An could not see anything, there were just too many people in her way.

Then a voice rang out, one of the Younger boys. "The Holly King issues challenge to the King of the lightening year. Hand over his queen and set aside your crown peaceful and we'll all escape a bruisin'!"

There was a ripple of laughter from the crowd. "An' who be this spike-headed upstart who doesn' even issue 'is own challenge?" Ian called.

There was a shuffling of bodies and then a collective gasp and murmur as the Holly King revealed himself. "**I** am the Holly King, Old Man. Step aside. It is time for younger, smarter men to lead." It was the voice of Patches.

Ian chuckled, arms folded over his chest. "So come an' take it, Berry-boi."

Patches laughed. "I'm not so great a fool as to lock branches with you directly. Men?"

There came a roar and the army of the Holly King surged forth. Ian bellowed, "MAKE ME A PATH!"

The armies went at it. None of the on-coming fighters engaged Ian directly, and he neither forced the issue nor changed form. He only struck those foolish enough to try him. For a little bit, the Oak army made headway. In the back, An and Skye felt strengthened as they waited for the fight to reach them as they knew eventually it would. They could not see how the main fight was going, but by paying attention to their own bodies they had a fair idea. They could at least tell when the tide turned and their side began to fall.

Aislynn had debated if she wanted to be involved in this at all, finally deciding to ride the Queen's shoulder, to protect her if things got too close before the fight ended. Then she felt something odd, heard something not right. She leapt from shoulder to the ground and began listening and sniffing. Liberty paid her no mind, trying to get an idea what was going on beyond her little circle. Suddenly, Aislynn flew at her, hissing and screeching, startling her enough to back her into Roulet.

"Aislynn, what th' devil...!" Liberty began, stopped as the ground collapsed where she had been standing. As it was, she still nearly slid in, but Roulet grabbed her in time.

An whirled when Aislynn shrieked, saw a dirty red hat pop up from the hole and gave it a sound crack with the shillelagh. Tam dropped back down and something else jumped out of the hole, going after Roulet who had pushed Liberty behind her. "Skye!" An yelled as she lunged for the badger man, made him turn to deal with her.

The Badger spun, saw the Highlander aiming for him and dodged, moving to deal with him and leaving An to struggle with the red cap coming out of the hole again. Roulet darted forward to help her. Danny ducked under the sword, twisting as he did to reach up and use his claws on the length of wood. This only served to royally piss Skye off, and he used the hilt of the now fragmented claymore to pound Danny in the solar plexus so conveniently offered up to him.

An darted forward, taking a swing at a man she did not know who had come up behind Skye, swinging a bokken. The wooden katana met her wooden shillelagh in the air and cracked loudly. She continued her swing in an arch, spinning inward and with a deft twist, sent the bokken flying. Someone nearby picked it up and began to use it. A crack to the disarmed man's leg was followed by one to his temple and he went down, only to get back up after a moment to fight on the Oak side.

An felt a brief surge of strength and lunged after another trying to attack her brother. She fought fiercely, making short work of those trying to get past her. Skye had dealt with Danny, chucking him into another fray and returned to deal with the forces trying to come up out of the hole. Roulet had her hands full with the red cap. Shocking him did not seem to faze him.

An was feeling the heat, and the drain on her limbs from the losses their side was taking. She had managed to push back one of the mortals as Skye wrestled with Coach and Four, when she was attacked from behind by Tam. She whirled, saw Roulet getting up from the ground, shaking her head and moving to once more protect Liberty, drawing her further away from Skye and the rest of her defenders. An swung at Tam, connecting but not hard enough. "Skye, th' Queen! Roulet's not....!"

Tam bore her to the ground, knocking the wind out of her.

Skye looked up, saw An down and Liberty being slowly spirited away and chose to go after the queen. With a surge of rage, he threw off Coach and chase after Roulet. He did not get far before he was swarmed by people coming out of the hole. They bore him to the ground, but could not manage to keep him there.

An came to, her shoulder feeling like hell from the bite she had sustained. Tam backed off, turned to jump someone else. She felt odd, looked around and knew who her enemies were. She saw the harp boy trying to help Skye get the masses off of him. She reached out with the shillelagh and tripped Billy. Then Patches was coming out of the hole and walked sedately towards the Queen. Roulet moved out of his way and Liberty just stood there.

Patches knelt in front of her. "Can we end this, my Queen?"

She sighed, glanced over at the dog pile which still bucked and surged as Skye tried to fight the weakness and the weight of many. "Aye." She bent, drawing a flower from her crown and entwining it in his, kissed his forehead.

Everything came to a halt as the healing began to spread. One by one, folk got off of Skye and he calmed down, straightening his jerkin and kilt. Liberty threw a glare in his direction. "Stubborn, cuss," she playfully growled.

"Aye, well, yer th' one what married him," Ian grunted, walking up rubbing his head. He stared down at the hole in the turf, looked over at Patches now standing beside his daughter. "Well, played. Usin' yar head. Now, get it filled in again."

Patches laughed. "Aye, chief. Tam! Danny! If you two will be so kind as to undo your handiwork? And thank you."

"It ain't gonna work twice, ya know that, aye?" Ian glared. He looked so much more comfortable without the crown of Oak on his head.

The wreath of Holly had become a spiked crown on Patches' uneven hair. He smiled. "Oh, I know. I'll just have to think of a different clever next summer. At Yule, I just have to avoid you."

Ian laughed, clapping him on the shoulder. Someone handed him a pint, which he passed immediately to Patches. "Well, yar majesty, 'tis yar shin-dig now."

Patches held up his drink, bellowed "Cheers!" and chugged about a third of it. "Now, you lot! Unless I've set you to something specific, get back to partying! I want some dancing!"

Skye ground his teeth, watching his wife and Patches walking arm in arm ahead of him, but kept his mouth shut. He followed the majority of the crowd off to the dancing green where the musicians were hastily tuning up. Jonny was of course ready before any of them and began a stately but spirited piece on his fiddle for the King and Queen to dance to. Everyone else waited a measure or two before joining them.

Raven landed on Skye's shoulder. He looked up at her, frowned but didn't say anything. After all, it was her husband out there dancing with his wife. He decided they could commiserate. He offered her a sip of his Guinness but she shook her head.

Then the first dance was over and Skye looked down to see Patches standing in front of him. "Trade you?" Patches said, holding up Liberty's hand. "A Queen for a Handmaiden?"

Skye chuckled. "Yar loss," he said, passing off his drink and reaching for his wife as Raven launched, dropping into a woman. The two couples spun back out onto the dance floor.

An watched the dancing, smiling. Roulet was out there with her white tiger, who was still wearing that collar. Leila was out there with anyone who would dance with her, and even Kyle was dancing with someone. There were new faces and old out in the crowd. Shannon's frog boy was looking far more princely now, and even asked for a dance, which An granted. He wasn't as ungainly as he looked, and was unsurprisingly good at the Kerry style. Solitaire danced with Mikey and seemed to be actually enjoying herself now, or at least paying more attention to him than to the fact that Ian was not paying any attention to her.

Jonny stayed on stage almost the whole night, playing or singing. Billy joined him, but it was more often Billy who dropped back. He was getting popular with the ladies. At one point, Billy appeared at An's elbow and led her to the stage, passing on the message that Jonny wanted her up there. She blushed, let herself be deposited on the stage and sang a few with Jonny and a few on her own, always following his lead. They sang old stuff, new stuff, all of it suited for her lullaby voice.

She headed home somewhere after two in the morning. The royal pair and their consorts had sought their own little corners of the world for more ancient rites hours before. She kept hoping that somewhere along the way she would be met by a particular highwayman, but her path remained empty. She dressed for bed slowly, taking her time, but in the end she went to bed alone, though she left her window open.

An saw precious little of Jonny during the summer months, which grew hotter than the first summer she had spent here, if that was possible. It was all she could do to breathe when she went out. She left most of the gardening to the pixies, venturing out only to feed them and that only in the evenings.

Once the Tallows returned from their vacation and went back to work, An had charge of Elizabeth most of the day. Sharon once made a comment how grateful she was of this, as this meant she could work through the summer instead of having to chose between daycare or staying home. Elizabeth was of course delighted with this, because every morning after she got up and her parents had left for work, she would have breakfast with An in the cottage and then disappear to play with the other kids. She made sure to be back at least forty-five minutes before either parent was due home. She was learning a lot and becoming a very well-adjusted and athletic young lady.

They only had one incident where they were almost found out. Sharon had gotten off work early and without warning decided to go home for lunch. She had gotten to the house and found it empty. When she called An, some quick tap-dancing had to be done. An sent Aislynn to find and fetch the girl and told her mother they would meet her at the creamery in half an hour. When they got there Elizabeth had spun a quick lie about being down at the park and changed the subject quickly, knowing it caused her governess discomfort. That was when An noticed she was getting very deft at not telling the truth without actually lying, something she was certain was Jonny's influence. She was not sure if this pleased her or not. Though no doubt it would be useful in her life, hiding what she was.

An alternated between the Hedge Gate and Courtz for her 'get out of the house', which Roulet and Solitaire insisted she get. She watched Serenity and Elaroush, the electrified stoneling, getting closer.

Brink eventually showed up at the Rest, mingled in with the rest of the residents like any one of the Taken. An did not enlighten anyone as to what he actually was. She would let him do that for himself. Eventually he stopped setting off her 'radar' (as Roulet put it) and she became more open with him, especially about Elizabeth. She watched him spending time with Kyle, who had eventually reconnected with his family. Apparently the woman Kyle had been dancing with at Mid-summer was his wife. She quickly figured out that the blue wolf was who Brink was here for.

Caleb was being even less welcomed than before, once his conversation with William about Jonny had gotten around. He put up with it, developed a rather surly attitude and spent most of his time with William and a few others who had once served the Northerner. An gave him the cold shoulder because every time she saw him, she began to worry that the reason she had not seen Jonny was his fault.

One Wednesday at Courtz, An got up on stage. She had a few new poems, but nothing she had felt like sharing until now. There was one she had written after the incident in the Dark City, but never read to anyone. She did not know why she was doing it now, but yielded to the impulse and went on stage. She was always nervous when she came up to read. There were precious few of the Touched here, and that helped a little.

"I... I wrote this a while ago, when I were in a bad patch," she began. "'Tis called Nightmare. I've gotten over it. But I know there are those for whom it might mean somethin'. Remember you are not alone. There are those who do understand.

> Horror
> in my soul
> terror
> in my mind
> ripped
> from my heart
> left
> the path behind
>
> the city burns
> its heart dark and searing
> its windows watch
> like eyes scarred and leering
>
> desperation panic despair
> I turn to look and you're not there
> cross the void and fall into hell
> ride the tide of asphalt swell

filth and tar and asphalt hungry
seeks to feast on flesh in umbrage
smoke cacophony bright light blaring
denizens pass beyond all caring

I toss and turn upon my bed
running from terrors in my head
the darkness comes steeped in red
I'll sleep again when I'm dead"

She accepted the applause with grace, found her way to her table and drank her tea, ate her dinner in relative quiet with Aislynn. She was surprised when, a little while later, a young woman approached her. It wasn't until the girl spoke that she realized she wasn't just standing there because she couldn't get where she wanted to go, a common problem at Courtz. "May… may I sit? Talk?" she asked timidly.

An gestured to an empty chair on her right. He hadn't come in some time, but she always left Jonny's chair empty just in case. "Please."

The girl pulled the seat out and sat. An offered her tea, which she gratefully accepted. The act seemed to calm her. "You remind me of my grandmother," she laughed. "With the tea. That's her fix for everything it seems."

An smiled. "Th' right tea'll fix just about everythin' but a broken heart. An' e'en that it'll help soothe fer a bit."

She sighed. "I love your accent. And your monkey," she smiled as Aislynn offered her the sugar.

"She is often more popular than I am," An replied. "This is Aislynn," she said, introducing them. "I'm An."

"Miss O'Keefe, I know," the girl nodded. "I'm sorry, where are my manners? I'm Rebecka."

"Pleased to meet you, Rebecka," she replied, beginning to realize that there were things about this woman she could sense, if not outright see. She was no where near as visible as Tori, but ...almost like she was seeing her shadow. "What brings ye to my table?"

"Yer... sorry, your poem. It... spoke to me on a... really deep level and I just needed to talk, and it makes me feel like you'd understand. When'd you write it?"

"It were around... oh, April, I think," An answered, lifting her cup for a sip of tea. "Before my brother got married."

"Why? ...did you write it I mean?" She shook her head. "I'm sorry, that's a really personal question." She sipped her own tea for courage. "But... there's a reason I ask."

"I had a bad experience," An replied softly. She took a deep breath, thought she smelled a hint of the City on the girl. Aislynn took the hint and timidly approached her, sniffing her, let the girl pet her for a few seconds before darting back into An's hair, playing at shy. What she did was whisper the word, "*City,*" in her ear. "I went to a big city with some friends. Ended up in th' wrong part o' town."

The girl took a deep breath and then plunged ahead. "You ever get the feeling that the city was alive? Ready to devour you? I mean... well, I'm sure getting lost anywhere is worse for you but..."

"I know what ye mean," An injected, calming the girl. "'Tis always worse in my nightmares. But tell me what happened to ye, Rebecka, that my little verse should speak so loud."

"I... you're going to think I'm crazy. I know the cops do."

"Try me. I'm Irish, luv. We'll believe anything so long as it makes fer a good story."

Rebecka gave a soft little laugh, drank her tea before getting up the courage to tell anyway. "My... girlfriend and I went into Atlanta a few weeks ago. We were going to a concert. We... ended up in a very bad part of town, so totally lost I don't even think it was Atlanta anymore. I looked up one of the streets we were on and it hasn't existed in that city for sixty years. We tried to use our GPS but we couldn't get a signal. It seemed darker than it should have been and really run-down."

"Almost as if th' street lights were dimmer than they shoulda been?"

"Yes. Well, we weren't exactly dressed... not to attract attention, and where we were it was the wrong kind of attention. Some guys started stalking us, so we ran. Tammy darted down an alley... I told her it was a bad idea, you *never* go down an alley when you're running from someone. You stay in the street and make as much noise as you can. They catch you down alleys.

"But I couldn't let her go alone. There were these mangy dogs down there. Well, we thought they were. Then they stood up and were just some homeless guys. Luckily, they spooked Tammy before she got too far down the alley and we were able to get out before the guys chasing us got too close. But... they had friends up the way, pinned us in against a van. One of them looked like something out of Lestat, I swear. He ...he grabbed me by the throat, then screamed in pain and threw me half way across the street. They ignored me after that.

"I screamed, threw things at them, but they grabbed her and shoved her into the van and drove off. There was no plate." She stopped talking a moment, overcome with emotion and An let her be, tried to think of some way to mark her. "I chased it about half a block before I saw something coming out of an alley that looked very hungry and ran looking for a cop. I had to hide behind a dumpster at one point. But when I found one, a cop, he thought I was crazy. I told him what street my friend had been kidnapped on and he told me there was no such street. I looked it up when I got home and turned out there *used* to be a street with that name, but they'd changed half a century ago."

"So yer friend is gone and ye think yer either crazy or t' blame?" An offered.

She heard the girl nodding by the jingling of her earrings. "I think I survived mostly 'cause of my cross."

An tipped her head. "Explain."

She heard the clitter of chain through a metal loop as the girl pulled out the pendant in question. "It was very hot. I felt the heat from it, but it didn't burn me. It got hotter when whatever was chasing me got too close. My mother gave me this crucifix before she died. Said it was a third degree relic. I'm not Catholic like she was, but I've always worn it. I'm of strong faith, just haven't..."

An smiled, "...decided on a denomination?"

"Yeah. Tammy used to tell me I was Agnostic. I don't even know what that means."

An set her hand on hers, to still the fidgeting she could hear.

"Now you listen, little girl," she said, using the governess tone, the one she used to calm the after-effects of nightmares. "You were incredibly lucky. Yer mother gave ye her blessing when she gave ye that, I take it."

"Yes," the voice was small, a little girl's.

"That and yer faith are the only reasons yer not still in that hell. And aye, m' dear, ye slipped sideways inta hell. Ye couldna protect yer friend. Th' best ye kin do fer her is ta remember her in th' best light ye can. There is nothin' ye can do for her save pray, and this is one case where it might do some real good. But live yer life. Don't let this drag ye down. There are folk aplenty ye can talk to. Folk who will understand. Ye've been touched by darkness. Yer not th' only one. God gave ye a chance. Don't waste it."

Rebecka remained silent a long time, drank her tea and then stared at the empty cup.

An let her ruminate, cast her attention to other places in the club. She saw Cass come in, without his partner, and head to the bar. He was off duty, as he ordered a beer, sat and drank it. He asked Sil a question that was answered by someone next to him. The response was apparently not something to his liking. She could practically hear the man's heart breaking from here.

She excused herself from Rebecka who did not even hear her, and got up. Before she had cleared the tables, Cass was leaving. She stepped up to the place he had vacated as Sil was taking away the nearly full bottle. Sil turned away to make a drink.

"Did he get a call?" she asked, knowing it was not the case.

Sil flicked his eyes at the man next to An, a regular by his voice, and a mortal. "Yeah, the wake up kind."

He set a Morning Dew in front of An, never having asked if she wanted anything. She sipped it as the guy beside her exclaimed,

"Hey, the guy had a right to know! God, I wish someone had told me *my* girlfriend was stepping out on me. I never would have married the bitch."

She sank onto the seat. "Ah. You told him about Serenity and El. He did need t' know, but it was her place t' tell him."

"They're getting married, An," Sil said flatly. "She was kinda running out of time to tell."

She sighed. "There are gentler ways." She stood. "Thank ye for the drink, Sil."

She headed back to her table but Rebecka was gone.

When An got home, the cottage was cold, in spite of the fire burning in the grate. She did not need the house to tell her Jonny was here. She slipped off her shoes and put them away. Setting down her bag, she went to the cabinet, fetched a glass and poured a healthy dram of honey whiskey. She crossed to the chair where he sat staring into the fire, and sank into his lap, handing him the glass.

He smiled his thanks, but the expression was sad and tired.

"I were beginning to think things were over," she sighed, content with his presence but concerned by his mood.

He sipped the whiskey, tilted his head against the wingback's corner to look at her. One uplifted eyebrow said a lot of things. "It would be better for you if I said that it were... but 'tis too late for that. What gives you such a notion?"

She tipped her head in a shrug, taking a sip of the whiskey herself. "Seems ye've been avoidin' me since Mid-Summer. Even then I got no more than a proxied request t' sing with ye."

"I've been avoiding *summer*."

She gave him a pained and ironic smile. "That I can understand. Though I was beginnin' t' think it were... me. Such th' fool I am. But then, I be new t' love."

"I told you I'd be difficult."

She laughed softly, "Aye. Aye ye did. An' I told ye, I'm new at this."

His voice was soft but the edges hard. "Better than jaded."

She leaned back, settled in his arms. "They say it's goin' to get hotter," she offered.

He let her guide the conversation. "Doesn't usually start to cool off 'til September."

"Ugh, how do ye survive?"

He gave a soft chuckle. "I hide. In places easy to keep cold."

She took the whiskey. "Like a barren little lodge in the wood made of snow and earth?" she smiled, took a sip before handing it back.

"Aye. 'Tis one place."

They sat in silence a little while longer, and she thought back on the events of the evening. "Do you... dream for mortals too?"

He looked at her. "Most of what I do. Making sure no one is using them. Why is it ye be askin'?"

"I met this girl... well. I read this poem I wrote about th' ...City. I wrote it back before ye helped me with those nightmares." She blushed remembering what had happened shortly after that. "Well, it drew a young woman to me, name was Rebecka. Apparently she an' her friend ended up in th' City. Her friend was snatched up and carried away, but they cast her off after one of them got burned by her crucifix. She had a blessin' on her. She managed to escape mostly unchanged but... she was disturbed enough that my poem had an effect. I was wonderin' if ye could... make sure he's not workin' her dreams t' make her easier t' take later?"

He thought a moment, reached up and brushed a lock of hair from her face. "I'll have t' find her in yers first. Then I might be able t' find her with only a first name."

She took the now empty glass from him, setting it on the table beside them. "Well, it is quite late, perhaps we should get dreamin'."

He held onto her tighter. "*First things first, Misty. I've been hiding from th' season, which means I've been deprived of soft company an' th' comforts of th' fairer.*"

"*Really, more than a month without? You? How ye must have suffered!*" she mocked, trying not to smile.

He stood, lifting her up easily. *"T'were terrible. Mind if I remedy that now?"*

"And if I do mind?" she teased as he carried her into the bedroom.

"Oh, I'm told I can be very convincin'," he said as he laid her on the bed.

14

Life moved apace. The war with the Russians slowly escalated, though it remained in the shadows. They never hit the Rest and the O'Keefe's never hit the building they all knew Spetznakov lived in. An never saw much of the give and take. Skye saw a great deal.

Lughnasadh came again, saw An enter more of the competitions than the previous year. She actually entered a couple of the fighting contests. Entering the 'Touched' matches, she progressed decently, but was taken out in the semi-finals. Skye won that one. For a lark, and at the agreement of the non-Taken, An also entered the mortal rounds. She got less far, but didn't do nearly as badly as expected, learned what she needed to from it. She lasted four rounds.

The bardic contest, as Liberty had discussed the year before, was split up into categories. An entered the dance just for the fun of it, but did not place. She placed third in the singing, losing out to a mortal with a well-trained voice and a young siren recently escaped from Haggard. The siren won, naturally.

An took only the poetry contest seriously. She had chosen the one she was going to recite with a great deal of care, agonized over it for a week. However, when she took the platform and turned to face the Holly King and his wife and the Bard, something else came out of her.

> "Drumbeats in the distance
> Vibrations in the air, humming
> the piper calls the dance
> ready war coming
>
> Blood in the air, burning
> ashes fill the sky, falling
> wheels spin in mud, churning
> ravens crowd the fields, calling
>
> Summer came with war on the wing
> but not with the glory of which bard's sing
> but with blood and bone and hell and fire
> broken limbs and peril dire
>
> From first to last of battle's refrain
> the fields lie watered in blood-soaked rain
> forgotten the fallen in victory's spire
> ground in the mud of battlefield's mire
>
> Drumbeats in the distance
> vibrate the air, thrumming
> the piper called the dancers
> ready   again."

An was more than a little startled when she stepped from the stage. She gave Patches a long and meaningful look as she did. She was guided to a seat and someone else pressed something to drink in her hand.

"Are ye all right?" the drink- giver asked, a young mortal man she knew in passing.

"I'm... fine," she stammered.

"Beggin' yer pardon, miss, but yer pale as a ghost. Ye went like paper up there."

Her hand fluttered to her brow. "I... I don't like it when that happens. But I'm physically fine."

"Stage fright can do that. If ye think ye might faint..."

She waved her hand at that thought. "I'm not faint, thank ye kind. Though were anythin' t' cause that, t'would be this infernal heat," she said, sipping the drink she had been handed. It was a cool, sweetened juice drink. It did seem to help a little. But the other... the other *burned* at her. She rose, headed for the house. Slipping into the solar and feeling her way through familiar territory, she sank into the corner chair by the window and pulled her book from its pouch. She began writing what she remembered of the poem. This she would have to send a copy of to the children. It reeked of that kind of warning.

Almost as if thoughts of them summoned them, she smelled warm summer grass and the distinctive hint of lion and looked up, half-expecting to see Lion before her, or the King. It was Ian. He arched an eyebrow as her reaction shifted from delight to confused disappointment.

"Not who yeh were expectin'? I can leave an' get th' bard, if yeh like..."

She flushed. "That's not... who I was..."

He chuckled as he straddled a chair he apparently carried over with him. "Who'd yeh expect?"

"I were thinkin' of Them an' th' smell o' ye... yer presence..."

"Ah. *Them* them," he nodded. "Why were yeh thinkin' o'em?"

"This. I... need to get it to them." She handed him the book, let him read the poem for himself. "I don't know if it were intended for us and Them or just Them, but..."

"Yeh feel th' need to warn Them, by all means, do." His eyes ran down the page swiftly, the light in them changing with the words they drank in. "This why yeh left th' contest s' quick?"

She nodded. "That and someone reminded me I'd been in th' heat too long."

"Worst comes I'll put yeh in th' office fer all that," he said, looking her over as if trying to decide if she did need a bit of air conditioning. "Tell me about th' poem."

"I... don't know. I was goin' t' recite a sweet little piece with a myriad of interpretations but... this came out instead." She blushed, looked away as she closed the book, setting it in her lap and folding her hands over it. "It happens sometimes... th' spontaneous poetry. An' when they do... there's a feel to them that's different from ...other types that just flow from th' pen. Sometimes it's an explanation, sometimes an expression of everythin' boilin' up inside, like that night at Courtz when th' dreams had become too much. But these... these I'd call an attack o' th' bard's tongue."

"They come true?" The way he said it was expectant, as if it was inconceivable that she would say no.

She merely nodded. Her voice was a near whisper when she said, "One way or another." She felt the weight of his eyes as he waited for her to say more, felt the pressing need to say something else. "I never understand them until it happens."

"Seems to me that, at some point this summer, we'll see a war that's either been repeating itself or will. Which could mean th' Red Queen or th' Russians."

"Not th' Dark Man?"

He tipped his head, considering that possibility. "Anything is possible, but... we don't often have issues with him. Though yer right, we should keep our options open."

"Are ya all right?" Liberty's voice came from the doorway. An looked up. "They said ya left th' poetry contest in a hurry. I were afraid..." She stopped, looking An over critically, then her father. "Yar a little flush at th' cheeks, a wee pale under that. But ya seem fine. No one said Serephina'd shown her mug..."

An blushed under the heat flush. "I'm fine. I... was disturbed by th' poem I wrote."

"Recited, ya mean," she corrected, frowning.

"No. Wrote. It was created on th' fly." An flipped open the book to the page and passed it over. "I hurried here fer a bit o' peace so I could write it down afore it flitted away from me."

She watched the blood fade from Liberty's face as she read. "I'm goin' t' stop sharin' it, I keep gettin' that reaction," she sighed.

"Is this..."

"A prediction?" Ian supplied.

"It's a warnin'," An corrected. "An' that's all I know of it."

Liberty shook her head, handing the book back to An as she looked at her father. "I'll have a talk with Solitaire... see if she's seen anything.... Get her sister to pull out her cards." She turned back to An. "Ya get no images with these?"

An shook her head. "Just a flow of words. I don't even know what they are until they're out. Often I'll pick up a pen, look down an' see th' poetry already on th' page and not remember writing it. Other times I'll say them and not be able to forget them for a bit."

"We'll remain vigilant," Ian said, covering her hands with his own. "Now. If Liberty's in here 'cause someone told her yeh'd run off, that means there's a Highlander out there not long from gettin' th' same message, so..."

An rose, blushing as she slipped the book back into her bag. "Aye, I'll find him, calm him down."

An managed to get to him before he found out, though someone's off-hand question to her if she was all right spoiled any chance of escaping completely. She then had to explain all over again. He wasn't completely convinced by her assurances.

When she got back to the bardic area, the contests were over and she was surprised to find out she had won the poetry contest. Jonny, of course, had completely disappeared. She wandered for the rest of the afternoon, indulging herself a little at the buffet. She stuck to the non-alcoholic drinks though. She was over-heated enough. Eventually, she retreated to the veranda with a plate, seeking shade. She found Ophelia also there, hiding in the shadows.

She let Aislynn guide her to a rocking chair and set down her drink on the table beside it. She set her plate in her lap and nibbled as she watched what she could see and listened to what she could hear and tried to piece together a picture from the two. Eventually, Ophelia sank into a chair beside her.

"Hi," she said quietly.

"Afternoon, Ophelia," An smiled. "And how are ye today?"

"Hot. And dry," she replied, rubbing her arms through her thin sweater.

An cocked an eyebrow at her attire. "Well, th' dry can be helped. There's th' river, a lake, plenty o' places to swim. Th' heat... well, I learned t' surrender long sleeves a while ago. Not even sheer sleeves helps in this heat."

"I'm too... I couldn't."

An tilted her head in acceptance. "'Tis a personal choice. Roulet and Liberty could help ye find a comfortable middle ground an' ye ask. They did so fer me. Ye should have seen me," she chuckled. "Wool stockin's, ankle boots, floor lengths skirts plus petticoat. High collars, long sleeves and tight bodice. Look at me now," she said, twitching a corner of her calico cotton skirts. The sundress she wore was very fifties-ish and satisfied her modesty. "I'd have fainted by now in what I prefer t' wear."

"I'll... have to think about it."

They sat in companionable silence for a little while before Ophelia tried small talk. She asked about Aislynn and the Rest and how An found a job and was getting on. An told her what she knew and how Ian had eventually found her a job she enjoyed. "I'm sure at some point they'll find somethin' fer you. What are ye good at?"

"Housekeeping. My mother always told me I'd make someone the perfect wife," she smiled sadly. "And I did, ...but I never got to the house part. His... unit got shipped out the afternoon of the wedding. We were supposed to have at least a day or two. But something changed." Her eyes grew hard. "Then that evil Old Man dragged me below the waves and turned me into ...this."

"And what is this?" An asked quietly, gently leading her.

"A thief. A killer. I'm not a siren; I don't sing sailors down, but... they see me floating and try to rescue me... And then I had to steal them or drown them. The Man in the Carrion Coat... had a hook." She shuddered. "I can't count how many times he's gutted me with it, ...cause I wouldn't... Then there were his cages."

She looked out over the green. "Everything here is so colourful," she sighed. "So..." her sentence went unfinished as something caught her eye.

An followed her gaze, saw her watching one of the wrestling matches. At the moment An could only see one combatant, Cullen, shirtless but still in his suit coat, and holding someone in a firm grip while the crowd cheered them on. Ophelia blushed, her hand drifting to the end of a chain which ended in something under the sweater.

"So," An prompted, leaning back in the chair and leaving the rest of her plate to Aislynn's mercy. "Have yer eye on someone, I see."

She snapped back to the present, looked at An with widened eyes. "Oh, absolutely not. I'm... a married woman!"

An nodded. "Fair enough. Though if yer husband still lives... he'd be too old t' be a proper husband. Not to mention likely remarried, believin' ye dead," she said gently.

The woman sighed, still fiddling with whatever was at the end of that chain. "I... don't think so. I feel... positive. I've had people looking into it.... His whole unit vanished. There's a chance... that he was taken, too."

"Ye remember his name?" An asked with surprise, more than a little envious.

She shook her head sadly. "No. Just ...his unit. I remember what ship he was on and... well.... It's complicated."

"Always is," An agreed.

Raven landed on the rail, shifting so that she was sitting on it instead. "Hi! Hey, 'Phelia! They're getting up a three-legged race over near the maze and I need a partner. Wanna?"

An smiled, nudging her. "Oh, go ahead. Have a little fun."

Ophelia smiled shyly, and let the younger woman drag her away.

An remained on the porch watching the two run off.

"You should take your own advice, missy," Aislynn chirruped.

"I've had plenty o' fun t'day, thank ye. I'll wait 'til th' dancin'."

Aislynn shrugged, went back to snacking. *"Suit yourself."*

Near twilight, An left the veranda, wandered along the outer edges of the festivities, enjoying the quieter part of the night. She found a place at the far end of the battlefield, sat and just listened to the oncoming night. Aislynn entertained herself by stalking mice, then chasing fireflies as they began to rise from the grasses. No one bothered them.

Eventually she heard the strains of music and got up, walking back to the dancing green. There, she let herself be pulled into the crowd, onto the floor by whatever young man took the fancy. She was a free-spirited dancer and loved the Irish styles and country reels.

Billy Younger was the main fiddler and singer for the first part of the evening. An wondered where Jonny had gotten off to, guessed it was the heat that had driven him off. She let herself be talked into getting up on stage with the harp to sing with him. She laughed, blushing, but allowed herself to be thrust in front of the microphone and followed his lead. It was at the end of one of the modern songs by Flogging Molly Jonny had taught her that An caught sight of the bard. He was off to the side, head to head with Serenity. She watched him lift her chin with a finger to look at him. The conversation seemed intense.

Without thinking what she was doing, she turned away from the sight and began to sing "Red is the Rose", leaving the band to catch up to her. She was heartbreaking. Her eyes were closed by the time she was done, so she did not see Jonny slip up onto the stage before she felt the sudden cold. She slowly turned as he took up his guitar, tempting her as he sang "Whiskey Lullabye". She glared at him at first, listened to him singing the pain of the betrayed. Finally, she took up the second half, finding the irony in the verses and their roles. When they were done, there were few dry eyes. It was the kind of song the Irish love.

Even Cullen was moved. He seized the watching Ophelia and pulled her onto the dance floor, half-drunk and tears streaming. Ophelia began blushing, becoming uncomfortable. By the end of the dance, she ran off and Cullen shrugged, turning to the stage and yelling for them to play 'Jonny, I Hardly Knew Ye'. Jonny sighed, nodding to the band and obliged.

An quietly slipped from the stage and followed after Ophelia. She had to get Aislynn to fly up and find her. The petty drake returned shortly and lead her to part of the river where the water ran deepest. Ophelia was sitting at the bottom of the hole where the boys were fondest of finding trout. She looked up as An's shadow blocked the moon, slowly rose 'til just her eyes were above the water.

"Ye ran off," An said flatly.

Ophelia nodded.

"Was Cullen not th' man ye thought he were?"

She rose just enough to blurt out, "I thought he might be…" and sank immediately.

An gave her a wan smile, understanding her more than the girl knew. "Ye thought he might be yer husband? Cause he and his whole battalion were lost?"

"Company, but yes." She repeated her bobbing to the surface to speak, sinking once more to the eyes after.

"Have ye talked t' him of it?"

She shook her head violently, causing hundreds of tiny, violent ripples to ring away from her.

'Of course, ye couldn't,' An thought. 'Should have known better.' "It doesna rule him out," she said instead. "War changes men. The Red Queen changes men."

Slowly she rose, staring at the reflection of the moon in the water. "Barry said… it's the coat, makes him so cold. In Boston, they call him Broken Thomas."

"But they name him Cullen here?"

She nodded. "His first name. Middle's Thomas."

"What does Barry mean 'Tis th' coat makes him cold'?"

Ophelia rose a little higher, folded her arms on the rock An was sitting on and rest her chin on them. "He... there was this bargain with... the Old Man. The coat's his. Apparently someone in the O'Keefe family has to wear it. Or something like that. It changes them. There's something it's supposed to do, but Barry won't tell me. If I could get it off him... I'd know... if he was or not. But it won't come off."

An thought a minute, watching the drowned girl in the water and running her fingers in the cold current. "Have ye asked Ian? If Cullen were ever married?"

She frowned. "He wouldn't know."

"He's th' man's uncle. If he were married, I think he'd know."

She shook her head. "It was kinda... last minute?" she said, her eyes telling An that it had been in secret.

"Hmm. I... might be able to find something out. Let me talk t' th' coat." She stood up but Ophelia's hand snaked out, grabbed her ankle in a grip that was surprisingly strong.

"What do you mean, 'talk to the coat'?"

An smiled, bent down to tenderly brush a lock of hair from the woman's eyes. "Things tell me things." She reached down and fingered the sleeve of her sweater, asking and receiving information in nano-second flashes. "Fer instance, ye've worn this sweater since.... It were sent to ye from England with th' last letter ye received of him. It also says, ye knew he was missin' when ye went t' th' dock, were contemplating..." Ophelia shot back in the water away from her, her eyes wide.

"I am sorry," An said. "I... things do not realize how much information is too much, what is too personal. But ye see what I mean."

The nod was hesitant and slow. "If you can... find out..."

"I make no promises but that I will try. And you,... don't hide yerself away. Cool off an' come back t' th' party. Or go home, but don't sulk and drown yer sorrows."

"I can't drown again," she said.

An smiled. "It's an expression."

"I know." She rose a little further in the water. "I can't drown that way either. It doesn't matter how much I drink. I can't get drunk. I want to. I can't. But if I don't drink... it hurts." The last was a bare whisper.

An nodded. "I'm familiar with th' problem." She stood. "I'm going back to see what I can find out. You... do what yer going t'. I'll let ye know if I discover anythin'."

Ophelia nodded and sank all the way under.

Having sat beside the river, An felt much cooler than she had earlier. She headed back to the festivities, slipping her way into the dancing crowd. She found Cullen, jitterbugging with Luminara and deeper into his cups than when she had left. Jonny and Billy were playing together. They were doing a song called the "Devil Went Down to Georgia" and Billy was playing the Devil's part. Together they were impressive.

As the song ended and they changed instruments, mostly to give the fiddles a chance to cool off, An saw William headed her way and marched up to Cullen to avoid him. "Might I have this dance, sir?"

Cullen looked down at her. "School marm's gettin' forward," he grinned. "Should I feel privileged or do I have th' bootle t' think... thank?" he asked as he pulled her into his arms.

She grunted as he crushed her a little too hard, managed to smile. "Liberty has introduced me t' th' concept of something called a Sadie Hawkin's Dance. I am exercisin' that right."

He laughed, roughly spinning her. "That's a whole dance, darlin', not one turn on th' floor. It's a dance party where the girls ask the guys out instead of the other way around. Was pretty daring in its day. Don't see a lot of it now."

"I stand corrected," she blushed. She fell silent after that, concentrating on her conversation with the coat.

Thankfully, the song did not last terribly long, and she was able to slip away from him. She had heard some of the things he said as they danced. He was insufferable, opinionated and full of himself. She also knew that the coat only made it worse.

Reeling from the information she had gathered, she slipped away from the party altogether. Aislynn informed her that Ophelia had sank to the bottom of the pool and wasn't coming back up, so there was no point in trying. An needed to digest the information anyway. She found herself on the path through the wood; realizing where she was only when she noticed she had sidestepped an incomplete mushroom ring because she had seen it. She stopped, oriented herself and continued on, only glancing at the rath through the trees.

Halfway past the fort, she heard wings fly over, felt a sudden, chill weight land on her shoulder and looked up at the white raven. She smiled. "Fleeing th' heat?" she asked.

He merely cawed and settled down on her shoulder, let her carry him back to the cottage. When they arrived, she realized why. Shifting to man, he sank into the nearest chair. He looked worn out and pale. Immediately worried, she ran her hand over his forehead and cheek. They were warm.

"What's wrong?"

He just looked up at her.

"Is it th' pain?"

"No," he croaked.

"Th' heat then," she surmised. She thought about it. Every time she had been near him today, he had been giving off a radius of cold. Now it was barely there, and only noticeable when she touched him. "It... takes a lot out o' ye t' stay cold? But..."

He gave her a rueful smile and a pained laugh. "I can't bloody turn it off, but th' hotter it is, th' more it takes out o' me."

She sank to the floor beside his chair and the temperature in the cottage began to drop. "Last summer I remember seeing quite a bit of you."

He sighed, becoming more comfortable as the air grew less warm. "Bit hotter this year. And I've... been working more."

"Workin'?" she frowned.

"Th' Russian's?" he said with a raised brow.

She understood suddenly. "Ye want anythin'?"

"Anythin' cold."

She got up, opened the refrigerator and saw two foggy bottles and grabbed them. She brought them to him and held them both out. "I don't know what these are. And if I glamour them so I kin see th' bottles I'll still not be able to read them."

He turned them so he could read the labels, gave her his lopsided smile. "Well, I imagine that one's yers," he said, passing it to her and pressing the other to his temple.

"What is it?" she asked, sitting in her chair and opening it. She took a whiff. It smelled of licorice and vanilla. "Ah, root beer."

"Kid's beer," he smiled.

She frowned at him. "So I don't like beer. Whiskey suits me fine." She sank back in her chair and slipped off her sandals. Her mind ran through everything she had encountered today. She watched him as he opened and drank his beer, paid attention as his colour came back and he looked less wilted. When she thought he had recovered enough, she asked quietly, "What know ye of Haggard?"

He looked over at her, frowned. "Why do ye ask?"

"Reasons. Many of them actually."

"Why don't I start with 'what do *you* know of Haggard'?" he countered, watching her with his earth-brown eye. There was no fire in the grate, but a pair of lamps sat on the mantle, giving off sufficient light.

An reached under her small table and pulled out her lace, began working with the fine thread as she thought and explained. "Well, Elizabeth showed me *Th' Last Unicorn* for starters."

"Movie or book?"

"Th' film first. I made her read me th' book." He nodded and she continued. "An' what little I remember from my service, th' book is close: King Haggard, castle by th' sea, though some tales have it under th' sea or on a crag in th' middle. Controls th' Red Bull t' keep th' unicorns in th' sea. I know there was something between him and Amalthea, but whether that was Haggard or Lir... He's both men, most like. Lir is th' father of Manannán mac Lir, who is in turn th' old man o' th' sea and..." she sighed. "That's rather circular."

"Tales of gods often are."

"There's Shakespeare's King Lear, but I don't know if that connects. Have I missed anything?"

"Th' Man in th' Carrion Coat."

She thought, glanced over. "I'm... not familiar with that one, though I've heard it. ...Recently."

"I've introduced ye t' Sting, have I not?"

"Aye. My favourite so far is "They Dance Alone"."

"Heartbreaking, that one. I'm referrin' t' "Th' Soul Cages". It speaks o' th' keeper in th' carrion coat. 'He's th' king o' th' ninth world. Th' twisted son o' th' fog bell's toll. In each an' every lobster cage, a tortured human soul.' That's also Haggard. He is all of them. He is sworn never t' love, though it is rumoured he broke that vow once."

"Amalthea."

"Aye. Now, why do ye ask?" He set aside his empty bottle and turned in the chair to regard her.

She took a deep breath, released it. "Ye saw Ophelia and Cullen, aye?" He nodded. "Well, I followed after her. Talked t' her. Have ye heard her tale?"

"Nae."

She explained what she knew so far of Ophelia's story. "...Then she said something Barry had said about th' coat an' Broken Thomas."

That brought Jonny's head up.

"Ye know of it then," she said, only glancing sidelong at him as she worked the thread into a delicate, filigreed leaf.

"Aye. Cullen were a... happier boy before it. It makes him cold, but it keeps him from feelin' guilt at th' things he does fer th' family, had t' do in th' war."

"Well, ye know where it came from?" She did not look up. She knew the answer already.

"I've heard... rumours."

"Haggard made a bargain. He made that coat to find his true love, then got some hapless soul t' wear it, t' search for his true love. Haggard's love. Only then will th' coat come off, save in death, an' even then th' coat must transfer to another. It was made to find love."

"Interesting."

"However, if th' man wearing it were t' meet his own true love an' know her fer such, th' coat will come off and Haggard will have t' make a new bargain." She finished off the leaf and set it in the basket, started a new flower.

Jonny regarded her in silence for a bit. "An' ye know this how?"

"Th' coat."

One white eyebrow arched. "So that's what ye were doin'. I'd wondered."

She left off her counting and looked over at him in surprise. "Surely that not be jealousy I'm hearin'."

He laughed softly. "No. But he seemed too crass for ye. I believe th' modern term is 'not yer type'."

Her brows went up in disapproval as she counted her stitches. "Most certainly not. But I had t' get close enough t' talk t' th' coat. And it required subterfuge lest th' coat make him resist getting free of it."

"Wise." He smiled as he leaned back in the chair, kicking off his sandals. "Amusin' nonetheless."

15

Jonny was gone when An woke. This did not surprise her. What would have surprised her was if he had still been in bed. The house said he had left in the coolest part of the morning, the best time for him to have done so. She was certain he had flown back to his snow lodge.

She rose, got dressed. She opened the carved box on her dressing table and looked in. Last night she had placed her poetry book inside with a note and a bookmark. Her book was still in it but the note was gone. She lifted the slim volume out of the very magical little box and flipped it open to the poem. There was a small folded note there in Eagle's handwriting, smelling delicately of lilies.

It said simply: "Keep us appraised. Other than minor testing of borders, we are experiencing peace. Since we have grown, we are in less direct danger. Someone will keep you informed if anything should change."

An smiled, set the book aside and went to the window. She threw open the sash and looked down to the roses peeking their gold and red-singed heads up at her. The wisteria had shifted around it, growing up the sides and over her window, draping clusters of fragrant purple blossoms in the now open frame. She reached down to the vamprick, coaxing a blossom loose in her hand and brought it in, setting it in the box for Eagle.

She headed through the door to the Tallows, Aislynn sailing down to land on her shoulder, passing her the meat pie she had taken from the cottage table as she shifted into a small monkey. An came into Elizabeth's room. The girl was already awake and working on an art project. She looked over her shoulder and saw nothing, stroked Elizabeth's head. "Have ye been down t' breakfast?"

Elizabeth shook her head. "I'll be down in a minute. Want to finish this."

"All right." An walked away, finishing her pie before getting to the stairs. She slipped into the kitchen and, with Aislynn's help, made herself a cup of tea.

An heard someone sitting at the table still, which surprised her just a little. "Not going in to work today?" An asked politely, bobbing her tea bag.

There was the rustling of paper as whoever it was turned around. It was Sharon. "Well, no. I'm taking a day off to take Elizabeth shopping for school. It starts soon and they're having a tax free week on back-to-school things. Would you like to come? Get out of the house? It's the best time to buy clothes."

An gave a little laugh. "Ah, no thanks. Out o' th' house means out in th' heat."

"Still not used to the temperatures?"

"I understand they take years to acclimate to properly. Besides, I've an errand or two o' my own I might do. It'll mean less in and out of air-conditioning than what ye've no doubt planned."

"Suit yourself. You change your mind, or decide you want to join us for lunch, just give me a call."

"If I change my mind," she agreed. "But don't count on it. One of my errands is fond of cookin'."

An took advantage of the free day. She waited until Sharon and Elizabeth had left before heading upstairs to her garret, slipping through the closet door into the cottage. Aislynn shifted back into dragon-form and flew out the back door. She followed along behind her, headed for the main house. She paused to check on the pixies, but they were fat and happy and buzzing about like little bees, which is what they sounded like: bees and bells.

The walk was less pleasant than in earlier months, though it was no where near as hot as it would get within a few hours. If there was no real breeze today, she would have to take the short-cut through the Mead Hall to get home. It was that or get home so late she'd have to walk from Courtz.

There was a light breeze picking up and sweeping through the open doors and windows of the antebellum manor when she stepped onto the veranda. Ophelia was sitting on the porch in the coolest, darkest corner with a cup of coffee, taking in the bright summer morning.

"You have no idea what colour is like when you live without it," Ophelia said without preamble.

An smiled. "I gather it is like seeing when you thought you never would again."

Ophelia looked over, shame registering. "Oh, I didn't mean to ... there I go, sticking my foot in. I'm... not used to social interaction."

An tipped her head in agreement. "Ye've not had a lot of practice. Ye'll get plenty o' that here. ...I spoke with th coat."

She suddenly had Ophelia's undivided. Her eyes were large over the rim of her mug. "And?" she whispered.

An felt around for a seat. Aislynn sailed in and found one for her, landing on the back of the rocking chair and swinging with it as it rocked wildly, enjoying herself, wings out for balance. When the chair slowed down some, she blew on it, frosting it over a little. An moved over to the chair and Ophelia followed, taking another. "Well, I know it's purpose. ...And how t' get it off, but it will be tricky."

"Tell me," she said eagerly.

"He has t' find his true love... and know her fer who she is," she added when Ophelia started to get excited. "Remember, he danced with ye and didn't know you fer her. So, either he isn't yer husband, ye aren't his true love, or he just is blind to it. He'll have t' be convinced. Do ye know th story of 'East of th' Sun, West of th' Moon'?"

Ophelia shook her head.

An settled back in her chair and told her the tale. "It is a love story about an enchanted prince who comes to a young maid as a beast and convinces her to marry him. At night, he comes to her as a man, though she never sees him as it is dark. Eventually she goes to see her parents and her mother convinces her she is married to a monster and to light a candle to see him while he sleeps. She does so and drips the candle wax on him, waking him. He tells her had she only waited 'til the first year were over he'd have been free.

"So, he is taken away. In some versions, he turns into a bird and flies away, in others he is taken. In all of them, the girl wanders the world over asking things if they had seen him. She asks the sky and the sun and the four winds, and each tells her no, but gives her a present. After seven long years she finds herself on a shore where she discovers that her true love is about to marry a sorceress princess. She sets herself below the princess's window and opens one of the gifts.

They are all magical toys: a bowl that makes whatever food you are craving; a golden hen and her little brass chicks; a mechanical nightingale that sings every song known to man, that sort of thing. Each day the princess asks her what she wants for the toy. Each day the girl replies, 'to sleep in the prince's bedchamber'. The princess agrees, but each night she gives him a sleeping draught in his wine. In some versions the girl meets him during the day and he does not know her at all. But each night the girl pours her heart out to him, telling him everything she has suffered to find him. But the prince sleeps through it all, and she goes away disheartened.

"Now the prince has been having the strangest dreams and tells his manservant. The man tells him about the girl and on the last night, the prince throws out the draught. Hearing everything from his true love's lips, he remembers her and they flee together."

Ophelia sat quietly, sipping the last, cold dregs of her coffee. "What does this have to do with the coat?"

"He met her and did not know her. She had to confront him with evidence, tell him things he remembered before the spell keeping them apart was broken. If he is your husband, there is every likelihood something is keeping him from remembering. You will have to find the one thing that will make him remember."

An sat, letting her digest the information, rocking quietly with Aislynn stretched out on her leg, sound asleep. Eventually Ophelia got up and wandered into the house after mumbling something An did not understand but took for a goodbye. The air was heavy with the smell of new mown grass and fragrant flowers. An remained in the chair, wishing she had brought her lace, but closed her eyes and drowsed in the slowly rising heat.

It was much later in the day when she woke, feeling very poorly. She rose, headed into the house to the kitchen, sank into one of the chairs. Martha was immediately fussing over her, pressing cold juice into her hand. An thanked her, told her not to fuss, but that she would like to pass some time with her if she could stand the company. "Just shoo me out if I'm in th' way. 'Tis about time I hear where my food comes from," she laughed.

"What on earth are ye blatherin' about?" Martha tutted, trying to sound as if she had no idea.

An smiled. "Oh, I know yer cookin'. I am full aware whence my supper comes. And thank ye."

Martha rattled the package she was opening and began chopping some kind of vegetable. "Oh, 'tis nothin'. Ye eat it here, ye eat it at home, 'tis all th' same save fer who does th' dishes."

"An' th' companionship," An offered.

"But sometimes a body needs a little time to themselves," she added. There was something in her voice that said she meant a bit more than she was saying. An decided to save herself some embarrassment and did not press.

The two women spent several hours chatting while Martha made supper. When dinner was ready, An was surprised to see so few people at the big table. Ian and Ophelia were there of course, and Shannon's frog prince, who was going by Freddy now. They were fixtures in the house. Cullen and Aiden were there, but there was no one else.

Conversation was intense, mostly dealing with how quiet the Russians had been recently and what plans were being made to find out what they were up to. Freddy managed to change the subject to the night's soccer match and was persistent enough that the men gave up talking about anything else. An smiled at the whole affair.

"So, how's your young ward coming along?" Cullen asked An suddenly.

She was a little thrown off by the question, as it had come out of the blue. "Fine. School starts soon, so I'll have more time during th' day an' less in th' afternoons. I'm actually busier in th' summer, as I've got her all day."

"I meant the other thing. What you're teaching her. The magic?" he asked, reaching across for a roll.

"Oh...," An blushed. "That's not my job. 'Tis Sean's. I just make sure she gets to her lessons. An' ...teach her when it's appropriate to use it and when not."

"So you're just a nanny, th' soccer mom without th' mom part."

Her eyes flashed, the fog within swirling. She felt the mists increase around her ankles. Ophelia's outburst of "Cullen!" allowed her to realize it and get herself under control.

"I am a governess, Mr. O'Keefe. I teach."

"But th' kid's in school during th' day, you said so yourself. What do you do? Have th' kid at lessons day and night?"

"Cullen," Ian warned.

An could handle herself. "Certainly not. I teach her more than that school does. I learn what she is learning and help her understand what the school fails to explain properly. I teach her how to control herself and comport herself."

"Manners and Math," he snorted. "She could go to finishing school for that."

The change in her accent should have warned him. "Certainly, she could. But then she would not have access to Sean, nor learn about Mab and witches and how not to insult your house elves; or that, for someone like her, mushroom rings could most certainly become gateways to places where she'd be eaten alive. I teach her that being polite and respectful can save you from witches or fey if you run across one unknowing, and sharing what little you have with a beggar or old lady can earn yourself help, a blessing or just plain save your life. I am also there to defend her against those things that would come to take her, that only she and I can see, and that her parents are certain are either pranks or her imagination. And what is it *you* do for the family, sir?" she countered, feeling the flush of her anger on her cheeks. "Besides order people around, blow things up, drink too much and behave inappropriately with young women you don't even know at family gatherings?"

Cullen's eyebrow went up in appreciation. He glanced over at his uncle who was buttering the last roll. "I warned yeh to be polite," Ian chuckled. "Yeh not see her at Lughnasadh?"

"I saw her getting her ass handed t' her by Melvin Donnelly."

Ian rolled his eyes, "But not her knocking some sense into Lipscomb, Howell and Finch?"

Cullen stopped with his wine glass halfway to his lips, looking over as his uncle ate his roll in two bites. "Lipscomb? Young Ian?" he said, doubtfully. "That lad's got an arm on him."

Freddy snorted, "Don't matter what kinda arm you got on ya if ya can't reach your target. She took his staff away from him in a single twisting move and then laid him out!" he crowed.

An blushed. "Now there's no call t' embarrass th' boys. They were very good. I got lucky."

"Yeh learned yeh kin deal wit' those what underestimate that yeh can't see," Ian corrected firmly. "It's th' ones what have seen yeh fight that give yeh trouble. She lasted longer against those she *could* see. She's no slouch with that shillelagh, Tommy-boy. Skye's seen t' that."

"And Juan. He's the one taught me th' escrima and th' fencing," An injected, settling into her dessert as Shannon set the crumble before her.

"Juan doesn't..." Cullen growled, then suddenly shut up. His eye had caught the knob of the shillelagh where its head rest on the table. "That isn't th' iron shod one, is it?" Cullen asked, pointing with his fork, panic on his face.

"Aye," Ian said calmly as he began eating his dessert.

"Ye never let me play with that as a kid!"

"Well, she's not a kid now, is she? It's taken to her and that's th' end o' that."

Cullen grumbled and began eating his dessert. He wasn't going to argue with that tone.

Aislynn drowsed on her shoulder, fat and happy and thoroughly stuffed, and An realized that it was too late to just go home. Sharon would worry. So, An took the portal shortcut to Skye's Mead Hall, and walked next door from there.

She could see the pale lights of the pixies among the flowers as they hid themselves at her passing. She paused to check on her rosemary, plucking a few stems of the dill to dry for later. As she headed into the house, she woke Aislynn up. *"Come on, sleepy head. We have to go t' th' Tallows first."*

"Why?" she grumped, tried to curl up tighter.

"Because it's too early. They'll still be awake."

"So? Stay out until they go t' bed."

An sighed, heading for the side door that only opened to other places. "Were tonight Wednesday or Friday I might get away with that. Not tonight. Now change. We're goin' t' have t' walk home from Courtz."

She sat up, grumbling as she shifted herself into the small service monkey and latched herself once more around An's neck and slipping back to sleep. As a monkey, her full stomach was a great deal more obvious. *"At least you took th' short-cut home,"* she mumbled.

An sighed, smiling and told the house she'd be back in a few hours. She opened the door to Courtz and stepped out into the lounge. There was a small party up here at the moment and An apologized profusely for intruding as she used Cipín to guide her to the far door. "Oh, don't mind me. Can I tell th' bartender if ye need anythin'?"

"Yeah," someone piped up, moving to get the door for her, "see if we can get either a menu or some kind of sandwich platter sent up?"

"Certainly," she smiled, thanked him for holding the door and felt her way downstairs.

She headed immediately to the bar and told Tori what was wanted. The woman nodded and left the bar to Brad, heading into the back. An proceeded down the path between the bar and the tables, moving slowly as it was a crowded night.

She was surprised to see Cass and Dukes here. Cass was at the near end of the bar having a tense conversation with Serenity.

"How did you expect me to react? What good does your concern do me? I want your love, but I got beat out by Ben Grimm hooked up to a car battery, because he doesn't have a job and because he 'understands you'. I think I have a little right to be bitter!"

An moved politely past the argument, disinclined to help Serenity out of her mess. She should have told Cass before things had progressed as far as they had. Her progress was stalled by someone fairly large. She was beginning to think he was a regular, because he always seemed to be in her way when she least needed it. As she skirted past him, she came upon a different scene, this one with Leila and Dukes. She stepped around just in time to see the djinni throw herself into Paul's startled arms squealing, "Baby!"

To her surprise, Paul threw her off again, snarling. "Don't 'baby' me, bitch. Your alimony check is in the mail. What the hell are you doing here? I thought you'd moved to Tallahassee with whatshiswipe?"

Leila was crestfallen. "Alimony? What?"

"Yeah, from the divorce? Exactly... thirteen months and six days ago... if you don't count the time between filing and judgement."

"I never.... Paul!" she cried, her voice suddenly very unlike the urban, hip hop girl she had sounded like every time An had dealt with her. "I was fuckin' kidnapped! Two years ago!"

An slipped past another patron, not wishing to intrude on their privacy even if it was in public. Aislynn tapped her to go left and she narrowly avoided a chair someone had left out. She continued on her way, not stopping until she was out on the street. She made herself take shallow breaths, trying not to suffocate in the sudden heat. It was nearly eight and the temperature was only down to eighty degrees. An turned towards her neighbourhood and began to walk slowly.

Aislynn lifted her head and looked back at the club. "*What I wouldn't give to be a fly on that wall.*"

"*Aye, well, we're not goin' t' eavesdrop. She's goin' t' have some explaining to do, and she's lucky he already knows about us. I'd be willin' t' bet th Dark put a changelin' in her place.*"

"*Sounded like it. I think I heard him say something about kids....*"

"*We're goin' t' leave it,*" An warned. "*Just concentrate on gettin' us home afore we melt. I'm goin' t' want a cool bath when we get there,*" she sighed.

16

Friday, Elizabeth spent her last free weekday getting as much training time in with Sean as she could. An was working in the other half of the hall with Skye and a few others, Lipscomb included. They were trying to find a way for her to sense, notice or otherwise defend herself from someone she couldn't see who was being sneaky. So far they weren't discovering much, and eventually settled with how to handle matters once she'd been attacked. An could at least tell that Elizabeth was enjoying herself.

They were both home in time for supper and An even stayed in that night, as George decided to order pizza and watch a movie with the family. An sat in the living room with them, working on her least complicated crochet and working without really looking. It was good practice to work by feel. The film was some animated thing about a little red riding hood and her granny in the snack business. An found it quite silly, though an interesting take on old fairy tales. She supposed it was not being able to see the prat-falls and silly expressions that left her less enthusiastic. Elizabeth loved it. Aislynn found it highly amusing, sitting on Elizabeth's head stealing her popcorn.

Soon enough it was time for bed and An took Elizabeth upstairs and got her ready, tucking her in. Before she left the room Aislynn cleared her throat from the bedside table. *"Might want t' call fer back up."*

An came to the window. *"What? Why, what do ye..."* she searched the street and the yard and the trees, saw nothing but the flashes of the gnomes in their places. *"I don't see anythin'."*

Elizabeth jumped up, stared out the window too. "What is it? What are you saying?"

An settled her back in the bed. "Hush now. Were there a danger ye'd have just made yerself a target. And ye need to learn yer Irish."

"Look now," Aislynn chittered. An obeyed, still saw nothing.

"What is it I'm supposed t' be seein'?" she growled.

Aislynn sank back on her haunches. *"That's what I was afraid of. Call Ian. You've got a black sedan casing th' neighbourhood."* She headed for the door. *"I'm going to slip out and follow it as a bird, see if I can get a plate. Tell th' chief he's passed by twice since you came up here to put her to bed, and twice more that I know of... I just hadn't seen th' pattern yet."*

An nodded, pulling her phone out of her pocket and telling it to send the message as a text. There was too much a risk to make that as a phone call. She tucked Elizabeth back in. "Now you stay here, ye hear me? I don't want them seeing ye if yer what they're looking fer."

Elizabeth nodded and buried herself in the covers. An slipped from the room and turned off the light, headed back downstairs in case of trouble.

A few minutes later she felt her phone vibrate and set her hand on it in her pocket. It told her that the message had been received and someone was coming. She went into the kitchen to make herself a cup of tea, more for something to do than a need for a drink.

Sharon had gotten up and gone to get a shower when Aislynn slipped back in through the kitchen door. An set the phone on the counter as she felt for the sugar container and the drake began pushing the buttons with her tiny little monkey fingers, sending Ian the licence plate. A few seconds and she handed An the phone back. The phone reported that Cass and Dukes had been dispatched to deal with the sedan. He would be sending someone else to watch the neighbourhood more discretely.

An sank back against the counter, relieved. It would most likely be Jonny or Samantha, or even Raven, all of whom could become animals that would not stand out in the neighbourhood.

It was then that her ears picked up something on the television. George was watching the news and there was a report of mob violence that had claimed the lives of at least eight men at a warehouse. Aislynn's paw latched onto An's arm tightly as the images flashed over the screen. "Police are not releasing the names or images of the victims as yet, but so far eight bodies have been removed from the warehouse. The only speculations we've been able to get is that a group of men were playing poker in the office after hours when the warehouse was hit. We believe this to be part of the on-going mob war between the Irish Mafia and the encroaching Russian Bratva...."

An stopped listening. She pulled out her phone and headed upstairs immediately. The moment they were at a safe distance Aislynn hissed, *"That were th' warehouse from th' manor... from when we went t' th' City?"*

An felt her heart tighten. *"It's also where we staged from th' night Reggie were killed."* She put the phone to her ear just as Ian picked up the line.

"I've got someone on their way, An. Have they tried to broach th' house?"

An thought the words would never come out of her mouth. It felt as if they had gotten stuck in her chest. *"Check th' warehouse. Now, uncle! I think... It's on th' news. Aislynn says it's ours. They've eight bodies, Ian! Who was there tonight?"*

She heard him moving, heard the jangle of the keys on his ring. She heard him stop. "*It... it's gone. Th' warehouse key is gone,*" An thought it sounded as if his heart was breaking.

"*Stolen?*" she asked, somehow knowing better.

"*That means th' magic's broke, An. It means th' door's no more. I... I've got ta get out there....*"

"*Mundane means, uncle,*" she warned. "*Ye don't want it t' appear ye were close enough t' have had a hand in it.*"

She wasn't sure he had listened as he clicked off. She moved to her door, opening it to the stairs but didn't go up them. Instead, she sank onto the second step and pulled the rose from her hair, began stroking the petals, not caring that she was being cut. Aislynn curled up in her lap, petting her hair.

It seemed like hours later when she heard footsteps on the stairs. She did not bother to look up, just sat there with her phone in her hand, waiting, willing it to ring. The poor thing was fretting its circuits wanting to ring for her. She heard George's voice, "Miss O'Keefe?"

It was not until she felt a breath of cold and Aislynn began tugging on her hair that she looked up. "Ceobhránach," Jonny said with a terrible softness, kneeling and taking her hands in his.

She saw the look on his face, and the fact that he had come down to her level instead of drawing her up nearly brought tears to her eyes. "Oh, this is not good. It can't be... Who?" She squeezed his hand, not caring how the cuts stung, or that she was getting blood on him.

His voice was barely above a whisper. "*I stopped by on th' way here,*" he said in Irish. "*There were ten in all. They took one t' th' hospital but... he's not going t' make it. And there isn't a healer close enough t' do any good. Such a waste.*"

She tightened her grip, shook his hand, angry. The tears spilled over. "*Did I know any of them?*"

"*Most of them. Ye fought a few o' them: Grim, Eli, Brian Murphy, Bryan Joyner, Conner, Nevin, Donnelly, Scott Dun, Ian Lipscomb...*" He stopped as she gasped, surging towards him without collapsing. She had indeed fought several of them and recently. She had spent most of the day with young Ian.

"I remember Conner, sweet kid. A little... shy. Donnelly... at th' games... Ian... oh that sweet boy!" She looked up, her face changing as her brain did the math, shifted unconsciously back to English. "That were only nine."

Jonny changed his grip on her, warning her it was the worst.

"Oh, god, Skye?"

"No," he said quickly. "It were... Sean."

An found herself unable to believe it. "Sean? Our Sean? Her... he... how'd they? Oh, sweet Mary, Mother of Pearl!" she gasped. "Elizabeth!"

This brought George's head up. "What about Elizabeth?" He had been standing quietly out of the way until his daughter's name.

An shot up, slipping around Jonny with more grace than she should have in front of George and ran towards the door she could see faintly glowing from the lock she had put on it. Behind her, she heard Jonny explaining things to Mr. Tallow.

Elizabeth sat up as the door opened, her eyes wide, terrified of what she was about to be told. "What? Did the people in the car..."

An drifted across the room, sat on the edge of the bed, set her hands on the girl's shoulders. Elizabeth was already crying, silently, the tears just rolling. "There was... I'm not sure what happened yet. But... Sean... Sean was killed tonight."

"NO!" she screamed. "Please be lying!" she begged. "Please tell me someone's lying. There was a mistake."

Jonny was in the doorway. "I'm sorry, *a stóirín*. I saw him myself."

Elizabeth looked from Jonny to An even as her father came around him. "He can't lie, can he?"

An shook her head. Elizabeth dissolved into sobs and wrapped her arms around her, burying her face in her chest. An rest her cheek against the top of her head.

George stood by ineffectively, finally, said quietly, "I'll... I'll go tell Sharon." He slipped quietly from the room.

An turned her head towards Jonny, but not fully. "*What'd ye tell him?*"

"*That th' gentleman who had been teaching her self-control and some self-defence was murdered tonight. Nothing less than th' truth.*"

She nodded. A minute later Sharon was there and An quietly backed out, letting Elizabeth take comfort in her mother's arms. She let Jonny take her hand, guide her around a few toys forgotten on the floor that An had miraculously missed rushing in.

George was waiting in the hall. He startled An when he took her by the arms and drew her into a hug. "We're terribly sorry for your loss. You take whatever time you need."

An swallowed her confusion. "Elizabeth will want to go t' th' funeral. May she?"

"She's a little young..." he said, from the sound of his voice he was looking into the bedroom at his sobbing daughter. "But you're right. She'll need the closure. Was she really close to him?"

An nodded. "She adored him. He taught her so much about how to focus her own energies..."

"We should go," Jonny said softly, placing a hand on her arm.

She nodded. Aislynn ran up, scampered up her dress with the snow rose in her hands. She handed it off quickly, sucking her little thumb with a glare in Jonny's direction. An let him lead her out of the house, not even paying attention until he guided her into a car pulled up to the curb. He helped her in and climbed in the back seat with her.

She turned to look at him, realizing she had to focus. She shouldn't have been taken away from Elizabeth at a time like this. Not with the Russians trolling the neighbourhood. "The car. Did Cass and Dukes..."

Jonny shook his head. "Car's gone."

She sighed in relief, sank back against the leather seat. "Where are we going?" she asked, forcefully pushing aside her emotions and shock and getting right to business. She was obviously needed somehow. Jonny never got in the car with her. He usually flew over-watch.

"Well, that all depends on yer answer to m' next question."

She met his brown eyes. "Which is?"

"Do ye remember th' conversation we had at th' riverside on Ostara?"

An felt a blush rising. "I remember discussing a great many things. I don't think this has ought t' do with Serephina."

There was a darkening in his eyes at the mention of that name. "No, it doesn't. We talked about ye bein' able t' become mist."

"Aye. I remember that. I remember almost succeedin' too. Until ye said something an' I lost my concentration."

He tipped his head. "Aye, well, I did that apurpose, t' prove t' yer mind ye *could* change back. So, what I need from ye now ...is t' try again. Go all th' way this time."

"Here, in th' car?"

He nodded. "Aye. 'Tis important. Charlie'll be driving 'round town in circles until we resolve this."

"But... this isn't a problem t' be resolved," she stammered, not liking being put on the spot.

Jonny reached out and touched her arm. "Ceobhránach, we need ye t' go inta th' warehouse, and since th' police are still there, we need ye t' be unseen."

Her mouth fell open. On her shoulder, Aislynn popped out from under her hair snarling. "*Too risky!*" the dragon growled.

"There are others who can be unseen! Ophelia is very good at sneakin' she said," An protested. "And supposedly Aiden..."

"Aiden can only make *things* unseen not himself, and while there are a good many who could slip in and never be noticed, none of them can see magic th' way ye do. Th' sight is a rare gift, Ceobhránach," he said softly, stroking her cheek with the back of his hand. "It's like They don't want us seein' th' truth o' things or sommat."

"Can't we wait 'til th' police are done?"

He sighed. "Th' magical evidence will fade fairly fast. We need to know if magics were used in th' attack and if Sean... got anything off."

"Who are you t' be asking her t' risk her very solidity..." Aislynn began.

"I would not ask were it neither important nor I uncertain she kin reform herself," he said firmly. The tightness of his mouth spoke to the slow rise of his temper.

"I'll... try," she said, wanting the two to stop arguing. She turned in her seat, taking Aislynn from her shoulder, under protest, and setting her in the rear window.

She concentrated on the mists that had already begun to puddle at her feet. She willed herself to gather it up, to surround her, become one with her. She wanted to be as light and ethereal. Slowly, her perceptions began to change, spreading out as if she was all eye.

She turned to Aislynn and Jonny, tried to ask if it had worked but found she had no means of voicing her thought. Aislynn's eyes were wide, Jonny merely nodded.

"Charlie, take us near th' warehouse."

He turned back to her. "Now, ye'll have to spread yerself fairly thin t' keep from bein' too noticed. Th' warehouse is near enough th' river there's a fog risin' tonight with a little help." He did not elaborate on what that help was.

An looked down, noted that while her clothes and everything she was wearing had changed with her, what had been in her pockets had not. On the seat was her cell phone and the little gnome figurine that was the remote for the alarms on the Tallows' property. She reached out to the phone, tried to talk to it. It lit up, happy to be of service. She told it to print on the screen a message and to buzz until it was picked up.

Aislynn looked down, dropped through An to the seat and grabbed it. She looked at the screen and, grumbling, handed it to Jonny, returning to the back of the seat to read over his shoulder. The message said: **I can still communicate with what I touch**.

"Good," Jonny said. "Ye kin find out what happened. Though I want ye t' be careful. It won't do fer ye t' be overwhelmed and solidify in th' middle o' a warehouse full o' inspectors."

Yes, the phone said. An took in her surroundings, realizing she was aware of the car around her in a way she hadn't been before. **I can sort of see the car. And Charlie. I'm aware of him now, though I still can't 'see'.**

He arched one delicate, white eyebrow. "Useful."

It is like I am all eye.

"Like ye've turned yerself inward into yer eyes?"

More like outward. ...But still kind of inside out.

He mused on that. He looked out the window for several minutes before he spoke again. "I'm goin' t' be near as th' raven, keepin' an eye out. Anything happens, just get out, go t' th' car. Have Aislynn find me."

"*And where am I to be?*" the small dragon huffed.

Jonny regarded her. "*How small can ye get?*"

She rolled her eyes. "*Not bug size. Though that'd be useful.*"

"*Aye, i'twould. Sparrow? Bat?*"

"*I can do a sparrow,*" she grumped, still irritated with the bard.

Bat. Sparrows don't fly at night.

"*Good point. Bat then. Where will you be?*" she asked Jonny.

"There's a blue building across from th' warehouse, used to be a wire mill. I kin see into th' warehouse from there. When she leaves, fly over there an' I'll meet ye at th' car."

Think that was where the Russians were watching the warehouse from?

He took a deep breath as the car slowed and pulled into a secluded parking space a block down from the warehouse. "Anythin' is possible. I'll be careful."

He opened the car door, held it for An to pour out. Aislynn shifted to bat and landed on top of the vehicle.

It was slow moving for An, trying to figure out how to do so. A light breeze sprang up and helped a little, though it drifted her off course a bit. Jonny wafted her in the right direction, warned her again to be careful and turned back to give final instructions to Charlie. An managed to start off towards the warehouse and figured out how to move more swiftly by gathering herself up more.

Aislynn flew on ahead, staying where she could see her to serve as a beacon. When she turned back to face An and hovered for a moment, An slowed and began to thin out, stretching herself as far as she dared and easing along the ground towards the building Aislynn was now hanging from.

All the doors were open and people were milling in and out, carrying small bags and plastic numbers and cameras. The fact that every light in the warehouse was on had no effect on her perceptions. She slipped past the people gathering evidence or standing around talking, completely unnoticed, mingling with the fog slipping in off the river several hundred metres away. She called to it, wanting it thicker and closer.

She paused in the doorway, connected with it, wanting to know what it saw. It told her to ask the pedestrian's door and she curled in and around, caressing it with a tendril. Spread out over the floor, she asked it what it witnessed, saw everything thinly and without being overwhelmed. In this way, she followed the path of events, almost as if she had been there, though her view was decidedly skewed:

A shadowy thing solidified inside the door, just enough that it could operate the controls. The door opened and several men in black poured in. The enemy took their places and waited. One of them walked on wolf feet, though he stood like a man, remained in the shadows near the door with someone else. He consulted something, used tools to peer into the office, signalled the man next to him. A gun came up, took careful aim as the rest slipped closer to the room where six men sat playing poker. Conner sat on the edge of the desk eating from a bag of pretzels, watching the game. Grim was in the refrigerator getting the beer. Sean was on the computer.

The gun by the door fired and Sean's head exploded against the monitor and chaos ensued. Guns went off but the shoot-out was fairly one-sided. The office was a barrel and the O'Keefes: trout. Grim shifted to a large man-like wolf and launched over the card table. The sniper by the door switched to a handgun and unloaded his clip. Grim turned back into a man and dropped like a stone, shock and surprise on his dead face; the wounds sizzling. Some of the bullets embedded in the wall behind where Grim had been. Those areas suddenly felt dead to her and she avoided them.

From upstairs someone began firing downward, hit one or two of the black-clad enemies before something slipped up behind and shoved them over the rail. It frustrated An that she could not see this other thing no matter how she tried, except when it solidified just enough to effect things. Young Ian Lipscomb landed on the concrete floor not far from where other dead had been laid out a year before, broken and bleeding but breathing.

There was shouting and the assailants began moving more swiftly. Someone took things from the office, while others broke open crates and peered in. Someone lit a rag in a bottle and threw it into the office, slamming the door to it as they fled. The bottle broke against a white canister near the fridge and covered it in flaming liquid. The fire began to spread quickly, eating everything it could reach, its hunger insatiable. Moments later, the white canister exploded, blowing out the fire and every window on the lower floor of the warehouse. An felt this as an overall, dull pain to her awareness.

Someone kicked in the door and looked around, made a phone call. Soon other people swarmed the building. Bodies were assessed and taken out. Young Ian had managed to survive his fall, had choked out 'They spoke Russian… just started shootin'. Planned. …We were just playin' poker.' She felt the lie, even though she had no body to feel it with. They had not been 'just playing poker'.

An drifted back outside, felt Ian in the parking lot, the gryphon's anger and grief barely contained. She brushed against his hand in passing, making herself just solid enough to feel different from the surrounding fog. She slipped off towards the river and, gathering herself only just enough, began drifting along it.

She was several kilometres down river when a large white raven landed on the bank ahead of her. She was floating on the current, letting herself thin out and become one with the mist rising from the cooler waters. He shifted, called out her name. When he got no response, he reached down and put his hand in the water, caused a crackle of short-lived rime to spread over the surface towards her. He called her name again, more forcefully. Finally, "...Ceobhránach." The word was almost a sigh, carried more weight to her senses than her own name had.

She gathered up again, stopped drifting. In the middle of the river a female figure began to form of the mist, regarded him. Jonny stood on the bank, white hair lifting at the edges, floating in non-existent wind. He held out his hand to her, his eyes dark in the faint light from the nearby city lights. There was little moon out, as if she had turned her face from the horrors of this night. An drifted closer, reached out to accept his hand, slipping up the bank and into his arms, collecting herself together. It was not until he folded his arms around her that she went solid and dissolved again, this time in tears.

He let her sob until she was completely spent, before gently leading her across the grass towards the car waiting on the side of the road. It was not the same one that had brought them to the warehouse. This one felt and smelled different and Ian was in it, holding Cipín. He looked angry and heartbroken and stunned. Jonny settled her across from the chief, sat beside her and kept his arm around her. There was an exchange between the two men, done in a glance, each reading the body language of the other.

An forced herself to regain her composure. Later she could break down. Right now she was in mixed company, the company of her chief, and needed to tell him what she had seen. She dabbed at her eyes with a kerchief and sat up straighter. Jonny removed his arm when it seemed she did not need it any more.

"I would not think th' inspectors would be done with ye yet," she said softly, trying to get her voice to obey her. It sounded as whispy as she felt.

He saw it for the ploy it was but allowed it. "Detective Torres suggested I go ta hospital ta ma livin' man an' they'd meet me there when they were done at th' warehouse. I think they wanted me out from underfoot,, so I wouldn't see what they were findin' in ma 'criminal hideout'." He gave a pained smile that was very predatory. "Little do they know that is not that kind o' warehouse. Nothing in there but emergency supplies. There were some crates upstairs to be shipped ta Cork but they are fully legitimate cargo." He regarded her with his eagle eyes for a moment more, the car filling with the scent of emotional gryphon and summer fields. "Are yeh ready ta tell me what happened?"

She nodded. "I... I turned t' mist," she began.

"So Charlie told me." He looked to Jonny. "This little mission yer doin'?" he asked.

Jonny nodded. "I was on m' way t' th' Tallows when I saw th' police lights at th' warehouse. There were a lot of 'em. I flew by, saw what had happened, counted th' bodies, took note of who they were and swung by Courtz. Got Charlie t' meet me at th' Tallows and got An. Th' car ye sent me t' watch for was no where t' be seen. So I went in and told An... what happened. Th' Tallows know about Sean."

"Elizabeth's heartbroken," An said quietly.

"I kin imagine."

"An and I talked once about how she might use th' mist and th' fog, cause o' th' way it reacts t' her. Once, she almost managed t' shift like a smokeling. I had her try again; asked her t' slip in with th' fog from th' river and see what could be seen, if magics had been used or not. Th' plan was sound. Aislynn were a bat inside keeping th' eye out. She was t' flag me when An left th' warehouse and we were t' meet at th' car. I were watching from th' opposin' roof. Which, by th' by, is where someone else has been keepin' an eye on th' place. Quite a few cigarette butts and debris moved t' make comfortable seatin'."

It was not until he mentioned Aislynn that her mind went to her drake and noticed that she was crouched on the back of the seat behind the driver, sucking on a silver coin like a child with a lolly. When she held her hand out to her, the petty drake leapt across the car and landed on her lap. She started stroking Aislynn between her wings and on the back of her neck, as much for the dragon's comfort as for her own. There was a tiny crack as she bit the coin in two.

Ian returned his attention to An. "And what did ye find out but that yeh can turn ta mist?"

"It's not sommat I'll be willin' t' do often or fer long," she admitted with a tip of her head. "But... I was able t' slip in with th' fog from th' river without notice. I spoke with th' buildin' and its components. Saw what it saw."

Ian stiffened. Beside her, she felt Jonny's muscle twitch.

"Th' boys were playin' poker. Two were watchin', young Lipscomb were upstairs and Sean on th' computer. Something even th' building could not sense until it became solid enough opened th' door from th' inside, let th' murderers in."

"Shadowling?" Jonny suggested.

"Possible," Ian admitted.

"That would make sense. I never asked Courtz what that one had felt like. But... th' enemy had a man-wolf with them. He seemed to be giving th' orders. They took up position. Sean was th' first shot. They were not takin' chances an' they knew what they were dealin' with. It were a massacre. Grim they shot with iron. Th' ...shadow, I guess, shoved young Ian off th' upper floor. He hit a couple of th' Russians before he fell. Not sure if he killed any; they were all dragged out." She told him the rest without emotion, her tone going to flat recital as she told of the attempted fire and the explosion which ended it. She withdrew after that.

She could smell Ian's anger, as it had begun to fill the car with a scent even she could not miss. "There will be hell ta pay fer this," he ground. "Spetznakov thinks I won't retaliate? I'm goin' ta prune his organization ta th' stump, then take a backhoe ta th' root. And it won't just be Florida where I'll burn 'im. No. Every connection he has will wither away on th' vine. There won't be a single Bratva member left alive in any city wit' an O'Keefe presence anywhere on this continent. I'll burn them out o' their rats nests an' leave th' rivers ta run with their blood."

There was an audible growl now, heard even over the engine of the car and the noises from outside of ambulances and other emergency vehicles. The car came to a stop and Ian passed Cipín to An, turning to the man who opened the limousine door for him.

"Take them ta Courtz an' see ta it they get back ta th' Rest." He leaned back in the open door. *"An, go home. Yeh feel yeh need ta go ta th' girl, fine, but take every precaution. I'll send fer yeh when I need. ...And I will. Jonny, get her home. Make sure she's completely solid,"* he said, meaning something else than the surface words, but An wasn't able to suss out what that might be. *"It's not uncommon fer a first ethereal shift,"* Ian added to An as she looked to him in confusion. *"Yer just full o' surprises, lass."* With that he stood and went into the hospital.

The driver returned to the car and pulled out of the loading zone, headed as he had been directed. An merely sank against Jonny, letting him put his arm around her and taking comfort in his cool, fresh snow on churned earth scent.

17

Wakes are never easy. This one was doubly hard due to logistics. Though the fire went out very soon after it started, the damage had been done. Out of respect for the boys who had to have closed caskets, everyone had closed caskets. They were lined up on planks spanning the pool tables, their pictures on the coffins. In the main room, the stage was lined with wreaths, ten in all, with a large photo of each of the fallen and their name on a glamoured banner in O'Keefe colours.

An and Elizabeth were picked up at the Tallows early that morning by Skye. Sharon had expressed a desire to go, to meet these people Elizabeth spent so much time with, but was talked out of it by Elizabeth, and, surprisingly, George. "There will be another occasion for us to mingle. This is not the time. She's fine with An and her brother. We would just be intruding today."

An had warned them that Irish wakes and funerals were two day affairs, and they had accepted this with an ease which made An suspect someone had 'assisted'.

Skye drove them to Courtz and from there through the door to the cottage. He took the child out into the garden while An changed for the wake. She had not been about to wear full Victorian funerary garb in front of Elizabeth's parents. She was just putting on her boots when she heard the honking of a horn out front. She tied the last lace as Skye came in from the garden with Elizabeth and an armful of roses.

"Who is that?" she asked, tilting her head towards the front walk. As it was on the street, the house could not tell her.

Aislynn flew in from the bedroom with a black ribbon, asking An to tie it for her.

"Liberty wi' th' car," Skye answered.

An stood, taking the ribbon from Aislynn and grabbing Cipín, "'Tis not that far a walk t' th' Gate, Skye. No need fer th' car."

Skye opened the front door for them and An felt the already high heat outside. "Really? Ya want tae walk tae th' pub in thon dress in this heat?"

She sighed, realizing he was right, went out to the waiting car.

"But... aren't you going to have to walk it tomorrow to the burial?" Elizabeth asked.

"Aye," she replied, climbing into the car after the girl. "But t'morra morn Jonny will be beside me an' he'll keep me from overheatin'. Granted, no one'll see hide nor hair o' him fer days after, I expect, but there ye go," she said, tying the ribbon into a bow around Aislynn's neck as she wanted. Even Elizabeth wore a bow of green and gold in her golden hair.

When they arrived, there were not many cars. Liberty pulled up to the front and let everyone out, driving the car back to the house so as not to take up one of the too few spaces. She tended to leave those for people coming from outside the Rest and those who lived on the farther side of the community.

An led Elizabeth into the pub. The girl looked around, wide-eyed, having never been in a bar or public house of any kind. She saw the wreaths on the stage and went immediately to Sean's. There were tears sparkling in her eyes as she whispered something; then she bent forward and laid a twinkling stone on a chain on the wreath, kissed it. She leaned back into An when she drifted up behind her and set her hands on her small shoulders.

An nodded to Jonny who was off to the side, setting up. His hair was loose and a little wild. An led Elizabeth over to the bar where Tori was doing a little last minute setting up. She smiled sadly at the woman. "Why is it yer always here at th' wakes? Don't ye work at Courtz?" she asked.

Tori smiled, making Elizabeth a Shirley Temple before pouring An a measure of her favourite honey whiskey. "Well, I know the family well enough, at least bits. And most of the normal staff here at the Gate... well, they're usually attending the wakes so... I fill in."

"Thank ye," An smiled. "Does Jonny have his nut brown?"

"Not yet. Will you take it to him for me?" Tori asked, opening a bottle and setting it on the bar near her hand.

"Aye. I was goin' t' ask. Also, might I borrow that brush?"

"Absolutely. I'll keep an eye on the young lady for you," Tori nodded, setting the brush beside the bottle, making sure it tinked against the glass, letting An know where it was. She collected both items and crossed to where Jonny was tuning his harp.

He looked up as she approached, gave her a sad, half smile and stroked the surface of a stool beside him. It sprang into view as frost crusted over it. She set his drink upon it and held the brush up. "Ye want it braided back or t' leave it wild?"

Jonny glanced back over his shoulder at the stage full of wreaths, sighed. "Fer now, I think wild will suit. I may reconsider fer th' march. I'll let ye know."

An nodded, headed back to the bar and returning the brush. "Thank ye. I may need it in th' mornin'."

Tori gave a rueful look as she put it away. "A lot of people will likely need it in the morning."

Elizabeth looked around the pub, taking it all in. She had the look on her face of a kid having been allowed into some secret adult clubhouse. "What's in there?" she asked, pointed to the back room.

An put a hand on her back. "That... that is th' game room. There are pool tables and dart boards back there; but today... t'day it holds th' dead."

Elizabeth frowned. "Why? Don't you use a funeral home?"

An smiled indulgently. "Here, we do it th' old way. We tend our own dead and don't embalm. Even th' coffins are plain wood. We intend to return t' th' earth when we're done like we're meant. Thing's'll be a wee different from yer granfer's funeral, love, all peaceful and quiet and orderly. Th' wake is called a 'wake' 'cause they laid out th' dead on th' table, burned candles, talked about him, drank, cried, laughed, made noise enough in general in hopes that if they weren't really dead, just in a coma or deeply unconscious, they'd wake up. It happened all too frequently in th' old days. We didn't have modern methods of bein' sure someone were truly dead. And if it turned out they were, speaking well of them, and laughing, and taking care of one another were a way to ensure th' soul would move on and not haunt th' livin'. Sometimes even fights break out, which ye'll stay clear of if it happens."

"So, Sean's in there?"

An took a deep breath. "Aye. But... ye don't want t' see him. There were a fire and... he were wounded in a way ye won't... recognize. I'll not be responsible fer exposin' ye t' that horror. Th' caskets are all closed an' they're stayin' that way. I'll let ye see th' coffin, but no more, understand?"

Elizabeth nodded and Aislynn flew on ahead, perching on the cue rack to stay out of the way. Elizabeth gave Echo a shy smile as she came in. He merely nodded to her, slipping out of the way, trying to remain unnoticed. The girl went straight to Sean's box without even glancing at the pictures. She looked around. "There's... a lot of them."

"Ye knew how many there were. Ye saw their pictures."

"I know but they seem ...more like this," she said, resting her hand on the simply carved, flat-topped coffin. "Did they all... at the same time? Did he hurt?"

An knelt beside Elizabeth, made her look at her. "I saw it in that way that I see what a thing has seen, th' way that things talk t' me. I saw it all, start t' finish. Sean were a dangerous man. Ye knew that. He taught ye t' be a dangerous little girl, so no one could hurt ye if they tried." Elizabeth nodded, not knowing where this was going. "Well, th' bad men knew he were a dangerous man, too. So they made sure they got him first. He felt nothin'."

She sniffled, nodded again; blew her nose on the lace edged handkerchief An had made for her. "But the others did. That's why I asked. Cause this one," she said, setting her hand on Lipscomb's coffin and then on Grim's. "And this one. They hurt a lot."

An gasped. "Ye can feel that even now?"

Elizabeth nodded. "It's dull, and fading, but there."

An let her stand there, looking over the caskets, her hand upon that of her mentor for several minutes before she asked softly, "Are ye ready to go back out front?"

"Yes, I think so."

An took her hand and led her out, nodded to Cullen who was standing in the doorway of the sidebar. He just followed her with his eyes, trying to figure her out.

When they entered the main room, there were more people there than before. Skye was near the bar, talking with someone An did not know but could clearly see, someone she thought she might have encountered in the grand melee at Midsummer. Skye looked sharp in his black kilt. Seamus was over in a corner with Elaroush and a couple of mortals from the parts of them that kept vanishing from her sight. Jonny was playing quietly on his harp.

Ian was before the wreaths, still in the same clothes An had seen him in two days ago when he had called her to his office to discuss the funeral. It had taken a while before the morgue had released the bodies. There had been a lot of questions. He had a fresh bottle of Jameson in hand and was halfway through his own private ritual, taking a drink and pouring one at the base of each wreath. He wasn't bothering with a glass.

Elizabeth leaned into An and whispered, "Why did he do that?"

"'Tis an Irish tradition, *a rún*, t' share a drink with th' departed."

The girl hesitated, thinking, then asked softly, "Can I...? You know... do that?" she asked, pointing to Ian.

An caressed her golden curls. "Aye, I think a sip won't hurt. And Sean would like that, I think. But this only one, it'll be. And mind ye drink it slow and not tell yer ma."

She took her over to the bar and requested four full shots of Irish Mist, and a fifth half-filled. Passing Aislynn hers, she handed the half and a whole to Elizabeth and had her lead them to the stage.

Elizabeth looked up at Ian a little nervously, as if afraid he was going to tell her she was too young, then glanced back at An who nodded encouragement. She sighed and stepped up to Sean's picture again, holding out the full glass to it.

"'Tis gone to soon, you are, my friend.
'Tis more you had to teach me.
And gone too far away you are,
where words can never reach me.
But in my heart still you be
and in my memory forever-more
but I'll walk the path you set me on..."

An stepped up behind her and set a hand on her shoulder. The girl took heart, and found the rest of the words she wanted.

"...though you'll walk with me no more." She held up her own shot glass. "I'll make you proud of me, Sean, I promise," and then, in spite of advice, poured the whiskey into her mouth and swallowed. An set her own second glass before the wreath and both she and Aislynn threw theirs back with a soft "Sláinte."

Elizabeth seemed all right for a second, then gasped and winced as the whiskey burned its way down. She suddenly remembered the second glass in her hand and poured it on the wreath as she saw Ian do, then turned and threw her arms around An, crying. Though she turned her face up at Ian as if daring him to say anything.

The man Skye had been talking with, silently moved from the bar to the stage where An, Ian and the girl stood. Looking down at Elizabeth, he said in a gentle voice, "Mourn not, *ferch*, your friend isn't really gone. I would like it greatly if you would tell me of this man, so that I can give him his proper place on the rolls this next Samhain. He rests in *Annwfn* now." Turning his gaze to An, he smiled, unfazed by Elizabeth darting behind her skirts. "You've done well with this one, *Filid*. She will grow up to be a strong woman one day."

An was stunned, looked at the man as if he had suddenly grown three heads, and placed her hands protectively around the girl, drew herself up. "I've no idea who ye are, sir, nor what ye called us, but I'll thank ye not to take such familiar tones with either o' us in th' future. I'll not be th' one t' initiate th' bairn t' th' Irish tradition o' donnybrooke, but I'll not hesitate if ye persist on intrudin' on our grief and makin' assumptions regardin' our beliefs." For good measure, she called Cipín from where she had been left resting against the bar.

Aislynn hissed at him from An's shoulder, snaking her neck out as far as she could to snarl. *"She will hesitate, but I will not. And if I start it..."*

Ian held his hand out, palm down, "Na, na, *calm down, be easy.* He's new out, and he's Welsh. Gi'e 'im time t' learn." He offered the man the bottle. "Take a swig, and sit and listen, boi."

The man seemed taken aback by An's outburst and the dragon's threat and turned, found himself staring up at a drunk and dishevelled Ian holding out a bottle to him. Looking him over, he leaned forward, pitched his voice low so that anyone not there with them would have a hard time hearing. "Shameful, sir! Is this how you honour your men? Look at yourself. You're a Chieftain! Clean yourself up and show your men the honour they deserve. You disrespect them, their memory, and the other men still under you by looking like this. Mourn their passing, but honour them by celebrating their accomplishments in this life. The young one and the *filid* have the right idea, though the custom is older than she thinks," he said, turning to smile at her.

Perhaps he thought he was complimenting her. It came off as patronizing. He turned back to Ian, unable to pass him and crossed his arms and gazed at him as if daring him to challenge his words.

An gasped at the idiot's daring, took a step back with Elizabeth to get her further out of the way of the fight she was certain was about to happen.

Ian looked at him levelly. "There is no shame in grief, boy, nor in fatigue. I'vena slept in a week, 'twixt th' police an' th' Russians an' th' needs o'ma people. My men an' my god understand if I'm a little worn 'round th' edges. An' yeh? Yeh've no right to speak to me so, in my own place, at a wake for my clan.... Yeh are not O'Keefe. Yeh stand here on sufferance. Take care, feat'er duster, that yeh dunnae spark as old a tradition at a wake." His voice had begun civil, and grown more forceful with every word until the other man seemed to shrink before him.

He dropped his hands down to his sides as he cleared his throat, "*Faddau 'm*. I apologize, I did not realize that you have not had any rest. I beg forgiveness. I didn't realize that this was your place. If I have breached hospitality, tell me what I may do to make amends."

An snapped, "Ye kin start by paying attention and learnin' th' local traditions afore ye deign to correct people ye don' even know. Or speakin' so familiarly to children ye've no' been introduced ta!"

The man bowed, the tanned skin of his face darkening in his embarrassment. "I beg yer pardon, both of ye." Withering in the face of her scowl and noting the tendrils of 'smoke' curling up from Aislynn's nostrils, he made a swift retreat.

Jonny raised an eyebrow at the exchange and traded his harp for his fiddle, began to play "Finnegan's Wake".

Ian stepped off the stage and wandered into the crowd, greeting people as they came in. An turned to each of the wreaths to have her say and Elizabeth sat on the edge of the stage, swinging her black, patent leather shoes in time with the fiddle. When he reached the part of the song where the fun begins, she started laughing.

Soon An sat beside her, smiling beneath her now lowered veil.

Elizabeth's eyes were bright. "That is sooo not 'Amazing Grace' or 'Go Rest High On That Mountain'," she laughed.

An set her arm around her shoulders. "Those can be arranged, ye know. A word t' th' bard..." she said, tipping her head towards him.

She shook her head. "Nah. I want the whole Irish thing this time. Who knows... I may put one of these in my will."

An chuckled. "Well, ye see anyone ye know, feel free t' talk or listen or question. I'll be required once and again t' sing. I've explained m' job in th' mornin'."

She nodded. "Hey, I see Kellain and Fitz. Can I go..."

An gave her a light push, telling her she was free to go to her friends.

Skye came up as she ran off. "Sorry aboot Cidrich," he said, handing her a whiskey. "Ah'd a warned th' nugget, but ah thoucht he'd gotten enouch a taste o' ya at th' changeover."

An frowned, trying to remember.

"Th' daft dobber wi' th' bokken, ...th' wooden katana? He tried fer m' back an' ye disarmed him wi' a deft wee twist an' cracked his skull."

An nodded, suddenly remembering the man. "Aye, ye'd a thought," she mused. "Cidrich, eh? Well, ye tell th' idjit that I'm a wee protective o' that lass, an' don't take kindly t' others tryin' t' do my job with her, 'less'n she or I ask."

"Ah've cleared his heid," Skye chuckled. "Thouch he's wantin' a proper introduction if yer willin'. Apologize?"

An thought about it, shook her head. "Not t'day. I've no head fer it. I've work t' do, th' child t' keep an eye on, an' grief o' my own t' gather afore I kin wail th' Rest's."

He nodded, gave her a brief hug. "I'll warn 'im t' stay clear."

"An' he gets near Elizabeth I'll let her jinx him," she added against his shoulder.

He paused, looked down at her. "She can dae that?"

There was something wicked in the swirling of her eye. "*He don't know one way or t'other, now do he?*"

He frowned. "*Ya... lie?*"

She tipped her head in a shrug. *"I didn't say I'd have her jinx him. Just that I'd let her. I've no idea really what she can do."*

He laughed, clinked his beer bottle to her empty glass and headed off down the bar.

Jonny started playing something she knew and she raised her clear, haunting voice to sing for him. She sang a few more songs, some sad and slow, some sad but spirited, some just rousing. The last managed to get her out on the dance floor for a turn with Billy Younger before he joined Jonny at the stage with his own instruments.

An headed to the bar, got drinks for both of them and set them on the stool between them. Billy flashed her a broad smile for it and Jonny just met her eyes with his earthy browns. She blushed and slipped away, headed back to the bar for some tea. Cullen approached while she was sitting there. His tie hung loose and his shirt was unbuttoned. His jacket pockets hung low with two liquor bottles. He reached behind the bar when Tori wasn't looking and snagged several empty pints and shot glasses.

"So," he said, beginning to work on his drinks, "ye were there?"

An sipped her tea, realizing he was probing her. "No."

"Ye said ye saw what happened."

"I did."

"How?" He grabbed the fountain hose and sprayed cola into the large glasses one by one. Ophelia slipped up silently on the other side of him, watching.

An sighed, her voice hard. "I speak to objects. They talk t' me. I slipped inta th' warehouse after and asked. Th' floor, th' walls... it all showed me what happened. I told Ian everythin'. Ye want details, ask him. I'd like t' get th' image o' Sean's head..." she stopped, eyes flitting to the mirror to find Elizabeth not terribly far away. "O' watchin' Grim die wi' an iron bullet in his craw."

Cullen nodded, began pouring a sickly sweet, licoricy, minty liquid into the shots. "Did ye see the faces o' the murderers?"

She just watched him as he picked up the first shot and dropped it into the soda and chugged it.

So that was what he was after. She sipped her tea. "Aye. I did. And no, I can't pick them out o' a line up or on th' street or a photo. Save fer th' wolfm'n, without th' eyes of things, I can't see them myself."

"Can't ye ask a computer t' show ye?"

She took a deep breath as he dropped another Jaegerbomb. "No. They can't show me what's on them, only what they themselves experience. Otherwise I wouldn' haf'ta get Elizabeth t' fix th' television box so I can watch whatever it is she wants t' share with me. And afore ye ask, I'll not subject that child to helpin' me pick out th' men what murdered her mentor."

Cullen growled, mostly to himself, dropped another bomb.

Beside him, Ophelia wrinkled her nose at what he was drinking. "Eww, how can you stand that stuff?" she asked, cradling her vodka as if it could protect her nose from the stench of his particular poison.

"I can't, but back in Europe beggars couldn't be choosers. Bad cola plus bad alcohol equals a fine little party drink." He shrugged and moved to the next shot, chugging another. "Never underestimate the ingenuity of a soldier in the field to take trash and turn it to treasure."

"But… you're not over there any more. There are things that taste better available. Why still drink it?"

"Habit?" he suggested, chugging the last one.

An finished her tea and slipped away. Her eyes fell on the stage and the row of ribbons and felt the pain all over again. She found a chair near and sank into it. There was a slight spark as Roulet set her hand on her back, sat next to her. "How are you holding up?" she asked.

An leaned over against her shoulder. "No nightmares, that's good. I still dream though."

"They'll pay for this. We'll find a way."

An gave a dry chuckle, shook her head. "This won't be th' last funeral this summer, Roulet. Before this war is over… we'll be so sick o' this place we can't set foot in it on a normal day."

"Yes. I'm sure there will be other funerals. Ones, maybe twos. But this has got to be the worst of it. Ten in one blow? We'll not be caught with our pants down again."

An buried her face in her hands. "This is going t' get so bloody."

Ian caught everyone's attention, standing on the edge of the stage. He looked more dishevelled than when he had arrived. He took a long pull from the bottle of Jameson in his grip. Someone pressed a glass into An's hand and Elizabeth sat on the other side of her from Roulet, something fizzy in her cup. They all turned to face the chief, waiting.

"Charles 'Grim' O'Keefe, Elijah Michael O'Keefe, Sean Oisín O'Keefe, Brian Murphy, Bryan Joyner, Nevin O'Dol, Melvin Donnelly, Scott Dunn, Ian Lipscomb, Jonny Conner," he intoned. "A good laugh an' a long sleep are th' two best cures, boys... sleep well. We'll have th' last laugh."

He paused to take a swig of whiskey from the mostly empty bottle. "Each and every one of yeh was a good lad. Loyal. Brave. True. All my boys. So many in th' ground. Yeh fought th' good fight, and went down swingin'. Yeh'll be missed... for a short while, before we join yeh in th' Summerlands where th' whiskey flows like water, all is light and laughter, and song fills every heart." He polished off the bottle, letting it drop from his fingers onto the stage as Jonny and Billy began playing the opening strains of "Danny Boy".

Ian sang, his voice rough with emotion and drink, tears rolling down his cheeks. Before he was done the whole pub was singing through tears. An heaved a heavy sigh. This meant the chief would want her to sing "Súil a Rún" at the grave side.

She saw Jonny wave her over as she looked up once "Danny Boy" was over. Before she had quite reached him, he began to play "The Green Fields of France" and An nodded, finding her way to the foot of the stage and singing, letting her keener's voice rouse the anger as well as the grief of the gathered. Thankfully, once that was done the pair launched into something more spirited. They kept up this pace, a few high, a few low, to keep the emotions from wandering too far in any one direction.

At one point, the two cousins, Harry and Peter, were at it, rolling on the floor trying to break each other's heads. Ian scruffed them both and tossed them out back into the grass and told them not to come back in until they were done. It did not take them long. They came in sporting matching shiners, arm in arm and hollering for more to drink.

Dawn found Elizabeth on the couch, curled up on An's lap with her shawl draped over her, and An asleep against the back of the sofa. Aislynn was tucked into Elizabeth's neck. They were awakened by Ian, standing, bleary-eyed, in the doorway. From the sound of things, An and Elizabeth were not the only souls to have fallen asleep in here. Mostly it was the young ones, which An did not mind.

"It's time," he said.

They sorted themselves out and headed into the bathrooms in small groups to straighten their clothes and wash faces, taming hair. Tori went around with bottles of Gatorade and breakfast biscuits. They were less sweet than tea-biscuits, better suited to a morning after drinking.

An took care of Elizabeth, straightening her out, giving her last minute instructions about what to expect at the church and the graveside, pressing Cipín into her care. Jonny chose to leave his hair wild, and somehow, it seemed fitting. His black patchwork vest was looking worn and slept in. The pants he wore had seen better days and his shirt had lost buttons on one sleeve. His feet were bare.

He gave her a wan smile as she looked him over. "Ye said 'all disarray or none'."

"Aye, that I did," she answered, taking a swallow from her flask and passing it to him. He took a swig and nodded in thanks, handing it back. Even Aislynn took a sip before the flashing silver vanished into a pocket of An's voluminous skirts.

It seemed no time at all they were watching the pallbearers filing into the room to collect their burdens. An left Elizabeth in the care of Sean's grandmother, his closest remaining relative, to walk in the place where a daughter would have. It seemed fitting as Elizabeth had become the closest to a daughter the man had possessed. An moved to stand beside Jonny, behind Father Thomas in the warm morning air.

This time, An called the mist. It came to her, curled at her feet, comforted her. Jonny struck the bodhrán and side by side they began the march, and An began to keen. The fog changed the pure notes of her wailing, echoed and played with it until it sounded like a bean sidhe striding through the Rest, calling people from their beds to mourn.

When An finally collapsed at the steps of the church, every dwelling in the Rest was empty and the little church was full to bursting. An had to admit, it was slightly hotter this morning than it had been the first time she had served as keener. Jonny's presence helped to keep her from overheating too quickly in the crepe dress, but it was still warm. She remained on the steps of the church, unwilling to get up until it was time.

While they waited, catching fragments of the mass from the open door, Jonny silently smoked and An played with the fog. She made tendrils and tried shaping it, giving Aislynn something to chase and pounce. She was developing a little skill. Jonny just watched, conserving his strength for the heat of the day later.

All too soon the bells were ringing and the altar boy came out, nodding to them. He held his lantern out for Jonny to glamour for An. He blew across the glass, covering it with a glowing frost that would light her way as she lead the procession through the fog to the cemetery through the little strip of woods and over the narrow river. This time, all of them were lain side by side, lowered with care one by one under Echo's obsessively watchful eye. How he had complained at what the coroners had done to the bodies. He was more protective of them than ever.

Father Thomas said his piece and benediction, and An sang "Súil a Rún" as the members of the Rest gathered handfuls of dirt and scattered them over the coffins. Half their work was done by the time the gravediggers moved to fill them in.

When An stopped keening, the air was frightfully still. The silence was a living thing, and not even the birds in the nearby trees seemed to want to break it. The gravediggers looked around, half afraid something was going to ride out of the haze and snatch them away. She saw their fear and dismissed the fog. Most of it followed her as she turned and walked back to her cottage, Elizabeth at her side and Aislynn flying on ahead to lead the way. Jonny had long since vanished.

18

That was not the last funeral by any means. By the time Mabon had come and gone, there had been no less than six others. Not all of them men, not all of them mortal. Mabon itself was less spectacular than the previous year. Even the bonfire and the straw man failed to get more than a momentary rise from people. Tensions ran so high there were numerous fights.

The only thing people seemed to be talking about was the war. An overheard someone discussing the latest excursion, talking about how they nearly got their asses handed to them while the white raven just stayed up in the air and watched. The man spat, saying Sorrow was a coward for always watching and never fighting, not even coming in to the rescue when it was so badly needed. Without warning, he found Cipín cracking across his calf, sending him hopping.

An growled, keeping her voice tight, "One, ye've no idea what his orders were. Ye have a problem th' way he conducted himself, talk t' th' bloody chief. Ye'd have no idea if he did sommat or not. Maybe he did. Maybe some o' ye are still breathin' thanks t' some unseen thing he did. Moren' a few out here are alive 'cause he stayed out o' it, and went fer help rather than divin' in.

"'Tis a far harder thing to watch people dying and not be able t' save them than t' be in th' thick o' things at risk o' dying, too. Doubt me? Ask any soldier's wife or mother. Ask any woman what ever waited on her man t' return home from th' wars. Waitin's bad enough, but t' hav' t' watch, helpless?" An had been unable to contain her rage at that and stormed off rather than give in to the violence wanting to boil up within her.

As she marched away she heard someone telling the man as they restrained him, "Rumour is she witnessed th' warehouse massacre... as if she'd been there in th' thick of it... an' helpless to stop it." An could feel the pitying eyes on her after that.

The O'Keefe's had set up a new warehouse for triage and An had gone with them more than once, whenever she was at the Rest when the alarm bells rang. It was one of the things she didn't like about spending most of her time with the Tallows. Everyone was doing their share, and she less than most, or so she felt.

Eventually Cullen had found Willy, the man who had made Liberty's security cameras, and got him to make a magical camera that took magical pictures and proceeded to photograph all of the current members of the Russian group. He had shown these to An and she had pointed out the individuals she had seen, including which one was the wolf. Less than a week later that particular man was found floating down river with a belly full of iron and a craw full of silver.

The war was taking its toll on everybody.

By the time Halloween came around, spirits were in need of serious lifting. Sharon came with Elizabeth to the Rest for the trick or treating and went on for days about the 'amazing costumes'. George would have come but for an emergency business trip.

Elizabeth was upset, but he promised to wear his Green Lantern costume under his suit to the meeting just for her. Sharon had dressed as Wonder Woman, and Elizabeth was Isis from an old TV show she had found on the internet. They had tried to get An to dress as a superhero, but she was too uncomfortable with brevity of the attire and ended up going as Tut, the Isis character's raven. She wore a raven headdress and a long, slim black dress with a feathered shawl for wings.

Halloween, while not the success it had been in previous years, was nonetheless successful at bringing up the emotional level of the Rest as a whole. There was hope, people were saying. And in the last hours before midnight everyone was listening for the bells to ring, praying they wouldn't. Midnight tolled and the whole community breathed in collective relief. They had managed to go an entire month without the death bell ringing. Some had come close. A few limbs had been lost. But no one had died, on their side.

She learned later that the same fight was going on in every city across the country where there was an O'Keefe presence and that particular branch of the Bratva.

All Saint's day dawned and An woke to the sounds of the death bell. The deep toned one rang slow and steady and the smaller, high-pitched bell rang twice. Two dead. She was out of bed and dressed and on her way to the manor in a trice. Elizabeth and her mother had thankfully gone home late the night before.

A number of people had the same idea, and she found herself stopped by a gathering crowd, most of which she could only feel. She could not get any closer and sighed, frustrated. Someone grabbed her arm less gently than they perhaps intended and she turned, saw Solitaire pulling her out of the mob towards the side, and out of the crush. They managed to make it to the veranda where Mikey was standing on the step preventing all passage. He started to deny them when Solitaire said, "Too many people she can't see crowding her."

He nodded and the two women went off to the side of the veranda, Solitaire putting her in a rocking chair and out of the way. They did not have to wait long before Ian came out of the house, his face dark and more beak than man. His anger was a tangible thing. "On th' eighteent' of August, Spetznakov made a grave error. He attacked wit'out provocation an' massacred ten o' our boys. We've been payin' 'em back since, an' wit' success in most places. This mornin'..." he paused to get his voice under control, his emotions raw. "This mornin' Rowdy were goin' in ta defend Young Fitzwarren who were arrested fer th' shootin' o' one o' th' Russian bastards. We were pretty confident he'd be home by dinner on self-defence. Now.... Someone put a bomb in Rowdy's car, took out him and his intern, Miss Becky Salver. Aye, she weren't one o' ours, but she died wit' him, and so I ordered th' bell fer her. There were several bystanders hurt, so what yeh can do fer those families I want yeh ta do as anonymous as yeh can. Yeh know I don't cotton t' collateral damage."

He turned to a woman in the front of the crowd. "Tiss, I'll be seein' yeh in my office now. Yeh'll be needin' ta take over fer Rowdy."

"Aye, uncle." An recognized her voice as the woman who had come with her to the Tallows that first day, set everything up.

"I'll be needin' yeh ta set up th' funeral expenses an' a trust fer Miss Salver's little sister. That family will not be wantin' fer a farthin'." Ian then disappeared into the house with Miss Jones at his heel and the crowd began to disperse.

Rowdy's wake and funeral went like so many others had, though there was more drinking than normal, and more people getting into fights. Ian's only words to Rowdy's image were, "They're not done payin' fer yeh yet, boi. They hit non-combatants this time. Yer man did for th' bastard what killed yeh. He's a good lad. We'll see 'em all ta hell fer this."

An was introduced eventually to the grieving boyfriend, a slim gentleman by the feel of his hand, and slightly effeminate by the sound of his voice. He was really sweet as he thanked people for their well wishes, and told stories that showed what a romantic Rowdy had been, in spite of his bad boy image and rough edges. Then he would drink and growl about his vengeance and An could hear something dark and dangerous in the thin man.

Samhain was two days later, on the seventh, and the Rest was ready to explode. The celebration was more intense than she had ever seen this community. The bonfires burned hotly, and from the smell An suspected they were further fuelled by fats from the recent slaughtering of livestock. Liberty and Patches went through the rite with passion and energy and the dance around the bonfires went on longer than previous years. Everyone was celebrating hard, looking around suddenly as if they had seen something or were hoping to see someone.

During the dancing, Jonny had sung Sting's 'They Dance Alone', and not a dry eye remained as women, and a couple of the men, took to the floor and danced with the memories of those they had lost. Jonny brought them slowly up from that one, playing something only slightly faster and a little less painful before moving them to a more spirited piece.

An noticed Cullen was in higher spirits than normal, was speaking in clusters with certain people, including Patches, who seemed to be in agreement with him. The two men toasted to something and went about enjoying their night. They were in a better mood than they had been in months, but there was something very bloodthirsty about their joy.

While Fox had put up the usual hedge this year just inside the gate, Ian had also ordered guards posted, just in case. So when an unknown woman looking like a life-sized plastic doll came walking out of the wood, there was a moment of panic.

The doll stopped near the edge of the festivities, staring at all the people and the fire.

Liberty approached her cautiously, not wanting to spook her. "Where are ye from?"

The doll looked at her in confusion, said something in what sounded like Spanish.

Aiden stepped out of the crowd at that, set a hand on Liberty's arm. "I got this. *You are safe,*" he said in Spanish. "*Where are you from?*"

"*I fell from the tree,*" she said, pointing back the way she had come. It was then someone noticed the broken noose hanging from her neck.

"*Ye were hung?*"

She looked confused. "*Well, yes. That's what you do with old dolls on the island of dolls. My rope broke and there was no one. Then it got colder and the woods looked different and ...I saw the fire. Fire means people. There is never fire on the island. ...I'm not in Mexico, am I?*"

Aiden gave a rueful little laugh. "*I somehow doubt you* were *in Mexico. What's your name?*"

"Adora."

Aiden turned to the people slowly beginning to gather. "She's from th' 'island a' dolls in Mexico, or so she believes. Her name is Adora. Th' noose broke an' she began walkin'. Somehow ended up here. I don't think she came through th' fort."

"Probably not," Jonny sighed. "There are places in those woods that'll serve fer gate fer a small soul. Especially on nights like this. One o' th' Gentry and their host couldnae get through, nor could they find one if they looked. They have t' be made or stumbled upon."

Fox piped up. "I... think I've seen this island of dolls. Creepiest place I ever passed."

Ian looked at him, frowning for an explanation.

"I was doing some scouting. I've been through that area plenty of times, never seen it before or since. Couldn't get onto it, either. That was back when I rescued Serenity, remember? I didn't mention it 'cause I forgot about it. Wouldn't have remembered it now but for..." he gestured in the doll's direction.

Ian nodded, set a hand on Aiden's shoulder. "Hate ta burden yeh, but, 'til we kin find someone else what speaks Spanish, I'll need yeh ta take care o' her, teach her up a bit."

Aiden nodded, and began to lead her nearer the food.

Meanwhile, Ian began shooing everyone back towards the fires and the dancing green.

At this point, An had had her fill and just went home.

An was called to Ian's office a few days later. As she approached, she heard an argument going on between Aiden, Cullen and Ian through the slightly open door. It was apparently about Kevin, the Late Rowdy's boyfriend.

"Th' lad has a right to his vengeance," Cullen was saying.

"Aye," Ian growled. "But those were non-combatants, Cullen! Mob molls are not viable targets."

"Neither was Becky or Rowdy," Cullen added.

"It makes us no better than them," Ian said with a snap of beak.

"We'll just have t' start directin' Kevin's anger," Aiden suggested. "He's been doin' this on his own. And he's gotten pretty good at it. That's three Russian officers, four goons an' th' two girls in less than a fortnight, Ian. He looks harmless with that stupid Hawaiian shirt of his. They let him just walk in where he pleases."

Ian sighed. "Soon enough that'll get around, an' they'll shoot before he can get close. His mind's anywhere I t'ink i'tis, he's brewin' a deat' wish," he growled. "Take him in hand, then. Start giving him official jobs."

An quietly pushed open the door and peered around it. Ian waved her in, gestured for Aiden to show her the chair. She walked over to where Aiden stood holding the arms of the chair and sat, Aislynn perched primly on her shoulder.

Ian began with a deep breath, rubbing his face. "An, ye ken how much I despise sendin' yeh out."

"Aye, uncle. Means th' need is real."

"Aye. This may sound odd, but I need ye t' go t' lunch wit' Aiden, here."

She glanced over her shoulder at him. He smiled sheepishly down at her. "All right. To what purpose? 'Cause I know there is one."

"There's a restaurant run by th' Russians. It's a bit of a hangout fer them. They don' know yeh, they don' know Aiden, and I know fer a fact both o' yeh kin ditch th' accents. Yeh'll need ta. There's a gentleman I want yeh to meet there. His name is Ivan. An, you'll be th' one t' point him out. He's a yeti."

An wracked her brain to remember what a yeti was, finally tripped over it, filed back with the myths and legends of Tibet. "One of th' Northerner's?"

Ian smiled, nodding. "One o' her beast trainers. He's been out a couple months, but I've had him stashed away somewhere really cold. Now th' weather's turnin', he's come back an'll be helping us from th' background."

"But he's not an O'Keefe," Cullen complained.

"No. He's Russian," Ian snapped, "which is why I'm askin' him in on this."

"Damned Ruskies," Cullen grumbled.

"And that be why you a'n't goin' t' lunch wit' An," Ian growled back.

An suppressed a smile. "I take it ye want me to check out th' restaurant for what I can see?"

"Aye. I've reason t' suspect there be more of late."

An was more than a little nervous when Aiden finally led her into the restaurant. Cipín was in the car and she had been given a traditional, collapsible tapstick. She found she did not like it as much as her solid shillelagh. Aislynn's absence on her shoulder was also keenly felt, but she would have drawn a lot of unwanted attention. She was currently a small ferret curled up in the large handbag on An's shoulder. As it was, she wasn't even wearing her own clothes, had been convinced into a simple pantsuit and business jacket. It was odd how naked she felt without her rose or her skirts. She felt vulnerable and exposed.

Her blind eyes roved over the medium-sized restaurant swiftly without appearing to. She whispered to Aiden that their contact was the gentleman in the tan coat at the first table on their left. Aiden turned, waved to the gentleman as if he knew him and guided her over, carefully putting her back to the window where she could easily watch the entire restaurant. Ivan already had his back to the room and seemed just a little nervous about it. To An, it was clear he would have preferred a rear table with his back to a wall, and Aiden did not seem comfortable with his back to the broad window. She did her best to put them both at ease.

She reached across the table blindly, smiling at the yeti, her accent lightly British. "So good to finally meet you, Ivan."

The man smiled, took her hand and shook it. "Mutual, Miss Cobrán. Aiden," he said, shaking his hand. His accent was very lightly Slavic.

The men picked up the menus and the single waitress brought over an old Braille version. "Sorry," she said. "It hasn't seen much use," and proceeded to tell her the changes. The waitress went away with their drink orders and An took the opportunity to look Ivan over as she read.

She assumed he looked human enough to normal eyes, though a bit grizzled. He was bearded, with general Eastern European features that could place him from any number of countries. His hair was rather shaggy, though combed back. From what she could tell he was very hirsute. At the same time as she saw the light brown hair and beard and dark eyes and rather bland features, she also saw white fur and long, ape-like arms, though she realized they were slightly longer than normal even on the mundane side of things, and his teeth, which he was very careful not to show too much of, were pointed.

"Finding everything to your satisfaction, Miss Cobrán?" he asked.

She smiled. "I find myself at odds," she said, carefully filtering out all traces of her lilt and sticking to her 'teaching' voice. "I have no idea what any of this is. I have heard of borscht, but that it is very spicy."

"It can be. Allow me to help you," he said and began to rattle off things on the menu for both of them, telling them what they were and tasted like. By the time the waitress came back with the samovar of tea, they were ready to order.

Ivan and Aiden began to chat about random things, like his trip here and what to expect from Florida weather. An could easily have commiserated but she was paying attention to other things as she sipped the strong Russian tea. She kept her head as still as possible, making it look more like she was listening in one direction than looking in the other.

What she discovered was that the man behind the counter was a werewolf, and there was something shadowy in the back room which she would catch glimpses of as the staff came in and out. There were several men at the back few tables that all were perceivable in whole or in part. The one that seemed to be the manager was fully visible, extremely attractive and charming in a way that set off alarms. There was one other individual seated closer to the door, who seemed to be made of glass. Other than that she was able to see three disembodied coats, a vest and the glint of a weapon when one of the coats moved just right.

She slipped her hand into her purse, 'feeling around for something' and Aislynn pressed her phone to her fingers. An asked it to send Aiden a text message of what she was viewing. She did a running description starting from the door and going clockwise around the restaurant, describing empty spaces as well as what she could see to keep from confusing him as to the location of the magical.

Aiden checked his phone, frowned and sighed, looking up at Ivan. "Henry won't be joining us, I'm afraid. Little sister crisis." His eyes flitted to note each thing An had pointed out.

Ivan smiled, beaming at the waitress as plates came to the table. "Ah well, Henry is missing out on this wonderful food. *Spasibo, vozl'ublennyj.*"

The woman tittered, said something back at him that An did not catch and sauntered off.

They ate with pleasant small talk, discussing nothing important, and the two men told enough lies that An couldn't be sure if the discomfort in her chest was evidence or indigestion from the food. Soon enough they ordered dessert and coffee, finished up, paid their tab and left together, An perched on Aiden's arm.

Ivan was a gentleman and helped her into the front seat of the car, leaning into the window to speak one last thing to Aiden. "I will meet you later, *da*?"

"Da," Aiden said, starting the vehicle.

In short order, they were back in Ian's office, in spite of the round about way Aiden took them.

"There are at least four touched that I could see," An reported, still using her British accent. "A werewolf behind th' counter, a glass elemental, a shadowlin' (I think) in th' back room, and I am not sure what th' manager was, but he was very... attractive in a dark way."

Ian groaned, "Bloody siren. Yeh hear him talk?"

She shook her head. "But there are magical coats, a vest and at least one weapon that I saw. A handgun. You can bet there were more I couldn't see. I only chanced a glance at that one."

Ian's hand hit the table. "They're gettin' more. He's selling his people fer power," he growled.

An frowned. "Maybe. Or this is what his daughter bought him. None of those men seemed unhappy with their condition from what I could tell. To men like that it would feel like power. They won't reckon th' price."

"How many of them were in a Russian Gulag?" Aiden sighed. "Th' Dark City might seem like a vacation compared."

"Maybe. It still worries me," Ian sighed. "His magical forces are growin' and I'm unwilling ta do th' same. I'm here ta save people from that fate, not send them ta it."

Ivan came in as they were leaving, smiled at them. "Enjoy your lunch, Miss O'Keefe?" he asked An.

She smiled back. "I am not sure. Th' flavours were pleasant but there were so many lies flyin' around I couldn't tell if it were quite disagreein' with me or if that were just th' two of you."

Aiden laughed, apologized as he guided her down the hall.

Ivan looked confused, glanced over his shoulder at Ian who just grinned. "She knows when yer lyin'. It can be... uncomfortable."

An did not go to Courtz that night, as Sharon and George decided they wanted a date night and left them with pizza money. The two of them enjoyed a quiet evening in, watched a movie and read until it was Elizabeth's bedtime. An put her to bed and went downstairs to read in the living room until the Tallows came home around midnight. Only then did she go upstairs to her own bed in her own cottage.

Friday, she went to Courtz as was her wont. She was at her usual table, watching the people she could see and enjoying most of the music. There were more people from the Rest here than there had been of late, mostly the non-Irish and the younger folk. Brink was back, drinking rum at the bar and Kyle wasn't far from him, apparently trying to talk him into coming out to the Rest for the Yule Ball.

Leila was bouncing between the dance floor and the bar drinking tequila shots. She made occasional sojourns up onto the stage to sing, mostly rap songs, though she managed to get Roulet and Solitaire both up to do something called "Lady Marmalade". Her voice was good, her dancing was better, between them both she was a hit with the crowd.

An decided she was not going up on stage at all tonight, not while that woman was around. She did not want a repeat of Bealtaine. Not here.

Jonny appeared beside her, a Nut Brown in hand and a cigarette burning in the ash tray. An had no idea how long he had been there. She gave him a soft smile and went back to her meal, taking a last bite or two before leaving the rest to Aislynn. Not that the monkey wasn't already helping herself to the plate.

Once An set it aside, Jonny took her hand, asked her to sing with him. An completely forgot that she had resolved not to tonight and allowed him to draw her up on stage. Together they sang the "Scarborough Fair/Canticle", each singing their own song but blending his clear tenor and her mellow alto with an easy grace. They politely ignored the applause and, with her right hand in his right and his left arm around her waist, Jonny guided An deftly back to their table, neatly avoiding those seeking to detain him for personal reasons.

Daphne had just brought them fresh drinks when someone else appeared at the table. An felt Jonny tense every so slightly and Aislynn ran up under her hair by her ear, whispering, "*Beautiful, blonde and pissed.*"

"This really isn't yer kind o' place, Cecilia," he said calmly and coldly.

"It is a bit low brow," she agreed. Her voice was sharp and An could tell from her speech patterns that she was upper class, wealthy and entitled. An imagined the woman could be extremely likeable if she wanted to be, and right now she didn't want to be. "So this mousy little librarian is what you leave me for?"

An frowned. She had gone back to her comfortable high collars and long sleeves the moment the weather had begun to turn, slow though that turning had been.

"If I had known you liked the type I'd have worn glasses instead of my contacts."

Jonny was outwardly calm, pausing the bottle inches from his lips to speak before taking a sip. "She's a teacher, not a librarian."

"What the fuck ever, Jonny! If it was brains you wanted, we could have just talked more and fucked less. I am smart, I am *hot*, and I love you enough to fight my father over you! I had actually just made arrangements..."

Jonny set the bottle down sharply, cutting her off. "This is neither th' time nor th' place fer this, Cecilia."

She set her hands on the table and leaned forward, no doubt giving Jonny a good view. But his eyes were on her eyes, and his... were cold. "And where and when would be the 'time and place fer this'?" she said, low and cool, mocking his accent.

He stretched his neck forward and An watched frost beginning to appear on his bottle. "Never. I told ye, we're done."

An noticed he was a lot more firm with her than he ever had been with Serephina. She also noticed this woman was as used to accepting 'no' as the succubus.

She turned on An, "Let me warn you about this smarmy bastard, sweetheart. He'll never stay. He'll pursue you, make you unable to live without him and then drop you like an out-dated suit. Whatever you do, don't fuck him. He's not even that good," she added cattily.

An felt that lie like a slap in the face, which it had been intended to be. However, it missed its target. She did not let the discomfort of the lie show, sipped her Morning Dew calmly.

"Wait, how long have you been seeing him?" the woman exclaimed as An's placid demeanour made her question.

Jonny was suddenly up and around the table, had Cecilia by the arm and pulled her close. She turned on him before he could speak, "How long have you been seeing her? Were you cheating on me with *her*?"

Aisylnn snorted by An's ear, "*Technically i'twere th' other way around.*"

His voice was dangerous and sent a chill up An's spine, followed by a tingle as she remembered the sensation of being pinned by him and that voice. "Ye leave her out of it, Cecilia."

"What does she have that I don't? Aside from about ...twenty extra pounds?"

An's hand unconsciously went to her less than flat stomach and ample hips, frowning. She had never thought of herself as overweight.

"Maybe I wanted somethin' pure fer a change," he snarled, so low An almost didn't catch it. He then dragged the woman away towards the back hall.

An drank her whiskey, Aislynn sitting high up on her shoulder, trying to see over people to watch the conversation. Shortly, she left the table, finding herself a perch from which she could see. An shoved her misgivings aside and listened to three young women on stage energetically singing about a fine man named Mickey who was less than gentle with hearts.

How ironic, she thought.

Aislynn dropped back onto her shoulder, pressing her head to the pulse point just behind her ear. It was something she was fond of doing as a dragon, and truthfully, it worked better with a dragon's longer face. She whispered rapidly, *"She was angry, then shocked, then teary-eyed but not crying. She ran out. I'm not sure if that's going to turn into anger or not. ...Ye still want to stay with a man like that?"*

"Depends," she whispered back as she saw Jonny returning. *"Did he warn her?"*

Aislynn snorted and pulled back as Jonny came up to the table, holding his hand out to An. "May I take ye home?" he asked. "I've a need for sommat stronger an' I'd rather..."

She stood before he could finish. She half expected him to walk her to the house the long way, but instead he led her to the stairs. An saw Skye watching them warily, giving her a concerned look regarding the woman who had just flown out the door and the man she was leaving with. She gave him a smile, and a slight shake of the head, telling him not to worry about it, and followed Jonny upstairs.

When they entered the cottage, she immediately dropped Cipín into her stand and headed into the kitchen, fetching one of her bottles of quad-distilled poitín and a pair of glasses. Pouring one deeper than the other, she brought the taller of the two to the chair he had dropped himself into. Setting aside her own drink she removed her boots and took them to their place on the coat stand at the door. She did not pick up her lace. Just sat with her glass in hand, watching him, not drinking.

Jonny stared into the fire, drank almost all of the alcohol in one go.

"Finish it an ye like," she said. "There's more."

He nodded, tossing back the last of it and set the glass on the table between them. She leaned forward and set hers in its place.

"Ye'll be wantin' an explanation," he said, his voice flat.

"I've learned wantin' and gettin' are not mutually inclusive. I'll accept what yer willin' t' give," she said simply. She observed him with a slight tilt of the head. "Though it seems t' me ye feel th' need to explain. Somethin' about not bein' seen as hypocritical, I would expect." The words bit him and she regretted them instantly. "I'm sorry. I meant that as an observation, not a catty remark. I'm... not like that."

"I know yer not," he said quickly, trying to set her at ease. "Though ye've an uncanny knack fer getting t' th' heart of a matter, however ye get there." He picked up her glass, drained it too.

An got up, drifted into the kitchen and fetched the bottle. Aislynn had stretched out on the back of An's chair, dragon once more and glared at him. An refilled both glasses and set the bottle down, not picking either of them up. She sat slightly sideways in the chair, her head resting in the corner of the wings, waiting him out.

"She may not need an explanation," Aislynn snarled, *"but I sure as hell do."*

Jonny sighed, chuckled. "Leave it t' th' drake t' demand what ye'll not ask. Ye should listen t' her, ye know, when she tells ye t' stay away from me."

"Is that what you want?" she asked. "Me t' stay away?"

He laughed again, that humourless chuckle she sometimes hated. "Ah, but I'm a selfish bastard," he said, taking a drink.

"I keep tellin' ye, ye deserve happiness and love. But ye never listen. Ye've an almost Catholic Guilt level of self-loathing."

That elicited a genuine laugh, short though it was. He sighed, leaned back in the chair. "That were... that were work."

"Cecilia was work?"

Aislynn frowned. *"You're a gigolo?"*

Jonny glared at the dragon. "Nae. 'Tis not an easy thing t' explain. Cecilia... Cecilia has a reputation. She's young, beautiful and entitled. She sees something or someone she wants and she goes after it; uses men fer everything she can get and when she's done, casts them off, regardless o' how they feel. She is careless with hearts. Left a string of broken men in her wake. Some of which will never trust a woman again, though I do what I can."

An listened, pulling the rose from her hair so she could lean back more comfortably. Without thinking what she was doing, her thumb began to play across the petals, not yet cutting.

"What she said about her and I were true. Over th' last two months I've obliquely pursued her, drawn her interest, made her love me and then, when I was certain she actually gave a damn, I began avoidin' her. Three days ago she confronted me and I told her I was done. I did to her exactly what she's done to at least four men I've talked with."

"So it were an object lesson t' her. A heart fer a heart?"

"Aye." He took a long minute, thinking, framing what he was going to say. She let him take all the time he needed. "There is a court, not really a secret court, but not exactly open, either."

"In other words, yer not forbidden t' speak of it, yet it is not generally known?"

He nodded. "The Court of the Snow Queen. ...I'm a member. Serephina... inducted me, years ago. Th' hard way."

An digested this before speaking. "Serephina is a member. And ye resent being part o' this secret court?"

"Sometimes. Sometimes I believe in it."

"So 'tisn't all punishin' th' guilty?"

"We also take those who don't know or understand love and show them. Th' kinder o' us teach them an' then make them move on. Th' more cruel are less gentle. Which can defeat th' purpose, ye ask me. ...Then there are th' times we take those who are afraid of love, refuse t' allow it cause they don't want t' be hurt... draw them out, show them that yes, love hurts, but wasn't it worth it?"

"An'... am I a victim o' yer Court?" she asked softly. Once she had fallen into that latter category. Though it wasn't avoiding love at all costs, just being mindful of her station and who she fell in love with, but that distinction might not matter to the Fae.

He did not answer her, which was neither confirmation nor denial. "Ye see now why I tell ye I'm unworthy?"

She shifted in the chair, getting more comfortable, thinking. "I take it Serephina does it fer th' joy?"

"Sometimes," he admitted. "Why I wouldn't help her with that last one. As far as I could tell he wasn't deservin'."

"So you subscribe t' th' more noble side o' this?"

He sighed. "I try. Only way I can live with it. She did it t' me, then dragged me in."

"Ye teach th' careless and malicious what it feels like, show them th' error o' their ways," she said, ticking her points off on her fingers. "Ye take those, perhaps like us, who don't remember or know what love is and teach them how t' feel. Ye make those what would deny their feelin's face them further, enriching their lives eventually. ...And how does this make ye a bad man? Sounds more like atonement t' me." She regarded him carefully, contemplating the possibility that she was a target. She discovered it didn't change anything. "Will Cecilia be a problem?"

He watched her, trying to fathom her response. "No," he finally said. "I've explained things to her in a way she won't ferget lightly."

She got up, set her rose down. walked over to him, took the half empty glass away and set it beside her rose. She reached out with two fingers and drew aside stray wisps of snow that had slipped his ponytail. Her fingers continued, tracing his jaw until she was tipping up his chin. She kissed him. For a moment he let her, his eyes closed and breathing deep. Then he pulled her into his arms as he stood, returning the kiss.

An tried to draw him off to the bedroom. They made it as far as the fur rug on the floor in front of the fire.

Rolling her eyes and growling, Aislynn threw herself off of the chair back and flew into the bedroom, slamming the door behind her.

19

The Yule ball came before Christmas this year. An, Skye, Liberty and the twins had gotten their costumes from Miss Moffett and her mother.

An had chosen to come as Dawn. It was a sleek column dress in gold, with rings that connected the top of the bodice to the golden collar at her throat. Her shoulders were bare except for the rings that connected the top of her long, matching gloves to the neckband. Silky fabric draped from the wrists to the back of the neck, in variegated shades of gold and red and purples, simulating the painted sky. Her mask was elaborate: Mardi Gras style with feathers, coppered and gilded branches that swept up and back. Even An had to admit, she was breathtaking, though she was a little uncomfortable in the form-fitted gown. She was unusually self conscious of the slight lumpiness of her middle, but Liberty had convinced her into a light corset.

Roulet and Solitaire had both chosen dragons, completely independent of one another. Solitaire was a dragonfish, and Roulet had dressed as a Chinese-styled dragon in red and gold. Liberty and Skye were Arthur and Guinevere. An thought the costumes somewhat thin, as the claymore passing for Excalibur was right there on Skye's back, but she said nothing, enjoying the evening and trying to impart as much hopeful feeling in the room as she could.

No one had bothered with the witch's charms this evening. No one had felt like going to such extremes this year. The costumes were good nonetheless, they always were. Even Aislynn had made an attempt, changing into a small vixen and wore a Maid Marion dress as an homage to an old animated Robin Hood film Elizabeth had watched recently.

The ballroom was hung with icicles and holly, with mistletoe in strategic places. The goblin band played as before and there was more food than anyone could eat. Lafayette had out done himself. He had baked a cake the size of a small card table, and decorated it as a snowy landscape complete with candy trees, a 'frozen' river of spun sugar with a chocolate bridge and a horse drawn, marzipan sleigh complete with bells and passengers. No one wanted to eat it, it was so beautiful. Lafayette had to cut it himself before people would partake.

An danced, enjoyed the refreshments, watched others. She found no one she might take for Jonny, but she was not really looking so desperately this year. She was searching for someone else. On her hand were two gold rings. One was so large she had to put it on her thumb and convince it to stay and the other so small she wore it on her pinky. She made sure she spoke with everyone, one way or another, subtly touching them with the hand wearing the rings.

Just before she started to get dressed for the evening, Ophelia had paid An a visit. The girl had been very nervous as she handed her the two rings. "Get them to tell you who he is, please?" she asked, her dark eyes full of unshed tears and terrified hope. "They were ours."

An had tried, but the rings were stubborn. They said they couldn't be sure unless they touched him. And so, here An was, touching as many people as possible, hoping one of them was the right one. The evening was wearing thin when An was finally approached by a man in a tuxedo who introduced himself as "Bond, James Bond, at your service, Bright Dawn."

An smiled, reaching out her hand to be led onto the dance floor. "Aurora, please." When her hand came into contact with his she felt the overwhelming, high-pitched, metallic screaming of 'Yes!' and nearly collapsed.

'James' caught her. "You all right?"

She righted herself, deflecting the question. "I am not used to these heels," she sighed.

He accepted that as the reason for her stumble and swept her onto the floor. He was a good dancer, and the waltz was easy, though half-way through she got this horrible fear of 'what if this is Jonny'? She tossed out a casual question, testing the waters, "So, what do you think of the music? I'm afraid I don't know this piece. I'm sure I've heard it before but..."

James shrugged. "It's music, and it has a good pace for dancing. You are marvellously light on your feet, Aurora."

She smiled, blushing a little. "I am only as good as my partner, Mr. Bond."

He chuckled at that and she relaxed, let herself be swept up into the music, made confident by his response that it could not possibly be Jonny.

When it was over, 'James' bowed and took his leave, and An began looking for the peacock mask. She found it fairly quickly, and hurried over, bumping into one or two people. The room and everything in it may have been magical, but a good number of the partiers most certainly weren't. In her haste, she had forgotten to look for those subtle clues which told her where the unmagical were standing.

Reaching the peacock mask, she lightly touched the woman's arm, making her jump. She recovered quickly as she realized who it was and what it might mean. "Did you?" she asked, breathlessly.

An slipped the rings off her fingers and into Ophelia's hand. She bent to her ear. "Ye'll want a word with Mr. Bond."

"Bond?"

An nodded, turned Ophelia in the right direction. "Gentleman in the black suit and bowtie standing next to the red dragon."

"Oh. Thank you!"

"Don't thank me yet," An whispered as she watched the girl weave her timid way across the room to where 'Bond' stood. Just before she got there, he stepped out onto the floor with the dragon and Ophelia shrank back, devastated.

An sighed and crossed to her, took her by hand and waist and began to dance without asking permission. "Follow my lead," she whispered.

She manoeuvred them close to where Roulet and Mr. Bond danced, waited for the right moment. When he put the dragon into a spin, as their hands were outstretched to their limits, An swept in, turning Ophelia into him and stealing off with Roulet. "Sorry about that, dear," she smiled. "Cupid's business."

The dragon's eyes went wide, "Oh really," she grinned, settled back to keep her eye on the couple. "If I had known that I wouldn't have asked him to dance. Though the way you traded us out was priceless."

An smiled shyly. "It helps to not be yourself every once in a while."

Roulet returned the grin. "Oh, the things you can get away with!" she crowed.

"Provided you aren't here for the unmasking," An added.

"True. ...Aw, damn it, they're going outside."

An looked over, watched the peacock lady and Bond heading out to the back patio for more private conversation. Bond had something in his off hand that he was fiddling with. "She gave it to him," she whispered.

"Who what?"

"Th' ring, she gave it t' him. If he recognizes her as his lost wife... remembers her... th' coat may come off."

Something else drew their attention before Roulet could ask what the devil she was talking about.

There was a woman in a black gown with a raven feather mask standing before the empty thrones. She had been mingling, dancing with a few people. An did not remember her from when she had been trying to touch everyone. That or she had unconsciously avoided her. No, she realized, her presence was growing stronger. She stopped dancing with Roulet, in spite of the still playing song and just stared, drew back slowly.

The bells began to toll midnight and the man dressed as the tin woodsman stepped up to one of the empty thrones. Masks started to come off. Patches seated himself on the throne and Raven, in a harlequin gown of black and white stepped up beside him, but did not sit in the other throne. They stared at the woman in black, who had yet to remove her mask. But as the bells tolled, it became less necessary.

An stepped back again, near 'Arthur and Guinevere', did a double take as their masks came off. Skye stood there in the dress, and Arthur's crown began to twist and shift into the crown of evergreen and snowdrops. There was a moment's shock as others realized what she had and laughed, but that was quickly stifled.

Ian shed his Scaramuccia mask and approached, stopping ten feet behind the woman in black who was now unquestionably the Morrigan. She stood a great deal taller than she had before the bells had rung, and her hair was now a dark red and seemed to drip with blood. She smiled, cold and hard.

"I see you defied me, daughter. I tell you to leave your ragdoll and come home and you marry it." Her voice was beautiful and terrifying all in the same breath.

An took a step closer to Skye, calling Cipín to her, praying she would arrive in time. Next year, she swore she would be leaving her in a quiet corner of the Manor. Aislynn landed on her shoulder, all dragon again, though still in her Maid Marion dress, wrapped her tail protectively around An's throat. She was trembling, but maintaining a brave, defensive front.

Raven grabbed Patches' hand and stood tall. "He's not a ragdoll, mother. He is a king."

The Northerner laughed, a sound felt as much as it was heard. It both drew and repelled. "A mummer king in your little mummer's play? What power wields he? This maker of changelings."

The comment struck An as odd. She had not known what it was Patches had done in Faery. She glanced around the room, worried, looking for Jonny among the unmasked. He was not there, though Tam was, and he was staring hard at the Red Queen.

Raven's lips were tight as she resisted the urge to answer her mother's question.

"Come, we are going home."

"No, mother," she finally dared. "I still love you. But I love him too, just... differently. I'm not a little girl anymore. I'm woman married. I'll stay with my husband."

"I tolerated your running off, because I knew you still loved me. But this," she raised her hand towards Patches with a sneer, "is defiance too far. Perhaps as a widow you will see reason."

At this Ian spoke. "I'd not recommend that course o' action, Morrigan," he said. His voice was cold and calm. The Northerner turned slowly, drew herself up as she regarded him.

"And why is that, griffin?"

"One, what love she holds for yeh might swiftly turn t' hate. Two, yer under Hospitality yet." That made her take a deep, slow breath as she seethed. "T'ree, those two swore their own vows before a priest on Holy Ground."

"So?" She seemed leery suddenly, of something in Ian's face and voice. He was too smug.

"What they swore might be of interest to yeh," he said with deceptive casualness. "I would have stopped them had I known what they planned... well, advised against it... but," he shrugged, grinning. "I believe th' phrase yer most interested in is 'our hearts beat as one'."

Several people gasped at that. The Northerner's eyes grew dark as she turned to her daughter. "Is this true?" she hissed.

"Yes." Raven lifted her chin, staring her mother down in open defiance.

An was confused for only a second or two before it struck her what that would mean. There were oaths and Oaths, and sometimes the Universe listened and held you to them. It was the stuff of which Geasa were forged. An ill-spoken word was often the end of a man, and when the speaker was magical or tied to magics for which wyrd things were known... the odds were high one would get what one wished for, though not always what one intended.

There was no question, looking at the pair, that such a tie had been forged. And An had no doubt it had been deliberate. If ever one heart stopped beating, so would the other.

The Northerner regarded the two of them hotly for a long moment before speaking again. "We are not done with this discussion, daughter." With that she turned from them, strode towards the veranda doors. Before she was even halfway there, she dissolved in to an unkindness of ravens and flew off into the night.

An trailed closer to the door, seeing Ophelia and a man whose identity she could not at the moment make out but could guess at. They were just standing after having ducked the angry flock. The man was in a white shirt, the black coat lying abandoned on the patio. The first of the guests to leave after The Northerner was an old man in a navy pea-coat, who bent and picked up 'Mr. Bond's' discarded jacket as he passed, glanced sadly at the pair now kissing just feet from him. Someone passed between An and the door and when the way was clear again, the man was gone.

An ran to the patio, stopped at the threshold, holding on to the frame. Ophelia was now clinging to Cullen in a panic, looking around, her nostrils wide. An could smell what had alarmed her: the sea. The air was filled with the scent of fish and salt and the bitter air of northern oceans. Looking down she could see wet footprints fading from view. But they ended before the steps.

She ducked back into the ballroom, leaning against the wall beside the door. Skye found his way over to her, Liberty on his arm. "Ya all richt?" he asked.

She blinked up at him. "Two. Two Gentry in one night an' both stayed fer th' unmaskin'. Ye have t' ask?"

"Twa?" he frowned.

"Haggard. Out there, just now. Took Cullen's coat. I... I have t' get home."

"But th' battle?" Liberty asked.

An shook her head, reaching out without looking as Cipín sailed into the ballroom to her hand. "I've no heart for it tonight. T' fight or t' watch. Jonny's nowhere t' be seen at th' unmaskin' and with Her here... I need t' find him."

"Ya shoudnae walk home on yar ane," Skye insisted. "She coud still be oot thare..."

Ian came up, escorting people out. "She'll not touch any tonight. Not wit'out violatin' old pacts. And that's sommat not even she'll do. He might be out in th' woods," he added. An could tell from his eyes that he was worried as well.

She set her hand on Skye's arm. "I'm not alone," she said, raising her shoulder to indicate the dragon there, and the hand holding the shillelagh. "And I'll be careful." She kissed Liberty's cheek. "Ye sittin' this one out, sister?"

Liberty gave a rueful chuckle. "I think Patches was a little too preoccupied t' find me. Da figgered it out."

"Long days of heat," An sighed. "Winter was too brief as it was." She stepped out into the night, doing her best to avoid the crowd headed for the battlefield.

It was not too hard to slip out of the mob. Her path and theirs were divergent after a certain point. If she had hoped to encounter him in the wood, she was disappointed. Nor was he at the cottage when she arrived.

Aislynn went on in the house as An stopped in the garden. She left her shoes by the door and walked back down towards the hollow, enjoying the scents of the stubborn vampricks which did insist on blooming year round. Even some of her less magical roses were blooming, as roses like cooler weather. She stood there, down near the brook, softly stroking the black velvet petals of one of her red roses when the lights of the pixies flew up from the lily beds, disturbed. She looked around, sliding the shillelagh up in her grasp.

There was a fluttering through the bare branches of the fruit trees and the landing of feet on the little wooden bridge. An relaxed, even before Jonny stepped out of the shadows into the moonlight.

She smiled. "Ye had me worried, a' chroí."

He did not speak, but took her in his arms and held her as if she were an anchor in a storm-tossed sea. He was shaken. His heartbeat was rapid and his skin warmer than usual. The light dance of her fingers across his back made him quiver and not with pleasure. She looked up at him, saw the pain in his eyes and started to draw away, realizing that even the lightest touch was hurtful. She could only imagine the agony that was the embrace he held her in.

He refused to let her go.

He said nothing, kissing her urgently, running his hands over the sleek fabric of her golden dress. She resisted at first, not wanting to be a source of pain for him; but he was so insistent, so desperate, wanting this for whatever reason. She knew if she refused him that he would go somewhere else. Perhaps even to Serephina. So she surrendered, allowing him to punish himself against her body.

20

Christmas eve saw An at the manor, mingling with the people there for the family party. Aislynn was delighted with the present she had been given. It was a box like one expects to find silverware in, but instead of fine silver forks, spoons and knives, there were metal lollipops stacked in the slots. There were four each of copper, silver, and gold, all just the right size for her.

Other presents were handed out and a marvellous dinner was laid upon the table. It was shaping up to be a better Christmas than the year before, until Shannon walked into the small ballroom where the Christmas presents were scattered among children playing with wrapping paper and new toys. She was pale.

Ian's face went from paternal joy to worried scowl instantly. "What?"

"A call from a neighbour o' th' Quilts," she breathed. Quilt was the surname Patches and Raven had taken upon marrying. "There... there was a horrible noise a bit ago, and bright lights.

They looked out th' window and… the whole house is covered in ice and snow. Mrs. O'Leary said her husband was tryin' th' door, but it willna open. She saw… she saw a flock of black birds flying away."

Ian was out the door in a breath and Skye rushed after him. Everyone followed them out but the children and Shannon.

Ian had taken flight, leaving Skye standing, frustrated, on the step. Less than a minute later, Roulet pulled up in front from the carriage house, revving the engine of Liberty's SUV. Liberty, Skye, and Mikey climbed in. An slipped into the back at the last minute. There was a thump on the roof as Roulet peeled out of the drive and down the road. Skye poked his head out, saw Freddy splayed out up there, clinging with froggy fingers.

When they finally pulled up, Ian had already ripped off the door. Neighbours were standing on their lawns, most in dressing gowns and slippers, some armed with whatever they had at hand. As Roulet cut the engine and everyone piled out, Ian came out of the shattered front door. He was pale and angry and generally not safe to be around. Skye gave him a wide berth as he stepped into the house himself, sword in hand.

Ian took a moment to get himself under some semblance of control, noticed who all was on the lawn. "An, I need yeh ta…"

She nodded without him having to finish and slipped in after her brother. She had no need of Cipín to guide her. She could see every inch of the house. It was all coated in a thin layer of dark ice. Snow crunched under foot. She followed her ears to where Skye was hacking at something. As she stepped into the Holly King's kitchen, she saw two ice statues sitting at the table, their Christmas dinner spread in front of them, frozen like everything else. Skye was hacking in frustration at the block of ice that had been the refrigerator.

Outside, on the lawn, An heard the heart-wrenching double thunder of the gryphon: high eagle scream filtering through the deep throated lion's roar. She reached out and cupped Raven's face. The couple were sitting at a corner from each other at their little square table, holding each other's hand and staring, determinedly, at some point on the opposite side of the table, taller than either An or Skye. An's hand felt only death and cold, and the ice told her nothing.

"Skye," she breathed, barely able to get her voice to work. He whirled. "I've seen yer claymore afire. Will ye oblige me?"

He nodded. At a thought, the blade erupted in flames. "Now whit?"

She stepped back, away from the table. "Thaw out a portion o' th' table for me. I need contact. And this ice," she pointed to the hands of the statues, "try not to burn it."

Skye damped back the flames some, held the blade over the table near their joined hands. The ice began to melt and run off, dripping onto the floor. When she could see the bare wood, An nodded and he dowsed the fire, stepping back. She set a trembling palm on the damp tabletop. After a few minutes she pulled back, tucking her hand under her arm to warm it. She wrapped her shawl more tightly around her and, taking up Cipín, left the house.

She went to Liberty's side, who stood by the car, staring skyward, waiting patiently for Ian to land. He had leaped into the sky, crying forth his rage and trying to find signs that the Red Queen was still in this world. It seemed forever before he landed.

While they waited, Skye had tried to press An, to find out what she had seen. Apparently he had called after her, asking as she walked out, but she hadn't heard him. She refused to say a single word until Ian finally landed.

The Griffon issued orders to Mikey and Seamus as they pulled up on Seamus' motorbike. They were to search the Rest and account for everyone. Roulet he sent to ring the bells. Only then did he cross to where An stood, surrounded by Skye and Liberty, with Freddy sitting on the roof, wide-eyed, looking it all over. Skye stepped back to give him access. He just stood over her, looking down at her.

She looked up, met his golden brown eyes with her own foggy orbs. It took her a moment to be able to articulate what she had seen, he patiently waited her out. "It was Her. She... I don't understand what were said. I can't comprehend th' words. But She was angry, ...sad, too. In the end, She said somethin'; they looked at each other, nodded, looked back at Her and... then they were ice. She burst into a ball of birds, th' house froze over an' She flew up th' chimney." She took a deep breath, trying to sort out her own feelings over the matter. "What is inside that ice... isn't alive. I am sorry, Uncail, that I can't give ye more. I don' understand why I cannot comprehend..."

He set his claw upon her shoulder. "She did not want yeh t' know. 'Tis enough we know this much."

The bells began to ring: five steady peals of the mid-tone bell. The people standing on their lawns immediately headed back to their houses, even as Mikey and Seamus began going from door to door accounting for everyone who was supposed to be there. Then the largest bell began pealing its deep, melancholy tone, slow and steady. As it rang, the smallest bell rang out two high notes, one for each lost soul. This pattern would echo out for the next few minutes, making certain every soul in the Rest knew that, once again, they had lost one of their own.

It was difficult to hold a funeral for statues of ice. In fact, when they melted, as they eventually did no matter what was done to preserve them, there was nothing left. As if what they had been had melted away with the ice. They held a wake though. The only notable thing about it was the off-hand comment that the Holly Crown seemed to have been cursed since Henry had worn it. There was discussion as to who would be taking it up six months down the line, but no one volunteered.

The Mafia war paced on. Cullen was less visible as far as An was concerned. She saw less and less of the war as movements became more subtle. Disappearances were more common than corpses and after a while, Ian began to suspect that it was not because the Russians were getting better at hiding the bodies.

An had confirmation of this one evening in late January when she came up to the manor to pay Martha a visit and bring her some fresh, winter herbs. She was sitting in the kitchen chatting, laying out a new set of crocheted trivets she had made for her when they heard the commotion. Both women peeked out of the kitchen door fairly quickly, saw the witch dragging what looked like a wooden man, trying stiffly to keep up with her. An followed, coming to the door of the living room where Ian was sitting on the couch scanning the news. Baba thrust the wooden man in front of Ian with a scowl.

Ian frowned. "What is this, Baba?"

"I bought. At Goblin Market. Look et heem!" she croaked, pointing.

Ian frowned, shaking his head, though An could tell something was bothering him. "I don't understand. Ye rescued someone. I'm glad, but... why are yeh pissed?"

Furious, the old lady grabbed the man's head in both hands and leaned him closer to Ian, as if bringing him nearer would make him more recognizable. "T'addeus McKellum!" she snapped. She shoved the man back. He staggered and straightened placidly. "Not two Samhains back I am givink heem cookies!"

Ian's eyes darkened, the head cocked. "T'addeus McKellum should be sixteen and in high school."

The boy looked up, dreamily. "School?" he said. "Prom..."

Ian sat forward. "Th' McKellums opted ta move ta th city last year. Tad?" he called. "Taddy?"

This appeared to spark a memory from the boy. He seemed to recognize the name, looking around as if he should know where he was. Then he slumped back into his wooden mannerisms and turned to the witch. "What would you like me to do first, mistress?"

The old lady grunted and began cursing in old Russian.

An could hear Ian's teeth grinding from the door as she turned away, heard him pick up the phone. *"I want a census done o' all our people, Rest and away. I want ta know where all of them are. I think we got some gone missing and I want to know who and how."*

Most of the run of the mill Taken, those not involved, seemed almost oblivious to the war. Serenity was spending more time at Courtz with Elaroush, especially since he started working outside the Rest. It was a mundane job, not related in anyway to the 'Family', but An knew he reported to Ian frequently, the things he saw and overheard. Cass and Dukes stopped by regularly, though they usually did not stay for long. An noticed Leila spending a little more time at the bar, especially when Dukes was due in. She would not stay much longer after he left. Adora had gotten a job at some sports bar across town and stopped in after work. Even Ophelia had started coming, feeling more comfortable around strangers who would ignore her. She had taken to sitting at the end of the bar, away from everyone.

A lot of those who *were* involved often used the club as a staging point. Some group of the 'boys' were always either coming or going from here. Cidrich was at the opposite end of the bar from Ophelia, and Caleb was hunched a stool or two down. Even Cullen and Seamus were lurking in the back somewhere.

One Friday night, just past Imbolc, An went to Courtz as usual. She had her dinner, drank her tea, indulged in a little whiskey. Mostly she watched the people, the ones she could see and listened to the ones she could not.

The stage grew dark, the house lights dimmed expectantly. Only a single, dim blue spot remained on the stage. Silence fell. Something small and glittery was tossed from the KJ booth to the centre of the stage and a thin stream of smoke began to hiss forth from it, building to a column as the music started. Leila formed from the smoke wearing black cargo pants with a pair of coined and belled belts criss-crossing her hips gunslinger style. Glittering, clear, stiletto pumps graced her feet, her gold vest and jewelled key momentarily hidden by a red hooded cloak. Balanced on her outstretched palm was an apple with a bite taken from it. The opening strains of Natalie Kills' "Wonderland" began and she moved her hips with the sharp beat.

"I'm not Snow White, but I'm lost inside this forest." She threw the apple into crowd on the dance floor, where it was caught. "I'm not Red Riding Hood, but I think the wolves have got me." She tore the cloak off and tossed it aside. "Don't want those stilettos, I'm not, not Cinderella," she sang as the shoes were kicked off over the audience where they exploded into confetti. She threw herself into the rest of the song.

Her dancing was hot and sensuous, a heated fusion of hip hop and belly dance, all styles. The crowd was eating it up, becoming almost a living thing. Near the end of the number she picked up the cloak and swirled it on, spinning with it, hiding herself. On the last note the cloak fell back to the stage floor, empty of all but a puff of escaping smoke.

She reappeared a few minutes later at the bar, sneaking up behind Sam and startling her. An frowned at the blatant and public use of magic, but everyone around them seemed to think it was just clever theatrics.

Leila had undergone a bit of a change over the last few months. Roulet had hooked her up with a friend of hers in the recording industry and the rumour was that she would be putting out an album of rap/dance music sometime in the near future. She was certainly an audience pleaser.

An had a song trapped in her head. George and Sharon had been watching Cold Mountain when she had left the house and the song from the film had haunted her all night. Finally she pulled her phone from her little shoulder bag and asked it if it could play it for her. She listened to it a couple of times, learning the lyrics easily. Finally, she was decided. She sent Roulet a text, requesting the song and got up from her table. Cipín guided her easily to the stage, Aislynn riding her shoulder happily.

Her entrance was nowhere near as theatric as the Djinni's had been, but the lead in of the music was dramatic enough. Only the thin trickle of fog about her ankles drifting across the black boards of the stage enhanced her performance. She began to sing "You Will Be My Ain True Love" with a haunting voice that, though lullaby soft, carried perfectly well without the microphone that she was no where near. The bar grew quiet as she sang.

While the general audience received it well, it wrought very different reactions from different people. Jonny applauded from their table, though his eyes were shell-shocked and distant. A few others at the bar, like Caleb, were similarly teary-eyed and uncomfortable.

Cullen on the other hand, reacted very badly. He shot to his feet, breathing rapid, his hand reaching for something not there at his left hip. He shot An a murderous look of abject rage through the narrowed lids of his wolfish eyes. A snarl of hate crossed his normally jovial face. He upended his beer bottle, draining the last of it and slamming the empty on the bar hard enough to crack the glass. He cut across to Jonny's table, pausing to speak to him before he stormed out of the bar altogether.

The reaction got the attention of several people as he brushed past An on his way out, not being careful at all. She reached out for her chair, confused and reeling. Jonny pulled it out for her, dragging it so that the sound would tell her where to find it. She sank into it, turned to him. "What... what did I... A chroí? Explain?"

He sighed, taking a swallow of his own beer. "That song, i'twere what She promised us. It is *everything* She promised. Would we but walk through th' fire an' th' swords for Her, nothing would harm us an' Her love was ours."

An frowned, confused. "But... it was written for a film, fer all it sounds traditional... I looked it up."

His eyes softened, his smile pained. "One of us. Don' know who penned it, but I myself have heard her sing it countless times. Played it fer her once, afore she..." he did not finish his sentence, nor did he need to.

"I..." she turned, watched Ophelia running out after Cullen. "Well, I'll never sing it again then. I'd no way of knowing."

She reached for the glass Aislynn was pushing towards her. It was whiskey. She sipped.

Jonny's hand covered her other. "That's th' trouble with us. No way of knowing what will set who off an' in what way. Th' lovely Leila could have set any number of people off with her little faery tale ditty had they been payin' attention t' more than her hips."

An nodded, still feeling low-spirited. She took a more full swallow. "I suppose I should just leave th' choices of what music I should learn t' yer expertise," she said glumly.

"No. Ye should explore what music ye like," he insisted. "Ye sang well, do not doubt that. An' it *is* a beautiful song."

An sat more stiffly in her chair, drained the last of her whiskey. "Thank ye, but... not knowin' what suits, what is taboo, and knowin' precious few others that machine knows... 'tis best I do not try again."

Jonny became angry at that, his jaw tightening. "I'll not have ye silence that voice 'cause one ass can't handle a wee reminder. Nor have ye turn to a submissive, limp rag only singin' what's been approved fer ye. I served th' same durance vile as he, heard th' song more oft... an' I've not berated ye fer it. I'd hear ye sing again, and a song o' yer own choosin'. There are times we should take th' risk, or They just win."

Before An could formulate a reply or even suss out how she felt about either outburst, she felt a faint buzzing in her pocket. She did not have to slip her hand into it to know it was the remote. She gathered Cipín, took Aislynn to her shoulder and rose. "I have t' go..."

Jonny's eyes flashed. "*Need a hand?*"

She shook her head. "*Be it what I suspect, no. I can handle it.*"

He watched her as she meandered purposefully through the crowd and headed for the private lounge upstairs. An swiftly opened the door to her garret, gliding through her empty room and down the stairs on near silent feet. The house was mostly quiet at this hour, but there were muffled sounds coming from the girl's bedroom. An slipped in, shillelagh at the ready, Aislynn in dragon-form again, ready to breathe on whatever it was.

The child lay on the bed, tossing restlessly, whimpering and unable to wake up. Whatever it had been had fled under the bed, and now lay there, lurking, waiting for the door to close.

An strode with clear purpose to the middle of the room, stepping into the square of moonlight streaming in from the window.

Aislynn flew to a shelf where an old doll sat forgotten. It was one of those toddler-sized plastic things intended to be a life-sized 'companion'. She carried the doll to the bed, dangling a leg over the side, lowering it slowly.

Several long seconds passed before the thing took the bait, reaching out to snatch the plastic leg with a tentacle. An noticed several blue rings on the back of that suckered coil. She would have to be careful. Elizabeth had been watching animal documentaries among other things lately, and the most recent involved a blue-ringed octopus that was purported to be one of the most venomous creatures on the planet.

She swung the end of the shillelagh at the tentacle as Aislynn engaged it in a tug of war over the doll. She connected, but the creature did not let go. Instead, it drew further out from under the bed, other tentacles reaching out for her. An let the thing have it, laying about swift and sharp with Cipín, if nothing else making it pull back as she struck. The iron end had no extra effect on the creature, telling her it wasn't a fey thing. But she already knew that.

Aislynn breathed on it, freezing the tentacle on the doll, then biting it viciously. Finally it withdrew that limb. Instead of retreating completely, it surged out from under the bed, grabbing An's ankle and using that to pull the rest of itself out. She was expecting a full blown octopus. She was disappointed.

The second half of the beast was more arachnid than cephalopod. At least two of the back appendages ended in scorpion stingers. An sighed, kept her foot anchored. She swung wide, cracking the carapace on at least one of the stingers and knocking the other back under the bed where it became entangled in the dangling sheets. Flipping the shillelagh, she stabbed downward, aiming for the soft joint between scorpion abdomen and the tentacles sprouting from what had to be its blind face. The thing had no eyes.

Aislynn began to breathe on the floor, putting down a layer of frost. The creature did not like that at all. It tried to scuttle towards the radiator, but An had it pinned. It tore at her legs, ripping her stockings and scratching her ankles and calf. With one stinger disabled, Aislynn launched herself at the other. An kicked at the beast with her free foot, applying all her weight to pin it down as she pried the shillelagh up and proceeded to smash it to pieces. After a minute or two it stopped thrashing and began to melt away to nothingness. On the bed, Elizabeth slipped into softer dreams and stopped whimpering.

Aislynn shook herself vigorously and leapt lightly to the bed, sniffing the girl. Elizabeth rolled onto her side, facing the wall and Aislynn dodged. She lifted her head to peer at An over the child's shoulder. *"I'll sleep here tonight,"* she whispered. *"Just in case."*

An nodded and drew the covers up over the girl as Aislynn curled up under her chin, trilling softly.

Tired now, emotionally and physically spent, An trudged back up to the garret, and slipped through the closet to the cottage. The fire in the grate was not a surprise. The man tuning a violin in the chair in front of it was. She smiled tiredly, crossed the room. He looked up as she sank into her own chair, taking a deep breath. His eyebrow arched as he took in her disarray.

An pulled the rose from her hair, setting it on the table beside her chair and bent to unlace her boots. She turned the dark, sueded leather over in her hand, frowning at the deep scuffs in the sides. She sighed and set it aside, pulled off her other, gasping as it tugged wounds she had been ignoring.

Jonny set aside the fiddle, laying it in its case and closing it. He knelt in front of her. Lifting the foot up onto his thigh, he turned it carefully to examine the deep gouges. He ran his fingers up her leg, firm but gentle, seeking the top of her stocking. Not finding one, he glanced up at her, capturing her eyes with his as he drew a small boot knife. Pulling some of the fabric up from her thigh, he made a slice, slipping his fingers into the new hole and tore it free of the top half of her hose. That done, he slid it gently off her leg, careful around the fresh scabbing.

An let him, gasping when she felt the cold of the blade under her skirt and the small jerk as the fabric gave. She gritted her teeth as he tenderly worked the hose off her wounded leg. Glancing down, she inhaled, long and slow, sank back against the chair. It was worse than she had thought.

Jonny fetched the bowl of water and the cloth steaming on the kitchen table, and bathed the wounds. He carefully laid the torn edges of her skin back in place and coated them with a thin film of frost. He took a roll of white linen and expertly wrapped the remainder. Her other leg received the same treatment: hose cut off, tenderly bathed and frost-healed. This leg did not need wrapping, having taken less damage. What little healing he could do was sufficient.

"Ye inclined t' tell me what did this?" he asked softly, his fingers playing with the foot he was still in possession of.

She tried not to squirm. "I don't rightly know what to call it. A nightmare-born chimera 'tis best I can describe."

He tilted his head.

An explained. "Elizabeth's been having nightmares, fer months now. Most times they're not bad and she doesn't need me. Lately.... She's beginnin' t' feel Sean's absence sore."

"Been a bit since he was murdered," he said softly.

"Aye, well, some folk... it takes a while to really hit them. She's been... suppressing a lot and it's finally found an outlet. She needs a new mentor. I can't fix this. All I can do is damage control."

"Against...?" he prompted.

"Her sweet self. Her infernal imagination. Her uncontrolled magic."

He frowned, began playing with her ankle and calf. "I thought she learned control. Was doin' so well."

"Well, only works when she's conscious, now doesn't it? She's started... creatin' her dreams. It's happening more often as time goes, and some of them...! T'night were part scorpion an' part octopus, an' not just any octopus. No, Elizabeth has to dream of blue-ringed octopi. An' afore ye ask, no, it dinna bite," she preempted as she caught the light in his eye. "Though apparently its suckers are razor edged," she groaned, gesturing to her wrapped limb. "That were th' leg it latched onta whilst I beat it inta submission."

His fingers had reached the inside of her knee and she was trying not to writhe. "And yer chaperone?"

She frowned, then it dawned on her what he'd meant. "Aislynn? She's... curled up with th' *cailín*. I'll get her in th' mornin'. ...Might start havin' Aislynn sleep with her 'til we manage t' get this under control. Been happenin' too often."

He shook his head. She moaned as his fingers began to threaten more northern climes, watched him as a mouse watches a cat slowly stalking up on it, mesmerized and helpless to stop him. "I don't know what they're called," he said, "ask Liberty, but ...they come in pairs. Ye put one in yer room an' one in th' child's... ye'll hear if there's trouble."

"That all depends on th' type of trouble," she breathed.

His grin was predatory. "Well, I highly doubt she'll be in th' kind of trouble yer in at th' moment."

21

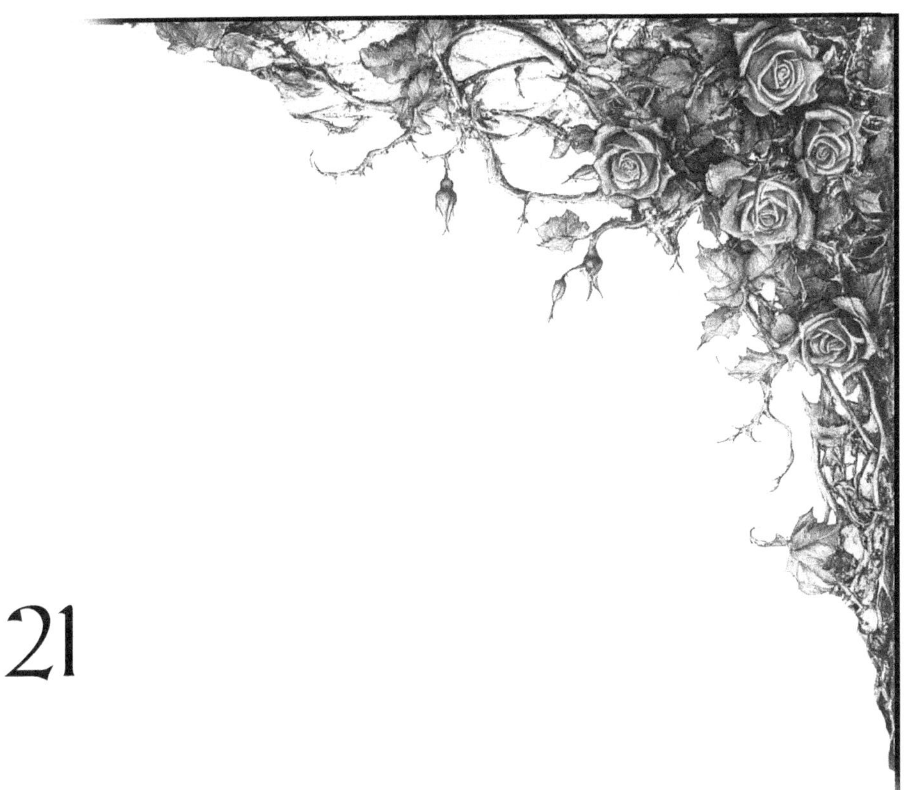

In the morning, An paid Ian a visit. She found him on the veranda, enjoying his morning coffee and a cigarette, gazing out over the fields and his face full of care. She paused as she came around the corner, watched him a moment, debating on whether or not to add to his worries.

"Come on up, An. Whatever i'tis yeh need is likely a small matter compared ta what else weighs."

She sighed and approached. He was a very astute man. "And as such, can wait or be handled elsewise," she said, still trying to resist. She felt her way up the steps and came over to stand beside him.

"There's coffee an yeh want. Maybe some tea if yeh ask."

She shook her head. "N'thank ye. Th' brownie's seen t' my breakfast. Anythin' I can do about what weighs ye?"

He gave an appreciative chuckle. "Unlikely. But thank yeh. What can I do fer yeh this fine morn'?"

An leaned back against the railing, half turned to face him. "I hate askin', but it's not for me. Elizabeth. She needs a new tutor."

Ian cocked an eyebrow as he lifted his coffee to his lips. "She that much a handful yeh no longer wan' th' job?"

"Oh, heaven's no!" she exclaimed, then noticed the grin creeping up the other half of his face. "Oh, ye great tease! No, she needs a magus o' some sort. I can only help her so much in that regard and... she's losing control o' her subconscious."

"How do yeh mean?"

"She's startin' t' have nightmares."

He shrugged. "Most children do. There are ways ta go in an' help an they're that bad. Would have t'ought yeh knew that, havin' required it in th' past. Yeh can even do it."

She shook her head. "I've already thought of that and Jonny's said th' dreams of a wizard are a dangerous place, even for one as skilled as he. Th' source o' them is something I can work on, but th' results... they're wearin' me out. Not to mention gettin' more dangerous."

He turned to her, leaning against a post. "How so?"

"She dreams o' these horrible creatures, chimera mostly..."

"She's told yeh o' them?" he interrupted.

She shook her head. "I've *seen* them." She waited, knowing he would ask.

"I thought yeh said i'twere too dangerous ta view them? Yeh haven't gone in, have yeh?"

"I've killed them, there in her bedroom. Somehow, while she's sleepin', she's less control over her abilities and she's makin' them real. So far I've killed a scorpion-poisonous-octopus thing, an alien clown and at least four jabberwocks, each more vicious than th' last."

Fox's voice came from the door, "Well that explains that," he said, crossing to the coffee service on a table and helping himself.

"Explains what?" Ian asked. His face was placid, but his eyes were sharp and attentive.

"I've been seeing some weird shit out in the in betweens and the borderlands. I mean weirder than normal. Gem mentioned complaints of vorpal bunnies in the suburbs, gremlins, too. And not the mythical, muck-with-mechanics kind. I'm talkin' 'fed it after midnight, allergic to sunlight' gremlins. And I've seen evidence of something the dryads say might be a jabberwock, might be a bandersnatch, but I don't think it's either. Frollywogs and mugglewumps," he added in a mutter.

"So ye think what she's dreamin' is leakin' into Faery?" An asked.

"Maybe," Fox shrugged. "You killing things every night?"

An shook her head. "Just every so often. But she's not tied to Faery."

Ian crushed out his cigarette between his fingers and balled up the filter, setting it on the coffee tray. "She's tied t' you. That's sometimes enough. 'Tis th' risk we take, gettin' involved. Aye, we've got ta get this under control."

"I can bring her to th' trainin' hall like always and have her run herself through th' meditations and other exercises Sean taught her, but that will only go so far."

Ian nodded. "Do that. Actually, we might be able to set her up wit' Juan for now. Some martial arts discipline might help. If nothing else, teach her ta fight them on her own. I can see if Luminara is willin' t' help her wit' some lucid dreamin'."

"Why not Jonny...?" she began, not having known there were other Dreamers at the Rest.

Ian shook his head. "Jonny's not as available at th' mo' as ye'd need right now, an' consistency is best. Meanwhile, I'll send upstate for someone t' continue where Sean left off. I'll let yeh know. Stay on th' alert. Yeh come ta th' point yeh need a break, let me know and I'll send someone who can be invisible ta watch from th' room itself. I might be able ta spare Jacob a night or twa."

She nodded. "Thank ye." She started to turn and then remembered. "Oh, Jonny spoke of these devices what can let ye listen to one room from another?"

Ian frowned, trying to think. It was Fox who suddenly realized what she meant. "Baby monitors?"

An waved her hand, "I guess."

Ian looked over at him in askance.

"They're like walkie talkies. You remember those, right? They were real popular with the kids a couple decades back. You push a button and talk to the other handset." Ian nodded. "Baby monitors work the same way, except one's always on send and the other receive."

"Isn't that a bit invasive?" An frowned.

Fox shrugged. "That's why you only use them in a baby's room and only when the child is alone. Though that's not going to reach from your cottage to the girl's room," Fox added. "They only have like a few hundred yards radius."

Ian turned back to An. "Willy. We'll ask him ta fix yeh a pair up. Unless yeh'd like ta start sleepin' in th' attic..." he added with the edges of a grin fighting the corners of his mouth.

She breathed, "No, thank ye. Th' house'd get jealous, I think."

Ian chuckled. "It might at that."

"If you hang around a few," Fox said, draining his coffee cup, "once Ian's done with me, I can take you down to Willy's shop and get you a set."

"I would appreciate that, thank ye."

The two men moved into the house and An wandered in after them, headed for the solar in the front of the house. She paused in front of the living room, remembering something she had seen nearly a year ago and forgotten about. High on the bookshelf near the large, flat-panelled television screen, were two books suspended in mid air. An drifted in, reached up and pulled the first one down.

She was not surprised to find she could read it. It was a book on the history of the Tuatha, handwritten in Gaelic in a vivid violet ink and an elegant, scrolled hand and beautifully illuminated. She set it down and fetched the other one. It was not in a language she could understand or recognize. The letters and the patterning of the words were none she was familiar with. While she spoke only two languages, English and Irish, she could read several and recognize what language they were even if she could not understand the words. This was not one of them.

She had sunk down onto the couch and was reading the history with the other on her lap when Fox finally found her. He'd had to sniff her out. "She's in here, chief!" he called.

An looked up as Ian appeared above and behind Fox's fiery head. "Not your usual perch," he grunted.

She stood, carried the books over to him. "I saw these last year and ...well, I only just remembered them. They're both magical and I meant to ask ye if ye knew and intended them to be in here. But there were things happenin' that day that sort o' made it... inconvenient to bring up."

Ian held out his hand and she set the books in it. He flipped through the history with a soft smile. "Was wonderin' where this had wandered off ta. Must have gotten put up there by accident. Thank yeh," he said as he handed it back to her. "Yeh kin borrow it an yeh like. Just get it inta m' office when yer done." He glanced at the other book and his expression went blank.

"Uncail?" she asked softly when he hadn't said anything for several minutes.

"This... this doesn't belong out here." Without another word he turned and wandered off, carefully turning the pages with a claw, reading through it as he disappeared around the flower arrangement.

"I hate it when he does that," Fox mumbled. He turned back to An. "Come on. I know where Willy's got his shop set up."

An tucked the book under her arm and followed Fox out the front door.

The 'baby monitors' were a little smaller and more discrete than actual baby monitors, and Elizabeth was happy to help An test them. She had been worried the girl might object to them, that they would make her feel like a infant; but she was actually grateful.

"Now it doesn't matter if they get past the alarms or I make something really bad. You'll hear and get to me."

She stroked the girl's hair at that, placed a kiss to her forehead. "'Tis all right, luv. Uncle's gettin' ye a new tutor and said ye can start workin' with Juan on physical self-defence an ye like while we wait. Could take some time. Meanwhile, we'll see what we can do about why yer havin' them."

"Too bad Mr. Sorrow can't go in my dreams like he does yours and just get whatever's causing them," she sulked.

An became a little more stern at that. "Now, Elizabeth," she chided, "we both know very well why yer havin' these nightmares, and his goin' in be too dangerous fer th' both o' ye, an' is not goin' t' help. We'll come t' grips with *that* wakin' an' with time, all right?"

With a sigh, Elizabeth nodded and An went to the cottage to test the monitors.

Several days later An stepped through the door from the attic only to be informed by the house that she had company. An frowned, slipping off her boots, seeing no one in the front room at all. She pulled off the first sock and the moment her bare foot touched the polished hardwood floor, an image flowed into her mind of Jonny staggering in, then of him on the bed. He was nodding and heavily. She sighed, undressed her other foot and crossed to the bedroom. Aislynn flew in from the open window and landed on the dresser, sulking.

Jonny was sprawled across the bedspread, unconscious, barely breathing and fully dressed in a dirty white t-shirt, jeans that had seen better days and one tattered sandal. She slipped her fingers beneath his mane of snow and felt for his pulse. It was there. She sighed, removed his remaining shoe. She had a word with his jeans, convincing them to assist her in peeling him out of them. She was not surprised to find nothing under them. She managed his shirt and shifted him enough to pull the covers out from under him and roll him beneath them. He was dirty, but there was no help for it. An whispered an apology to the brownie for the dirty sheets and began to undress herself.

As she got into her night dress, Aislynn closed the window, and the fireplace began putting off more heat. An slipped into the bed beside him. No sooner had she pulled the heavy blankets up over her shoulders and snuggled in, than he began to seek her warmth. He was still unconscious, but the arm came out, wrapped around her waist and pulled her in. She sighed, half-content, half-frustrated with his condition. The most telling signs of his affection were unconsciously made. Ruminating upon the possible meanings of the latest gesture, she drifted off herself.

IShe had not been asleep an hour when something woke her. An opened her eyes, saw that the moon had moved halfway across the room, telling her that it had been more like four hours. She listened, tense. Jonny still slept like the dead beside her, arm draped over her, face buried in the crook of her neck. Then she heard it again, a soft "What the fuck?" from the device on the nightstand. It was not a voice she knew. It was followed by sounds of a struggle.

An shot out of the bed, pulling herself free of his grasp. Jonny did not even twitch. She grabbed her dressing gown and threw it on as she headed for the door to the attic. Her bare feet on the boards told her that the alarm was what had awaken her, but the house had turned it down, so she could hear the sound from the monitor and know what she was heading into. An still did not know, but that did not matter. She knew it was a single person and female. Her hand snatched Cipín from the air as the door opened and she rushed across the tiny room. Aislynn flew ahead of her, landing on the door and pulling it open.

Leaving the stairs, An followed the dragon's path, knowing it would be safe from obstacles.

Aislynn did not stop to open Elizabeth's door. She didn't have to. She flew in the open doorway, stopped, reversed and flew down the stairs to the first floor with only a quick, *"I'll get th' parents' door before they wake up."*

An stepped into the threshold and tilted her head in confusion.

In the middle of the room was a woman. She had wild blonde hair that just brushed her shoulders and clothes that covered most of her body. Whatever she had on had a plunging neckline that exposed a great deal of her breast and increasingly more as a creature that was little more than a ball of fur hung from something on the front of it and sank towards the floor. The creature was half mouth with fluffy, red-brown fur and a long tail. And there were eight of them swarming the intruder.

She stood there a moment in the opening, lit only by the moonlight pouring through Elizabeth's two windows, and nearly incandescent in her flowing white night dress and dressing gown. Mist began to curl up from her feet and she set the tip of the shillelagh on the ground and rest her hands upon its knob. An knew how to take an intimidating stance, just stood there and glared, waiting to be noticed. Meanwhile she studied what it was that enabled her to see the woman.

She was not one of the Taken, nor magical in the way Elizabeth was and Sean had been. There was something dark and pale and cold about her. It was not until she bared her fangs and bit one of the snarling, growling critters than An understood. The woman was a vampire. A real one.

The bitten creature screamed and An wondered how anyone was still asleep in this house. That was when Aislynn landed on her shoulder and leaned forward, neck snaked out and wings half spread in a menacing pose.

The woman ripped another creature off her body and threw it at the wall over Elizabeth's bed, where it landed with a thunk. It rolled, hopped over the sleeping child and crouched between her and the vampire, snarling and growling. She shook off another one and stomped on it as she turned and saw An. She froze. Even the critters stopped gnawing and attacking. The ones on the floor backed off the vampire with low growling noises, watching her with narrowed eyes. The ones still attached just hung there. A yap from the ones on the floor and they dropped off, making a ring around the vampire with only one opening.

The vampire met An's foggy eyes, tried staring her down. An felt something attempting to prick at her mind, but then the vampire shook her head and tore her gaze from hers. An never wavered. She took a step into the room and the door closed itself behind her.

They remained in a face off for several minutes, each trying to intimidate the other. The woman eventually reached down to her belly, grabbed something and pulled it upwards with a long ripping sound. Her body disappeared up to her cleavage as she rezipped her outfit. She ran her hands through her hair, smoothing it out and trying to come off nonchalant. Then she blurred for a second and bolted for the door to the study, seeking escape.

She was stopped by a wall of black carapace and clicking mandibles and at the sight of it, An knew what the furry things were. "Garthim," An ordered, "do not let her pass." There was a moment as the Garthim decided if she was something to be obeyed, and which of the beings in the room was its target. When it settled to completely block the doorway, An was satisfied it would obey her. She snapped her fingers at the balls of fur. "Fizzgig, guard yon *cailín*," and as one, they all piled onto the bed and glared, fanged mouths open, at the vampire. Some of them sat on the mountain ridge that was Elizabeth's side. It was a fearsome array; the bloody mouths breathing lie to the wall of cute.

The vampire turned, her eyes dark and flashing, stared at the governess armed only with a cane and a miniature dragon.

"You have one option, vampire," An said, her tone clipped and formal, "that allows you to leave this house with what passes for your life. You swear on whatever it is you still hold sacred, on pain of your destruction, that you will never again darken this house with your presence nor bring injury or harm to any member within it. Do so, and I will let you pass. Refuse and I will destroy you. Lie and I will destroy you. And do not mistake that I can. Greater than you have fallen beneath this shillelagh."

The vampire thought about the matter. She closed her eyes, tilting her head. An could tell she was doing something, she became... well, not exactly brighter, but *more*. An braced, sliding the shillelagh up in her hand, locking the door by setting her bare heel back against it and asking nicely.

She had about a second to wonder what else Elizabeth had lurking around the room waiting to hinder or help before the vampire blurred again, lunging. She moved faster than An could react, even though she had been ready for her to do something. She was behind An, seized her in a grip of iron and sank her fangs into the arch of her shoulder, just above the bone. The pain was explosive, white hot and draining. An did not scream. Aislynn did that for her, shrieking and breathing frost into the vampire's face as An became one with the fog that had built up in the room.

The vampire struck blindly at the dragon, made a lucky connection that sent her flying back against the shelves. Aislynn fell with a dull thud. An, on the floor and made of mist, solidified enough of herself to slide the petty drake to safety under the bed.

The vampire looked around, saw only the sleeping girl and her army of Fizzgigs, the Garthim and the shillelagh standing on its own in the middle of the room. Her eyes were beginning to dilate, her senses to reel. To An's eyes, she looked as Jonny looked when the drug was sliding into his veins and taking its effect, wild and ecstatic; though without the mellowing, sinking bliss.

An rose up, a ghostly figure made of fog, took up the shillelagh and swung. The knob cracked against the vampire's jaw, but it felt as if she had struck stone. The woman seemed surprised, but lunged at her, falling to the floor as she fell through An; rolled and rose just in time to avoid the tip as it slammed onto the carpet where her chest had just been. Panic was beginning to override the ecstasy.

She blurred again, tried the door to the hall and snarled when it refused to open. She put her back to it and faced her foe. Again, the shillelagh stood alone in the centre of the room. Having no other target, she attacked Cipín. An was there at the last second, swinging, just solid enough to wield her, to make the blows count. An knew this would not be a contest of strength. No strike from Cipín would make enough of an impact to affect the outcome of the fight, so An did not put her full weight behind them. She aimed to annoy, to harass, to batter the vampire into making a mistake that would allow impalement.

An had the perfect target. The zip had wandered again, presenting to the air a perfect V of fully visible flesh. It was better than a bullseye. After several blows from different directions, An sank back into the fog on the floor, this time laying Cipín down with her. She felt the woman turn, wary, not knowing where An had gone. An had noticed the woman blurring less as the fight wore on, and waited for her moment. When the timing was right, she rose up, using the shillelagh like a sword and completely solidified, throwing all her weight behind the iron tip as it plunged through her chest and out the back.

An stood there, panting in a night dress now splattered with blood, both hers and the vampire's, staring at the limp form on the carpet with the shillelagh sticking up out of the fog like a flagpole. She heard the shuffling of the Garthim at the door to the study and turned, told it to stay put. It obeyed, settling back down again.

An moved to the bed, shooed the Fizzgigs to make room for her and sat on the edge. She gently looked Elizabeth over. Other than a small bite mark on her wrist and the too deep, evenness of her breathing, she was perfectly normal. An guessed the vampire had made her sleep more deeply, if such things were within their power, and was, for the moment, content to leave her thus. She needed her asleep to keep the Garthim and the Fizzgigs, and right now they were very helpful.

Three of the Fizzgigs had gone under the bed and brought Aislynn out, setting her on An's lap as she reached into the nightstand drawer for the phone she had given Elizabeth. She told the device to call Ian even as she looked over the unconscious dragon.

Ian was awake, a fact which did not make An feel any better about disturbing him. It meant he was dealing with important things that could not wait. "Aye," he answered. His voice sounded a little harried, as if this was just one more fire he'd have to put out.

"*Don't panic, th' battle's done,*" An said. "*But I'll need a clean-up crew. I've got a vampire pinned t' th' floor with Cipín in her chest and I'm not sure if she's destroyed or not. It's not one of th' Dark's. This is a real vampire.*"

There was a muttered expletive from Ian's end and an admonition to someone in the room to hold their horses. "*I'll send yeh sommat as fast as I kin. I think Seamus is in th' Lakeside area wit' a van. I'll have Aiden meet ye there. He knows vampires pretty well, real an' th' Dark's. She get what she came fer?*"

"*Well that all depends on what she came for. She's bitten th' girl's wrist, I think, and my shoulder. Aislynn's pretty bad, but no one's life or death. I'll be calling Roulet as soon as I'm off with ye. A healer wouldn't go amiss an' she can open th' door for th' boys. I'm not takin' my eyes off this trollop until she's taken out in a box.*"

There was a chuckle from Ian at that and a rattle of keys as he selected one and handed it off. She could hear his instructions to someone to head to Courtz and call Seamus to meet them there. "*Boys'll be there in about ten. Five if I can light th' right fires.*"

"*Thank ye, uncail,*" she said, telling the phone to ring off and call Roulet.

The response to this call was a little sleepy. "*Bonsoir?*"

"Roulet," An said gently. "I need ye a moment. Can ye zip through th' phone? Aislynn's been hurt an' I could use a mite o' patchin' m'self."

She heard the crackle which preluded the arrival of the lightning woman and tossed the phone into the fog on the floor. An instant later Roulet was standing on top of the vampire, trying to get her balance from the unexpectedly uneven surface and hopped to the floor. She was in a tank top and a pair of ice blue, Chinese silk pyjama pants with tigers embroidered on them. She looked down at the vampire and frowned, turned, saw the Garthim and jumped back, ready to fire a bolt at it when the Fizzgigs snarled at her and she spun again.

An glared at the furballs. "Shush, you. She's here t' help."

They sulked, but let her approach.

Roulet kept her body facing the Garthim, and glanced down at An's calm demeanour. "Um... that thing yours?" she swallowed.

An shook her head. "Elizabeth's."

Roulet saw the dragon lying limp on her lap and knelt, forgetting the monster in the doorway as she checked her over. She sighed. "I need you to hold her just above her back legs and resist me, but don't pull. I'll do that." An did as she was told and Roulet took hold of the dragon's front half, careful of her wings and tugged. An heard the clicking of bone just as the crackle of electricity began and covered the little body. Even after Roulet let go, little micro-bolts of lightning wandered over the drake's scales, crackling and popping.

As Aislynn lifted her head, blinked and groaned, An heard the sound of a vehicle pulling up to the front of the house. She leaned forward enough to see the street from the window and saw Seamus appearing. "Roulet, luv, if yer done, would ye be so kind as t' go let th' boys in?"

"Sure. She should be fine in a little while. Broke her back, and knocked her senseless, but she's ok."

"Thank ye," An said.

Roulet nodded as she left, had to use the electrical outlet to do so, as the magical lock was still on the door. An picked up the dragon as gently as she could, cradling her in the crook of her arm like an injured cat. Aislynn snuggled down and closed her eyes, whimpered quietly. "It's all right, luv," An whispered. "I have ye."

She rose, crossed to the door and opened it, then went to stand before the Garthim. When Roulet zipped back into the room, An heard footsteps on the stairs behind her and the crackling of a large amount of plastic. An held up her hand in front of the Garthim's face as Aiden followed Roulet into the room, though at a much slower pace, with Seamus and two other people An could not see trailing behind.

An pulled back the fog and Aiden bent beside the vampire on the floor, began looking her over.

"Nope, she's destroyed. Bit young though. Not a whole lot of decomp yet. Not a bad job, Miss O'...." The word trailed off into a different kind of 'Oh' as he turned to An and saw what stood behind her.

She gave him a short nod and turned to the Garthim. "You can go now, back into the dream whence ye came," she ordered. "Ye'll not attack the girl or disobey her, understand?" There was a shuffling and clicking from the gargantuan. The eyes flared with purple light for a second. "If she needs like this again, ye'll appear in this room and defend her, aye?" Again the shuffle and click. "Good, now flit," she said, waving her hand in a shooing motion.

The creature drew itself up, the light went out in its eyes and it began to fold in on itself like the creatures from the film had, only this one turned to sparkling purple dust that burned away before the pieces hit the floor.

An sincerely hoped the orders she had given the creature had sunk into the girl's subconscious enough that she would summon it herself in her own defence. She closed the door to the study and crossed back to the bed.

"Thank ye, Aiden. And I apologize fer that. I needed to send it on its way afore it took objection t' anything." She indicated the body on the floor, " Do ye know ought of their powers?Fer I think she might have done somethin' t' th' girl." An gestured to the bed and Aiden started to cross to it but drew up short at the row of toothy balls of fur. Impatient, An snapped her fingers at them, pointing to the corners of the bed sternly. The six remaining Fizzgigs sulked, but obeyed, eyeing Aiden with narrowed and suspicious eyes.

Hesitant, with a glance over at An, Aiden bent over Elizabeth. He looked at her wrist, listened to her heart, counted her pulse and watched her breathing. Finally, he bent to her ear and whispered something, listened to the slow, long release of her breath, then the return of her regular rhythms. He stood, spoke quietly. "She's all right. I've brought her out o' the sleep trance. Some vampires are really good at that, changing a sleeping victim from normal sleep to trance states. They can input suggestions at that time and feed at will. But I'm of the impression she didn't have time," he chuckled, glancing over at the bloody fluffballs.

An submitted to Roulet's patching up of her shoulder, holding her dressing gown closed as she realized it had been open this whole time. She blushed and Aiden politely looked away. He pulled Cipín from the body and held it out to An without looking back. Seamus and the two invisible men lifted up the body and set it onto a plastic sheet, rolling her up and tucking in the ends. They carried it down to the van.

Aiden looked around at the room and what little evidence of the fight there was. It was mostly just splatters of blood and fur. "I take it the mage," he said softly, aiming a thumb at the sleeping child, "called up th' Dark Crystal critters?"

An nodded. "She's been manifestin' her dreams. Just fortunate that she was under attack tonight or I might have had t' fight th' Garthim. And that one I'd have had to call in back up on," she sighed. "Don't fancy my chances on it."

He chuckled, taking note of the DVD case of the Dark Crystal on the nightstand. "Just be glad she wasn't watching Naruto or Dragonball Z. Her rescuers would have made a bigger mess than the vampire."

An frowned, not sure what those things were, but glad that had not been the case.

He jerked his thumb at the Fizzgigs. "You goin' t' do somethin' about them?"

An crossed to the bed and addressed the six remaining creatures. They huddled together, looking up at her with soulful eyes. "You lot," she said, soft in volume but firm in tone, "will be allowed to stay..." They immediately became a hopping, hissing, barking ball of joy which An silenced with a single gesture and glare. They clustered again, clinging to one another and looking up at her, terrified they would now be told to leave. "On th' condition," she continued, "that ye snuggle up to her, stay out o' trouble, make no messes and guard her. Ye leave when th' sun comes up."

They looked at one another, then back at her and nodded as one.

"Then ye can stay." They all opened their mouths and let out a near silent, hissing cheer.

An pointed out the baby monitor. "Anythin' happens again, one o' ye yell at this thing. Ye make as much noise as ye can, ye hear?"

They paused in their searching for the best places to curl up and looked over, nodding. Some of them burrowed in under the blankets.

An proceeded to tuck Elizabeth in, working around the Fizzgigs neatly, all while using only one hand. There was a quiet throat clearing from behind her and she turned, saw a nondescript, small man standing in the doorway with a broom in his hand in dust-coloured, baggy clothes.

"Excuse me. Hello, Miss An," he smiled shyly.

She stood. "Ev'nin', Billy," she smiled. This was Billy Broom. The man was almost a brownie himself, so rarely was he seen. He was painfully shy and was extremely uncomfortable around beautiful people. An had only seen him once or twice at the manor. He cleaned. As far as she could tell, he liked cleaning. He had done it for so long in Mr. Sawgrass's plantation house, sweeping out the constant influx of swamp mud and dirt, that anything else he might have been or considered doing had been burned out of him decades ago. "Did Ian ask ye t' come?" she asked, as gently as she could.

He nodded, clutching his broom as if it was all that kept him anchored. It probably was. "You... you asked for a ... clean up crew," he stammered.

"That I did," she smiled.

"I'm happy to... but... you, you have to, to leave. I work... faster that way."

An nodded, turned back to the Fizzgigs. "You let him work, you understand?" One of them snorted and buried itself deeper in the covers. She turned back, gesturing for Aiden to go ahead. Roulet had already left, phoning herself home after she had healed An. "They shouldn't bother y', should they?" An asked, pausing beside him.

He shook his head. "They're not really real. They don't count. Ttttell Seamus I'll be... down in a... few minutes?" he asked Aiden and moved further into the room, assessing the mess.

An quietly closed the door behind him. She followed Aiden to the door, thanked him for coming, watched him warily cross the walkway to the waiting van. She closed the door and went to George and Sharon's room, undoing the magic that Aislynn had activated for her. Over a year ago, Sean had put a magical ward on their doorframe so that, if necessary, An could put the parents into a sleep deep enough that any noises of combat would not wake them.

Finished with that, she headed back up, all the while cradling the drake in her arm. She passed Billy on the stairs.

"All done. Good night, Miss An," he said meekly, lifting an imaginary hat to her and shuffling out to the van. An heard the door click and lock behind him. Tired beyond belief now, An headed up to bed.

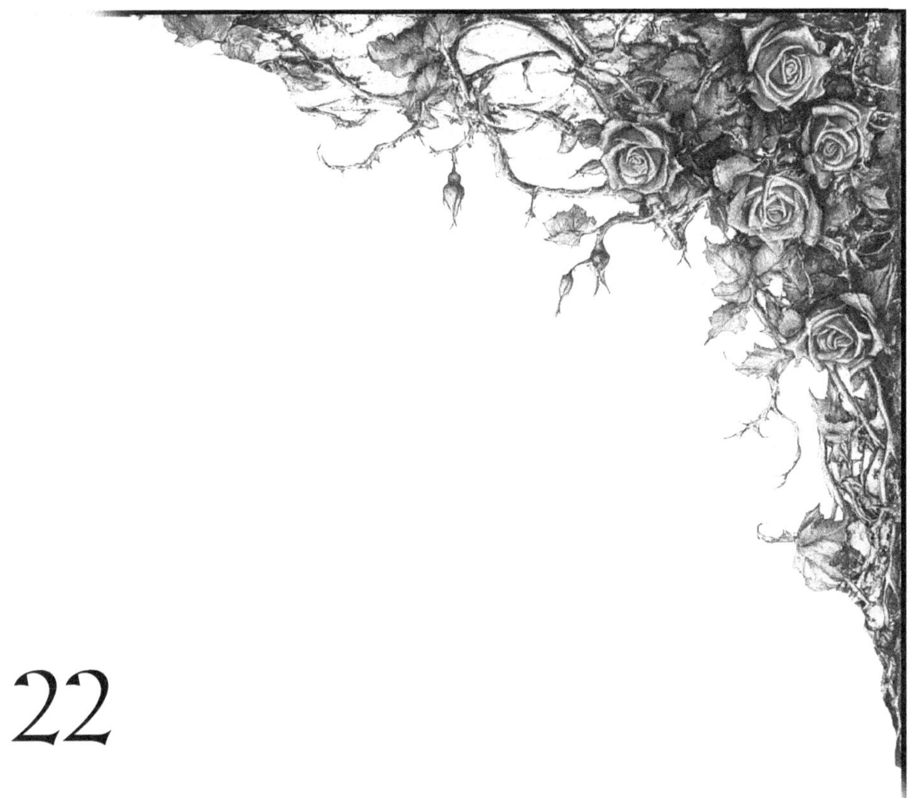

22

A few weeks later, An was at Karaoke when she saw another vampire. She was at her table with Jonny, enjoying the music and contemplating singing herself. It had been a while since she had taken the stage, since the débâcle with "My Ain True Love", and it was past time. Jonny had already flicked his eyes between her and the stage more than once. She was just trying to think of what to sing. She knew he would not make a suggestion.

She was sipping her tea, toying with various ideas when the speakers began spewing something very aggressive and bouncy. The music was not quite grinding but it came close. The singer was incoherent. Well, that was not completely true. He sang well, and there were recognizable words here and there, but between the style of the music and his accent, An just couldn't follow him. She looked up as Jonny muttered, "Punk," as he rolled his eyes and groaned. "At least it's not 80's thrash metal."

She looked up, but what An saw on the stage made everything else fall away. She saw the singer. He was dark-haired, light-skinned and extremely handsome. His dark curls were in artful disarray and his shirt was half-untucked and hanging low on one shoulder. His black pants looked painted on. He was breathtaking, if you liked the sort. The sort being a blood-sucker. He looked the same as the woman in Elizabeth's room.

Without a word, An got up and followed a very round-about path to her destination. She headed towards the bar, turned to the door. At the back of the bar she turned right again, going along the wall to the last booth where she could see Liberty sitting with the accounting books. She slid into the opposite seat with just a preliminary feel for where things were and leaned forward, keeping her voice down as Liberty looked up concerned.

"What is it, luv?" she asked.

"The gent on th' stage."

Liberty looked over as the man was taking his bow. She smiled. "Aye. That's Simon. He's a regular, though this is th' first karaoke I've seen him at. He's usually a Monday sort. Not a bad voice."

An frowned, shifting to Irish. *"Did ye know he were a vampire?"*

Liberty froze, turned slowly to look at An. *"Ya sure?"*

"Aye. Dealt with one up close and personal few weeks back, remember? Looks different than us or Elizabeth. I'm certain."

Liberty flagged a passing waitress. "Daphne!" The girl nodded and delivered the drinks she was carrying to the table beside them, making sure her customers didn't need anything else before sauntering over.

"Yes, boss?" she asked cheerfully.

"You know Simon, right?"

Daphne smiled. "Oh sure! He's a great guy. Fantastic tipper! Can never finish a drink, though."

"Would ya be a love and ask him ta join me, please?"

"Sure!"

Liberty shifted over a little and gestured for An to move to her side of the table. An was just sliding in when Simon arrived.

He smiled broadly, his British accent making him sound charming. "Summoned by the mistress of the house," he grinned. "This is either a great honour or trouble of some sort. With the luck I've had this past week, I'm more inclined to believe the latter. So please feel free to disabuse me of that notion."

Liberty gave him a smile. "An, luv, will ya draw th' curtain?"

An looked up beside her and saw a limp fabric hanging on the inside of the high booth wall that separated it from the ones around it. She reached up and pulled it about halfway closed, asking it nicely to continue its journey. Once it reached the far side the noise beyond the booth dropped off to an unintelligible murmur.

Liberty smiled broader, sighed. "Oh good, they work. And they don't cut out th' light, nice. I'll have ta thank Arachne an' her daughter."

An looked over at her. "Miss Moffett made these?"

"Aye." She turned back to Simon. "Now that we can't be understood beyond th' curtain, we can be candid. I know what ya are, Simon." She held up her hand as he drew back. "Fret not. I don't care. Not really."

He frowned at that, then let his curiosity get the better of him. "All right, I've been coming for months... granted, not normally Fridays, but... why're you only just now bringing this up?"

"Let's say my methods o' discoverin' such things only just saw ya an' leave it at that."

Simon's eyes flicked to An.

Liberty continued. "I don't mind having other supernatural types in here. If ya didn't know, I'm fey-touched myself."

He squinted at her, breathing deeply of the air in the booth. When his eyes flitted once more to An, they opened wider as he noticed the true nature of her eyes. When he looked back at Liberty, she looked more doll-like. He relaxed, leaning back in the booth. "I should have known. Hell, shoulda noticed. Lot of you?"

Liberty nodded. "A great many of my people come here. Some of them need practice mingling with mortals. Are ya familiar with th' rules o' Hospitality?"

"If you mean the Celtic ones? Aye. Lived a hop-skip from Eire most of my life. I've known my share of Scots, too."

"Well, they apply here, ta all. Supernaturals are welcome so long as they obey Hospitality. Now obviously, I can't run a true *brughaidh* here in th' states, and this isn't a traditional situation, but th' entertainment is free and I expect th' other rules ta be obeyed. No violence. In yar case, no feedin'. If, fer any reason ya find yarself in a spot o' trouble, ya kin ask for a day's hospitality. Ya can get three days without explanation. That goes against th' grain, but in these modern times I have ta be careful, and th' laws... well they interfere, don't they?" she smiled, shrugging with her hands. "I have rooms upstairs if ya ever have th' need. And aye, they have no windas."

"A bit open of you," he commented. "A little risky, wouldn't you say?"

Liberty's smile turned predatory, "Not if ya abide by Hospitality. Break it and ya won't walk out alive... well, dependin' on what ya did and why. At th' very least ya might find yerself on th' street regardless o' th' hour. It all depends on how much I like ya."

"Fair enough. Though I've a place of my own," he said, leaning back again.

"Most do. There are emergencies, however. I've slept here myself once or twice. So, do tell yar friends about th' policy. Contingent welcome. Th' only other real rule is not ta let th' masses know yer different, but that goes without sayin'."

"I think I can abide by that. Though lettin' the rest know... I'm not the best for that. But I'll put out what feelers I can. I'm... not a pack animal."

An leaned in to Liberty, "May I?" she asked, indicating she wanted to say something.

"A'carse, luv."

An ran her thumb over the small nicks in the head of the shillelagh for comfort, not really knowing she was doing it. "So long as yer spreadin' word, there's a word I'd like t' go around. There's a house on Tallyrand, just down th' way, two-story, nestled in trees."

"Describes quite a few in Lakeside," he said casually.

"This one ye'll know. There's a great deal o' magic there. It tends to attract attention," she said, locking her gaze with that of the vampire.

"The power child," he whispered.

"Aye. I've heard her called that. I want it known she's off limits and under extensive protection. Any I catch in that house I'll kill, like th' last one o' your kind what tried it." Her voice was cold and hard.

He leaned forward. "*You* killed a vampire? One who managed to get into *that* house?"

An could not decide if she should be insulted or flattered by his incredulity. "Aye. I did. Blonde hair t' here," she brushed her hand across her shoulder. "Curvy, wearing something that covered almost all of her, but zipped down th' front."

"Chastity," he snarled. "That empty headed idiot! Did she bite the child?"

An felt her heart drop into her belly. "Aye. There were small marks on her wrist but she brought no harm to her as we can tell."

"Good thing you got her off then... though it changes my assessment of you," he said with a tilt of his head.

"And why is that?"

"She was stupid to drink from the child. And no reason to think she was in there for any other purpose. While the child would be useful to one of ...us... it would not be as food. There is too much power in the blood of supernaturals. It makes us ...crazy. Did she say anything?"

An shook her head. "No, but she didn't look rabid. She actually thought about what she was going to do."

"She only tasted then. You got lucky. Bitch is fast. Was... Dead you say?" he grinned.

"Aye. She decomposed a bit, or so I was told."

He stopped at that, panic in his green eyes. "Told? You didn't see it for yourself?"

She smiled. "That's just it, I didn't see her after that. She... lost that which enabled me t' see her in th' first place."

He laughed suddenly. "That bitch can go invisible. I would love to have seen her face when she realized you could see her anyway."

"She did seem disconcerted," An said nonchalantly. "So, ye'll spread th' word?"

"That Chastity bit the big one at the hands of a blind nanny? Abso-bloody-lutely!"

An bristled at the word 'nanny'. "I have not said my capacity in this matter and I am not a nanny."

He shrugged. "You seem the type. Explains an Irish woman guarding an American child. Governess, then, if you prefer."

She nodded. "Thank ye. Now if ye'll excuse me, I've left my table in a bit of a... rush and I fear my company will worry."

Liberty immediately reached over and twitched the curtain open. "Go! I don't want m' husband panickin'!"

An smiled as she rose, bent to kiss Liberty's cheek. She turned back to the vampire and nodded, "Simon."

He smiled, flashing the tips of rather sharp eye teeth. "You know my name, governess. But I've not yours."

An blushed a little at her loss of manners, extended her hand. "An Ceobhrán O'Keefe."

He took the hand, kissing the air above it even as he quirked an eyebrow at the name. "My pleasure."

At that, An returned to her table. When she sat back down Aislynn put her tiny monkey fists on her hips and fussed at her in monkey gibberish. Jonny merely lifted an eyebrow and sipped whatever he was drinking. "Punk bother ye that much?"

She frowned. "Turns out he wasn't such a punk. Decent enough gentleman."

He gave a soft laugh. "No, lass. While they use it these days to describe hooligans who like the culture, 'punk' is a type o' music. Very rebellious."

"Oh. Sorry," she sighed, lowering her voice and shifting to Gaelic. *"I felt th' need t' let Liberty know that th' 'punk' was a vampire. She felt th' need t' explain Hospitality. I then asked him t' spread warnin' amongst his kind that th' next one I find in*

Elizabeth's bedroom will suffer th' same fate as this last one; who's name was Chastity by th' by."

Jonny stopped, looked over at her, setting the beer bottle down. *"'This last one'? When was this?"*

She blushed. *"Th' last time ye were over. Ye never woke up. Not when I came t' bed, nor when th' alarm went off, not when I left, nor when I came back. Don't fret. I had help."*

He frowned. *"What kind a' help?"*

An actually giggled, picking up her now cold tea. "Garthim."

Aislynn snickered at Jonny's expression.

An smiled, feeling coy all of a sudden. *"If ye come home with me tonight I'll tell ye th' tale. Quite entertainin', if I do say so myself. I'm surprised ye havena heard it. What with Seamus having been one o' them as fetched th' body."*

Jonny gave a snort and reached for his cigarette. *"If Seamus had been involved in th' killin' or seen any o' th' fight, ye'd be right. Th' story'd be all over th' Rest."* He drew down the last of the cigarette and slowly exhaled it. "Whenever yer ready then. But don't think this is gettin' ye out o' singin' again."

She smiled enigmatically. "No, but it does buy me time t' think of what t' sing," she said, standing.

An had just stepped out her back door, prepared for a bit of morning gardening when she heard Liberty's front door open. She stepped around the side of the house to see her coming down the walk towards her gate. Smiling, she called out, "Back here!"

Liberty looked up, nodded and pointed back at her own house. "Meet me in m' livin' room," she called. "I'm goin' t' get th' twins. Skye has somethin' he wants t' talk to us about."

An nodded and pulled her gloves off. She crossed to her little, open potting 'shed' and tossed them onto a shelf. She saw Aislynn clinging to the wall and reaching into one of the red rose bushes to pick a ripe rose hip. "I'm headed t' Skye's. He's got sommat for us. Join us if ye've a mind."

The petty drake politely declined.

There was a Gaelic curse and An walked around the house to the neighbour's, laughing. When she felt her way into the living room, her brother was pacing on the far side. This was a benefit to her, as the absence of his lower half gave her an idea of where the furniture was. She found her way to a chair at the end of a low table and perched quietly. He noticed her but said nothing, crossing to the window and looking out. It gave her time to study him.

He was excited about something, and somehow anxious at the same time. When he saw the twins on the front walk with his wife he almost sprang over An's chair in his rush to get to the door. He ushered them in with a patience reminiscent of a five-year-old trying to get the adults downstairs on Christmas morning. There were French and Romany complaints uttered as the only half-awake twins settled on the couch and Liberty took the chair opposite An. She swept her hand toward her husband in a grand gesture, grinning. "Well, we're all here. Spill it."

Skye took a few seconds to calm himself before speaking. "A'richt. A bit back Ian asked me tae carry some boxes up intae th' family archives. Ah dropped ane an' spilt it hither an' yon. Ah noted a book as ah were recollectin' shite. Whit caught m'eye wis thon it were written in Ogham."

An's head came up. "Ogham?" she asked, shocked. When the twins looked at each other in askance, An explained. "'Tis an ancient form o' Celtic writin'. Fifth century, maybe as early as first. Ye'll see it all over Ireland an' Scotland in th' old places, some parts o' Britain. Often used as a scout's tongue t' leave cryptic messages fer following forces. I didna' know ye ken it," she said, turning back to Skye.

He shook that matter off as unimportant. "Larned it in Service. It on'y matters cause ya doan see it much, an' niver here. So ah haed a peek. Turns oot t'were a diary. A really auld ane an' fair cryptic but... it mentioned th' loss o' a castle an' thon th' denizens hid their valuables sae th' invaders wouldnae get it. Ah showed it tae Liberty."

She smiled, giving him a look full of sweetness and love, "Roulet, ya know I've been researchin' th' O'Keefe's fer th' last few years?"

Roulet nodded, laughing, "I remember the obsession, yeah."

"Well, this diary ties inta all that. I'd found it... mebbe th' Imbolc before they came out," she said, indicating her husband and An. "I couldna read it an' set it down, in th' livin' room, ah think. Never gave it another thought fer some reason. I were delighted that Skye could read it. He's been translating it an' readin' it t' me like a bedtime story," she laughed.

He blushed a little. "Aye, turns oot, 'tis th' diary o' someun wha were close tae th' O'Keefe's. Took me a bit o' time tae translate, bein' ancient an' hand-written an' fadin' in places, but ah've done it. Ah've been wantin' tae dae sommat fer this man whit gives up everythin' fer us, an' this is perfect. There's a s'ard, th' O'Keefe ancestral. Accardin' th' diary, it were seen wi' th' king in a battle prior to th' abandonment o' th' castle, but niver again a'ter. And this is whit I want: Ah want tae find oot which castle this were, go there an' find that s'ard. Ah know how important ancestral blades are... more sae fer a chieftain. Ah want us tae find it an' gi'e it him."

An held out her hand and he placed the well worn, leather bound book on her palm. It was the same book she had handed Ian not so very long ago that had been misplaced onto the living room shelves. She looked it over with something akin to reverence. The lines of symbols were hard to make out, even if you knew what they meant. It had taken a great deal of work in the translating. "This explains why ye've been all but absent lately. Thought ye working fer th' Family. But this... is a worthy endeavour. Though why ye bring it to us..." she said with a shrugging tilt of her head as she handed it back to him.

He took a hard breath. "Ah would think it obvious. Ah want yer help. One, ah doan ken which castle or where it lies. And twa, we'd have th' folk whit mean th' most tae us an' him in on th' doin'. Thon an'... it may tak more than brawn t' acquire."

Liberty smiled at that. "As I said, I've been lookin' inta th' family fer years. Ah've ev'n traced th' tree all th' way up ta Da (an' that were eight months labour right there), but I've no idea which castle this were or when. There's no mention o' th' battle or which war th' castle were lost in."

"Not as coud be read anyhoo," Skye added.

Liberty continued. "It might go faster if we had help tryin' ta figure oot what war, what castle, etc. If we can find that, mebbe we kin figure out where th' sword got ta."

"We'd be glad to help," Roulet said. "I have some resources I can use that might help us dig up a location. Worst to worst, I can find out who has the sword now, if anyone does."

An felt useless as far as the matter was concerned. She had no means of researching. The records that would contain the appropriate information were all written and no amount of glamouring would make the words visible to her. As for getting someone to read it to her... they might as well just do the research themselves.

About a week later An found herself at Courtz again. It was a typical Friday night and as she came downstairs she paused at the bar to ask Tori if her table was free.

Tori looked over her shoulder out into the mid-sized crowd. "Yup. You want the usual?"

An nodded. "Scotch eggs this time?"

"Done. Need guiding?"

An shook her head. "I'm goin' t' detour by way o' th' stage."

"'Bout damned time." She chuckled at the blush on An's cheek. "Here," she said and placed a tall glass into An's outreaching hand. "Be a dear and hand that to Roulet?"

An turned towards the stage, slipping up the side of it to the KJ booth. She found the two steps and mounted them, holding up the glass as Aislynn whistled for Roulet's attention.

"Oh, perfect timing!" she exclaimed, taking the glass. "I love you, woman." She took a long sip from it.

"Actually, Tori made it. I'm just th' delivery girl. Got time t' put sommat in fer me?"

"Absolutely. Whatcha want?"

"Jethro Tull's "Pibroch"?"

An heard the clicking of keys. "Yup, got that one. You'll be on right after this guy," she said gesturing to the stage where a half-drunk man was mauling "I've Got Friends In Low Places".

"Thank ye, luv. Any luck so far?"

Roulet shook her head, then tilted it. "Maybe. Every time I think I find something it turns out to be a false trail. Get ready."

An stepped down from the booth and crossed the few feet of floor to the steps of the stage as the man staggered down, laughing, into the arms of his raucous friends. An drifted up the stairs, finding her way to the mike with Aislynn and Cipín's help. The music began and her haunting voice filled the club, full of the emotions at first of homecoming, then hesitation and finally soul-deep grief. The mists clinging to her skirts seemed to perfume the air nearest the stage with a slight, cool damp.

Ignoring the applause beyond a faint smile and a fierce blush she followed her usual path to her table. She had to pause for a few seconds as someone large passed in front of her, then she knew where her table was without having to feel. Jonny was there, where he had not been a second before, raising his Guinness in salute, that enigmatic, half-grin on his face. An's blush grew more furious, but she also smiled. She sank into her chair and picked up the waiting whiskey.

"See," he said softly, teasing. "Nothin' t' fear."

"Och, just m' head explodin' when all the blood rushes to m' cheeks," she countered, pressing the cold glass to her temple. Her skin felt the cooler air around him but beneath it she was on fire.

He merely chuckled and drank his stout.

Shortly after the sausage wrapped eggs arrived, Roulet came over to the table in a state of excitement. "I found it! I had to follow some obscure damn paths, but I got it!"

An's eyes lit up even as Jonny's brow raised. "Where?"

"Northern Cork, just outside of Duhallow. It's called Dromaigh Castle. I couldn't find it cause it's been in the hands of the Leaders more recently and the O'Learys at current. But it's one of three that the family lost over like a thirty year period, but I'm sure it's this one."

"What be ye wantin' th' O'Keefe ancestral fer?"

Roulet gave a look of complete exasperation. "Oh, of course the walking encyclopedia of ancient lores knew all along," she groaned.

An looked over at him. "Ye knew where th' castle lay?" She asked.

"Aye," he replied. "I know a lot of things historical. Bard, remember?"

She looked at Roulet who just sighed, "Why didn't you just ask him?"

"Cause 'tis th' first time I've seen hide nor snowy hair since th' day Skye brought it up," An snapped.

"I've been going crazy for the last week!" Roulet exclaimed.

Jonny's voice came again, soft as rain. "Can I ask why ye be wantin' t' know? Might be as I know more ye be in need of."

Roulet scooted in closer to the table, leaning in. "We're looking for something that was last seen there. An heirloom."

"Be as a lot of those lie at th' bottom o' th' keep well. Th' castle lay under siege by Cromwell's army in 1651. For some reason, they were allowed to march out en masse. 'Tis rumoured all manner of family treasures were thrown down th' well t' keep it out o' enemy hands. Many a treasure seeker has gone huntin', and all come home empty-handed... those what come back. There are some as never come home a'tall." He shrugged. "But then ruins are dangerous. And Irish ones fer different reasons." There was something hard in his eye as he took in the two women, a warning.

Roulet lifted her head as she realized what song was playing. "We'll be careful. Promise." She turned from Jonny to An as she stood. "Meet you at Skye and Liberty's in the morning."

An nodded and watched the gypsy girl rush off to set up another round of singers before what was queued up ran out. She smiled after her. "Skye will be pleased."

"If this is his intent, aye."

An looked at him, saw real concern in his earth-coloured eyes. *"What is it ye fear for me?"*

Jonny took a moment, drew a long, thoughtful pull from the frosted bottle. *"There are dangers in th' home country not present here. Especially in th' old places like Dromaigh. There's rumour o' fey blood in th O'Keefe line, datin' as far back as Caoimh, Son of Fionguine, who married th' daughter o' th' Druid Mogh Ruith, a lass it is said were th' ruler o' th' Muster Gentry. Which means, empty or no, it might not be completely abandoned an' th' O'Keefe protections do not extend t' walkin' inta their places. I'd have ye take adequate precaution."*

An nodded, thankful for the warnings. *"We'll be careful. An' I'll have Cipín. We'll find our way back."*

He said nothing more, and An was not sure if he was satisfied or merely no longer inclined to press the matter. Jonny got up near midnight and sang. It was a very happy and upbeat song... normally, but the way Jonny sang it, with less pop and more soul, it changed the meaning completely to something deeper and more mournful without being emo. Just as he was setting the microphone down, he caught Aiden's eye from across the bar and nodded. Instead of returning to the table, he gave An an apologetic tilt of his head and went down the back hall towards the loading dock. It was not hard for An to guess that he would be taking flight the moment he'd cleared mortal sight.

She sighed, remained a bare hour longer before heading back upstairs and towards home.

23

It was surprisingly only three days later that An, Skye, Liberty and the twins were being driven down a very minor Irish road towards the Dromaigh Castle Farm. When Liberty had approached her father about taking a trip to Ireland the long way, he was more than happy to accommodate. The speed at which he arranged the passports for Skye and An and the twins could not have been exactly legitimate, from what Solitaire had said. If it were, everyone had the wisdom not to ask.

The moment her feet touched Irish soil, An felt the change. She could smell it. The air was cleaner, cooler, more magical. Once they left the city and the urban areas, An began to see shadows of the countryside; even the occasional cottage or garden; and certainly the odd hill here and there. There was an odd familiarity to it all while at the same time being almost completely foreign.

When they pulled up to the old, two-story farmhouse, Skye held the door for the women while the driver went to the trunk to get their luggage. Once they were out, he headed to the back to help the driver as Liberty took An by the arm and guided her up the steps of the little Bed and Breakfast. Aislynn hid herself in An's hair, once more disguised as a monkey.

The proprietor greeted them on the front porch, calmly shelling peas as she sat in her rocker. She was a round, pleasant woman, which An could tell solely from her voice, as there wasn't a drop of the magical on her. "Ye must be th' O'Keefe's."

"Aye," Liberty beamed, shaking the woman's hand as she set aside her peas and stood. "I'm Liberty. This is my sister, An; our close friends, Solitaire and Roulet. And the Highland ninny over yon is ma husband, Skye."

Apparently the woman was admiring either the cut of the Scot or the way he manhandled several of the bags at once. "Och, they do grow them braw in th' Highlan's."

"That they do," Liberty chuckled.

"I'm Margaret O'Leary. I'll just show ye up to yer rooms." She opened the door for them and led them into the house. "Mind the stairs, Miss O'Keefe. They're about ten feet in front of ye, banister's on the right."

"Thank ye," An said as she heard the woman set foot on the first step a tad more forcefully than really necessary, to make sure An heard where they were. Once they were at the top of the stairs, she opened the first door on the left. "Mr. and Mrs. O'Keefe, ye'll be in here in the family bedroom. Plenty o' room and I dare say th' bed's big enough even fer th' like o' him."

Liberty laughed and An smiled. Behind them, Skye only grunted.

"Miss O'Keefe, yer across th' hall on th' right," she said opening the door. "Double bed, should be comfortable. Th' bath is next door on th' right and th' bannister immediately on th' left, so there'll be no danger o' ye findin' th' stair th' hard way. And you ladies will be at th' end in th' 'twin's room'. It actually has th' best view of th' old castle."

She stood out of the way to allow her guests to enter their rooms. "Supper is on the table at eight. Breakfast as early as seven, but that's the only meal I make 'as ye come down'."

Liberty gave her a broad smile. "'Tis all lovely, dear. We'll be down. Would it be possible t' have a picnic lunch for tomorrow?"

The woman smiled. "Not a problem a'tall."

Dinner was a quiet, family-styled affair, with just Mrs. O'Leary and her husband, who had been out in the fields all day. Conversation was polite and Mr. O'Leary was happy to give them all the information he and his family had gathered about the castle over the years it had been in their possession. After coffee in the parlour, they left their hosts to their knitting and evening paper and went upstairs to bed.

An was awakened somewhere before midnight by something that she felt more than heard. Aislynn pulled her fully awake by shooting across the bed and curling up into her neck under her hair in an attempt to hide from what had made the noise. An sat up and the petty drake slipped under the covers and refused to come back out. That was when An heard it again.

It was a long, high wailing that seemed to come from across the countryside. She got out of bed and slipped into her dressing gown, was in the hall before the cry ended. Moving purely on instinct, her hands out before her, An headed for the end of the hall where the twins had been settled. Skye appeared behind her in only a hastily wrapped utili-kilt as she pushed open the twins' door. Solitaire was just beginning to sit up, frowning. Roulet was already at the window, wearing only a pair of bikinis and a camisole. An used what she could not see of Roulet to navigate the room to the window. She was drawn to it and what she could now see outside.

Beyond the pane, the castle rising above the trees, was now magical enough An could even see the oaks surrounding it. What was more, she could see a woman standing on the tower, her dress and hair flowing back as if caught up in a fierce wind. An set her hand to the cold glass, almost hypnotized by the bean sidhe, feeling her pain as she began wailing again. She was prevented from being drawn too far in by the sudden presence of Skye behind her.

There were two windows in the room. Liberty stepped to the other with Solitaire, leaving An and Roulet with Skye looming over them.

"Do you see what I see? Or am I seeing things?" Roulet asked.

"Is that a banshee?" Solitaire asked, her voice quivering.

"Aye," Liberty breathed.

"Does this mean we're all going to die? Isn't what that it means? If you hear a banshee?"

Liberty set her hand on Solitaire's shoulder to calm her. "Not necessarily..."

"She's not that kind o' bean sidhe," said An softly. Her voice cut through the tension and fear in the room perhaps more effectively because of its quietness. "Somethin's off about her. I've seen..." Before she could complete her sentence, the woman leapt from the tower and sailed downward, vanishing from view beyond the treeline. Her wail was cut short.

Roulet shuddered. Solitaire buried her face in Liberty's shoulder. Skye set his arms around both the women at his window, trying to draw them away. An would not turn. She kept her eyes on the castle tower until it had faded from her view. Only then did she let Skye pull her back, though she did not fold into his embrace for comfort. Instead, she found her way to the nearest of the beds and sat, thinking about what she had seen.

Liberty came over to her, leaned against the bedpost. "Ya were sayin'?"

"I've seen a bean sidhe. One o' th' type what warns a family of a comin' death. They don't bring death themselves, just th' warnin'. There were somethin' odd about this one. I can't place it, but I'll trust my instincts on't."

The twins huddled together on the other bed and Skye just loomed, uncertain what to do.

Liberty had had enough. "All right," she growled. "Our hosts are either used ta this or dinna hear a thing. We've an early mornin' and then we'll likely have all th' answers we're bound ta get, so, ta bed, all o' ya." She took An's hand and drew her up, leading her towards the door. She shooed Skye on ahead.

Roulet refused to get into her own bed, choosing, instead, to curl up with her sister on the narrow mattress farthest from the windows. Liberty quietly closed the door. At An's room, she stopped in the open frame, not sure what it was she was seeing on the bed in the dark room. She laughed when it moved and she realized Aislynn was peeking out from beneath the covers. She bade An a good night, making sure she reached the bed all right before closing the door and heading to her own chamber.

The next morning, they asked their hostess about the bean sidhe. Mr. O'Leary had already gotten his meal and gone to the fields, so it was just the five of them over ham, eggs and fresh soda bread. She smiled indulgently. "We used t' hear her more frequently years back. But I think we're used t' th' drama. Occasionally, she'll wail fer guests. 'Tis thinkin' their presence calls t' her. She's a harmless ghost. Story is she's th' wife o' th' last O'Keefe laird t' hold Dromaigh. Threw herself from th' tower in despair, though there's not a soul who can agree to why. They abandoned th' castle just after."

She closed up the heavy wicker hamper and handed it to Skye as he stood back from putting his dishes in the sink. "Here. Now shoo. Be careful round th' castle, some bits an't as solid as they appear. Especially you, Miss," she said to An. "Ground's rocky in places."

"I'll be fine, Mrs. O'Leary, thank ye kind. What I can't see I can feel."

"I'd just bet you can," she smiled, shooing them amiably out of the house.

They took their time walking over to the castle. It wasn't far, just up a short little road. The walk brought forth buried memories for An: the sensations of walking along a country road, a pail of blackberries in hand and few cares in the world. The smell of fresh mown grass and the creep of ivy and moss was heavy in the air and set her at ease, beginning to melt away the long held sensation of not fitting into the world.

All too soon they were approaching the wooden gate in the ivied wall and Skye was pushing it open.

There was nothing untoward about the place. An could see nothing, though she slowly began to feel on the edge of something. They went first to the place where the bean sidhe would have fallen, saw no sign, old or recent, of the suicide. The twins headed off in one direction, exploring the side buildings and the rest of the courtyard. Skye, Liberty and An took to the battlements and what remained of the main building. Aislynn flew through the castle, exploring the high places. Aside from a heavy sense of history and Liberty sensing a familial connection, they found nothing out of the ordinary.

Fighting disappointment, they stopped for lunch in the courtyard, using the capped surface of the old well as a picnic table.

"The O'Learys are at least trying to keep it up, though," Roulet said. "There's some newly repaired beams in the stable and one of the side buildings."

"Makes me a little less irritated about it no longer bein' in family hands," Liberty sighed. "I like that couple."

An ran her fingers over the weathered surface of their table. "This is th' well, isn't it? Th' one th' books say everythin' was thrown down?"

"Aye," Skye answered, grabbing another piece of chicken.

"So... ye think there be sommat th' treasure hunters missed? Sommat our eyes could see?"

He stopped, stared at her. "Ya mean yar eyes," he sighed.

She spread her hands. "Not necessarily. We also have Aislynn, who could just fly down an' take a peek."

"*I could do that,*" she agreed through a mouthful of strawberry.

"So, why don't ya pull th' cover off after we finish lunch and we'll start lookin' in earnest?" Liberty smiled, giving Skye's collar a playful tug.

He growled devilishly, shrugging her playfully off. "Ya needn't sweet talk me, woman. Th' whole buggin' party's ma own idea an' ah ken ye cannae haul aff th' boardin' on yar own."

They laughed, finished up their lunch and cleared away their things. Everything was folded away neatly into the basket and set aside as Skye rolled up his sleeves and got himself set to remove the well-cap. It was sturdy and not more than a few decades old. Apparently there were still folk hoping to find ancient treasures at the bottom of the Dromaigh well. It crossed their minds that they were hardly any different, save for the supernatural aspect.

Roulet used her staff to provide a bit of leverage, so that Skye could get his fingers beneath the planks, hoping to pull up the whole instead of tearing it or the well apart. An stood back with Liberty and Solitaire, out of the way. Aislynn wrapped herself around An's neck and watched with interest.

Slowly, the seal cracked, iron nails giving way at the four corners where they had gone unnoticed. Roulet yelped when she accidentally brushed against one as the whole thing lifted up like a cellar door. Liberty started to move to her, when An's hand shot out and grabbed her arm, the fingers tightening painfully. Liberty turned, saw An's eyes open wide and the mists whirling madly.

Slowly, as the air from the well rose up like escaping smoke, everything billowed into view. It was as if there was a layer of magic settling over the whole castle. Even their mundane clothing was growing visible.

Aislynn sat up, smelling something in the air that made her nose twitch.

An stepped forward next to her brother. He was standing at the edge of the well, staring into the depths, dumbfounded. What curved away below them was not an ordinary well, but a sloping cave mouth. From deep within it came scents both alien and ancient with a touch of the familiar.

An took a step back as Aislynn began to shrink into herself on her shoulder. "Ohhhh," murmured the tiny dragon.

She turned to look at her, concerned what it was she had realized, and caught a glimpse of Liberty walking away from them. She was striding towards the tower, her walk not quite her own, her eyes intent on something not visible to any one else, not even An. There was something regal and self-possessed about that stride. An followed, aware Liberty was caught up in some magical thing. She could see it all over her. She did not think it immediately dangerous, but at the same time, felt she should not be left unsupervised.

As she approached the tower door, Liberty nodded to someone unseen beside it, calling out in a Gaelic that sounded archaic even to An's ears. An turned, calling to Skye as she slipped through the tower door in her wake, following her quickly lest she lose her. Liberty slowly began to climb the tower stairs, winding her way to the top. Occasionally, she stepped aside as if to let someone by, and An would feel the breath of ghostly passing, but see nothing.

"All right. I'm officially weirded out," Aislynn breathed in her ear, clinging to her vest with all four sets of claws.

An started to say something calming, but at that moment she happened to glance out the window they were passing. She looked down on the courtyard and could see neither Skye nor the twins, though she could hear his voice bellowing from below. She paused, setting her hands on the sill and looking out over the wall at what had caught her attention. Beyond the ramparts of the castle lay a dark, seething mass of men and animals under the banner of Cromwell's Protectorate. The castle lay under siege by what could only be an unseelie horde. "Skye! Do ye see th' army?"

Skye turned, looking out the open castle gates at the recently cut lawn and the gravelled road. "Whit bloody army?!" he growled.

She suppressed the quivering in her gut. "Liberty's caught in some ...memory, I'm thinkin'. I've got t' follow. Get up here!"

She turned and rushed up the rest of the steps, hoping the thought that had seeded itself in her mind was not what was going on. Liberty could not be allowed to follow the ghost woman over the ramparts. She burst out into the open air at the top of the tower and the siege was no longer just the superimposed illusion beyond the window frame. It was real and oppressive and all around as far as she could see. In the air, at a great distance, flew something she feared was an actual dragon.

Liberty stood at the parapet, looking out over the sea of hostiles, her hand upon something beside her and unseen at her hip. She did not look about to jump, but An was uncomfortable with her nearness to the edge and reached out for her. As her hand touched her shoulder, An could hear Skye's footsteps pounding on the stairs, just yards behind her, and then the world as she knew it dissolved. The nurse stood back from Lady O'Keefe, kept her worry contained. There was something about the seething army outside their gates that disturbed her on a level beyond living under siege should have.

Her charge, eight-year-old Ian, stood at his mother's hip, peering over the side, fearless.

"I wish ye wouldn't let him so close, M'lady," she said. "Makes me nervous, it does."

"And the army at the gates doesn't?" came the deep voice of Laird O'Keefe as he stepped out onto the top of the tower.

Nurse sank immediately into a deep curtsey as the boy turned and threw himself into his father's arms. She stepped back, out of the way and observed the mother. She had been her nurse too, when she had been young. She kept the family secrets. It was true what they said of the Lady, that she was of fey blood, and when you looked at her at times like this you could see it shining clearly in her. Her red hair was dark, not the bright copper of many Irish. You only realized it was red when the light hit it. Her green eyes settled on the nurse's dumpy frame and smiled indulgently. Her rose petal lips curved in a different smile for her husband and his heir, something deeper and more passionate. One could forget Cromwell's army, or that damned dragon in the sky above them in the wake of that smile.

Suddenly that glorious expression melted, the eyes going wide in horror as an arrow sprouted from the boy's back and he slumped in his father's arms. The nurse watched, mesmerized by the drops of blood hanging in the air below the Laird's hand. The Lady screamed. The Laird roared in shock as the arrow bit him too and he realized what had happened. Beside them, on the battlements, one of the archers turned, bow drawn, and picked out a single enemy archer grinning at him from the field. He let the arrow slip through his fingers, watched as it sailed through air heavy with smoke and heat, and slid though the ribs of the crowing enemy. An impossible shot for an impossible shot. But the boy was still dead.

They finally separated father and son. The Laird roared in rage as a chirurgeon moved to staunch his bleeding. The Lady wailed in anguish as she pulled her son's lifeless body to her. Finally able to react, Nurse reached over the Lady's shoulder and closed the boy's eyes. Everyone on the tower was numb with the shock and several minutes passed with no one aware of them. Then the Lady began speaking in a language the nurse felt she should understand. But there was a quality to it that made it difficult to comprehend the words, much less their meaning; as if she were speaking underwater, or through some other, equally fluid medium. As if she were holding conversation with something in another world.

What was clear was that she was begging, arguing, even yelling at something elsewhere. And there was a response, Nurse could feel it in the air, though not a word was heard. And then the bargain was struck like a tolling bell.

With a kiss to her son's forehead, the Lady clutched him to her breast and stood. Her movements were graceful and flowing as she carried his lifeless body to the tower wall, onto the crenellation and stepped off. She made no sound as she fell.

The Laird cried out, reaching his hand towards her even as her dress fluttered out of view. His hand was taken by his Lady's frail, and somehow less real hand. She still knelt before him, curled over the body of their son who had opened his brown eyes, weeping for some loss he did not yet understand.

Nurse stifled her own cry, clamping her hands over her mouth as she realized what had just happened.

Her fey-half gone, the Lady looked… lessened, older, her beauty fading, her hair a dark, lifeless brown with streaks of grey. Even her spirits seemed dampened, though she smiled as she clutched her living child to her breast.

The Laird stood, shrugged off the chirurgeon and began to bellow orders. A pall descended upon the castle, weighing heavy on every heart whether or not they understood what was going on. In short order, all were gathered in the courtyard, what meagre belongings they would require for survival in whatever sack or box they could manage. Nothing of value could be taken. Laird O'Keefe stood at the well, speaking ancient words, calling upon family guardians. Ungirding his father's sword from his hip, he held it over the open well and dropped it in. It was followed quickly by the keys to the castle and his crown. "'Tis yours now. Let's see them wrest it from *your* hands." Then, more quietly, "Forgive my failure."

He turned his back on the well, moving to where his horse stood waiting. Behind him, as he mounted, his people filed past the well, dropping their valuables into it. The enemy was letting them ride out, but their gold would be taken. Lady O'Keefe sat rigid in the saddle of her grey palfrey, every inch a queen of Celts. Nurse could have sworn the horse had been white, and glossier just days past. But then the siege had taken its toll on all of them; even the young lord held firmly in the saddle before her. She wrapped her arms tightly around him, careful not to put too much pressure upon his chest. Though it remained unmarked, she remembered a wound there, as did the boy. He was a little weak and dizzy, confused, or he would have ridden his own horse.

At a word from the Laird, the gates were opened. Before them lay Cromwell's hordes, parted like the Red Sea before Moses. A young man, the archer who had made the impossible shot from the tower, rode out ahead of the O'Keefe's carrying the golden griffin rampant on its green field. Laird O'Keefe rode out, his Lady at his side. Slowly, the rest of the denizens of his last castle flowed out after him through the dark gauntlet of the enemy. There was an acute sense of loss washing over them, turning the day nearly to night; leaving them with the feeling of a storm in the air which refused to break.

And they found themselves once more before the open well, reeling from foreign sensations and the memories of people they had never been. Liberty gasped, reaching out for her husband, tears streaming from her face. He pulled her in, nearly crushing her as she wept for something she herself had not lost.

"What just happened?" Solitaire finally managed. "It was like one of my visions but not. I still feel his blood on my hands," she said, staring down at them, rubbing her clean fingers together.

"I think... we just got caught in a ghostly re-enactment," Roulet offered.

An shook her head. "No. We were shared of a memory. Like I do objects? Only this were th' people who left this place, th' ones we were tied to. We just saw Ian die and be saved."

"I... I gave up our fey blood for his life. Mine and his," Liberty sobbed, trying to get herself under control. "I... his mother... my grandmother was half-fey."

"Her father was some fey lord, dallied with an' never again seen," An added. "I know. I were there, her mother's lady in waiting, privy t' th' secret of her lover. I birthed th' daughter as beautiful as th' dawn and just as wild. Nursed her as I later nursed her son.... Then watched him die. I... I am still seeing him falling from that tower. Though I walked beside them out of it, I still saw their bodies lyin' broken on th' stones of th' steps."

"I ...I made him mortal," came Liberty's hollow voice from the depths of Skye's jerkin.

"Ah made th' devil's bargain," Skye said. "It were part o' th' deal. Ma part o' th' deal. She gave up her immortality an' half her soul fer his life. Ah'd no leave it under siege an' subject tae starvation, tae die yet again. Ah made th' hard choice. But ah denied them i' th' end," he growled with grim satisfaction.

On An's shoulder, Aislynn was shivering. "*Stop talking as if yer them,*" she ordered. "*Get back to yerselves! Yer Roulet and Solitaire, a pair o' French gypsy twins, not a chirurgeon and an archer. Yer Liberty and Skye O'Keefe, Ian's daughter and her*

Highland lummox, not his mother an' father. Yer Bean An Ceobhrán, a mage child's governess, not Ian's nurse."

Skye frowned, beginning to pull himself back together. "An' whit were ya?"

"Objective Observer," Aislynn snorted. *"Now, get yer heads together. Ye'll want it afore ye go in there,"* she said, pointing at the well with the tip of her tail, *"with* Him."

Almost as one, they turned and looked at the well mouth, at the long, rocky slope that should have gotten darker as it progressed and seemed to be having the opposite effect. Without thinking, An's hands went out, taking up Skye's in one and Roulet's in the other. They looked at her a moment, then nodded and as one, they began the descent.

At first, it was just your average walk down a rocky, widening slope. An did not need to glance back to know that the door wasn't there any more... not visibly anyway, and wouldn't be until their business here was done. It was then that she realized what had happened to her, and where they were. She felt... like she had when she was over There, serving with her full powers as a faery governess. She needn't turn to see what was behind her, and knew that small movements of someone trying to be sneaky or hide something would catch her attention. She knew that someone even *thinking* of lying in her presence would be obvious, and lying to her face would not be possible. She also knew it would not cause her pain as it did in the real world. Its manifestation would be different here, in a Fey Realm. Though there was something about this place that seemed different... deeper... older, though no less potent.

She turned her attention to her companions without turning her head. Skye was much larger here, and feeling invincible from the way he held himself. This must be how he had looked the day he had rescued her, strong, handsome, eyes like steel, the epitome of the invincible Scottish warrior. The twins, for split seconds, were indistinguishable from each other and the stereotypical gypsy beauties. But in between those flashes, Roulet became a being of pure electricity, making it tingly and difficult to hold her hand, and

Solitaire became incredibly sexual and desirable, attractive to An even though she had no interest in women in that way.

Liberty was the most changed. She had become a wooden marionette, complete with pins in her joints which An suddenly realized were always there, just carefully hidden, and that they always hurt.

Her attention was drawn away from her companions by the change in terrain. The area was brighter and the ceiling so far above as to be invisible. They were surrounded by treasures in increasing amounts, walking upon a road of gold coin that thankfully did not slip or slide under their feet. Ahead there was a shifting and the creak of ancient scales moving against each other, and the soft sound of some monstrous cat stretching.

The brightness dimmed even as Skye's hands tightened, perhaps in an attempt to keep himself from drawing his sword. The gold ahead of them moved and then they realized it was neither gold, nor yellow, but the reflection of gold upon a mirror-bright, white scaled face. Aislynn's tail tightened uncomfortably around An's neck.

Liberty spoke first. "Forgive us, great dragon, fer our intrusion..."

The dragon cut her off with a chuckle. "You were not unexpected." Its voice was cool and ancient, almost dusty like an old book, but still had a well oiled tone to it that made it mellow and comfortable to listen to. "You did knock. I have been here since before Time. No one enters against my will. Had I not wanted you here, you would have found only an empty well. Now, what I want to know is: *why* you are here? What is it you were looking for in this ancient and forgotten place?"

His eye seemed to pierce through each of them, seeing through to their bared souls. What he found there he kept to himself. Aislynn may as well have been a statue on An's shoulder for all she moved.

Skye spoke up. "We come seeking somethin' given ya th' nicht th' O'Keefe's abandoned th' castle. Th' sword o' th' last O'Keefe Laird o' Dromaigh."

The ridge above one eye arched. "And what would you be wanting with that little fragment of metal? Surely there were greater treasures thrown to me that fateful night."

"We aren't treasure hunters," Solitaire piped up.

The dragon's gaze shifted uncomfortably to her. "No," he smirked, "*you* hunt something else entirely."

Solitaire shifted uncomfortably under that gaze at those words.

"We seek it no' fer ourselves," Skye continued, "but as a gift fer his son, our current chieftain an' king."

The dragon shifted his whole gaze to Skye. "He is still alive?" The pointed nose came closer, breathed deep. "You smell of newer times, centuries removed from that night. Yet you tell me the child still lives? I thought they had surrendered their fairy halves."

Liberty shivered, remembering that bargain intimately, and the pain of it. "They did. But when he came to an adult, he traded time ta th' Gryphon King ta protect his people. Th' unseelie kept stealin' th' family." There was no expression upon her wooden face as the dragon turned to her, breathing so deeply of her that the tail of her blouse raised towards a snout wider than her whole body.

The dragon chuckled suddenly, pulling back and settling in on himself, like a cat sitting in the sun. "That bitch," he laughed softly. "Oh, there is more to that story than I will tell you. Though I will say that fairy blood had already well tainted that line, made them vulnerable, desirable. And not just to the Morrigan. I tell you, the Aesir got the better end of *that* trade."

An noticed, without turning her head, Solitaire and Roulet's frown at that. Without even really being aware that she knew, she explained. "It is believed, and apparently rightly so, that the Aesir and the de Danann traded members. The Aesir, the Norse gods, got Freyr and Freya, and the de Danann got the Morrigan."

The dragon's only response was a low, near in-audible chuckle.

There was a shuffling of treasure off to their left and she felt Skye tense, though she realized it was only the dragon shifting other parts of its body. "So, will ye allow us th' blade?" she asked, trying to distract Skye. "Since 'tis only a 'fragment of metal'?"

The head shifted, much like a cat reconsidering if it wanted to be bothered by something. "Why do you want it? It is not yours."

They knew without thinking about it, that there was more to that question than the answer they'd already given. The dragon's eye fell on each of them in turn but it was An who answered him. "It was Skye's idea an' choice. Th' rest of us just came with him."

The dragon turned to the Scot, amusement clear in his eye as Skye twisted his head to pop his neck. Feeling that An had just thrown him under the proverbial bus, he sought for the best way to answer the question, knowing without thought that the dragon would wait however long it took.

"Th' man has gi'en me a home whan ah haed no expectation o' ane. Allowit me tae attend th' duty assigned me by th' King an' helped me facilitate tha'. He allowed me tae hav' his daughter. Though he couldnae stopped us... permission made it easier. He's gi'en so much o' himself fer his people, been a father tae them fer centuries... an' he has nothin' o' his own father an' family. An' ah ken whit ancestral blades mean tae a warrior. Ah thoucht... t'would be a noice gesture an' ah coud return a bit o' his father tae 'im. Let him see himself as th' Laird we see him t'be."

The dragon's eye did not leave Skye for several minutes, but Skye did not have anything else to say. That had been it in a nutshell and pretty words. Eventually, the great, slit eye roved over to Liberty. "And you. Why did you join him on this fool's errand?"

She actually snorted, though her face showed none of the emotion carried in her voice, "I don't find it a fool's errand. I've been huntin' my lost past since I escaped. Skye's m' husband an' Ian m'father fer all I never knew him growin'. As his only child..."

This the dragon interrupted with a narrowing of his eye. "You are not his only child. Nor will you remain the youngest." With that the dragon turned to the twins, leaving Liberty stunned to silence. "And you?"

Solitaire shrugged. "He's the chief. He takes care of us. I love him... more than a little. When Skye suggested it, asked for our help..." she shrugged again, "it sounded like an adventure."

There was a soft chuckle. "Would have thought you've had your fill of that," he said snidely, his gaze shifting to her sister in a less than subtle dismissal.

Roulet did not wait to be asked. "Liberty is family. Not blood family, the deeper kind. What she needs, I provide." She shrugged, "I've spent the last few years watching her back. No reason to stop now."

Satisfied, perhaps, the great eye swung to An. He said nothing, merely waiting for her answer. Eventually she gave it to him.

"I cannot say much that has not already been said," she answered with a tilt of her head. "He is my brother, though no blood lies between us. An' Ian my king. I thought it a wonderful idea an' am glad t' help. An' 'tis good t' be home, or as close to it as I'll ever know. Ian gave me a home when I surrendered mine out of duty and love. I owe him no less."

"Loyalty and Love." The dragon's deep voice rumbled through the cave, though whether he meant the words as a sneer or pleasure none of them could tell. "The two most dangerous emotions in the universe. The most personally damning," he chuckled.

"You have swayed me." The huge body began to shift with a great noise of spilling treasure and sliding coin. "You may take but one. See to it you take the right one." There was hidden menace in the last. An realized he had moved the entire bulk of his body to surround them and was big enough to do so without being noticed.

The dragon moved his head, opening a path and revealing a small hill of gold upon which stood a large, clear crystal on a marble pedestal. Embedded in which, were five swords. They stepped closer to examine them and An stifled a small gasp as she saw what appeared to be a heart embedded within the crystal. Not the hallmark shape representative of love and sentiment, but an actual organ. She could not tell if it was beating or not.

Skye either overlooked the heart altogether or found no significance in it, concentrating on the array of blades.

The centre sword was unmistakable. An had seen its like in countless engravings and tapestries depicting a particular faerie lady and an immortalized knight: Excalibur. Skye did not look at that one twice.

Solitaire resisted the urge to run her finger along the golden hilt of the one on the end. "Do we even know what the sword was supposed to look like? I can't remember. I feel like I should. I just saw it a little while ago."

"That's Durendal," An said softly. "Given to Charlemagne by an angel to give to Roland." An was only a little surprised by her knowledge. She was more startled by the fact that she had ever forgotten them than that she knew them at all. She pointed to another, more ancient shaped blade. "Gram, unless I miss my guess. Used by Sigurd to slay the dragon Fafnir." A still older sword, "Hrunting," she said, her fingers hovering an inch off the iron surface with its 'ill-boding patterns' and a faint red gleam from the blood that had tempered it. "The sword that failed Beowulf and was abandoned in Grendel's horde."

There was only one left.

It was an unassuming blade, yet seemed to fit between the gleaming brilliance of the French Durendal and the simple magnificence of Excalibur. It was even in harmony with the two Viking blades that flanked it. It was a simple Celtic long sword, battle-worn and well-used.

Without questioning his choice, Skye stepped forth and took the sword by the hilt, prepared to pull it from the crystal. An reached out and stopped him by simply laying her hand on his shoulder. He looked at her. She silently took Liberty's hand and set it on the hilt beside his. "Blood," she explained.

He nodded, shifting his grip to the left quillon while Liberty took the right. Between the two of them, they pushed upwards, sliding the great sword from the rocky sheathe with a grating noise that seemed over-loud in the quiet, echoy chamber. They stood there, holding it between them for a long moment.

The twins turned to watch the dragon, though An did not need to turn to do so. She could see it clearly behind her, scaled head resting on ancient paws, silently amused. Its tail raised itself into an arch revealing the cavern's only exit.

"Go." He said flatly. "The rest is mine."

An began to silently usher the others towards the entrance, before the beast could become bored and seek other entertainment. As she followed the others out, she wondered whether the faerie admonition against thanks applied to dragons, turned and gave him a small curtsey and nod.

There was a smirk on the finely scaled face. "I wish you well of it." There was something hidden in the dragon's words, but An could not tease their meaning from them. Swallowing the dim sense of foreboding, she yielded to the less than gentle squeezings of the opalescent tail around her throat and followed her family up the cavern slope towards the well.

Aislynn did not loosen her grip until she and An were drawn from the well mouth into the growing twilight world of the castle courtyard. Once more wrapped in a dark, misty haze, she felt suddenly devastated and weak. The sense of being omni-aware and able to recall any fact to her mind had faded, leaving her acutely aware of its absence. She realized what a blessing the kiss of forgetfulness the King had given her when she left him had been. It had eased the passing from one world to another and the sudden reduction of such powers. Now more than ever, she felt the loss of what she had left behind in the King's realm, though for the first time it was a selfish thought, a longing for what she had been. A memory flash of white snow-hair and the chill but heating touch of lips to hers drove such longings from her mind. No matter what may come, she would not trade back. Life in heaven was not worth her few moments of well-earned bliss here.

She felt a cool hand touch her arm and was startled when she realized it was Roulet. She had come to expect the tingle of surging electricity. That was gone now. There was sadness in the sound Liberty's breathing and An knew that she was leaning into Skye's jerkin. She imagined he was feeling suddenly very... mortal.

Slowly, as Aislynn loosened her grip and nuzzled her behind her ear, the people An loved began to fade into view through the dark mist. Nothing else was visible, but she assumed the sudden loss of seeing everything had temporarily overridden the faery gift that allowed her to see magic. That or her body simply had to remember that it needed to.

She let Roulet lead her a few steps away from the well, saw Liberty holding the large sword to her as Skye moved to put the lid back on the well. In moments it was as if they had never moved it.

The feeling of loss and sadness was mollified a little by proof of their success. And their new knowledge weighed upon them as Skye led the little party out of the castle gate and down to the farmhouse.

24

That evening, they held their silence about what had transpired at the castle. They were just not ready to discuss it. They did speak long enough to decide that it was not exactly worth the hassle of trying to get the sword through customs and opted to go home via the magical door in Dublin.

But first: shopping.

Without question, they stopped in at the Moffets' for brunch, much to the consternation of the shop-girl, Mavis, who was more than a little jealous of the privilege. When An made a comment about it to Deirdre, the woman had sighed and answered. "We've tried, really. But th' poor dear just can't handle it. We've had to have her memory altered twice already."

"May be time to hire one of the Touched," Arachne said sadly.

"Makes me so glad we found Tori," Roulet commented. "She can sort of see us, *really*, and just takes all the weirdness in stride."

"And there's a lot of that," her sister added.

"Aye," An laughed. "Deirdre, I simply must have th' recipe fer these pies. M' brownie'd be head over heels fer these."

"Can ye get mutton in America?" she frowned, pulling some paper and a nub of a pencil from a drawer full of odds and ends.

Liberty smiled. "At th' Rest, ya can. Helps we raise our own."

"That it does," she smiled, began writing the recipe.

Later, after an excellent early lunch, and a second round of gift shopping for Christmas presents, the group ended up in a bookstore.

They scattered in various directions, though one or another of them stayed near enough to An to help when needed.

She was looking for new and interesting things to send Eagle, as well as some personal reading material. She chose a book on oriental myths and legends for pleasure and a book on the evolution of warfare for education. Turning a corner, she was shocked to see three books hovering in the fog. She let her fingers slide across the spines until she came to the slimmest of the volumes. Pulling it out, she was thrilled to find it an instruction manual on Ogham. She slipped it into her shopping basket and moved to the next one.

It turned out to be a book on different types of fey creatures. An was a little surprised at first that it would be a magical book. But flipping through it showed her why: it was accurate. Most of the types of fey were listed alphabetically, with a lot of helpful tips about how to deal with them if you had no choice. The page on brownies was especially enlightening. The third book was another fey volume, with emphasis on fey types and other 'invisible people' of every other culture around the world. An could not attest for the veracity of this one, but it was likely as good as the first. She put them both in her basket and moved on to their Braille collection.

She was perusing their selections of classic novels when she felt it. It was as if the entire city just ...shuddered.

It was noon, but the light pouring through the window suddenly dimmed, then became brighter than ever, bright enough even An noticed. Aislynn nearly shifted to dragon, and wrapped herself tightly around An's neck. Roulet came running around the shelves from where she had been browsing and grabbed her. An clung to her, looking around, trying to find the source of the growing discomfort.

"What do ye sense?" Roulet breathed.

"Th' whole world is shaking. Feels like something's burnin' away around us," An whispered. "Like th' people in those films about nuclear bombs Elizabeth was watching last week."

"Well, I can tell you *that*'s not happening."

An looked up at her, uncertain what she was feeling. "Not here, ...but somewhere? Like ...over There?" An got a sudden chill even as she said that. Aislynn dug her face out of An's hair long enough to give her a wide-eyed, terrified stare at that thought. An slipped her hand to her phone, asked it to send a text to Ian, asking if he had felt it and what it might have been.

Solitaire came around the end of the aisle, made a sound of relief and added herself to the pile, wrapping her arms around her sister and slipping her hand into An's.

"Something...," An began. She did not get a chance to say anything further when there came a loud, low, deep sound that rattled the windows. Several knick-knacks shuddered off their shelves and shattered on the floor. It sounded almost like an implosion, and was felt far more intently than it was heard. An aisle over, someone collapsed and people rushed to the rescue, calling for an ambulance. Roulet grabbed hold of the nearest shelf.

"Was that an earthquake," she gasped, "or an explosion?"

Someone near by answered. "I don't think anything was slated for demolition today. I usually keep track of those things. Hold on."

An heard the tapping of a screen and assumed the man was going on the internet on a phone or a tablet. Shortly: "No. Nothing. No reports of an explosion or anything. Not much on it yet, but I found one news station speculating it might have been a gas main or something underground. We'll know by tonight, I guess. Oh, wait... there's something here about the Loopline Viaduct... powers out to the railways. And both the East-link and the West-link bridges are closed, reporting accidents when the bridges shuddered. May be some structural damage to the struts. That's gonna muddle up traffic for months."

An's blood ran cold. She told the phone to text Deirdre to have some of the local Taken check on the bridge trolls. 'I've a gut feeling something is terribly wrong,' she added at the end of the message.

Skye passed the other end of the row, bellowing An's name. Liberty, hanging on to his belt to keep from losing him, saw their cluster and pulled him back. "Here they are! Ya ladies all right?"

An and Solitaire nodded.

"I think it might be time to go home," Roulet said, her voice shaking.

Suddenly Solitaire grabbed her eyes and hit the floor, cutting off a sharp exclamation of pain. She was immediately swarmed. After a few minutes, her eyes shut tight, she swatted off the reaching, concerned hands. "I'm fine... it was... bright..." She lowered her voice so that only the four of them could hear her. "I saw a pyramid, and not the Egyptian kind... and then a flash of blinding light from all around and felt... like I was on fire and burning up like a paper doll. Something fell, but I don't think it was the pyramid..."

An gasped, met Skye's worried steel eyes. They both knew that landscape.

They gathered themselves up, paid for their books and swiftly left the store, going back to the hotel they had engaged for the day. Grabbing their slight baggage, An turned the bathroom door into a gateway to her cottage and everyone fed through. Once home, An severed the connection to the hotel room.

Leaving their things there in An's living room, they took the shortcut to the main house. They were surprised to find that the events seem to have been repeated even here. Several people were crowded into the living room watching the news, which failed to put forth any viable explanations though they were full of theories. There had been a similar event in the nearby cities, shaking buildings, breaking windows, setting off car alarms and car wrecks everywhere. Several of the bridges were closed. Everything was, so far, being blamed on whatever caused the damage to the bridges. And it was not just the Matthews that took damage. Main Street near the outskirts and the large one on Taylor, downtown, had taken damage as well.

It did not take long to find out what had happened. It was Cullen's fault and Ian was livid. Beneath her hand on the ancient wainscotting, An could feel the house tremble in the face of his wrath. It was not long before the entire Rest knew, those that had not had a hand in it. An knew Ian was leaving his office before he had passed the dining room and darted quickly out to the wide veranda and out of the way.

Several vehicles were pulling up to the front roundabout as An found her way to the far corner of the porch to watch. Cullen and quite a few of the other Taken spilled out, hooting and hollaring their triumph.

When Ian burst forth from the house, he went from man to full gryphon in the eight strides it took him to cross the white-washed boards. As Cullen started towards the steps, arms spread, crowing "UNCLE!", Ian roared.

An winced as his front talons dug into the top step, biting the old wood, watched the feathers on his neck stand up as that ferocious beak opened and loosed a sound that was part eagle shriek, part lion roar and part screaming tornado. The victory party went silent and even Cullen froze in place. The people who had been in the house quietly began to press in the open doorway, too afraid to get closer but dying to watch.

"What have you done?" Ian managed to snarl.

Cullen managed to find pride and courage even in the face of Ian's obvious rage. "I've struck a blow that that bastard Dark Man will not soon forget!" he said, drawing himself up. Ian said nothing, just watched him with murderous eyes. "I gathered parabolic mirrors and positioned them at every gate in the city, angled them to catch the sun, and then shone that sun, intensified by the powers of certain individuals," he added, inclining his head behind him, acknowledging the help without pointing them out for Ian's wrath, "directly into the Dark City itself."

He added in a somewhat smaller voice, trying to gloss over the fact, "I was not expecting the city to explode."

An was a little afraid Ian was going to explode. From the crowd An heard a faint squeak and the shuffling of feet as something sharp and metal bit into the wooden floor. Glancing over, she could see people moving out of the way of the tip of a claymore that had materialized in Skye's hand. Liberty rest her own hand on his, holding him back easily, but An could see the rage boiling up behind those steely eyes.

Ian's voice ground, recalling An's attention. "Do ya have any idea what ya've done?"

"Vanquished th' Dark Man. Or at th' very least ended his help to th' bloody Russians," Cullen said.

"Aye," Ian spat with a twist of his eagle's head. "Th' last ya've likely done. But vanquished him? Ya've likely driven him inta hidin' an' when he recollects himself... he'll wage a war on us we're not like ta win. Worse than th' war I fought when we stole ya an' yar unit from th' bloody Northerner!" To his credit, Cullen flinched at that. "I thought we'd learned our lesson after that, wit' near a third o' this community dead, but I guess not. D'ya have any idea how many innocent lives ya've snuffed with yar little coup?"

Cullen paled, swallowed, scowling. "No one in th' Dark City is innocent."

"Tell that ta Spetznakov's daughter!" Ian roared. He took a step off the porch. "Innocent ar not they deserved a chance ya didna give them! Why'd ya just do this? Instead o' runnin' it by me?"

"I... ta...," he deflated visibly, his eyes only flicking momentarily to the crowd, "prove m'self. Ye had so many other worries I thought this would take th' weight off. A decisive victory."

"Pyrrhic," Ian said. "Not decisive. Pyrrhic."

"I thought..."

"Ya *didn't* think," the great beak snapped. "Not beyond yer own glory an' th' desire ta prove yerself still a general. Yer impatient, Cullen! Always were. Now others'll pay th' price fer it."

Ian stepped off the porch onto the drive and Cullen instinctively stepped back. Everyone's breath was held. His voice was lower, closer to a growl as he issued his orders. "Get back out there, in intelligent groups an' scout. I want ta know th' extent o' th' damage an' what can and can't be salvaged. That is yar responsibility." Then he crouched and threw himself into the air, flying off in a fury.

Most of the people by the cars ducked, except for Cullen, who stood there stoically, prepared to face the brunt of his uncle's wrath. In a tree not far away, An caught the flash of white feathers and looked up to see Jonny watching the exchange. She did not have to read his expression to know that he was angry as well. He dipped his head, sharpening his beak on the branch with a few strokes and then flew off in another direction. An had the feeling it would be a while before she saw him again.

An Oeireadh
(The End)

Dance of Devils

An opened her eyes in the darkness. The room was dim, the fire out and the hearth swept clean. Moonlight filtered weakly in through the louvred edges of the closed shutters. Aislynn lay curled up on the empty pillow beside her, snoring so lightly it came out more as a purr.

She turned over, tried to settle back into sleep. There was no reason for her to be awake. The petty drake had not woken her, nor had the house or her brownie. The room was neither too cold nor too warm. She had not been dreaming. The baby monitor on her nightstand was silent and cold, telling her that Elizabeth had not created anything from her dreams tonight. An made a mental note to have Jonny teach the child the art of lucid dreaming. It would only help her in the long run.

Finally, she gave up, slipping out from under the covers without disturbing the tiny white dragon. While she reached for a dressing gown to cover the white eyelet nightdress she wore, she did not put on slippers. She owned none. The house preferred her bare-foot and she had long ago accepted this.

As she tied the sash of her dressing gown, she crossed to the window and unlatched the shutters, throwing them open to the side garden. Her house underwent frequent, subtle shifts and changes, something else she had gotten used to. So it was no surprise to her that there was no glass to lift out of her way, no barrier but the shutters to the cool air of an early Spring night.

The moon was high overhead and bright, cast a shadow from her cottage over the little side garden, though it left the rows of hollyhocks and early primroses to glint silvery in the bright light. She could glimpse coloured flickers in and out of the flowers. By the light buzzing of bees and the chiming of miniature bells, An knew they were pixies, not fireflies. The Vamprick roses framing her window sighed against the stones of the cottage as they inched towards the now open window. Their scent was heavenly and relaxing, blending flawlessly with the fragrance of the wisteria just beginning to bloom above her.

Beyond the low stone wall across from her window, she could see nothing but a bank of fog, though she knew Liberty and Skye's house was only twenty metres beyond it. Little outside her garden was magical, and thus was invisible to her eyes. She saw no movement across the way, where she knew her brother's window lay, and heard no other sound but the pixies and the wind in the trees. All the world but she seemed to still lie sleeping.

She resigned herself to wakefulness, began humming a familiar melody as she leaned on the sill. The roses turned towards her but otherwise grew still. She reached out to touch the red lipped petals of the nearest blossom, smiling softly. From somewhere near she heard an owl calling.

She heard the thrumming of feathers through the air seconds before she saw the shadow swoop out from the eaves above her. She looked up, hopeful, leaned back as a large, white raven landed roughly on the sill in front of her. She looked down at him in the circle of her arms and smiled; an expression which faded quickly.

The bird was in terrible condition. As she began to smooth down disarrayed feathers, the bird leaned into her, wings spreading; and she found herself straightening hair instead, encircled in the arms of the most beautiful man she had ever known.

"Jonny," she breathed, and just held him.

She could feel the ache in his body, the tiredness, the tension born of ever-present pain. She wanted to check him for other hurts, to tend to him, but let him hold her instead. There would be time enough for that. She breathed deep of him, taking guesses at where he had been and what he had been up to by the smell of him. He still smelled of snow and earth; but also of asphalt and diesel and smoke. She did not smell blood.

Finally his arms loosened and she drew back a little. "Just let me get a good look at ye," she whispered.

His smile was weak but teasing, "So long as it affords me m' fill o' ye."

She blushed at that, but looked him over. He had a few stains and tears on his shirt and a button missing on his vest. The patchwork pocket had been torn, leaving a frayed mouth that yawned open. His jeans were dirty and scorched in a few places, and his feet were bare. His knuckles were scraped and he had a slight bruise upon one cheek, but that seemed to be the extent of his injuries.

"What would ye have first? Food or bath?"

"Sleep and surcease of pain," he sighed.

She wanted to yield, but knew that was not what he needed right now. "Neither of which are options," she answered firmly. A faint tingling through her feet bore a message from the house. "Though the latter can be managed after. Come on," she said, slipping under his arm and helping him into the front room where a fire and a bath stood ready and steaming.

She helped him to undress, taking advantage of the opportunity to check him for further hurts. His lean, tanned body was perfect, unmarred by any new scars; just the artistic tracery of thin white lines that decorated his skin. A few bruises, no more. As he eased into the water, she crossed to the kitchen to begin putting together something for him to eat. The brownie could have done it, would have if Jonny had been worse off; but they had been together long enough the lass knew when to let An do something for herself.

She made him a sandwich with finely sliced mutton and a thick slice of cheddar which she toasted over the fire before adding it to the bread. Ice crystals formed on the bottle of brown beer she had brought him as he closed his fingers upon it. While he ate, she sat at the head of the tub and combed out his long, snow-white hair.

"Yer too good fer me, Ceobhránach," came his soft voice.

She smiled, but did not deign to answer. "An' where've ye been th' last month and more?" she asked softly, changing the subject.

He sighed and began to spin her tales of the bordermarches, detailing out some of the things he had seen, what had become of the great sprawl of the Dark City since its destruction. "ChinaTown has splintered off into a realm all its own. Though we don't know yet if th' Tong or th' Triad'll run it."

"They'll probably fight over it for eternity," she said softly.

Jonny nodded, sipping his beer. "There's a valley o' overgrown city which melts eventually into a dense jungle, within which I think I saw th' ruins of a ziggurat. Hummingbirds th' size of hawks, so I dinnae fly too close.

"Not far from where th' Battery once stood is a city of mirrors. Not sure quite what to make of it yet."

"So, in short, th' inmates are runnin' th' asylum."

He nodded. She finished off the braid she had worked his now clean hair into and moved to where she could see him. "Have ye gone t' Ian yet?" He gave her a look that said everything. "Of course not," she answered herself. "Well, ye've told me nothing that cannae wait until morn', so unless ye've left out anythin' urgent..."

He answered her unspoken question with a small shake of his head as he drained the last of his beer.

She noticed the black box on the table beside her, sitting innocently next to her lacework. She closed her eyes against it, hating the need for that box and what it held. She set her hand on it, calling his attention to it without a word. She rose, fetching the thick towel from the hearth and set it on the low stool she had been sitting on. Without another word or meeting his eyes, she drifted back into her bedchamber.

A pair of opaline eyes greeted her out of the dim corner. Aislynn's voice was only a little sullen as she asked in her accustomed Irish, *"Is he hale?"*

An nodded. *"A mite th' worse for his travels, but hale enough."*

Without another word, Aislynn launched into the air, slipping into the other room to find somewhere else to sleep. An felt suddenly bereft at her abandonment, but that feeling did not last long as cool arms slipped around her from behind and cooler lips pressed to her neck. She sighed happily, even knowing that nothing more would happen tonight.

She guided Jonny into bed and lay her dressing gown across the foot. Slipping between the sheets herself, she let him pull her into him, wrapping his cold arms around her warm body. It was not long before his breathing was long and even and he lay still against her. She pressed her fingers to his wrist, carefully counting the beats, measuring the rhythm, making sure he had not taken too much.

Eventually, she too slept.

An was sitting in the solar with her lace, waiting while Jonny was cloistered in Ian's study giving a more detailed report. Kellain was sitting nearby, filling her in on the plans for the upcoming Ostara celebration. An was only half listening. Jonny had been away for more than a month this last time and she was anxious to know if she was soon to do without again. Long absences were a matter of course with the bard, but lately, with everything going on, they worried her.

The peace of the house was interrupted by the arrival of someone coming in the front door. An could hear Samantha's voice chattering constant encouragement to someone, and then the lights in the hallway going out. Kelly poked her head out into the atrium and nearly fell backwards over An in a panic. An grabbed her, kept her from falling, whispered calming words. She felt the girl's arm pointing out into the hallway, her other hand covering her mouth to hold in the scream.

An held Cipín in an easy grip, ready for defence if necessary. She took a step out the door and saw Samantha huddled in a corner with a figure in rags that smelled of tar and decay. "Samantha?" she called softly. "And who would yer friend be?"

The raccoon girl looked relieved to see her, stepping aside just enough for An to see that the being huddled in the corner was a zombie. His skull was partly exposed by his left temple, and a patch of scalp with stringy grey hair hung down over his ear, which he kept pressing back into place. His grey eyes bored into An's mist filled orbs, revealing his uncertainty and confusion.

Sam sighed. "He doesn't have a name right yet, but... I found him behind a dumpster this morning and it's taken all my cunning and charm to get him here."

"And ye've brought him here why?" she asked calmly.

"So Ian could help him," she said innocently.

From the hallway to the kitchen she heard slowing footsteps and turned to wave Shannon back. "I'll get Ian, Shannon. Just keep everyone back. Sam, ye think ye kin get him t' Ian's office?"

She shook her head. "I think he doesn't trust the narrow halls. Alleys were... ambush points," she shuddered. "He's a little spooked right now. We've made huge progress with 'not eat people'."

To which the zombie's voice parroted in a grating voice, "Not eat people. ...Not eat 'coon."

Sam perked up and smiled. "See! Progress."

An nodded, motioned to Kelly to stay were she was. "I'll get Ian."

Slowly, she turned and felt her way to the hall, following her nose past the vase of carnations that marked the east wing. She counted the doors, let her senses tell her when she reached the sealed areas of the house. His door even felt different than the others near it, perhaps because it was one of the only ones with air conditioning. She rapped her knuckles upon it firmly, not as timid as she might once have been. She was a little surprised that it was Jonny who opened the door.

"Aye?" he asked softly, opening it far enough for Ian to see who was there.

She caught her smile before it had gone too far, suddenly remembering the feel of those lips on hers not a few hours past. She schooled her expression for her chieftain. Ian was leaning back in his chair behind his desk, his feet up and a cigarette in hand. "Uncle," she said, nodding her apology. "I'd not interrupt but there is someone new here to see you and... it best ye come t' him."

It was the wince in her face as she said it that made him get up, more than the words themselves. She stepped back as he ap-proached, began to lead the way. "Samantha brought him in but couldn't get him past the door. He spooked Kellain quite a bit, so I'm guessin' he's no fey face a'tall. If she sees what I see..." she let her words drift away.

As they approached the darkened atrium, An stepped to the side, fell in with Jonny as Ian slowly crossed the foyer. As he came around the large round table that held an enormous bouquet of lilies and roses year-round, he stopped.

"How came yeh t' bring him here?" he asked, keeping his voice low and easy, though An could hear the stress in it.

Even Samantha must have sensed it as she tensed, turning to face Ian, protecting the zombie behind her. The undead thing merely looked at him over her shoulder. "I found him behind a dumpster downtown," she said, trying to sound defiant.

Ian did not say anything, continued to watch her. Behind him, Jonny slipped his arm around An, ready to make whatever move would be necessary. An merely held her breath.

"He looked scared. I know what he is... and... I've been scared of them myself, run like crazy from them over there... but... I've never seen one on this side before."

"I have," An whispered. Jonny's fingers tightened comfortingly.

"He didn't behave right. So..." she shrugged, "I tried talking. When he spoke back, I just knew."

"Knew what?" Ian asked softly.

"That he might be waking up. Becoming a person again. Like I did. There's some of the man left in him. He hasn't even tried to bite me yet."

"No bite raccoon," the zombie said firmly. "No eat people."

For the first time, Ian's eyes flicked to the zombie. "Who told yeh this?"

"Ss-am," he stammered. "But I know... if moves... not food. Food not move. Eat move is... wrong. I want... I... hunger... but... no. Is wrong. Have. Won't. Stay?"

There was a tense moment as Ian took a deep breath, let it out slowly. "Do yeh have a name?"

"No. No name. Sam," he said, pointing to Samantha. He hesitated, pointed at Ian. "Een?"

"I-an," he corrected, drawing out the word to be better understood. He turned to Sam. "Yeh'll be responsible fer him? Might be slow goin'. An' he can't leave th' Rest, ...or be seen by most o' th' kin. Not til we kin find a way t'... obscure th' rot."

"Th' witch?" Jonny suggested. "Or maybe Mags. If anyone's heard o' one o' 'em... findin' himself again... she'll know. 'Tis not somethin' *I've* heard tell of."

Ian nodded. "Good idea."

An looked up at Jonny, "You get Mags, I'll get Baba?"

He gave her a measured look. "Mags might be easier fer ye..."

She shook her head. "I don't think Mags likes me much, and I know m' way t'th' witch. She and I have a... relationship o' sorts. I have cabbages for her anyway."

He opened his mouth to say something but she shook her head with a soft laugh. "As a rule, I don' ask. I just grow them."

He arched an eyebrow at her, then nodded. He exchanged a look with Ian before escorting An out the back way. He walked her as far as a white door in the side of the house beneath a sycamore tree before pressing a kiss to her hand, shifting into Raven and flying off in another direction.

An smiled softly, reaching for the knob. The door led nowhere, unless you knew how to open it. If you did, then one stepped from the side lawn into what Skye called his mead hall, but everyone else called the training hall. High ceilinged and filled with every conceivable weapon, and capable of providing any sort of indoor terrain, it was a well-used and valuable resource to the Rest.

There were a few people there, warming up or sparring. No one paid attention to her as she simply turned around and opened the door again, mundanely this time. Stepping out, she turned down the short path that led to the gate at the bottom of her garden next door.

There were new leaves and fresh blossoms on her fruit and nut trees, and they rustled pleasantly as she walked up the little path. Bells and buzzing greeted her from the patch of lily-of-the-valley near the stream and she smiled, nodding in their direction. She was beginning to understand them.

The sun was only just beginning to burn off the light mist from the stream as she crossed the footbridge, dappling the light across the grass. She smiled. She loved early mornings in her garden, almost as much as she loved twilight anywhere.

The air was full of the scent of fresh cut grass and new flowers as she approached the back of her little Irish cottage. Aislynn landed on the bottom of the kitchen door, peering around at her as she entered the little potting shed beside the split door.

"Whatchup to?" she trilled.

An emerged with a basket on her arm, a small, sharp knife in hand. "Hmm? Oh, I need to visit Baba this morning for Ian and since some of her cabbages are ripe, I thought I'd bring them with me."

Aislynn frowned as she walked past her towards the vegetable patch. "*Vamprick that way's getting a mite nippy,*" she warned in Irish.

An glanced over at the roses growing against the nearest wall. They were getting a little yellow, not much of a blush to their edges at all, and the dark red thorns on their tangle looked long and particularly sharp in the morning light. "They do look a wee pale. Th' others faring well? Or is this th' only one what's hungry?"

Aislynn landed in the grass and crept closer to the rows of cabbages and lettuce, keeping a sullen eye on the roses. *"Just that one."* She had a beef with that one in particular.

An nodded as she bent in the cabbage row, selecting a nice head and neatly removing it from the folds of leaves. "I'll get a feeder rat from th' pet store this afternoon, then. Or you could hunt squirrels," she suggested.

Aislynn thought about it. *"More in th' mood for pigeon pie,"* she trilled.

An selected another cabbage. "So long as there's enough for th' roses, too."

She popped her head up. *"You think if you brought her some sugar, she might have some cookies?"*

An laughed, setting another head in her basket. *"Too close to Ostara, pet. She's baking fer th' feast by now."*

She stood, stretching her back. "That should do for today." A warning hiss from Aislynn and she turned, Cipín in hand and aimed threateningly at the wayward roses. It shrank back from the iron tip of the shillelagh. "Ye'll have yer feed this evenin', greedy-guts. Though why yer hungry and yer sisters aren't..."

Aislynn snorted. *"'Cause th' bogarts've got smart and stay away from this part of th' garden. That witch's herb you laid out on th' edges o' that patch worked. Ye've had other little pests near th' others."*

An picked up her basket. "Maybe I'll get a rabbit then. You coming with me t' Baba's?"

Aislynn shook her head, stretched out in the grass in a particularly sunny patch. *"I'll pass. Don't like th' way she looks at me."*

She nodded. "Suit yerself. Warn th' pixies fer me?" she asked, jerking a thumb in the thirsty Vamprick's direction.

"Trust me. They know."

An closed the bone gate behind her with a small breath of relief. She did not mind dealing with the witch, had a regular arrangement with her to grow certain vegetables and herbs that her witchly proximity would contaminate. But she always walked away from the twisted little house with a sense of relief. She knew it was the magic, that it was designed to put one at odds.

Her basket was lighter than when she had arrived, but still held a few treats; a special tea, and some cookies for Aislynn. The witch had bought some trinkets on the goblin market and needed An to 'have a chat with them' to determine their function. One of the items had not even been magical, and another was not yet but was primed to magical purpose. One of these days, An was determined to go to the market herself.

As Cipín guided her to the right, she heard the rustle of feathers and the slight weight of a raven landed on her shoulder. She smiled up at Jonny. "Mags?"

"On her way," his raven's voice was more hoarse than his normal one, yet somehow still beautiful and alluring. It was another thing she had gotten used to. "Baba?"

She nodded. "She'll see what she can dig up to help make him appear... more intact. As fer his humanity... she'll have a chat with him on that matter. She'll pop up at th' house t'night. Shall I meet ye at th' Manor or will ye walk with me?" she blushed a little at that.

He shook his feathers, half spread his wings. "Hedge Gate. I'll deliver both messages and meet ye there. I'm in a mood fer a pint."

She nodded, changing direction slightly. "I'll just swing by th' cottage and put this away."

He leapt from her shoulder and flew off through the wood, quickly disappearing from her sight.

The rest coming soon!

Other Books By
S.L. Thorne

Love In Ruins
The Speaker
Mercy's Ransom
Fang and Bone

The Gryphon's Rest Series:
Lady of the Mist
The Gloaming

SHIFT
Books 1 & 2
Stag's Heart
Dragon's Bride

The Portswain Saga
Books 1 & 2
Midnight and Amber
Sagavis

All Available in hardback, paperback and ebook
at:
Thornewoodstudios.com/books
or
Amazon.com